MIRROR IMAGE

BOOKS BY ICE-T

The Ice Opinion

Ice: A Memoir of Gangster Life and Redemption—from South Central to Hollywood (with Douglas Century)

*Kings of Vice** (with Mal Radcliff)

*Mirror Image** (with Jorge Hinojosa)

*A Forge Book

MIRROR IMAGE

ICE-T
AND JORGE HINOJOSA

A TOM DOHERTY ASSOCIATES BOOK

NEW YORK

MIRROR IMAGE

Copyright © 2013 by Ice Touring Inc.

Management: Jorge Hinojosa

A Forge Book
Published by Tom Doherty Associates, LLC
175 Fifth Avenue
New York, NY 10010

www.tor-forge.com

Forge® is a registered trademark of Tom Doherty Associates, LLC.

The Library of Congress Cataloging-in-Publication Data

Ice-T (Musician).
  Mirror image / Ice-T and Jorge Hinojosa.—1st ed.
    p. cm.
  "A Tom Doherty Associates book."
  ISBN 978-0-7653-2514-3 (hardcover)
  ISBN 978-0-7653-3219-6 (trade paperback)
  ISBN 978-1-4299-4487-8 (e-book)
  1. Organized crime—New York (State)—New York—Fiction. 2. Street life—New York (State)—New York—Fiction. I. Hinojosa, Jorge. II. Title.
PS3609.C4 M57 2013
813'.6—dc23

                                                                    2012043279

Forge books may be purchased for educational, business, or promotional use. For information on bulk purchases, please contact Macmillan Corporate and Premium Sales Department at 1-800-221-7945 extension 5442 or write specialmarkets@macmillan.com.

First Edition: May 2013

Printed in the United States of America

0 9 8 7 6 5 4 3 2 1

Special thanks to everyone who's supported me for twenty-five years and counting. Love to all my fallen homeys, dead and locked away in prison. You are missed dearly. Eternal love to my inner circle of friends, family, and my wife, who really know what I go through and work to keep me focused and healthy. Peace to all the young street hustlers, players, and gangstas. To win the game you must devise an exit strategy. We all saw the last scene in *Scarface*.

—ICEBERG

I want to thank Ice-T for creating and introducing me to such an incredible cast of characters that made working on this book a lot of fun. I also want to acknowledge John Helfers, who took a chance on an untested writer and provided crucial guidance throughout this whole process. To Sabrina Koster, who read every chapter as soon as it was completed, and gave me valuable notes and encouragement. A big thanks to the real Micky Bentson, Al Patrome, Sean E Sean, Hen Gee, Evil E, and Big Rich: you have all been big characters in my life and I appreciate your friendship. To Bob Gleason, for making this whole thing happen and his belief in this project. And finally to my daughter, Ava, Sabrina, my family, and friends who I love dearly.

—JORGE HINOJOSA

I know which is the road that leads home and if I weave like a drunken man as I go down it that does not mean the road is the wrong one.

—LEO TOLSTOY

MIRROR IMAGE

1

Crush Casey had been up for hours; sometimes sleep didn't come easy, and this was one of those times. Today would have been Antonio's twenty-eighth birthday, and that thought had kept him tossing and turning all night. It was hard to imagine his boy being twenty-eight. In Casey's mind, Antonio would always be frozen in time as the sixteen-year-old who had visited him that last time in prison. On top of that, it was a month since Casey had visited his son's grave—'bout thirty days too long, far as he was concerned—and this morning, he was gonna make it right.

He glanced over at Carla, sleeping soundly next to him, a peaceful look on her face. She was a beautiful woman who understood him better than most—hell, maybe better than himself sometimes. Casey tried to be stealthy as he slipped out of bed like he was making an escape, hoping not to wake her, but he wasn't smooth enough to make it work.

"Morning, baby," Carla said in a sleepy, honeyed voice.

He leaned over and gently kissed her cheek. "It's early, baby. Go back to sleep."

It was too late, though; she was already up, and asked where he was going. Usually Casey admired how quick Carla's mind worked in the morning, but today it was a definite drag. He thought of making up a story, but even as he hesitated, he knew he'd have to come clean.

Casey dropped a shoulder at the door. "I'ma go see Antonio, it's been a minute."

He watched her examine his face, searching for a clue as to what his temperature might be, but it was pointless. She nodded and quickly jumped out of bed. "Okay, it won't take but a hot second for me to get ready. You want a quick breakfast?"

Casey had hoped to do this visit solo, but didn't care enough to open up a can of worms over it. "Just coffee, baby. I wanna bounce in twenty."

Exactly nineteen minutes later, they hit the road in Casey's black Escalade. The streets were quiet that early on a Sunday morning. New York, the city that never sleeps, was at least taking a break on God's day before revving up to do it all over again.

It was about an hour's drive to the graveyard, and Casey was silent for most of it. Carla was quiet, too, letting him contemplate. He appreciated that—her giving him space to do what he had to do was a big part of their relationship, and she knew it well.

As they crossed the bridge to Long Island, Casey reflected on his life and did a mental inventory of all the players in it, past and present. He was glad to reconnect with Champa Muñoz; he knew that, above everyone else, the man had his back and would always be straight up. They had been friends ever since they met at juvie, when they were twelve years old. Shinzo Becker was also a down brotha; he'd proved his loyalty on the battlefield when they forced the final showdown with his backstabbing ex-partner Gulliver Rono.

He thought of Rono, his former right-hand man, who'd betrayed him and got him sent to Attica for twenty years. In the end, that bastard had gotten his in spades, but nothing could pay back the twenty years behind bars and the loss of Casey's son. He wondered what had turned Gulliver out and made him a snitch and a sucka—he could understand if Rono had wanted to kill him so that he could take over the Kings, but to cut a deal with the feds—that was a real bitch move. Under his breath, Casey said, "Fuck 'em, who cares." Carla glanced at him and he shook his head so she left it alone. Casey changed lanes and went back into his head again.

Then there was the woman in his life. Casey couldn't help smiling as he stole a glance at Carla: even in just tight jeans and a T-shirt, she looked amazing. She was one bad bitch—a wildcat in the sack, whose body was a magnet he simply couldn't resist. Along with her brainpower, she was also a mind reader who knew how to interpret his vibe and act accordingly. That didn't mean she wasn't also a bit of work, however. But the fact remained that Carla was the first woman since Danielle, Antonio's mother, whom he felt he really connected with. It was a different relationship, though—it was more complete, more multidimensional . . . a result of his age and time. He recalled Mack D, his guru in the joint, speaking on relationships once: "Look here, nigga, when a woman meets a man, it's always the right time, and only when it's the right time will a man meet the right woman, you dig?"

Lately, however, there'd been a bit of a hiccup in paradise. Casey knew Carla wanted a baby—the hints she'd been dropping were becoming less subtle with each passing day—and that conversation was gonna make them or break them. It wasn't that he didn't love her, or that he had a problem with kids—quite the opposite. He just knew his lifestyle—leader of the most powerful gang in NYC—wasn't conducive to babies and all that domestic shit, because everyone knew a gangsta's biggest weakness was his seed.

The truth was, when Antonio was murdered, he'd 'bout lost his mind over it, and going through that shit again was not an option. He remembered how he'd transformed that pain into anger in the joint, and how he went to sleep having dreams of literally tearing Rono apart, limb by muthafuckin' limb. He was on the short road to insanity till Mack D had gotten him straight.

In Attica, you either had enemies or allies, but Mack D was different. He was the father figure Casey'd never had, a man with an impressive criminal pedigree and a profound intellect that made him untouchable. He was also a master communicator who always had everyone's attention. Mack had transcended the yard and gang bullshit and figured out more than most. He was a true samurai warrior, Buddhist monk, and Goldie from *The Mack* all rolled into one. He'd seen Casey through the ups and downs of prison life, got him to get his head on straight and start using his brains instead of his fists to not only survive in Attica, but make plans for what was gonna go down after he got out.

Then there was Lomax, his fat-assed, wise-crackin' parole officer, whose little hints had led Casey to breaking the back of his former gang, the Vicetown Kings, and killing his betrayer, Gulliver Rono, by chocking the life out of his betrayin' ass. Casey couldn't figure out Lomax: On one hand, he'd serendipitously helped him with his Rono beef without batting an eye. Course, that might have been due to the fact that Casey had a hand in destroying two other gangs on that blood-soaked night in Parkenbush. On the other, he'd also let Casey know—in his own delicate way—that he had the man's Saint Jude's medal that could get him indicted for the murder and mayhem of the VK and Rono drama. But over the last three months, Lomax hadn't jerked his chain once.

That bit with his medal irked Casey—typical po-po bullshit. The nigga could have given him back his shit, but instead, he was using it as not-so-subtle blackmail. The Saint Jude's medal was a gift from Antonio's mother, a link to his past that now was choking him. He knew Lomax had an agenda, and Casey was a part of it whether he liked it or not. At the moment, it looked like their mutual interests jibed, but the second they didn't, that was when he knew the shit would get critical, and hey, there was no way Casey was ever going back to the joint. He was out for good, be it alive or dead!

He thought about that final showdown with Rono, and how he was able to unleash the fury inside him and choke the life out of that double-crossin' nigga with only his bare hands. He had enjoyed staring into the chump's panicked eyes as his life was snuffed out. At that moment, he'd lost all concern for his own well-being and was solely focused on retribution. It was only a brief moment of sweet satisfaction, though; his killing of Rono was just a temporary fix from the pain of losing his son. He could have exterminated that sonofabitch every single day for a thousand years and it still wouldn't make things right, but it was something that needed to be done.

As he drove and replayed that night in his mind, he gripped the steering wheel like he had Rono's flabby neck in his fingers again. It wasn't until Carla put her hand on his shoulder that he relaxed up, and blew a breath out as he tried to calm down.

"You okay, baby? It's the next exit, right?"

"Huh, yeah. Just—just thinkin' on some things, thasall. Ain't no thang."

Carla returned her gaze to the streets around them. Casey scowled, annoyed that he'd put his shit out there like that. He was back on top—the undisputed leader of the Vicetown Kings, and head of a gang syndicate that covered most of the city. He should have been on top of the muthafuckin' world . . . but he wasn't.

Coming up on the exit for the Washington Memorial Park Cemetery, Casey pumped his brakes and eased the SUV down the off-ramp. They drove for a few more minutes, and pulled up at the majestic gates of the home of the dead. When Casey first heard about Antonio's death, he'd reached out to Champa and had him make sure that his son was laid to rest someplace remote and peaceful. The cemetery looked like a park: lush, green, and very quiet. There were no headstones, only markers set into the ground on the rolling hills.

Casey drove through the maze of streets with their corny names— Path to Light Drive, Court of Freedom, Sanctuary of Heritage Way—and felt his stomach roil and churn the farther they went. When they reached Antonio's location, he pulled over, turned off the car, and just sat there, in contemplation. It was absolutely silent; the graveyard was empty at this hour. Not even a birdcall broke the stillness. Casey lifted his head and looked around—he'd put a lot of muthafuckas in the dirt over the years, and wondered how many of them were buried in this field.

Casey and Carla got out of the car together, but Casey—anxious, angry, and grief-stricken—walked ahead up to Antonio's plot. The grass was still wet as he ascended the hill. When he got to Antonio's resting place, a simple stone marker, he looked down and squeezed his fists tightly and drew in a startled breath. He felt Carla come up behind him and saw her react to the strange, dark look on his face. It was an expression of pure, bottled rage. She stepped next to him and looked down at Antonio's granite grave marker. On the bottom corner was the reason for Casey's fury—scratched crudely into the stone in inch-high block letters were the words FUCK YOU CRUSH.

Carla took a quick intake of breath as Casey suddenly turned, took her arm, and through clenched teeth said, "Let's go." As they headed to the car, he tried to ease his grip on Carla's arm, mindful of the fact that he felt like breaking something, smashing anything and everything he could get his hands on.

They got in the car and Casey slammed his door shut, then screamed a bloodcurdling, *"Fuck, motherfucker, let me catch the muthafucka that did this shit!"* at the top of his lungs. Striking his large fists over and over into the Caddy's ceiling, he pounded the cloth and metal hard enough to rock the entire SUV.

Carla was visibly shaken; he knew she'd never seen him this angry and hurt before. Her body language showed that she was too scared to say anything, and scared to death that he might accidentally hit her. She pushed herself into the corner of the car, trembling with quiet sobs, her face in her hands.

A faraway part of Crush screamed that he needed to get himself under control, but it was lost in the tidal wave of ferocity crashing over him. He wanted blood, goddamnit, he wanted revenge! He wanted to find the muthafucka who did this and torture his ass until he cried to be murdered. He squeezed his fists tight around the steering wheel and gritted his teeth as he rapidly took deep breaths, trying to get a grip on his emotions.

Casey tamped down his rage long enough to search his mind for who would dare to do this, and how he would exact his vengeance. His mind was like a computer running through scenarios and options on how to get the muthafucka. Was it one of Rono's former men fuckin' with him? Was it someone else that had a beef with him and this was their clever way of calling him out? Was it the cops or maybe someone who he thought was a friend? He knew he'd probably never find out, and that made him even more angry. His instinct was to go to the cemetery's caretaker and do whatever it took to get some answers, but that was when he noticed Carla hugging herself as she sobbed and hitched in a breath, tears running down her cheeks. *Oh, shit.*

"Carla."

She flinched at hearing her own name, and looked at him with fearful eyes. *Now she knows what kind of monster I really am,* he thought. He took another deep breath, steadying himself, and turned to her again.

In a low, calm voice, he said, "Look . . . better you found this out sooner rather than later. This is who I am, this type of hate is what I inspire. My son paid the price for that, and many around me have paid it as well," he said as he looked away from her. Then he quietly said, "I can't change that or my past." Casey wanted to comfort her, but he held back, not entirely sure of how she'd react and also not wanting to be even more vulnerable than he already was.

Carla wiped her eyes and reached out to put her hand on his shoulder. Her touch calmed him even further, like it usually did. "I can handle it, I . . . just can't . . . imagine what kind of person would do that."

Casey looked at her and nodded his head once more. "There's a lotta cats out there that have good reason to hate or fear me. This is a small way for some punk-ass nigga to get some satisfaction without comin' at me straight up."

"I'm sorry, baby," Carla said.

"Yeah, well . . . it is what it is, and I can't do shit about it," Casey replied. He looked past her and out her window in the direction of Antonio's plot and paused. Once again, his actions had impacted his son. He looked down and exhaled, as grief and regret consumed him. *Sorry, son, for this and everything else.* He turned over the engine and they headed home in silence, with him staring out the windshield at everything and nothing. On Monday, he would call the cemetery and have them remove the marker and not replace it, leaving Antonio's grave unmarked. He wouldn't let his son be used again, either to pay for his sins or as a pawn to get to him.

An hour later, as they pulled back into the city, Casey's cell rang. It was Champa. He let it go to voice mail; he was in no mood to talk business. As soon as the ringtone stopped, it rang again; Champa again.

Fuck. Casey picked it up. "Yeah?"

"Hey, what's up, player? I heard they got a pickup game in the Bronx at two. You wanna go show these fools how it's done?"

Translation: *Two of our guys just got busted in the Bronx for slanging dope and we need to spring 'em.*

Casey gripped the phone so hard, the plastic case creaked under the strain. *The shit never stops.*

"A'ight, sounds good, we'll give those youngsters a ten-point advantage so it's interesting."

Translation: *What's the bail amount, ten Gs?*

"Shit, nigga, for it to be interesting, they need fifteen points. Anyway, I'll grab a bite and meet you there."

Translation: *Bail is fifteen Gs, and I'll get a lawyer on it.*

Carla looked puzzled as Casey hung up the phone. He figured she knew there was no basketball game and knew to let well enough alone.

2

Casey pulled up to Carla's place after circling the block twice to make sure he wasn't being followed, his mind bouncing between their visit to Antonio's grave and the trouble in the Bronx. Since taking back the Kings, it seemed like his phone was always ringing with some bullshit or other, and today was no different. At the same time, he figured it was to be expected; they were all criminals, after all. His grand plan of organizing them and ridding them of the more heinous crimes, like trafficking in sex slavery and dealing hard drugs, was ambitious at best. Like any good military organization, they needed structure, and that's what the Kings and he were both struggling with, because until now they'd all been used to operating as independent units.

"Okay, baby, I'll catch you later. I gotta put some work in," Casey said as he leaned over and kissed her.

"Okay, Daddy, baby will wait for you to come home," Carla said, giggling. Casey chuckled at that. Carla always knew how to make him laugh—especially when he needed to.

She hopped out of the Escalade, and Casey smiled as he watched her phat ass bounce while she walked to the front door of her apartment building. He always loved that view, as did the other passersby, with dudes up and down the street craning their necks to get a better look. Carla glanced back over her shoulder—she must have known he was looking—and gave him a saucy wink. He knew she loved him and wouldn't let the shit at the cemetery spin her out.

With that, Casey was off. His expression turned serious as he put his game face on. He was in business mode now and on a mission to take some people to church. His first call was to Shinzo Becker. Half black and half Korean, Shinzo was about fifteen years younger than Casey, and a straight street hustler always looking for a chance to prove himself. When the Rono beef had gone down, he proved himself in spades. He was smart, calm under pressure, and fiercely loyal to Casey. Case knew one day Shin would be the boss—and rightly so, he was a natural leader. Shin didn't know it yet, but he was about to get himself some stripes.

"What up, nigga, we got a pickup game in the Bronx," Casey said on his Bluetooth earpiece, talking slightly louder over the city noise around him.

"Yeah, so I heard. I'm already in motion—got this Korean kid who played college ball with me before, so the shit will get handled," Shinzo replied.

"No shit." Casey grinned—as usual, Shinzo was already on the clock. "Okay, inna minute," he said, then hung up.

To anyone eavesdropping on their brief conversation—and Casey always assumed someone was—they'd be clueless that Shinzo was meeting the guys at a Korean mini mart in the Bronx for a strategy meeting with their lawyer. The word "kid" always meant specific locations—"Italian kid" meant Roberto's Italian restaurant, "Thai kid" meant the Thai boxing ring in the Bronx, and so on, and "college ball" was short for "college baller," their nickname for a lawyer.

This kind of coded talk had been developed way back, starting when Casey and Champa were in juvie together. Early on, they'd realized if they were gonna thrive and not just survive, they'd need to be able to operate in plain sight. Within months, they had a flourishing black market business in full swing in the kiddie joint, offering everything from protection to cigarettes, pot to porno mags. Not bad for a couple of thirteen-year-olds, but then again, they were anything but your average kids.

Champa did his first juvie bid for setting his alcoholic stepfather on fire. He'd doused the muthafucka with 151 when he was passed out on the couch, lit a match, and *poof!* He hadn't killed him, but the sonofabitch was left so disfigured, he probably wished he were dead. Champa did it in retaliation for that chump beating his mother so bad, she'd been in the hospital for three days with her broken jaw wired up. That kind of shit stuck with a man—even today, Casey always noticed that whenever Champa saw cats drunk, it brought out something sinister in his childhood friend, and of course, everyone knew that you never cracked "yo mama" jokes around him. On more than one occasion, some dumb bastard had made that mistake and got a busted lip.

Casey's story was different, but just as fucked up. Both his parents were decent people who had caught bad breaks. His mother was a secretary for a law firm, worked hard, yet always had time and patience for her son. One night at dinner she complained of a severe headache, then started getting violently ill. She was rushed to Bronx-Lebanon Hospital, but died three hours later from a brain aneurysm. She was twenty-eight years old. Five-year-old Casey had watched in horror as his father frantically tried to bring her back to life. It was the only time he'd ever seen his father cry.

His father had a rough year after that, but eventually pulled it together to survive. He remembered his dad saying to him, "When life pushes you around, son, you got to push back." They were the only family each other had—no siblings, uncles or aunts, or grandparents. So there was no one to lean on or give a helping hand. His father worked for the transit authority; he was in middle management and was respected and well liked. One day when Casey's father was coming home late from work and waiting on the train platform, two white teenagers demanded money, which his father refused to hand over. The kids attacked him, and a fight ensued.

Casey's father knocked one of the little bastards on his ass and was wrestling with the other one when they all accidentally fell on the live train tracks. One was electrocuted instantly. The surviving kid made up a story that his friend and he were pounced on by Casey's father, the cops bought that bullshit, and that was that.

At the time, Casey was eight years old and suddenly an orphan. A friend's mom took him in for a couple days, but then Children's Services stepped in and tried to place him, which was tough. Most people wanted babies, not an eight-year-old traumatized by the loss of both his parents. For years, he was bounced from place to place. Some foster parents took him in for the short-term cash from the state; others, because they wanted an extra pair of hands to help around the house. Over the ensuing years, Casey went from being a happy, extroverted kid to an introverted, angry young loner.

At thirteen, he got transferred to his sixth family, which meant a new school and another nightmare. His new foster parents had seven other adopted kids, so clearly this was a business to them. Being the new kid in school, he was always getting pushed around and bullied by kids two and three years older than him. One day one of the kids, called Bulldog, and his two partners caught Casey off guard and beat the shit out of him by the school lockers. If that wasn't enough, they held Casey's legs open so Bulldog could kick him hard in the nuts, twice. It was painful and humiliating.

Casey got little sympathy from his foster parents and pissed blood all day. He was out of school for the next three days, and when asked who did it, Casey held his water and didn't snitch on any of his attackers. After being back at school for two weeks, Casey exacted his revenge on all three boys in one glorious day. The first boy, he stalked and caught in the bathroom during study hall. After throwing bleach in his eyes, he proceeded to stomp the living shit out of him. The sounds of the boy whimpering and begging him to stop were like a drug to Casey, and it felt fucking great. It was the first time in his life that he'd ever felt powerful, and he loved it. He fantasized that he was killing all the bastards who ever fucked with him as he jumped up and down on his head. He left the boy in a bloody heap out cold on the tile floor and bounced before anyone could catch him. In his mind, he'd killed him. The boy wasn't dead, but he lost sight in his right eye. The other two fared far worse.

From there, Casey went to the gym and found his next target. Grabbing a baseball bat, he walked up behind him and hit the second kid in the back of the head with all his might. *Crack!* The rest of the kids jumped the fuck back when they saw and heard the sickening blow. After the boy fell, Casey flipped him over and repeatedly swung at his face, breaking his nose and jaw and knocking out the whole front row of his teeth. He felt nothing but hate as the bat sent the kid's teeth flying across the gym. A couple of nearby kids were so freaked out by the brutality of the assault that they started to vomit, with one girl peeing in her pants.

By the time the coaches got hip to what was going on, Casey was already running out the door, dropping the bloody bat on the way out. He ran through the hallways until he was sure no one was doggin' him, then slowed down, breathing hard, his pulse racing. He was in a zone unlike anything he'd ever experienced. He felt like he had been living in slow motion until that day. All those years of being fucked around with and being shit on were over, forever. He fantasized that he was The Punisher, exacting justice. Fuck the consequences—no one was gonna fuck with him without payin' for it ever again. Fuck that!

The young Casey rounded the hallway corner and saw Bulldog talking to some girl, trying to be a little pimp. Perfect! Calm and cool, Casey reached into his back pocket and pulled out and opened his knife. Gritting his teeth, he walked up behind Bulldog and plunged the blade into the boy's neck as hard as he could. He was so strung out, it was a wonder he didn't miss.

Bulldog let out a cry and fell to his knees and just started shaking as he collapsed to the ground. He looked up from the ground to see Casey standing above him, his face expressionless. Casey had thought the kid was dying as he convulsed on the floor, but he didn't. He was paralyzed from the neck down for life.

Casey was immediately tackled by a schoolteacher. And soon a swarm of cops and ambulances converged on the school and tended to the victims and took Casey into custody. The cops were shocked by how calm yet defiant he was at the same time. He heard one cop say he was a "little psychopath."

The press covered the story for weeks, calling Casey a monster and the product of a shitty foster care system. Politicans used the incident as currency to get elected. The court of public opinion wanted him tried as an adult, but the judge overruled that and sentenced him to four years in juvie. After sentencing, he was soon forgotten by the outside world as a new headline dominated the press and the public's mind.

All that publicity did a lot for his rep in juvie, however. The young Casey had walked in with a lot of respect—something he'd never felt before and quickly became addicted to. From then on, he never walked away from trouble, but toward it. After his four-year stint, Casey came out ready for the big leagues.

Casey drove through the Bronx. It used to be home; now it was just another piece of his territory. The projects and the playgrounds were all a battlefield he'd both waged war and done business on at some point or another. Crime statistics still rated the Bronx as the most dangerous borough in NY, but like everything else in life, that seemed exaggerated.

Rolling down the familiar streets brought back more memories— meeting Antonio's mother at the National Puerto Rican Day Parade, taking Antonio to the Bronx Zoo. *Man, too many memories*, his expression turned hard as he thought of his lost boy yet again.

Pulling up to Kimchi's Mini Mart and Deli, Casey scoped out the area from his car and spotted both Champa's and Shin's rides. He took a magnet from the center divider and placed it below the steering column, opening a secret compartment that held a SIG 226 and a baby Glock 9 millimeter. He grabbed the baby 9 and from its weight knew it was fully loaded. The tiny but deadly pistol was compact enough to fit into his front pocket. Casey opened the Escalade's door and felt thick humidity envelop him as he got out and crossed the street; it was a hot day in more ways than one.

He walked into Kimchi's, enjoying the cool breeze from the air conditioner. Casey nodded to Mr. Kim, a skinny older Korean man who was always behind the register. No words were spoken as he headed to the back room. The storage room was filled with shelves full of boxes, foodstuffs, and everything else a person would expect in a Korean corner store—except for the two master criminals and their crooked attorney sitting at a card table, that was.

Shinzo, Champa, and Alejandro Hernandez all looked up and greeted Casey. After the what'sups had been exchanged, Casey hooked the fourth chair, sat down, and looked at Champa. "Okay, what the fuck happened?"

"Rodrigo and Ernesto were at that strip joint, the Crazy Horse Cabaret, getting loaded on I don't know what and got into a beef with some guys that were there for a bachelor party. After some shouting and a scuffle, Rodrigo and Ernesto got thrown out on their asses," said Champa.

"Are these niggas never not in some bullshit?" asked Casey rhetorically.

"Hold on, it gets better. They decide to wait for the guys to leave the club, right? When they come out, they jolly stomp these niggas, right then and there. Of course, the parking lot has closed-circuit—"

"Of course," said Casey.

"—the club owner calls the cops, they show up on time for once, Rodrigo and Ernesto resist arrest 'cause they're higher than kites, cops pat 'em down and find some rock on Ernesto, and then they go downtown."

Alejandro looked at Casey. "Bottom line, Crush, is that bail was set at seventy-five K for each of them. I'm sure I can get 'em something light for the assult and resisting arrest, but the possession, given that they both have priors, means they could be facing ten years, *and* that's with me using some grease."

"Shee-it! Okay, let's get their dumb asses out." Casey then turned to Shin. "You bring that bread?"

Shin nodded and tossed four stacks of money on the table. "Yeah, fifteen K for the bail bondsman plus five K retainer for the counselor here."

Casey watched Alejandro as he spied the money, but their mouthpiece waited for Casey to give him the nod, then took the dough. Casey respected Alejandro's intelligence, but at the end of the day, he knew the man was a criminal, too, and would sell him and anyone else out in a heartbeat to save his own ass. Alejandro had heard and seen too many stories about being in the joint to even think twice about doing a stretch. But Casey also knew Alejandro enjoyed his role as the VK's legal counsel and the perks it got him—plenty of power, boatloads of undeclared cash, and all the women he could handle. The shifty lawyer had always been straight up with them, and as long as he wasn't compromised, he would never be a problem.

Alejandro scooped the money up and placed it into his alligator-skin briefcase. Standing, he said, "They'll be out by dinnertime. As far as the other details, I'll let you know what the ticket is for leniency. By the way, I heard you got Lomax as a PO?"

"Yeah, what of it?" Casey looked at him sideways.

"I remember when he was a cop, rumor was that he was dirty, but they never could pin anything on him, so they bumped him to corrections."

"Yeah, that's a story I heard before. Do me a favor—dig on that for me on the DL and let me know what you find," Casey said.

"Yeah, all right. I think his old partner is still active. I'll see what I can get, no charge," Alejandro said with a half-joking smile on his face.

Casey looked at him and said sardonically, "You're a funny guy, Alejandro."

Casey and Alejandro bumped fists, and with that, the lawyer left out the back door.

Casey stared at Champa and Shinzo, took a deep breath, and exhaled. "If those guys think they gonna pull a dime, will they hold their water?"

"Yeah, they're tight with their families and each have kids. They know they'd lose that if they said shit," said Champa.

Shinzo nodded. "They're also both in their early twenties—with good behavior, all they're looking at is seven years max."

"Besides, they don't really know shit about shit," added Champa.

"Well, let's assume they're still set on stupid, and remind them of the consequences of spilling shit to anyone. Shin, I'ma leave that to you," Casey said. He didn't need to spell it out—everyone in the VKs knew the penalty for turning rat—snitches always ended up facedown in the gutter, no matter where they were.

Satisfied, Casey rose to his feet. "Okay, let's get all the major players at the Urban Victory office tonight at nine. These niggas all need to have a tighter rein on the baby OGs they got reportin' to them. Also, I'm guessin' Ern and Rodrigo were probably slanging shit on the side, so that's gonna have to be dealt with as well."

Champa and Shinzo both nodded. Casey looked at Champa. "It's past time we got our house in order. Our organization needs more organization, and I'm putting you in charge of making sure everything runs smooth from here on out. Make sure the sets don't get out of line and stay in check. You hear of anything that might rock the boat, you let me know quick fast."

Casey made sure both his captains felt his gaze. "Now that we got everyone consolidated, it's important that it sticks. A lotta these cats ain't used to really reporting to anyone. Not only do we have that to deal with, but we're also demanding they do business in a different way." Casey said, "Shinzo, you gonna be my eyes and ears on the street. I want you always movin' among your connects, going from hood to hood and making sure shit's adhered to, squashing any beefs before they get outta control, and reporting back to me on who the liabilities are and who's got skills. Got it?"

Shinzo nodded soberly. "I'm yer dawg."

With that business handled, they all split, Shinzo and Champa through the back door and Casey back through the deli.

On his way out, Casey grabbed an OJ from the refrigerator, walked to the counter, and handed Mr. Kim two bucks.

"That's not necessary, Mr. Casey," Kim humbly said.

"But it's appropriate, my man. Thanks for the use of your back room," said Casey.

"Anytime, Mr. Casey. As you Americans say, 'That's what friends are for.'"

"And as you Koreans say, 'A close neighbor is better than a far-off relative,'" Casey replied.

"Indeed, you are correct, sir, your friendship is always appreciated," said Mr. Kim as he bowed. Casey bowed back, took the money and his OJ, and left.

As he walked back to his Caddy, Casey remembered when Mr. Kim had come to him long ago with a problem. Casey owned the apartment above Kimchi's Deli, using it as a crash spot on regular occasion. Mr. Kim was smart enough to see what kind of man Casey was, and came to him one day when his only daughter had gotten involved with one of Casey's enforcers. Casey made the girl off-limits to everyone, not because he liked Kim or gave a shit, but because he wanted the insurance of knowing the store owner would never speak about what he saw or overheard.

Casey knew tomorrow's meeting was gonna be a battle of wills. A lot of the sets he now controlled were eventually gonna have to walk away from dealing hard drugs. That was gonna be a tough financial hit. It also meant that other independent crews would see opportunity and try and set up crack and heroin operations in his territories. Casey had to make it worthwhile for them to play ball because none of these guys had a moral compass worth a shit. He had less than six hours to figure it all out, but he was a pressure player, always had been, and knew he'd come through.

He pulled up in front of his place, glad to have some alone time to contemplate. As fine a woman as Carla was, sometimes a brotha just needed to sort some shit out all by hisself.

Casey rode the elevator up to his crib; the elevator doors pinged like the bell for the start of a title fight and opened. As Casey walked to his door, he heard music; either someone had broke into his crib and was messin' around, or Carla was there. He reached into his right pocket for the baby 9, pulled out his keys with his left hand, and opened the door slowly.

As the music grew louder, he heard Carla singing. Casey relaxed, put the 9 away, walked in, and shut the door. Casey's pad was pimped out in a modern Japanese style, with plenty of gleaming black lacquer and soft cushions for relaxing. Not only did it suit his sense of style, but he dug the clean lines and efficiency of it. Of course, he had the latest gadgets and guns hidden all over the place, as if he was gonna have a gangsta Easter egg hunt.

Carla saw him and bounced over, giving him a wet kiss. She looked fine as fuck: barefoot and wearing some white booty shorts and a tight spaghetti-strap top that made her tits look even bigger than they already were.

"What's up, baby?" Carla asked when she saw the look on his face.

"Ain't no thang . . . but in the future, I need you to drop a dime when you rolling through," Casey said.

Carla gave him a WTF look and was about to get into it before Casey interrupted her. "Hold up, now. Before you go left, you know what I do. . . . I heard noise in here and went into combat mode. A simple text would have taken that stress off my neck."

Carla still had a trace of a salty look on her face as she stared at him. "Are you *sure* that's all it is, Crush?"

"No, it ain't, and you best drop that eyeballin' right now. I'm in the middle of some shit at the moment, and sometimes a nigga needs some time to think *alone*!" Casey took a breath before he went any further off the deep end. "Look, we got a good thing, baby, so this doesn't have to be no drama."

Still glaring at Casey coldly, Carla said, "You got that right, nigga. Fuck it, let me get the hell outta your way, then." She stormed past him and headed for the door.

Casey was two seconds from completely losing his shit with the day he'd had and the shit still to come. The last thing he needed right now was his bitch trippin' and causing needless drama.

"Carla . . ." She kept walking toward the door, grabbing her purse. *"Carla!"* he said in a tone that made her jump and then freeze in her tracks. She turned slowly, clearly hurt, biting her bottom lip while looking at the ground.

Casey let a breath out between his teeth—he hated all this female drama shit, but he knew every woman was the same. Stepping closer to her, he reached down and tilted her face up to look at him. "Look, baby, we're good—shit, we're great. You're it for me, okay? I just got some heavy shit goin' on right now, and you already know 'bout my morning. I'm just sayin' let a brotha know when you're coming through because I got a hectic life and I wanna make sure what's important to me is safe, you dig?"

"That all sounds good, Crush, but sometimes . . ." Carla stared back at him again, but still had that vulnerable look on her face.

Casey narrowed his eyes and figured he knew what was comin'. "Come on, say what you gotta say, baby girl."

"It's just sometimes I feel like you takin' me for granted. You know, you come by when you wanna come by, we hang, which is great and all, but then you bust a nut and bounce out the door. Now, don't get me wrong, the lovin' is all good, but sometimes your leavin' makes me wonder if that's all you about, y'know?"

"Is that what's doggin' you?" Casey asked, his eyebrows shooting up in surprise. "You know you it for me, baby, don't ever doubt that! Shit, it's not like I don't like seeing your fine booty greetin' me as I come in the door. But I got 99 problems with putting the

VKs and everything else together, and I don't need some wannabe boss-baller thinkin' he can get to me by comin' after you. I ain't gonna let anything happen to you, a'ight?"

She nodded slowly while easing closer to him. "I hear you, baby."

"A'ight, then. I got some thinking to do, then I got a big meeting that's gonna go late. I'll call you after that, and stop by for a late dinner, cool?" He put his arms around her and kissed her. Carla melted into his embrace, and Casey just held her for a few moments.

When he pulled back a bit, Carla asked, "You promise?"

"Yeah, baby," Casey said, and with that he sucked on her bottom lip and squeezed her butt hard. "Mm-mm! Damn, woman, how could you think I'd ever wanna leave this?"

Carla laughed softly, smacking Casey in the chest. "'Cause you stoopid, like all men, that's why." She pulled the door open. Halfway out, she turned to look at Casey one last time. "Later tonight . . . right?"

Casey smiled and said, "Come on, girl, get outta here." The door shut and she was gone.

He went to the window and looked at the light of the city gleaming below him. His turf, all of it. How long could he keep the Kings on point, his girl chilled, and himself out of the joint and breathing?

Fuck, what a day.

3

The next morning, Casey got up early and hit the gym. While pushing weights around, he spied in the mirror two detectives coming his way. He ignored them until they tapped him on the shoulder. Casey turned and said nothing. The two detectives flashed their badges and started peppering him with questions about Rono's murder. Everyone around him gawked as the two pigs talked loud enough for the whole gym to hear. It was typical cop shit to try and embarrass him, but Casey didn't give a flying fuck.

"Look, Casey, we know you were involved, we just haven't figured it out . . . yet," one of the detectives said.

Casey kept bench-pressin' his three hundred pounds. "Well, till you do, get the fuck out my face!"

The cops eventually split and Casey finished his workout.

For the rest of the afternoon and into the evening, Casey contemplated his situation and the fate of the VKs. He'd been out of the pen for all of three months, and this gangsta lifestyle was already threatening both his freedom and life. He had gotten his revenge—for all the good it had done him—but he had got it. He had the Kings under his control and he had a great broad by his side. But in the end, his trip to Antonio's resting place had made him realize any personal peace he could find would be elusive at best, and a dangerous trap at worst.

So what's the point—it's a fuckin' losing battle. Doing a quick accounting in his head, Casey figured he was sittin' on close to $2.3 million in cash—enough to get him gone and give him time to figure out how to survive as a square. As far as the Kings were concerned, he could turn them over to Champa to run, and if he didn't want 'em, well, it wouldn't be his muthafuckin' problem.

Casey mulled over the issues that would crop up if he decided to stay, mainly, how to keep the guys on point and how to make sure there was no splintering off. How was he gonna make sure the cops, the FBI, the DEA, and anyone else with a badge was not gonna destroy what he created? Casey caught himself and thought, *What the fuck is this shit? I feel like I'm having a gangsta's midlife crisis.*

As Casey leaned back on his sofa, he exhaled and surveyed his apartment. On the wall was a copy of the famous Japanese print, *The Great Wave off Kanagawa.* He studied the picture intently: The waves looked like great claws, and in the background was the seemingly very small Mount Fuji. It almost looked like the waves were about to swallow Mount Fuji because of the perspective. Mack D always said "life is all about perspective." And then it hit him.

"Sonofabitch." Casey slowly sat up as Mack D's voice echoed in his head: *"The opportunity to secure ourselves against defeat lies in our own hands, but the opportunity of defeating the enemy is provided by the enemy himself."*

When he'd first heard that quote in Attica, Casey had been knocked out. "Oh shit, nigga, that's a jewel right there, wow." It was one of Mack's favorite Sun Tzu quotes. Mack often spoke passionately about how, in any conflict, you needed to see the weakness in others and do to them what they're trying to do to you. He explained that the enemies' strategy against you needed to be applied against their weakness for you to defeat them.

Casey ran over all of this once more in his mind, crystallizing what his next move would be. Glancing at his watch, he realized he needed to get to the office for the powwow with his field generals. He grabbed his jacket and headed out the door. As he pulled onto the street, he was formulating his master plan and what he would say to the guys. It was too early to let everyone in on what he had planned, but it was important that all the guys knew how shit was gonna work from here on out.

He drove to the office, constantly and unconsciously checking his rearview mirror. Casey pulled his black Escalade into the garage and saw Champa, who was just parking his gleaming silver Aston Martin DB9.

Casey got out and whistled at his brotha's new wheels. "Whassup, nigga, that the new whip?"

Champa smiled. "Yeah, man, some of the spoils from that little escapade of ours."

Casey surveyed the car admiringly; Champ had customized the interior, splashed it with a new paint job, added bigger wheels, and put fresh CEC rims on it.

"Damn, that shit is tight. Who did the work, Hans?" he asked.

"None other. He also installed bulletproof glass and added some voice-activated benefits," said Champa.

Casey knew that besides doing hella custom work, Hans was great at adding other "benefits," such as secret compartments that concealed guns.

Casey and Champa got in the car and shut the doors. Champa smiled big and said, "Are you ready for this shit, nigga?" He paused, making sure he had Casey's attention, then said, "Düsseldorf." On the dash, a panel slid up, and the handle of a SIG Sauer P226 popped out. Casey smiled at Hans's handiwork—he never would have guessed the dash had been customized—it looked that natural. Champa explained that he'd originally had the password set to "gun," but the damn thing was opening all the time, triggered by the rap lyrics he was listening to and by his phone conversations. He could just imagine a cop pulling him over, asking him if he had any guns in the car and that damn compartment opening. "So I changed it to 'Düsseldorf,' 'cause most niggas is clueless to that shit." Casey laughed and they got out of the car.

They kept the talk light as they walked to the elevator and rode up to Casey's Urban Victory office on the tenth floor. The garage couldn't be trusted to be secure, but once in Casey's office, they'd dispense with the small talk.

The office looked like most nonprofits in the city: cheap desks crowded together in a drab interior, a bit disheveled, and one step away from shutting down. It was exactly the way Casey liked it—deceptive. They walked into the Urban Victory lobby and past the gold logo on the wall, which looked like it was seconds from falling down. Underneath was written the organization's motto:

> *If you want to lift yourself up, lift up someone else.*
> —BOOKER T. WASHINGTON

Shinzo was waiting in the shabby lobby. "Whassup, boss man?"

"Hey, Shin, what it do?"

"Just waiting on these guys to arrive—you want 'em in the conference room?"

"Yeah, it's nice and clean, right?"

Shin knew by "clean," his boss meant that there were no bugs. "Yeah, the cleaning crew left it nice and tidy."

"Okay, you know the drill—when everyone arrives, call me on the cell."

He and Champa walked past the windowless conference room and into the back office. He shut and locked the door, and rather than sit at the desk, Casey walked to the bookshelf and called a number on his iPhone that triggered the floor-to-ceiling bookshelf to pop out. Casey pulled the bookshelf farther out on noiseless hinges, revealing a heavy wood-paneled door with a retinal scanner next to it. Casey put his eye on the scanner, the door opened, and he stepped into his plush office.

As he walked in, Champa chuckled and said, "James fuckin' Bond."

Casey smiled and said, "Come on, nigga, you know how we do."

The carpet was jet black, as was the furniture; the door and windows were bulletproof, and the windows heavily tinted as well. This was Casey's sanctuary and, if need be, his safe room. Casey sat down at the desk and turned on two fifty-inch LED flat screens mounted on the far wall. One showed the conference room and the outside of his door on split screen, and the other showed the lobby, garage, and elevator. All the cameras were HD and had the ability to pan, zoom, and provide audio if Casey wanted to listen to whoever was talking.

Casey sat behind his desk while Champa sat on the plush black suede sofa. They had about twenty minutes until everyone showed up. Casey leaned his elbows on the desk, looked at Champa, and said, "The opportunity to secure ourselves against defeat lies in our own hands, but the opportunity of defeating the enemy is provided by the enemy himself."

Champa looked at Casey cockeyed. "Nigga, what the fuck you talking about?"

"I got a plan to keep the cops in check. But I'm gonna need your help," Casey said.

Champa arched an eyebrow in surprise. "Oh, really? Well, damn, nigga, let's hear it."

"This is some next-level shit we've never played before, Champa. We gonna need to create our own special ops units. We gonna need top-flight computer guys to hack into systems all around the city, not just personal computers, but businesses' computers and government computers as well."

Champa focused intently on Casey, intrigued. "Uh-huh, okay, I'm down with you so far."

"I'ma need guys that can record audio and video in different locations undetected, as well as record phone conversations on landlines and mobile phones," Casey continued.

"Damn, nigga, you really are goin' James Bond, that's some hella stealth shit. Who we settin' up for the takedown?" Champa asked.

Casey looked at Champa for a beat and coolly said, "The N . . . Y . . . P . . . D!"

Champa stared at Casey, caught totally off guard. He opened his mouth, closed it, then opened it again and started laughing his ass off. Casey just leaned back and let him get it out of his system.

"Wow, nigga! Damn, that's some shit," Champa said once he'd caught his breath. "How the fuck we gonna do that and why? I mean, how's that fit into your grand plan? I don't get it."

"Champa, what are the cops always trying to do to us?"

"Shee-it! Catch us out of pocket!"

"Specifically . . ."

"Catch us breaking the law so they can put us under—"

"Exactly, but now we gonna turn the tables on 'em. We gonna compile evidence on all the dirty cops and their loved ones and, at the right moment, let 'em have it."

"Turn it in to their internal affairs people?"

"Not just them, brotha . . ."

And then it hit Champa like a thunderbolt. He sprang to his feet. *Ohhh shit! The press—awww, nigga, I love it!* Champa was dancing and jumping around. "It's gonna be like our own—what's that shit called?—y'know, run by that crazy English muthafucka—"

Casey smiled and said, "WikiLeaks, and he's Australian—"

"Exactly! We gonna target the cops that're already watching our asses. And at the right moment, we put 'em on blast. Those cops we put on the hot seat will need to be put on leave or fired on the spot 'cause there'll be too much public pressure, which means we won't be having anyone on our ass the minute we spring shit. It's our Get Out of Jail Free card. When shit starts getting hot, we drop that bomb, which creates a hella diversion."

Casey could tell the beauty and the brilliance of the plan were not lost on his friend. Champa fell back onto the sofa, deep in thought, before looking at Casey again. "Nigga, you a stone-cold genius."

Casey laughed and bumped fists with his second-in-command. "First things first: We gonna need to find out who the dirty cops are as well as see which ones are assigned to us."

Champa stopped laughing at that. "What if the cops watching us all ain't dirty?"

"Well, then, nigga, we'll create some evidence that makes them look like they are, just like their punk asses do to us all the mutha-fuckin' time!" Casey said.

"That's right, nigga, I got you," Champa said, smiling back at him.

Casey looked up at the flat screens. "Looks like they're almost all here—we gotta make this quick. I want to keep this plan on the DL, just you and me for now, a'ight? Once things start to get set up, then we start clueing in other people, but right now it is on a need-to-know basis *only*."

"I hear ya, nigga. So what's shakin' tonight?"

"For this meeting, I'm lettin' everyone know that you're my right-hand man, and that Shinzo's their day-to-day cat. Any problems, they talk to Shin, then Shin talks to you, and if you think it warrants it, I will step in."

As if on cue, Casey's cell phone rang. He read the caller ID and picked it up. "Yeah, Shin, they all here? Okay, we're coming now." Casey closed his phone and said, "Let's do this."

Champa got up, but turned to Casey and said, "You really think Shin is up to handlin' his weight?"

"Yeah, of course. I wouldn't put him in place if I didn't. Why?"

"Well, he's a bit new to the inner circle, Crush—"

"Yeah, well, he showed a lotta heart when the Rono shit went down. He could have gone left, but didn't."

"True dat, I don't want you to think I'm hatin' or anythin'—I mean, I like the dude, I'm just not a hundred percent sure on the nigga at the moment."

"You obviously goin' somewhere with this shit, so spit it the fuck out."

"Look, I'm just asking the question, tha's all."

"Okay, well, he reports to you, and if he doesn't work out, then handle it how you see fit, but you *talk to me first before any shit goes down*, Champa."

"Okay, I feel you."

Crush rose from his desk and headed for the door with Champa falling into step beside him. As they left the office, Champa chuckled and said, "What, no password or eye scanner to leave?"

Shaking his head, Casey laughed, too, and said, "That's actually a good idea."

Shin met Casey and Champa in the lobby, and the three men walked back to the conference room. Inside were Casey's six generals—all were ruthless, street smart, and complete egomaniacs. When Casey walked in the room, every guy there gave him a "whassup, nigga," and did their gangsta hugs with him.

Casey sat at the head of the table, with Shin and Champa on either side of him. He surveyed the room, looking at New York's criminal elite in front of him. Most of them he'd known for thirty years or more; they were all down because they believed that Casey was the one guy that could keep the peace and make everyone big paper. Smiling slowly, he leaned forward and said, "Man, this is a fuckin' treacherous crew if I ever saw one."

The room erupted with laughter, and someone hollered, "You got that shit right, nigga!"

Casey let the laughter die down before continuing. "Okay, before we get down to 'serious' business, I wanna let you all know 'bout a little hiccup that happened last night that we handled. Big Rich's guys, Rodrigo and Ernesto, got busted being stupid. Now, I got my college baller on the case, so they out now, but I need you guys to make sure all these baby OGs don't bring any extra heat to this situation."

Big Rich raised his hand and spoke. "Crush, I hear what you sayin' and I agree one hundred percent. I'm gonna deal with those niggas and make 'em an example so the rest of my crew understands the situation." Big Rich was probably the biggest player in the room, and he was certainly the best dressed. His suits were always custom tailored and his nails exquisitely manicured. He was known for having a strong pimp hand and was always talking that pimp shit. The nigga was no joke.

Sitting next to Big Rich was Sean E Sean, who gave him a look and asked what everyone else was thinking. "Damn, nigga, you gonna take 'em out cold like that?" Sean E Sean had actually known Crush longer than anyone else in the room, even Champa. He would've been Crush's right-hand man, but he wasn't around enough, because he was too busy boosting shit all over the city. Regardless, he was a trusted accomplice who put in the work and had a bullshit detector that was second to none. Unlike a lotta Casey's crew, he didn't speak much, but when he did, everyone shut the fuck up and listened.

Big Rich laughed. "Nah, I'm just gonna scare the shit outta 'em. But my point is that we all know what it's like to be young and cocky, and the fact is, there's only so much influence we got on these young ballers, y'all feel me?"

Casey looked at Big Rich and nodded. "Yeah, I do, but control is the key to us all making bigger paper, so you do what you gotta do. All I'ma say is I can only bail out so many niggas, and that's real talk."

"Speaking of paper, what's the next big payday?" Mick Benzo asked. Mick was about five foot eight, all muscle, and tended to always be pissed off about something or at someone. He got his name because when he was younger, he drove a Benz that was always breaking down. When anyone would say anything about it, his reply was always, "Yeah, nigga, but it's a Benz—what, you think I'ma drive a Chevy?"

"Inna minute, Mick, we got an agenda we need to follow. The paper's gonna come, believe that, but first up is protocol. Now, you all know Champa. Well, from this point on, he's gonna be my right-hand guy—"

Mick cut Casey off with a sneer. "Are you sayin' I gotta talk to him insteada you? Nigga, please, that's some bullshit right there. How you gonna tell me—?"

"*Nigga,* will you let me finish saying what the fuck I got to say! You all got access to me, that ain't changing. It's just that Champa's gonna make sure everyone's on the same page and that if anything needs to get done, it gets done. I'm not always gonna be available, but Champa will be, so if I can't be reached, talk to Champa so he can make shit happen."

Mick nodded, but he didn't seem completely satisfied. Ultimately, Casey knew he was a down dude, it was just his personality to be fucking sour. That nigga was either on cloud nine or pissed off, and most of the time it was the latter.

"Now, I'm gonna have Shin as my man in the streets. He's gonna be doing pickups and drop-offs and handling some other sensitive shit. Shin is relatively new to our group, but he's a real nigga."

Hen Gee from the Garcia brothers slowly stood and held up his hand. "Crush, you know you my brotha and I respect what you sayin' and all, and we been down for years and shit, but we don't really know this cat, so if it's all the same to you, we'd rather handle that business with you or Champa." Hen Gee and his brother Big E came from a prominent Honduran family. Both were big, about six feet three inches, and dark skinned. They controlled Crown Heights and Bed–Stuy; Hen Gee was the brains and Big E was the muscle. They worked out of their family-owned restaurant called Casa de Honduras.

Casey looked at Hen and didn't say anything right away; the two men had a lot of history and a lot of respect for each other. Casey knew the same rules needed to apply to everyone, otherwise there'd be chaos, but at the same time, Hen brought up a valid point.

Casey checked Shinzo out of the corner of his eye; he was just sittin' there like he didn't have a care in the world—calm, cool, and collected. *My nigga,* Crush thought, knowing he'd made the right choice and smiling a little at it. "Shinzo's my man, Hen, and he's the guy I tapped for this gig."

Hen nodded and exchanged a glance with his brother before looking back at Casey. "A'ight, Crush, on your word. Let's see how this goes."

Casey kept his stare even on Hen. "Thanks, brotha. For the next few weeks, Champa's gonna roll with Shin, but after that, he'll be ridin' solo." Having Champa shadow Shin was not a part of Casey's original plan, but from his guys' reactions, he'd realized he'd need some insurance to make sure everybody's shit ran smooth and that Shin would be accepted. He had no doubt that these cats would test his boy in the field to make sure he was worthy—and he had no doubt that Shin would handle himself just fine.

Sean E Sean said, "Okay, it seems like we all down with your plan, but speakin' to what Mick brought up earlier, what's the recipe for some major paper? I mean the whole reason we got this collective up and running in the first place was to leverage it for big shit. Am I right, or am I right?"

Casey nodded. "True dat, but I need all y'all niggas to hang tight for a minute or two while the logistics get worked out. We're not gonna be doing any more of that nickel-and-dime, smash-and-grab shit. I'm engineering this for over-the-top success, ya feel me? That kind of business don't shake itself out in a day or two. So till then, it's business as usual."

With that, everyone got up and mingled with each other and talked a little bullshit. Mick wandered over to Crush, cheesed up and gave him a hug, laughed and said, "Nigga, it's good to see your black ass back in good form."

Casey smiled. "Good to see you, too, Willie Dynamite." Mick laughed his ass off at that. Casey addressed the group: "Look here, this the only nigga I know who wears a mink coat with matching hat when it's ninety muthafuckin' degrees out." The whole room, including Mick, erupted in laughter.

Big Rich came up to Champa and Casey and said, "Whassup, playas, good to see you, Crush, it's been a minute."

"Yeah, man, thanks. I see you keeping it dapper as always," Casey said as the men embraced.

Rich smiled. "Well, you know there no business like ho business."

Casey tossed his head back and laughed. "True dat, my brotha."

Champa stepped up to Rich and gave him a pound and asked what the latest was on his cousin Jacob.

"He's still around, still doin' that computer shit. Every once in a while, he does some covert shit for me, fixin' tickets and bullshit like that."

"Cool, can you do me a solid and gimme his math? Let him know I'ma reach out to him soon."

"Yeah, no sweat, I'll text him now," Rich replied as he took out his phone. After texting, he gave Champa his cell to copy the number, then bounced with everyone else.

After everyone had left, Shin and Champa sat back down at the table and started chopping it up. Casey looked at Shinzo. "You just gotta whole eyeful of who you gonna be dealin' with, brotha. Now, you know I got your back, but you gonna have to prove yourself to those cats if you want their respect. Believe me, they gonna be watchin' your ass close for the next few weeks."

"I read you loud and clear, Crush. Don't you worry, I ain't gonna disappoint."

"Nigga, you say that like it's gonna be easy." Champa sounded a bit annoyed.

Casey was about to say something but decided to see how Shin would handle his shit with the OG.

Shin turned to him. "Look, I ain't gonna bullshit anyone, I'm confident. I got no distractions and I'm all about this shit. I'm gonna keep it one hunded and take no bullshit. At the same time, I'ma give you and these other triple OGs the respect you all earned. I know this is my shot, and I know you got jewels for me. So all I'm sayin' is give a nigga a shot and I'll show and prove."

Champa looked at Shin, sizing him up. "You got heart, nigga, I'll give you that. Now let's see if you can walk that talk."

Casey stood up and grabbed his keys off the desk. "Okay, it's quittin' time, let's get the fuck outta here. Do me a favor, Shin, check all the doors and lock up."

Casey and Champa took the elevator down. "So, what you think about that meeting?" Champa asked.

"These guys are down 'cause they respect my pedigree and 'cause they believe I can bring them big paper and make their lives less dramatic, so . . . if I don't deliver some serious shit just like I promised, then they'll bounce," Casey replied.

"How much time you got till that happens—two, three weeks?" asked Champa.

"Maybe not even that long, we'll see. In the meantime, put some feelers out there and see what's good."

The elevator doors opened, and the guys clicked the alarms on their key fobs, their vehicles chirping in response.

"Okay, I got some shit I'm investigatin', but I don't wanna speak on it just yet. You wanna get something to eat?" Champa asked.

"Nah, I promised Carla we'd do dinner."

"A'ight, in a minute."

It was 10:30 P.M., so technically Casey was supposed to be at home per his parole, but he figured with the unspoken agreement he had with Lomax, he could risk being out late every once in a while. He speed-dialed Carla and let her know he was a few minutes away.

When he pulled up to her building, Carla was waiting behind the glass doors of the lobby. She came out and jumped in Casey's ride and gave him a kiss and said, "What's for dinner, baby?"

"I was thinking . . . Casa de Honduras."

"Ohhh, baby, I heard about that place. How fun!" Carla said as she buckled her seat belt.

Casey hit the BQE and was at the restaurant in ten minutes. They pulled up and valet-parked the SUV. Casa de Honduras was a small restaurant with about nine tables, but was always packed with notables, actors, businessmen, politicians, or anyone else with pull. The front door had a prominent sign that said CASH ONLY, and the decor inside was like your grandmother's living room, but the food was legendary. Outside, there was always at least a half-dozen paparazzi wanting to pounce on the hottest celebrity. Crush and Carla walked in and were greeted by a pretty Latin girl; she smiled and said hello politely and then excused herself.

Carla looked at Casey and said, "Wow, that was strange. She didn't ask if we had a reservation or if we wanted to be seated." At that moment, Big E walked out with a big smile and loudly said, "What's up, fam, who is this gorgeous lady? A present for me, you shouldn't have!"

"Carla, this is Big E, and this restaurant has been in his family for over seventy-five years."

Carla smiled and said, "I've heard so much about this place, I'm so excited to be here."

Big E gave Carla an extra-long hug, winking at Casey as he did. Casey smiled and pretended to be hot. "Nigga, do I gotta put a cap in yo' ass at your own damn restaurant?" Big E held his hands up and laughed as he led them back to the kitchen. As they walked, Casey could hear Hen arguing with his mother in rapid-fire Spanish. Although Hen towered over his tiny mother, he was trying to calm her down, holding up his hands in an attempt to placate her. All around them, cooks and assistants ran everywhere, creating huge plates of the food the restaurant was famous for across the city.

When Hen saw Casey, he gave him a dap as he rolled his eyes and smiled from ear to ear. "Whassup, man, good to see you, do you see what I'm dealing with here?"

Mama Garcia, barely five feet tall, came up to Casey and gave him a big kiss on both cheeks. "*Hola,* Casey, you came at the perfect time. My son is driving me to an early grave—he wants to tear down my restaurant!" At that, Hen and his mother started goin' at it again louder than before, and talking even faster.

Big E managed to squeeze between his mother and brother. "Hey hey hey, come on, you two, let's do this later—we don't often see Casey anymore."

"True, true," Mama Garcia said, turning to Carla with a broad smile. "So, Casey, who is this lovely lady? Your wife, I hope?"

Casey cocked his head slyly to the side and smiled and said, "Mrs. Garcia, are you trying to get me in trouble? This is Carla Aquila, Carla, this is Mama Garcia, and that other big stump is Hen Gee, Big E's brother. By the way, Mama, I'm on your side. I don't think you should tear this place down."

Mama Garcia glanced at Carla slyly and said, "Casey, always the charmer, no? You best watch out for him, darling. Come with me, let me show you the restaurant before my son ruins it." Without waiting for an answer, she took Carla by the hand and went back into the dining room.

With a sigh, Hen Gee turned back to Casey. "I'm glad you came by, man. C'mon, let's go in the back." He led Casey to the back office, which looked like it'd been hit by a tornado. Hen sat down behind the desk, and Casey sat in a chair against the wall.

"You really thinking of tearin' this place down, dude?" Casey asked.

"Hell no, just redecorate, maybe expand it a little, but she always likes to spin it like I wanna level the place! Christ, dealing with my mom is a full-time job. She only just let me do a Web site last month!"

"Did you run down the meeting we had tonight with her?" Casey asked, knowing Mama Garcia was really the boss of their outfit. That little five-foot-nothing old woman had been running both the restaurant and their crime business since before her sons were born. Beneath her motherly facade was a stone-cold criminal, who was no joke.

"Of course I did. She's cool, she likes you, dude, always has. Knowing Champa's gonna be Shin's training wheels didn't hurt either. I appreciate that, by the way."

"Yeah, well, we gotta make sure it's smooth if we're gonna make this shit big, right?"

"I heard you gonna have a 'no hard drugs' rule, that true?"

"Where'd you hear that?"

"Come on, Case, I'm just doing the math in my head, let me have that."

"Yeah, well, that's comin' down the pike."

"That's cool with us, you know we don't play with that shit anyway, so it ain't gonna affect our biz, but people like that bullheaded Micky Benzo gonna lose their cool over it."

"Yeah, well, don't worry about him. He'll be making enough loot to keep him only mildly pissed off."

Hen Gee laughed and said, "Same old Crush, you a funny nigga, man."

"Come on, let's go to my table before your mom puts my ass in the mix with Carla."

Both men walked to the front of the restaurant, where Casey took a seat next to Carla.

Mama Garcia was still talking a mile a minute to Carla. When Casey appeared, she looked hard at him and said, "You . . . I will talk to later. Don't blow it." She walked back to the kitchen, her big ass swaying back and forth.

Carla looked at Casey and smiled and said, "Wow, I love her! Okay. She's a trip."

"You have no idea," Casey said.

Carla scanned the menu and frowned after a few seconds. "That's weird—there's no prices listed."

Casey laughed. "Yeah, Mama Garcia arbitrarily decides what to charge, based on whether or not she likes the people she's serving.

I remember back in the day when Mike Tyson came in here, a week after he was defeated by Buster Douglas. She gave him a bill for a thousand dollars. Hen and E were losin' their minds, tryin' to tell her she couldn't do that. She was pissed 'cause she bet a lot of money on him and he lost."

"Oh my God, what happened?"

"He told her to bet big on his next fight and guaranteed he would win and he did against Tillman."

Carla laughed with him. "What are you getting?"

Casey smiled again—he hadn't even touched his menu. "That's another thing: You can order whatever you want, but Mama Garcia's gonna serve you what she thinks you should eat."

"Jesus, this woman! I mean, I love it, but damn!" Carla said.

"It's all part of what makes this place great. It's not just the food, it's the experience," Casey replied.

"So, how'd you meet the family?" Carla asked.

Casey shifted in his chair. "I'd gotten to know the Garcias through Antonio's mother. She'd been waitressing at the restaurant for five years." He could tell she wished she hadn't asked, but fuck it, that how it goes sometimes.

They had an incredible meal of plantain soup, miniature pupusas, and poached tilapia in a spinach cream sauce. For dessert they had fried coconut ice cream with a chocolate fudge sauce that had every table drooling. When a fellow patron asked for the same thing, Mama Garcia turned to the table and curtly said, "We're out!"

Mama Garcia visited their table throughout the night to see how they were enjoying their meal. By the time they were finished, it was almost midnight, and Casa de Honduras was still seating people. Casey and Carla got up and went to the kitchen to say their good-byes. On the way out, Casey tipped their waitress fifty dollars—the meal was no charge, of course.

Carla was quiet on the drive home. Normally, Casey would have attributed that to the fine meal and good company, but he could tell something was building inside her.

As he parked in front of her building, Carla turned to him. "I had a wonderful time tonight, Crush."

Casey nodded but stayed silent; he knew women well enough to know there was more coming—most likely a lot more. And he was right.

"You know when you were handlin' your business with Hen, Mama Garcia was talking about her kids and how it bonded her and her late husband together. That really struck home baby," Carla said as she interlaced her fingers with his. "I love what we have, and the idea of having a little one with you is, well . . ." Carla paused as Casey's face tightened.

"Carla, as far as kids go, there is no way I'm gonna put anyone I care about—especially flesh and blood—in harm's way again. As Sunday will attest, you see the potential results. I can only handle so much." Casey tried to let go of the tension in his body and wished she had just left well enough alone instead of singing this tune again.

"That either means you don't care about me, or you don't think I'm already in harm's way," Carla snapped.

"You know what I meant, Carla!"

"Yeah, I'm afraid I do."

"Look, you have a daughter, you've been down that road. What we have is cool, having a child would be nice but it's not necessary."

"Nigga, are you for real right now? Just because I have a daughter doesn't mean I'm done! I want a child with you! Trust me, I wish I could banish those feelings, but I can't. What happened to Antonio was horrible, but life is for the living, Crush! I know how you are, you push the envelope in everything but in a calculated way. That doesn't work in relationships. A child is worth the risk—"

"*Look*, Carla, I'm not that guy. Not now at least, and maybe never. If that's what you want, I don't know what to tell you. Maybe that means you got to make a decision." He regretted saying those words as soon as they hit the air, and knew he had fucked up.

The moment Carla heard that, she flipped. "Fine, nigga, have it your way." Pissed, hurt, and frustrated, she jumped out of the SUV and slammed the door.

Casey was too wiped out from his day to give a fuck at this point. He popped his SUV into drive and turned his phone off. The day was finally over, and it looked like his relationship was, too.

4

The next afternoon, Casey took a cab downtown to meet with Lomax. He never took his own ride there; he didn't need anyone to start asking questions on how he could afford an Escalade still fresh out of the joint.

He stepped into the waiting room with all the other parolees, checked in, did his pee test, then sat in the waiting room again. The windowless room was crowded as usual, filled with about twenty guys waiting to see their POs.

The waiting room was a drag for everyone; it was very likely that all the parolees had been there for a few hours just for a three-minute interview. On top of that, a lotta the guys were sweating their piss-test results. There were always rumors that cough medicine or even Mountain Dew could give you a false positive. The other thing that could jack you up was a warrant you didn't know about. Casey knew more than one person who'd shown up and was violated back into the joint for a traffic ticket that had turned into a warrant.

As he cooled his heels, Casey surveyed the room to make sure nobody he had beef with was there. A couple unlucky bastards were already in cuffs for breaking parole, and would be sitting there all day until they went to lockup. Casey overheard one violated Puerto Rican guy telling his sob story about how he got busted. Apparently, he was a tattoo artist and was working at an apartment he shared with his girl and their six-year-old kid. One of his customers showed up with a twelve-pack to calm his nerves, because he knew he was gonna be tortured by the needle for three hours. The guy drank half the beers, but the tattoo man didn't touch a drop, knowin' he'd be tested the next day. The Puerto Rican worked on the dude for a few hours and sent him home around midnight. At 7 A.M. the next morning, his PO walked right into the apartment—no knock, just walks right in, went straight to the fridge, and found the beer. He then walked in the bedroom, cuffed the guy, and dragged him out while his wife's screaming her head off and his kid's bawling his eyes out. Now the guy's gonna do two more years behind bars, and the dumb-ass who brought the beer's stuck with a half-finished tattoo.

The guard broke up this sad tale and announced, "Hekimyan and Casey for Lomax."

Casey and a Middle Eastern–looking guy with a scar across his face both got up and walked to the guard, who took them past a room of cubicles filled with POs interviewing their cons. The guard told them sarcastically they must be something special to be assigned to the boss man.

At Lomax's office, the guard told Casey to sit outside the door while Hekimyan walked inside. After about five minutes, Hekimyan came back out and said to Casey in a thick accent, "You're next, sunshine."

Casey eyed the dude for a second, then ignored him, thinking, *It's comments like that probably got your dumb ass that scar.*

As Casey opened the office door, he was hit with the stench of Lomax's lunch. As always, the PO's fat ass was overflowing his chair while he chowed down on a thick corned beef sandwich. He was looking at files on his desk, and told Casey to sit down. Without looking up, he asked, "Have you had any recent contact with the law, Mr. Casey?"

"Nope."

"Employment the same?"

"Yes."

"Residence the same?"

"Yeah."

Lomax looked up at Casey and after a moment said, "Shut the door." Working his teeth with a toothpick, Lomax leaned back and regarded Casey for a few more seconds. "You gotta pretty easy parole, Mr. Casey. No spot checks, no GPS ankle bracelet, and your curfew isn't until nine P.M. That's a lot of free time to be productive, don't you think?"

Casey knew this was Lomax's way of pushing him to get the next target, Alek Petrosian. When Casey had visited Lomax a month ago, the PO made a big deal of how Rono had been taken off the streets and that he hoped Petrosian would meet the same fate. Alek Petrosian was an Armenian mobster who, for the past two years, had flooded the streets with heroin and Eastern European prostitutes. Casey'd heard of him while he was doing time in Attica. The word was that he was ruthless and a bad muthafucka and blah blah blah.

Casey stared at Lomax. "I assumed I got the parole I got because I did what I was supposed to do."

"That's right, your dedication to playing by the rules is the difference between you wearing an ankle bracelet or worse, Mr. Casey. In two weeks, I'll want to see you again and review your performance. Who knows—if all goes well, you could graduate to mail-in status. Good day, Mr. Casey."

Annoyed, but careful not to show it, Casey left the office. On top of everything else, now he had to deal with Lomax's increasing pressure on him to take out Alek Petrosian. The only reason Casey'd played ball to begin with was because Lomax, in his own subtle way, had let it be known that he had Casey's St. Jude medal. That medal could link Casey to the murder of Gulliver Rono.

As he left Lomax's office and walked through the waiting room, he heard the Puerto Rican guy telling his story again. He put on his shades and headed outside, glad to be out of the stench and presence of that fat fuck.

Casey hailed a cab and dialed Shinzo on the way to the office. He knew Shin's sister-in-law was Armenian; maybe she was the key to facilitating a meeting between Casey and Petrosian. It was a long shot, but what the fuck. When Shin answered, he sounded like he was out of breath.

"What the fuck's going on?" Casey asked.

"Me and Champa were meeting with Big Rich when a shoot-out erupted. One of Rich's customers got tagged in the leg, but everyone else's good—"

Casey could tell Shin was about to go into more detail and interrupted him. "Kill game and meet me at the office." Holding up a twenty, he told the cabbie to step on it. His biggest concern was that the shoot-out was a hit attempt on Big Rich. He wasn't gonna jump to conclusions, however, because it could have been as simple one of Rich's girls losing her mind and trying to kill a nigga.

Casey pulled up to the office and hopped the elevator to the Urban Victory offices, walking into a mild flurry of activity. Urban Victory was a nonprofit whose focus was to help at-risk kids stay out of trouble. It organized events at schools and parks, primarily in the Bronx, consisting of ex-cons speaking to kids about prison, staying away from a life of crime, and how to deal with potentially violent or dangerous situations. Funded by "anonymous donations," it was where Casey told Lomax he worked. It was the perfect cover, because it allowed him to be around ex-cons without violating his parole. Casey's "job" was to file papers, do miscellaneous office work, run errands, and sometimes talk at the events. If there was a spot check by a PO while Casey was handling something, well, then, he was on an "errand," and would be back later.

The head of Urban Victory was Joe Pica, a white guy who was also an ex-con, and who took the job very seriously. He'd met

Casey through Shin, who'd done time with him at Sing Sing. Joe had landed there when he was sixteen years old because he'd murdered a friend's uncle who was a molester. The State tried him as an adult and gave him twenty years, but he only served seventeen. When Shin introduced him to Casey, he already knew who Casey was by reputation. And for his part, Casey knew from Shin that Joe had a nonprofit struggling to stay afloat.

At their first meeting, Casey told him that his funding problems were over and that he already had office space set up for him and his staff. Casey said that the nonprofit would continue doing its thing; the only stipulations were that Joe needed to change the name to Urban Victory, cover for Casey at any time if needed, and run it like a legit nonprofit. It was hard for anyone to say no to Casey, and Joe was no different. The fact that he was on the verge of shutting down and that Shin co-signed for Casey made it a no-brainer. The next day, Joe walked into his new office space, it was laid out with desks, chairs, and phones, even a sign on the wall that read URBAN VICTORY. As far as Casey's secret office and his real plans, Joe was completely clueless to that, and Casey aimed to keep it that way.

As Casey walked back to his office, Joe came over to him. "Mr. Casey, I got a call from Officer Lomax to verify your employment. I told him what he needed to hear."

"Okay, cool, good lookin' out, Joe," said Casey.

Two minutes later, Shin and Champa walked in and quickly went back to Crush's office. Shin was covered in blood and a goddamn mess. Casey looked at him in disbelief. "What the fuck happened? Are you shot?"

Before Shin could get a word in Champa started talking. "Nigga, you will not believe the wild shit that just went down at Big Rich's—"

Casey held up one hand. "Just hang for a second, Champa." He walked to the door and hollered for Joe. When he came over, Casey peeled off two C-notes and instructed him to get Shin some

ICE-T AND JORGE HINOJOSA

new pants, shirt, socks, and shoes—pronto. Joe looked over Casey's shoulder to Shin covered in blood, his eyes widening, but before he could say a word, Casey snapped his fingers twice to get his attention. "It's nothin', just be cool, no cops are showing up. Get him some gear and when you get back, don't knock, call my cell. Go right now." Not waiting for a response, Casey closed the door and turned to Champa. "Okay, what the fuck happened?"

"Okay, me and Shin went to see Big Rich at his massage parlor, The Good Times. Rich and us were chopping it up—you know, bullshittin' and whatnot—when in the middle of our conversatin' we all hear one of his broads bitchin' from one of the back rooms. Well, we both looked at Rich and started laughing, *till*—"

"We heard a gunshot," Shinzo broke in.

Champa frowned briefly, then continued. "Then we heard some dude screaming like a bitch—'Oh shit, I been shot'—but it's from a totally different room. Then this big country-lookin' nigga that's been shot in the leg stumbles out of the room butt naked with a gun. He looks at us and thinks we shot him. So this nigga starts busting caps off like a fucking maniac. Bullets're flying all over the goddamn place while the dude's slippin' in his own blood leakin' from his leg. We all scatter, but there's no real place to hide because the walls are like paper thin. Then *this* crazy muthafucka—" Champa waved at Shin, who smiled and looked embarrassed. "—figures the nigga's outta bullets, rushes him and nails him in the jaw with a right hook, and wrestles him down to the floor. There's blood all over the fucking place!"

Shin picked up the story from there. "Meanwhile, the guy who fired first comes running out of the room in a rage, so Rich and Champa draw down on his ass and say, 'Drop your piece, nigga!' The guy thinks they're undercover cops or whatever and does it. Before they can say anything, the guy sees me on the ground with this naked nigga covered in blood and completely loses his shit. He runs over to us, screamin', *'Oh my God, oh my God, what have I done, shit, shit, shit!'*"

Laughing, Champa said, "Now, get this—apparently this dumb muthafucka shot his own *brotha*! Those dumb-asses went to get a rub and tug and now the nigga realizes he shot his own brotha!"

Casey looked at Champa and said, "Wait a minute, why'd he start shootin' to begin with?"

Shin said, "Rich's girl told us he was pissed 'cause he said she made him 'pop' too quick. So he's like, 'Bitch, you need to give me another one for free.' She told him to fuck off and said *he* was the only bitch in the room. He got pissed, pulled out his shit to scare her, and fired it into the wall . . . and, well, you know the rest."

Casey stared at them both in amazement. "What about the pigs?"

Champa shrugged. "After all that bullshit, we got the fuck outta there and left it in Big Rich's hands."

Shin nodded. "Crush, all that shit went down in about three minutes, I swear."

"Get Rich on the phone."

Shin did just that and handed it to him after Rich was on. "Whatssup, nigga?"

Rich said, "Ahh shit, Crush, you gotta get this playa a big pay-day. I can't handle this retail shit no more."

"I hear that. You get any visitors after your little party?"

"Nah, it's cool, my neighbors know what the fuck time it is. I got my cleanup crew to tidy things up quick fast and sent that nigga around the corner to a guy that does body work, so that's that."

"All right, nigga. Well, keep me posted—I'm out."

"Hold up, Crush. That young nigga showed his stuff today, he was a good call."

"You got that right. Okay, movin'." Casey hung up.

Casey's phone buzzed with a call from Joe Pica, who said he had the clothes for Shin. Casey told Shin to go to the bathroom and clean up. When he was out of the room, Casey looked at Champa. "So, how you feelin' Shin now?"

Champa nodded. "Yeah, my man put it in today. I know word's gonna spread about this, so that's a good look for him."

After a few moments, Shin came back in. Casey told him to lock the door, then introduced him to the secret back office.

Shin looked around, clearly impressed. "Man, this is some real double-oh-seven shit!"

Champa laughed. "Nigga, I said the same damn thing!"

They all sat down, and Casey asked both men if they knew an Armenian named Alek Petrosian. "This is the guy I gotta tag for Lomax. He's supposed to be a helluva baller."

"The only Armenian I ever knew was Luca Bagramian, who was killed ten months ago in a drive-by hit," Champa said. "Luca was a bad muthafucka, always runnin' a lot of big shit. I actually pulled a couple jobs with him back in the day."

Casey turned to Shin, who said, "I don't know him, but I know of him. He runs a lot of H and supposedly imports broads from the Ukraine. My sister-in-law could probably find out who he runs with or where he hangs out. It's a pretty tight-knit community, for the most part."

"Talk to her on the DL and get back to me as soon as you hear anything." Casey turned back to Champa. "What's the status of that team I asked you to pull together?"

"I gotta phone guy and I also called Jacob to set up a meet to check him out."

"Okay, I wanna see the phone guy, so make that happen for tomorrow. I'll tell you a location later."

Casey walked Shin and Champa out and locked the door behind them. He walked back and sat behind his desk, running over the plan in his head and taking stock of where he was at. As he did, however, thoughts of Carla crept into his mind. He hadn't heard from her today, but then again, he hadn't reached out to her, either. He went back and forth on whether he should text or call her, and decided to text, given she was probably at work and couldn't talk anyway. It also meant he didn't have to deal with voice mail.

Casey wrote, *Our communication got twisted up last night, you do-*

ing ok? and sent it. He rose, left his office, and decided to pay a visit to Mick Benzo in West Harlem.

On the ride there, he dialed Mick and let him know he wanted to do a one-on-one. Mick was down and told him to meet him at his crib. Casey knew what he was gonna say, but didn't know the exact script yet. However, working on the fly always was his strong suit, so he figured the words would come when he needed them.

Twenty minutes later, he drove down Strivers' Row in Harlem. Strivers' was a group of beautiful town houses originally built for whites only back in the day. When the development had finally been finished, Harlem was primarily a black neighborhood, and as a result, nobody white had wanted to move in. After the development company went bankrupt, they'd let brothas and sistas start living there.

Casey pulled up to Mick's spot and spotted a couple of his guys outside. They immediately recognized Casey and told him to go on in. Casey walked in and was greeted by Mick at the door.

"Whassup, my nigga?" Mick said with a smile.

"Chillin', man—this is a tight spot you got, baby." Casey admired the hardwood floors and neoclassical moldings throughout the crib.

"Yeah, Harry Wills used to live here."

"I'm not hip—who's that?"

"He was a boxer back in the day, one of the best, but you know he got jerked around by the white man 'cause after Jack Johnson won the title in 1910, whitey wasn't about ta give niggas another shot at the crown." Mick always had a bit of a chip on his shoulder; he was also a Five Percenter, as were a lot of his guys.

They went into the living room, where some of Mick's guys were hangin' out. Mick told 'em all to scatter and to close the door.

Once they were alone, Casey got down to it. "Look, Mick, I got where you was comin' from the other day and I appreciate your support in our endeavor. The truth is that without you, this won't work, so I need you to be totally in on this. You got a serious rep, so what you say and do matters to everybody."

Mick looked at Casey and said, "Come on, man, you a triple OG, how'm I not gonna give you my support? 'Sides, nigga, we go way back."

Casey nodded. "That's cool, brotha. But there's one more thing—"

Mick held up a hand. "If it's about Champa, that's cool, Crush, I ain't sweatin' that."

Casey looked at Mick and said, "Right on . . . it's something else, though, a certain part of your business that's eatin' up our own people."

Mick jerked his head back and looked at Casey incredulously but said nothing. Guys like Mick weren't used to being confronted like that, and when they were, blows and gunshots usually ensued.

Casey held his gaze and said, "In the end, it's about paper, right? We only do the shit we do 'cause we want that paper." He could tell Mick was pissed but was holding it together—he had too much respect for Crush to go left on his ass.

Mick put his fingertips together very carefully and said, "Nigga, are you tellin' me to give up—?"

"No, Mick . . . I'm *askin'* you to do something that will make you more paper in the end, as well as ensure that our people don't continue to get fucked. Ultimately, you know the white man is really behind all this shit. We've had enough Harry Wills in our culture, Mick."

Casey kept his stare cool as Mick squinted back at him. "You a clever muthafucka and you right . . . but, nigga, I'm pulling five hundred K a month off this shit! It's a goddamn paper train!"

Casey quickly jumped in. "I know the economics, Mick. Your cost of goods is 'bout twenty percent off that five hundred K, but you also got the headache and high cost of distribution to figure into the mix. What I'm talkin' 'bout is no cakewalk, either, but it's a better business."

There was a knock on the door, and one of Mick's lieutenants walked in. Mick whirled around and unloaded on him. *"Nigga, when that door is closed, it means stay the fuck out or get shot! Now, get out of my fuckin' face!"* Mick's lieutenant jumped the fuck out of his skin and damn near busted his ass getting outta the room.

Casey let Mick pull his shit together, then stood and walked over to him. "I'm settin' up some fly shit, and you know I'm the nigga to do it. I got a plan for both the paper and the pigs."

Still fuming, Mick cocked his head and looked at Casey in disbelief. "The pigs? What the fuck you talking 'bout?"

Casey ran his whole plan down in detail over the next thirty minutes while Mick sat and listened without saying a word. Holding Mick's attention was no easy feat, but he did it. During that time, Casey's phone buzzed more than once, but he ignored it, knowing he was dealing with something fragile that could fall apart easily.

At the end of Casey's breakdown, Mick nodded and said in a low voice, "That's a good plan, and you *might* be able to pull it off, but if you don't, then what—I'm left with jack shit? How am I supposed to eat then?"

Casey sat back in his seat. He knew Mick was down to play ball; now it was just logistics—once Mick agreed, so would everyone else. "The proof's in the doin', my man. Till I pull this off, it's business as usual, that way there's no risk. When I prove my plan works—and it will—you'll need to give up selling the hard shit. Pot's cool, but everything else has to go."

"What about some other cat coming in and picking up where I left off?" Mick asked.

"As far as other people trying to move into your territory and start a business, you handle them like you do every other muthafucka who tries to challenge you." Casey smiled. "Only difference now is that you gonna have some helluva backup."

Mick looked at Casey and said, "I'ma sleep on this, but if you can deliver what you say, then I'm good. But I'm gonna need to see this shit in action before I change up my game plan, you dig?"

Casey gave Mick a nod, bumped fists with him, and said, "My man." Mick walked Casey out, passing the guy that had interrupted their meeting, who now wallpapered himself against the wall.

Mick turned to him. "Nigga, would you relax?"

Casey chuckled. "Mick, you still a goddamn trip."

In false modesty, Mick replied, "Who, me?" then laughed his ass off at his own joke.

Casey got in his car and rode out a few blocks, then checked his messages. There were two missed calls from Champa and Shin, and a text from Carla that said, *Whatever Crush, I'm tired of being on the hamster wheel to nowhere.*

Casey replied, *That's not what's happening, I know you're working, I'll call you later, and we will sort this out.* He wasn't gonna let this drama with Carla distract him; there was too much goin' on to not be on point. He listened to the voice mails from Shin and Champa, each one letting Casey know that everything was on track to meet the phone guy, Jacob, and Shin's Armenian sister-in-law that night.

5

The next day, Casey got a text from Champa saying he had a meeting set up that night at the Arthur Avenue Bakery in the Bronx with the phone guy.

The Arthur Avenue Bakery was a world-class bakery that sold the best bread in the city. Casey remembered being a kid and smelling it a block away. It was a little hole in the wall that had two tables in front and also sold pastries and coffee. The bakery was a low-key place that afforded privacy, unlike Palombo's down the street, which always seemed to be packed with firemen. Not that he had beef with firemen; it's just that they carried badges, and he wasn't down with dudes that carried badges, cops or not.

Champa had set the meeting for 5:30 P.M. Casey got there a little early and parked down the block and walked there. Across the street from the bakery was the War Memorial Park. As Casey passed the park, he paused for a second and looked at the kids and their parents. They all seemed very happy, the kids playing on the monkey bars and swings while the parents looked on contentedly. He wondered if that could ever be his reality—kids, family, the domestic life. He knew Carla was the right woman for him, but he probably wasn't the right man for her. Whenever she brought up family, it triggered thoughts about how things had all gone wrong with Antonio. Even if he hadn't been locked up when his son got killed, would that have really changed anything? His son would have been surrounded by gangsters and crime 24/7 had he been free. How could he tell a kid to forsake the life his father led, when it wasn't important enough to him to leave it behind for himself and his family? That hypocrite shit fucked with Casey's head—the "do what I say, but not do what I do" was total bullshit!

He knew his relationship with Carla was coming to a head, and decisions would be made, one way or the other. He didn't want to lose Carla, but the only way he felt Carla and he had a shot at having a family was if he squared up and moved to a new locale. Away from the memories and the drama that he knew would always find him, no matter what. *Maybe I should just walk away and spare her any more disappointment or worse. Let her find a square cat that's a solid earner and gung ho on having a family and shit.* Carla was thirty-eight, still young enough to have another kid. The idea of him having another kid just made him feel vulnerable to his core. If something happened to him or the kid, then what? And what if something happened to Carla? Then he'd be raising a kid solo—that shit seemed insane. Crush Casey, single father and gangsta? *Nah, fuck that.*

Casey walked across to the bakery and took a seat outside and realized he had to compartmentalize that train of thought so he could keep his head in the game. He called Shin and told him to meet Champa and him at the bakery in forty-five minutes and just chill in his ride when he got there.

A minute later, Champa rolled up in his Aston Martin with the phone guy in the passenger seat. He popped out and walked over to Casey with his usual swagger. "Whassup, Case, this is Al P., Mr. Telephone Man."

Casey stayed silent and seated, bumped fists with Al P. Then the guys sat down and ordered coffee.

Al had been a fixture in the hood for a long time. Champa and

Casey both knew of him, but didn't really know him. His rep in the hood was clean: He wasn't a troublemaker or a snitch. He'd worked at the phone company for many years until a car plowed into a pole he was working on. Al plummeted forty feet to the ground, and had been in the hospital for a month. After that, he had a bit of a limp and went on disability, but he was far from disabled. He just constantly complained to the insurance company about aches and pains for a year until they finally said fuck it, put him on permanent disability, and sent him a check every month.

With a lot of free time on his hands, Al cultivated a pretty shitty dice game that always kept him in debt. As a result, he got into every type of phone scam possible to make money to feed his dice habit. He ran fake calling cards, 809 frauds, and used a war dialer on a VOIP service to steal people's credit card numbers.

The credit card scam was social engineering at its best, because people willingly gave up their information. Al had programmed a computer to auto-call numbers all over the U.S. over the Internet. When a person picked up the phone, a computerized voice would tell them the credit card company suspected illegal charges were being made to their card, and it was investigating. The computer voice prompted them to say yes or no if they had recently charged three hundred dollars at an auto parts store, invariably they would say no, and the computer would ask them to confirm the credit card number and their billing zip code. After that, the computer would inform them that the charge would be credited back to their account after the next bill. One out of ten people would fall for this scam, and with the war dialer constantly dialing people, Al averaged about six hundred credit card numbers a month. He had a couple guys he sold numbers to and pocketed about $1,500 a week. A nice little scam, but it hardly made him rich.

Casey sized up Al P. He was a dark-skinned brotha in his mid-forties. He was also one of the few guys who was slick enough not to have done any time—a bold distinction in this day and age. Casey squinted at him. "You been pretty good at dodging the police and not getting popped." What he was really asking was, *Are you rattin' muthafuckas out to stay outta the joint?*

Al P. was noticeably taken aback. Having someone like Crush Casey lean on you like that was enough to get anyone a bit unglued. Casey knew people were more likely to be truthful when they were caught off guard. Al cleared his throat and replied, "I'm a one-man operation—I stay on the move and I don't get greedy."

Casey worked the silence a bit, knowing that Al was already uncomfortable and on the defensive. "So why you wanna be down with us, then?"

A ghost of a smile flitted across Al's face. "When I spoke with Champa, it didn't sound like I had a choice."

"Nah, this meeting's mandatory, but joining up is a choice," Casey said. "I'm fixin' to do some real fly shit on a lot of levels, and I need a guy with your skills to make sure it goes off without a hitch."

Al leaned forward. "What's the proposition?"

Casey eyed the slender man. "Nigga, you gonna have to roll them bones and commit on my word or walk away."

Al stared back at him for a moment, then burst out laughing, breaking the tension at the table. He shot Casey a grin and said, "Well, Casey, I guess my reputation precedes me."

"Uh-huh, you gotta commit right here, right now, all or nothing. The details'll come once you're down. All I can tell you at the moment is that the job would be for a few weeks and it'll be long hours. Also, when I give the word, you'll need to hold off on all your other activities and devote one hundred percent of your time to the operation."

"What's the paper look like?"

"For that, I'll pay you fifty K."

Al P. couldn't contain his excitement over a score like that. "Hell yeah, I'm in," he said loudly.

"Calm down, nigga!" Casey looked him over one last time. "Gimme a minute with my man over here."

Al P. got up and strolled across the street to the park, grinning the whole way. When Casey was sure he was out of earshot, he turned to Champa. "Are you sure this cat's as good as it gets and ain't gonna put us in the mix?"

"Yeah, the nigga's tip-top. I've known him for a while—besides, he knows your pedigree, so believe me, he ain't gonna fuck any of this up. Hell, I kinda feel like he was glad you're interested in him. Flying solo has its hazards, so he knows he's gotta affiliate with someone sooner or later. Last but not least, he's in a bit of a spot with Sean E Sean right now."

"How's that?"

"He owes him eight Gs, and from what Sean tells me, he's been duckin' his calls lately."

Casey shot Champa a look. "Well, there's a vote of confidence. Okay, wave him back in."

Champa raised his hand and Al came over.

"Okay, nigga, this is what's up. I'm gonna lace you with five K now and square your debt with Sean E Sean. That's a nigga you don't need to be owin' anything to, you feel me?"

Al just nodded as Casey spoke.

"You gonna need to keep your nose clean, so lay off that gambling shit until we done." The slender man just kept nodding. Then Casey broke the whole plan down for Al. He told him he'd have his list of targets in the next couple days and there'd be a lot of 'em. When Casey pulled the trigger, he'd want all their phones tapped 24/7.

Al's grin grew from wide to shit-eating in thirty seconds. "Sheeit, man, not only can I do that, but I can track their movements minute-to-minute, see all their text messages and e-mails, and turn any cell phone into a high-tech, long-range listening device."

Casey said, "Hold up. Speak on the last part, the listenin-in bit."

"Once I install the right program, all I gotta do is dial a number to tap into that phone's mic and hear everything goin' on around it. The phone don't even ring, and its owner has no idea you're virtually there. Even if they change the SIM card, I can still get 'em, and be totally undetected. I can constantly gather as much data as you need and keep it on a remote server. The hard part's gonna be reviewing everything I get. If you have that many phones tapped, the manpower to listen to it all will be huge, and I'm just one guy."

Casey was unconcerned by this. "Leave that to me. So, how you gonna put the program on the target's phone without 'em gettin' wise?"

Al snapped his fingers. "Hell, that's the easiest part. I just shadow the target and load the software by Bluesnarfing." Off Casey's frown, he continued. "I wait for the target to pass a bar, and then send 'em a Bluetooth message with a photo ad about Happy Hour. When the target sees the message, he'll think it's a new tech campaign the bar's running. On the message, there will be an X in the corner that the target thinks will close the message, but it actually accepts the app and downloads it into the phone."

Out of the corner of his eye Casey saw Shin drive up, but he stayed focused on the task at hand.

Champa whistled at this. "Pretty goddamn sneaky. And you're sure there's no way to check the phone to see if it's been hacked?"

Al P. feigned a hurt look. "Nigga, who you think you dealin' with? Ain't no one gonna know, not with my apps. The only way to make sure their phone's clean would be to take it to the dealer and have them do a factory reset. Even the virtual shields you can buy won't stop my programs from being loaded."

Casey got up. "Okay, we're done here. Champa will reach out to you when we're ready." Al P. and Casey bumped fists.

Casey was impressed with his skills, and knew $50K was nothing compared to the results he was gonna get, not to mention the hell he was gonna raise. He wasn't worried about his or Champa's phones being tagged with this Dick Tracy software 'cause they always talked in code about their shit or used burners. But in the back of his mind, he always wondered if someone was eavesdrop-pin'; knowing who he was talking to was a puzzle piece he didn't want anyone to have.

As Casey signaled Shin to pull up, he turned to Al P. and said, "This is Shinzo, he's gonna take you back to your spot and give you your bread." Al glanced at Casey, a little suspicion crossing his face, and Casey said, "Nigga, you can take a cab if you want."

Champa laughed and said, "I'll take you back if you're worried, Al, don't sweat it."

Al P. looked at the guys, nervously laughed, and said, "Nah, it's cool. I just been ridin' solo awhile, so a nigga tends to be a bit cautious."

Champa opened the door and Al got in Shin's car. Casey looked at Shin and said, "Bless this nigga with five K and drop him wher-ever he needs to go."

Shin already had an envelope ready and gave it to Al. "Buckle up, you in for a helluva ride." And he pulled away from the curb.

Champa looked at Casey and laughed. "Nigga, you did *that* on purpose!"

"Hell yeah! A dude like *that* likes to be in control, but this time he's gotta know that he's not—I'm the fuckin' shot caller. But look, he talked a good game, let's make sure he can deliver. Have him get a couple phones bugged so we can see that shit in action. Once we know they're good, we'll be able to place them strategically."

"I was thinking the same thing. It would be good to have phones to eavesdrop for us, you know, when a nigga goes into a hairy situ-ation. Maybe you could also give one to Carla." Champa looked at Casey with a straight face, but couldn't hold it and started laughing.

Casey laughed back and said, "Now, how'd I know you would go there, Champa. Whassup with Rich's cousin Jacob?"

"I went by his spot this afternoon and told 'em we wanted to do a meeting tomorrow around two P.M."

"Is he cool?"

"Yeah, he's a Rasta computer geek, spends all his time at a keyboard, he wants to be down. 'Sides, Rich told him what's up and he's not tryin' to get him pissed off, otherwise he'd *never* get laid again."

Casey laughed and said, "Okay, text Shin and see what's up with his sister-in-law and have him meet us at the office after he drops Al."

Both Champa and Casey hopped in their rides and were at the Urban Victory offices in a few minutes. Inside Casey's stealth office, he ran down the progress to Shin, then got down to business about setting a meeting to meet Alek Petrosian. Shin told him that his brother's wife wasn't much help, or maybe she just didn't want to get involved. The only thing she said that was of any use was that she'd seen the man a couple times at an Armenian restaurant in Queens called Marat's. Shin had been there before, because it was where his brother had held the wedding reception.

"Shit, now what?" Champa asked.

Casey sat quietly rubbing his chin, thinking of a way to get at Alek Petrosian. On one hand, he could just have him shadowed and orchestrate a hit, but that would only temporarily solve the problem, as he would surely have a number-two guy ready to take his place. Besides, if he did that and anyone found out he was behind it, there'd be a full-scale war, and Casey had too much on his plate to deal with that shit now. That meant he'd have to take out Petrosian's whole fucking crew. That didn't really sit well with him, as his guys would want to know why they were doing it. His crew wasn't in the vigilante business unless it paid paper. Also, for Casey to put their lives at risk—to handle his dirty business with no upside to them—seemed really foul.

As he mulled over every unappealing option, Casey wondered how he'd let himself get into this fucking mess. His concentration was broken by his second-in-command. "So what you wanna do, man?"

Casey looked up, took a breath, and said, "Shin . . . have one of our soldiers get a job washing dishes up in that spot, have him go in desperate, sayin' he'll work for next to no money. Make sure it's someone who knows to shut up and listen and not question what he's been told to do."

Shin nodded his head. "I got it. I know a couple of guys, I'll have one of them apply tomorrow morning."

"Tell 'em it's a grand if they land the gig, plus a grand for every week they gotta work there. Make sure they show up, shut up, and don't make friends. Get them a picture of Alek Petrosian and report to you ASAP if he shows up there." Casey checked the time; it was about 7 P.M. "Okay, Champa, let's go see Jacob."

Champa looked at Casey funny. "Hold up, I set the meeting up for tomorrow, what if he's not there?"

"I want all these cats working for us to be on their toes at all times, so just consider this a surprise inspection. I'm willing to bet he rarely leaves his house and is always glued to the computer, so I'm sure he'll be there."

"Okay, I dig it, that's tight."

The guys rode the elevator down to the garage, where Casey told Shin to meet Champa and him at Jacob's and gave him the address. Casey told him when he got there to hang outside and keep an eye on things. Casey jumped in the passenger side of Champa's black-on-black DB9 Aston Martin. Champa turned on the monster, its growling engine echoing in the enclosed garage. He had Sly Stone bumping as the Aston slowly crept out onto the street. They went a few blocks to the Cross Bronx Expressway, where Champa opened it up. The sports car rocketed down the expressway, with Champa confidently weaving in and out between the cars with flicks of his wrist on the leather-wrapped steering wheel.

As his man drove, Casey admired the car's custom interior. All the wood paneling had been replaced with custom black carbon fiber; the seats were done in black Alcantara leather with red stitching and Champa's initials were embroidered on the headrests. "How much did Hans charge for all this?"

"Twenty-five Gs, including the hiding spot for the 9 milly."

"That's tight. I'm too hot right now to drive anything but the Escalade, and even that's pushin' it."

As they drove to Jacob's spot, they passed the Bronx-Lebanon Hospital Center. Champa said, "Remember I was laid up there for two weeks after I got stabbed by that Dominican bitch?"

"Yeah . . . that's also where Antonio was born."

"Right, I remember." Champa pretended to check his cell phone while he drove.

Casey remembered being at the hospital for thirteen hours, waiting for his son to be born, hoping he was gonna have ten fingers and ten toes and all that other stuff parents fret about. He wondered if his son had been brought there when he was shot up. He knew Champa would probably know, but he didn't want to ask. That type of curiosity just took him to a dark place.

They pulled up to Jacob's spot and chilled in silence while waiting for Shin. A few minutes later, they saw him pull up in his dark gray Mercedes G-Wagen. Champa and Casey got out and walked over to him. Shin rolled down his window and Casey said, "Call me if you see anything."

"And if you see any niggas next to my shit, put a cap in their ass!" Champa added. He cackled as they headed to Jacob's, while Casey just shook his head. *That nigga's his own best audience.*

Jacob's building was a small four-story walk-up. On the bottom floor was an Afro-Caribbean restaurant called Uncle Charlie's, packed with Rastafarians and with a big picture of Haile Selassie in the front window. Casey smelled the strong aroma of jerk chicken as they passed the restaurant and walked into the lobby. They climbed the stairs to the top floor, and before they could knock, Jacob answered the door.

"Hi, Champa. I thought we were supposed to meet tomorrow at two?"

Jacob was a light-skinned brotha of medium build, with dreadlocks to his shoulders and black horn-rimmed glasses. He wore jeans, Birkenstocks, and a T-shirt that read, MIT FOOSBALL. Unlike most people who got a surprise visit from Crush Casey, Jacob didn't seem nervous or intimidated. Casey liked that.

Champa hesitated, then said, "Yeah, well . . . how'd you know we were here?"

Casey quickly interjected, "He has microcameras set up with motion sensors."

Clearly impressed, Jacob turned his attention to Casey. "Yeah, good eye. It's nice to meet you—my uncle's told me a lot of stories about you." He stepped out of the way and waved them into to the living room. "Come on in."

Jacob's apartment was immaculate, actually antiseptic. On the coffee table were neatly arranged magazines: *CoEvolution Quarterly*, *Scientific American*, and *Whole Earth*. In the corner of the living room there was a huge, elaborate cat tree house covered in brown shag carpet that reached from the floor to the ceiling. The apartment had two bedrooms, with the smaller one holding only a twin bed and nightstand. The bigger bedroom had all the computer shit in it, including six huge monitors. It was a geek's paradise.

Casey had actually met Jacob very briefly back in the day, when he was a toddler. Rumor had it that Jacob's mom had wanted a baby bad, but didn't want a dude to come with it. Supposedly, she'd heard of a computer convention taking place at the Javits Center and went down there to find the smartest cat she could. Given that those guys probably never got laid, it was like shooting fish in a barrel. The folklore was that she'd landed a guy who eventually became the chief scientist at the National Computer Security Center, a onetime division of the National Security Agency. After Jacob was born, she did nothing but point him in the direction of computers, hoping for big results. And it had worked, sort of.

Jacob had been into computers since he could walk. He'd gotten his first computer when he was nine, a TRS-80 MC-10 that you had to hook up to your TV. It was one of those joints that you had to load and save programs on a cassette tape recorder. He lived on it, doing nothing but pecking keys morning, noon, and night. His aptitude was evident, along with his mischievousness, and by the time he was twelve, he was hacking the NY transit system to get free rides. At fourteen, he hacked into the school computer to give his friends passing grades, and when he was sixteen, his mom got cancer. She didn't have insurance, so he hacked into an insurance company's computer system and overnight she had the best care possible. Nine months into her treatment, Jacob got busted and charged with computer tampering and trespassing in the first degree.

That was during the '80s, so there was a lot of "gray area" when it came to the law and information security. Also, the fact that he was sixteen—but looked like he was twelve—and trying to help out his mom made it even more complicated. He pleaded not guilty, but accepted a plea agreement to a lesser misdemeanor charge, and was sentenced to two hundred hours of community service. His mother still got her treatment, because of the possibility of malpractice, and her cancer eventually went into remission.

Now, he spent his days being an anonymous cyber Robin Hood. He'd recently released an application that successfully searched for registered sex offenders using different social networks to solicit sex from children. So far, his app had exposed more than 2,600 registered offenders, and had led to the arrest of a half-dozen scumbags.

Dispensing with the small talk, Casey and Champa sat down in Jacob's living room and started running down the list of things that needed to be done. "The first thing I need is a system that can record multiple conversations at once instigated by a preprogrammed VOIP call."

Jacob instantly flipped into nerd mode. "How many calls and how many hours? And how many people? You're talking both cell phones and landlines?"

"As many as thirty people, and about fourteen hours a day worth of audio for three or four weeks, all cell phones."

Jacob's eyebrows rose until they almost touched his dreads.

"Whooooa, that's a huge amount of data. Wow . . . okay, so that's about three thousand hours a week. I think I'd need about eight terabytes of memory, that should be more than enough. I could have the system also delete dead air and convert the audio from .wav files to MP3s to increase storage capacity. Everything would be time stamped, of course."

Casey instantly knew he had the right guy and kept talking. "I also need a program that transcribes the audio conversations on the fly and simultaneously scans for specific phrases and words, then sends alerts once matches are made."

"Okay, I can do that, too. I'm gonna need to get more hardware to handle all that processing, but I'm guessing that won't be a problem."

Casey ignored that. "I also want e-mails and SMS messages, on the targets' phones, scanned for keywords, too—can you handle that?"

Jacob began pacing the room, rubbing his hands together. Casey could tell he was pumped at the prospect of doing some spy shit.

"I also want a phone and computer app that shows me where all the targets are in relation to where I am. That program should also alert me when any target is within a quarter-mile of me or anyone else that has the app installed."

"Okay, that's doable, too. I can do a Google Maps thing and have you be able to tap on the dots representing the targets to see who they are and where they're at."

"Dope! I also want to be able to tap into cameras in specific lo-cations around Harlem, Brooklyn, and the Bronx, record video, and sync that with the audio from the targets' phones."

At that, Jacob stopped pacing the room and sat down. "Damn . . . okay . . . I can do that if the cameras are IP cameras. I've already got a database of hundreds of unprotected cameras all over the city. Even if they're password protected, I can crack them pretty easily."

"The last thing's a bit more complicated—"

"More complicated than what you've told me so far?"

"Can you tap into a cop car's computer and pull a live video feed?"

Jacob took a deep breath and stared at Casey for a long moment, making him think he might have asked the wrong question. The hacker sat back and closed his eyes, deep in thought. He started talking out loud to no one, looking like a fucking madman. Casey watched him go into what almost looked like *Rain Man* mode.

"The cars probably have a Linux device, so . . . I'd need to hack the police department's FTP and telnet servers for access to those grids. . . . I could scan IP addresses that the police department uses. Holy shit, I can do this! I bet I could also hack directly into a police cruiser's DVR and watch, delete, and even add video." He turned to Casey, his eyes wide. "I can do it. Why don't you guys bounce, and I'll get started now and let you know when I got that all working."

Champa laughed and said, "Hold on, nigga, we dig your enthusiasm, but we still got to go over logistics."

Casey looked at Jacob, who was obviously amped. He'd given the guy a helluva challenge, and this geek was eatin' it up. "Okay, so how long to set everything up?"

"Well, my existing gear isn't gonna be able to handle everything. I'm gonna need about fifteen grand in additional equipment. Is that cool?"

"Absolutely," Casey replied.

"Excellent, I can order it today. It will be here in two days and take a half a day to set up. Meanwhile, I'll write a program that can eavesdrop, transcribe, set alerts, and test it while I wait for the equipment to arrive. To perfect tapping into the police cruisers, that shit could take anywhere from a few hours to a few days, depending on how complicated and protected their tech is. As for the mapping application that lets you see where you are in relation to the targets, that's easy, I can do that in a couple hours."

Casey nodded and said, "I want you to do all the work yourself, no subcontracting to anyone."

Jacob looked slightly offended. "I'm not some script kiddie. All of this work will be coded one hundred percent by me, no one else."

"So this'll take about four days on the outside?" Champa asked. Jacob nodded.

"Okay, cool. Champa's gonna be your contact on this. I want you to understand that you cannot brag on this shit under any circumstances. You need to keep your mouth shut, got it?"

"I got it, I got it," said a distracted Jacob.

Casey leaned forward and got in the hacker's face. "Jacob, listen up. I ain't bullshittin' here. I am not your average guy, you know this. If you listened to those stories your uncle told, you know I'm not a man to fuck with. Don't . . . say . . . shit."

Jacob was completely focused on Casey now. "I understand, I won't say anything to anyone, and I won't get caught."

"That's what I wanted to hear. Now, how much you want for setting this up and monitoring everything twenty-four/seven for the next three to four weeks?"

Jacob looked at his shoes and mumbled a bit. Casey could tell that he was uncomfortable negotiating, or maybe it was something else. Casey remembered Champa telling him that he'd done stuff for Rich, and in return, he'd gotten the computer geek laid.

"How about this? I'll give you ten grand now; as far as the equipment goes, order it online and e-mail a link to Champa and he'll take care of the bill. After that, I'll give you ten Gs a week, cool?"

Jacob perked up and agreed immediately. Casey nodded to Champa, who pulled a knot out of his pocket that weighed ten grand. He handed it to Jacob and followed Casey to the door. Casey was reaching for the doorknob, when Jacob tentatively said, "Oh . . . uh . . . Mr. Casey, would you mind, I mean . . . can I keep the equipment, too?"

Casey looked at Champa, then back at Jacob. "Sure . . . *if* you deliver and don't cause me problems."

When they got downstairs, they walked over to Shin, who rolled down his window. Casey told him to put together a team of guys to watch Jacob's place around the clock ASAP, but by no means should they talk to him or make contact. He told him to make sure Jacob knew that he had eyes on him for his protection; he didn't need him getting paranoid.

Casey pulled back his coat sleeve and looked at his watch. It was 8:40 P.M., and he had a 9 P.M. parole curfew he didn't want to blow. He didn't think Lomax would check on him, but now that he was building his pyramid, he wanted to limit any exposure that could fuck his shit up. He got in Champa's ride and told him to step on it.

Casey made it back to his crib at 9:10 P.M. As he walked in, the doorman told him he had a visitor. *Fuck,* he thought—he'd had a feeling all day that Lomax might pull a surprise visit and sweat him about Petrosian. Casey's concern evaporated when the doorman told him his visitor was Carla, and that she was up in his crib.

Casey walked into his spot to find Carla waiting for him in a tight-fitting business suit and skirt that showed off all her assets to maximum effect. He walked over to her. "Didn't expect to see you here."

Carla's expression and tone showed she was a bit bummed out. "Oh yeah, right, I forgot to give you a heads-up I was coming over."

Casey held up both hands. "Hey, it's cool, baby, I didn't say I wasn't glad to see you. I don't like this fussin'."

Carla nodded, but Casey knew she had something more to tell him. "So, after your text this afternoon, I had a meeting with Nicole, the head of food services for the hotel. She went to the doctor, and it turns out she can't get pregnant. Her man really wants a kid bad, and she's freaked out that he's gonna split when he finds out."

"That's heavy."

"Yeah, well, anyway, it just got me thinking about the pressure I've been putting on you about a baby."

Casey was about to speak but held back.

"The fact is: I love you, and I want us to be a family, but I can't help feeling that deep down, you don't want the same thing."

Casey felt a quick jolt of anger at her trying to put words in his mouth, but restrained himself. "Look, baby, I'm three months out the joint with a whole lotta shit goin' on. I'm still trying to get my head straight. I'm not saying a baby's out of the question, but a brotha just needs some time, that's all."

Carla blew out a breath. "That's cool and I get it—I just feel like maybe you wanted more space."

"Nah, baby, that's one of the things I like about you is that you do give me space, when I need it." Casey put his arms around her and said, "But right at this moment, I don't want any space 'tween you and me, ya feel me?"

Carla giggled as she snuggled into him. "I sure do."

6

Casey woke up at 6 A.M., got his two-hour workout in, and showered. His night with Carla was memorable in more ways than one, and things seemed to be back on track with her, which was a relief. At nine thirty, Casey called Champa and woke him up. He told him he wanted to see Alejandro Hernandez that morning and had him find out if he was in court or in his office. He got dressed and drove to Champa's crib. All the pieces were starting to come together, and today was gonna be a big day.

Casey rolled up to Champa's apartment, which was in a heavily Latin part of the South Bronx. Champa loved his Latinas, so he was right where he needed to be. Casey called and let him know he was downstairs and in seconds Champa came out wearing a classic old-school Adidas sweatsuit that was black with red stripes. He came up to the car and talked to Casey through the open passenger window.

"Ay, man—I called Alejandro's office and he's in court for the next hour and a half. I told his secretary we'd be rolling through so she could put us on the book. So, you wanna park and come up for a bit?"

Casey parked the SUV and they both took the stairs up to

Champa's crib. Walking into his apartment was like stepping back into the 1970s. Champa loved everything about that era: blaxploitation movies, the music, the furniture, everything. He even had vintage *Playboy* magazines on his coffee table. On his walls, he had a few original Andy Warhols and Roy Lichtensteins that he'd carefully stolen as well as some photographic prints of the nightlife of Studio 54. His prized possession, though, was a first edition of Iceberg Slim's autobiographical novel *Pimp*. The book was in a gold ornate frame with red crushed velvet matting. On the cover of the book was an inscription from Iceberg: *To Champa, my Nigga from the Bx. Iceberg!*

"So what was this dude like?" Casey asked.

"He was tight, old school, droppin' jewels left and right."

"In the joint, this shit is required reading."

Champa walked back to the kitchen while Casey checked out his pimpin' crib. The song "Whatcha See Is Whatcha Get" by the Dramatics was playing on the stereo. Champa hollered to Casey, asking if he wanted coffee. Casey declined and sat on a well-worn brown leather sectional sofa. Champa walked in, lowered the music, and sat down across from him with an espresso.

Casey looked at a photo of Champa's mom on the side table. "How's your mom doin'?"

"She just celebrated her eightieth birthday, she lives in Georgia now with my aunt." Champa laughed. "She squeaks when she walks, but for the most part, she's doing good. You think about your parents much?"

Casey hated talking about his parents; it made him feel uncomfortable unless he was talking to Carla. "Ya know, here and there, what occupies my mind today is how we gonna figure out what cops to target."

Champa polished off his espresso. "And that's why you wanna meet with Alejandro?"

"Correct, I need to get an inside track on who does what and who's assigned to any of us."

"Man, that's a needle in a muthafuckin' haystack. Alejandro'll probably know something about a couple precincts, but as far as Harlem and whatnot, he's gonna be clueless."

"Yeah, I know. It could take months to figure this out, and we only have a few days." Casey leaned forward, elbows on his knees. "My guess is the detectives assigned to me are probably based out of the Forty-eighth Precinct, 'cause when I went under, that's where they took me. Anyway, get dressed. I'll meet you out front."

Casey left the apartment and called Shin when he hit the street. "Any news on our man getting a job at the restaurant?"

"Everything's set. The owner put my man to work immediately, washing dishes for half of the legal minimum wage. He's on notice to report to me after every shift."

Ten minutes later, Champa came down, wearing a pin-striped suit and chattering on his cell phone to some broad. He got in the Escalade and they headed out.

The law offices of Alejandro Hernandez were on the top floor of a six-story building on 161st, a block away from the Bronx Supreme Criminal Court, a building Casey and Champa knew all too well. When they walked in, an older Asian couple was talking to Alejandro in the waiting room. The couple looked at Champa and Casey a bit cockeyed, but didn't interrupt their conversation. Casey gave Alejandro a nod and the space to do his business. The couple had a son who was "innocent" of robbing a jewelry store, even though the jewels were in his pocket. After the couple split, Alejandro walked the guys back to his office.

Alejandro was of Dominican descent, in his mid-forties, and a little overweight. His high-end office was, in its subtle way, a tribute to his success. He'd worked hard and bent a lot of rules to get where he was at today. He was a deal maker, and had no problem representing any client, as long as they had the loot to pay. He had strong relationships with everyone at the courthouse, from the parking attendant to the secretaries and clerks. He was always overgenerous at Christmas to all the support staff, and as a result, if there was information he needed, he always had a few people that would willingly give it to him. He knew which judges cheated on their wives or drank too much, and which ones could be influenced with a little dough. For their part, the judges respected his acumen and knew he was a winner, but none of them liked him. He was way too slick and cocky. Alejandro was a master manipulator who got a lot of criminals off, and his conscience had no problem with that. He was fascinated with his clients, and lived vicariously through them. In many ways, he was just like them except his hustle was legal—well, mostly.

As a kid, Alejandro got into a lot of trouble, but nothing major: a little stealing, shooting out windows with a BB gun, and bullshit like that. At fifteen, his cherry got popped for selling weed. Afterwards, his father sat him down and said, "Since you seem to like to run with criminals, why not get paid to do it and become a criminal lawyer?" The alternative, his father calmly explained, was if Alejandro didn't, he would "beat him to death if he *ever* got in trouble again." His father made it clear that he wasn't gonna stand for his mother going through hell anymore because of her son's criminal and mischievous ways. From then on, his father had a noose around his son's neck until he graduated from law school.

Afterwards, he got hired by a respectable midsize firm in Manhattan. But the long hours and clientele didn't suit him, so he went to work for a local lawyer who had clients that were more to his liking . . . thieves, hustlers, murderers, pimps, and con men. For the next three years, his boss taught him all the dirty tricks of the trade: how to work the system, how to make sure you got paid, and how not to cross the line but dance on it instead. Then one afternoon, an angry client came into the office and shot his boss point-blank in the head. He died instantly, and just like that, Alejandro inherited a law firm.

He quickly grew both the business and his reputation over the next few years. Because he was a kid from the streets, he spoke his clients' language and couldn't get punked. This brought him respect and a lot of street cats looking for a down mouthpiece. He also insisted on being paid in cash, of which he declared maybe 30 percent. Around this time was when he met the already notorious Crush Casey.

Casey saw him work his magic firsthand when Alejandro represented him on a gun beef. Alejandro got it dismissed by greasing a judge. Casey was impressed and relieved, given that the charge could have easily landed him in jail for five years. After that, Hernandez defended Casey and his crew for many years, getting them off numerous times. But like everything, one day Casey's luck ran out and he landed in Attica for twenty years. He should have gotten life, but Alejandro had pulled out all the stops and got him a deal. The deal had cost Casey a lot—250 large in legal fees, twenty years of his life, and his relationship with his son. Still, Casey knew that's the way the game was played, and he wasn't trippin' about it.

The guys sat on the two couches, and Casey opened up the conversation. "Do you have any idea which detectives are watching me, Champa, or the guys?"

"Specifically, no, but given that your old partner was only taken out recently, my guess is that they are still watching you."

"What about Mick Benzo, Big Rich, the Garcia brothers, or Sean E Sean?"

"Benzo, I have no idea; that's Harlem, I don't know what's going on over there. As far as the other guys, if they're being watched, it would probably be by the same detectives assigned to you, given that you all are known associates."

Casey was hoping he'd at least get some useful information, but that didn't look like it was gonna be the case. "Okay, well, how many detectives are there in the Forty-eighth Precinct?"

"More than anywhere else because it's where the Detective Bureau headquarters is located. So, maybe three or four hundred detectives?"

Alejandro went on to break it all down. He said that each precinct had about thirty detectives that did "ground ball" cases—those were cut-and-dried crimes. Crimes that needed more investigation got bumped up to the Detective Bureau. That bureau had a bunch of units, the main ones being SVU for sex crimes, Homicide, and Robbery. The SVU department probably had about forty detectives, where the Homicide and Robbery squads each had about sixty-five.

Alejandro sat on the corner of his large mahogany desk. "Given that the Rono shit involved multiple murders, there's a possibility that both you and everyone else are being watched by the Homicide Unit, but it's more likely that they're being investigated by someone at the OCCB, the Organized Crime Control Bureau." The OCCB was headquartered in Manhattan at 1 Police Plaza, otherwise known as the Puzzle Towers.

Casey asked where narcotics fell in all this, and Alejandro said that the Narcotics Division and its sixty detectives were under the OCCB, but located in an old brewery near the Mount Vernon and Bronx border.

Alejandro didn't know everything Casey wanted to know, but he knew a shitload. Casey sat back, doing the math and constructing a strategy while the other guys held their tongues and waited. Finally he inhaled, satisfied that he had the info he needed for now, then asked, "What'd you find out about Lomax's old partner?"

"Lots, actually . . ." Alejandro walked around his desk, grabbed a yellow pad, flipped back a few pages, and started reading out loud. "John Fordham, fifty-six years old, he and Lomax were partners for six years and worked in the OCCB—"

"How long ago was that?

"Uh . . . let's see, twelve years ago."

"Okay, so what happened?"

"On paper, the story is that both guys were investigating a known Colombian drug dealer. They ended up busting him with over fifty pounds of cocaine. After the coke was checked into the department property room, someone stole five pounds of it; at the time, it had a street value of around six hundred grand. Fordham and Lomax came under suspicion because it was their case, and Internal Affairs got involved. IA investigated some of their previous cases and discovered nine additional instances of suspicious cocaine transfers. When they tested the cocaine from some of the evidence still remaining, they found out half of it was Bisquick."

"Daaaayum," said Champa, "these muthafuckas is slick."

Alejandro continued. "The investigation widened to the whole department, all the way up to the captain. In the end, nobody was charged, but Lomax got busted down to being a parole officer because they found twenty-five grand in cash in his trunk that he couldn't explain."

"Why would anyone under investigation stash twenty-five K in their trunk? That's bullshit. Lomax may be an asshole, but even he ain't that stupid," Casey said. "Okay, what's the unofficial version?"

"I gotta guy on my payroll, Carl Jimenez, who does investigations for me. He was on the force for thirty years, and worked out of the Puzzle Towers in the Counter-Terrorism Bureau. He knows both guys, and told me Fordham was always a loudmouth and a bit of a prick, whereas Lomax was the coolheaded one who took care of business. He said their partnership wasn't made in heaven, far from it—apparently there was a lot of animosity between them from the very beginning. When the investigation heated up, things got even worse, with the two of them getting into a fistfight in the middle of the squad room. The next afternoon, they found the twenty-five K in Lomax's ride. When I asked Carl if he thought Lomax was dirty, he was quick to say 'absolutely not.' He said Lomax got into being a cop because when he was a kid, his sister OD'd on drugs, so there was no way in hell he would ever deal or be involved in that type of shit."

Casey thought it was ironic that Lomax had gotten fucked over by his partner just like he did. The difference being that Lomax

did a different kind of time and didn't get the satisfaction of choking his partner's ass to death.

"What's Fordham doin' now?" asked Casey.

"That's the kicker: Two years after the investigation, Fordham's
captain took early retirement and moved to some ballin' crib in
the Bahamas. Then Fordham became the new case captain of the
bureau. He oversees all the detectives and reports directly to the
chief."

"He's runnin' thangs while his old partner's low man on the to-
tem pole. That's some good intel, Alejandro. Call up your man Carl
on the DL and ask him if he knows the names of the senior detectives that report to Fordham."

"No sweat." Alejandro picked his phone up and hit a speed
dial. He turned to his computer and pecked at the keys as he
cradled the phone between his neck and shoulder. "Hey, Carl, it's
me. . . . Yeah, your check's ready. . . . Let me ask you something—
remember that Fordham conversation we had . . . Yeah, who're
the old-school detectives still in that department?" Alejandro
quickly typed and he listened intently on the phone. At the end,
he hung up the phone, printed the list, and handed it to Casey.
On the paper were twenty-two names, plus Lomax's old partner,
Fordham. Casey looked it over, recognizing the names of the two
detectives who had questioned him about Rono's death earlier in
the week.

Casey folded the paper, stood, and put it in his front pocket.
"Thanks, Counselor, we're gonna bounce."

"No problem, glad I could help."

Casey reached into the breast pocket of his jacket and pulled out
an envelope. Inside were fifty crisp one-hundred-dollar bills. The
lawyer had said he'd look into Lomax for free, so Casey wasn't
obliged to pay him, but he hated being in anyone's debt, and knew
the money would always keep Alejandro attentive and happy.

"An early Christmas bonus—"

Champa interjected, "Just don't blow it all on one broad."

ICE-T and JORGE HINOJOSA

Alejandro laughed as he took the envelope and said, "Thanks, Case."

Champa and Casey drove back to the Urban Victory Office.

"Whatchu think? Do we target Fordham and these other cats Alejandro gave us?" Champa asked while darting through the light morning traffic.

"Yeah—in a way it could play out in our favor, 'cause if we find out it's all under the OCCB, that's a much smaller target than multiple precincts and divisions all over the city. The next step is to get a visual on these guys so we know what they look like, then get Al P. close enough to load the program on their phones. The logistics of that are gonna be fuckin' complicated unless we can come up with a way to streamline this shit."

"No doubt," Champa said.

7

For the next two days, Casey had Champa check on Jacob's progress while Shin's guy washed dishes at Marat's and watched for Alek Petrosian. He also had Champa scour the Web for photos and videos of the detectives on the list Alejandro had given him. This would be critical in making sure they were able to recognize the right guys to target.

Casey had a lot at stake: To begin with, he had to satisfy Lomax by taking out Alek Petrosian. Killing Rono was one thing, but taking out a nigga he'd never met and had no beef with was another, and that was a problem. There was also the question of would this shit stop after he took Alek out, or would he be Lomax's personal hit man indefinitely? *Fuck that.*

Casey knew he was in the mix, but in a way, he liked it. Having shit run smooth was great, but he got off even more by overcoming insurmountable odds. It was at those times that he felt the most focused and alive. He liked pushing himself well beyond what he felt was his capacity. Casey was an all-or-nothing nigga, and if shit didn't pan out because he wasn't focused—well, then, fuck it, point seen money gone. Another issue was to find a big takedown for the crew, something high-dollar that would keep them focused. His niggas, like him, needed action and something to work toward. If they didn't have that, there'd be no solidarity. And then there was his plan to take down the cops, which would both cover his ass and fuck over the hypocrites that had been on him for years. The idea of putting those bastards on blast for everyone to see was fucking intoxicating.

And finally, there was Carla. She was the key to Casey keeping his head tight and he knew it, but he still didn't know if he really had the capacity to be in a relationship for the long haul. He remembered back when he'd first entered Attica—he was twenty-nine and already a legend on the street. Back then, nobody could tell him shit.

When he'd had his mandatory psychiatry evaluation, the shrink told him that in his opinion, Casey would always be uncomfortable in intimate relationships because of his parents' deaths and the numerous bad experiences he'd had in the foster care system. *"When that happens to a kid, he often becomes detached or violent or an addict. And that means you have someone that can never give one hundred percent to anyone else."* Casey remembered hearing those words and being pissed. The longer the shrink spoke, the more he was sure he had Casey pegged. He suspected that Casey formed relationships through shared violent experiences; being in shoot-outs or fights bonded him to his guys because he identified with the "take no shit from anyone" attitude.

For Casey, respect was earned in combat; until he'd seen a nigga in battle, he would never really trust them. The shrink had told him that the trauma of his youth would follow him like a dark shadow unless he did something about it. He told him that through talk therapy and treatments like EMDR and hypnotherapy, he could help him minimize the past's influence on the present and, in some instances, eliminate it altogether. Casey wanted no part of his treatments or to be anyone's experiment, but he knew that consenting increased his odds on getting an early parole and reuniting with Antonio.

For the first three months, he'd played along with the shrink's plan, or at least that's what he told himself, but after that he saw the benefits of treatment. Seven months into his sessions, budget cutbacks eliminated the visits. It was then that Mack D, a sixty-five-year-old master criminal, had entered the picture. He had waited and baited Casey like a master chess player—had he not, Casey would have dismissed him. Mack elevated Casey's game with his gangsta metaphysics and put him on a positive path. And it was a good thing, too, because eight years into his sentence, he'd gotten a visit from his son, who told Casey he was following in his father's footsteps with his first job. His boy was sixteen at the time and, just like his father, couldn't be told shit. Casey tried everything to get his kid to call off the job, but to no avail. Stuck behind bars, he tormented himself about the potential consequences and his lack of influence on his own son. On the outside, no one would have defied him, but things had changed.

Five days later came the news that Antonio had been shot robbing a store with another kid. Antonio died in the hospital within hours. On hearing this, Casey went into a dark hole of hate and depression. Had it not been for Mack D, Casey knew he wouldn't have survived that devastating loss.

Casey felt his phone buzz. It was Champa, who said he was outside the office with Shin. Casey let them in and asked for an update on the day's activities.

"Jacob will be ready to do some test runs on the tech tomorrow afternoon," Champa said.

"Reach out to Al P. and make sure he's on deck for tomorrow's meeting with Jacob. Have 'em bring five phones that we can do tests on," Casey said, then turned to Shinzo. "Whassup with our man at the restaurant?"

"He hasn't seen Petrosian at Marat's, but it's only been a couple days. I expect he'll show up sooner or later."

"All right, we all got shit to do, so let's go do it." With that, Casey broke up the meeting, and they all went their separate ways.

. . .

Casey didn't sleep much that night—his mind was buzzing with details and logistics. That next morning, he hit the weights hard, and while working out he got a text from Champa: *I got phone problems, my connection's weak, I'm gonna need a repair guy.*

Casey knew that was Champa's coded way of sayin' Al P. was locked up and that he was reaching out to Alejandro to spring him. Casey stared at the phone, resisting the urge to smash it against the wall. It seemed like everywhere he looked, niggas just couldn't help shooting themselves in the foot. Casey texted back: *I'd be pissed as hell if I got a new phone and it was fucking up already. Maybe you should toss that shit and just start over.*

Champa quickly texted back. *Nah, the phone's good, just a bit of interference, that's all.*

Which meant whatever the po-po had Al P. on, it wasn't major, like a murder rap or some shit. Casey toweled off and sat down, wondering what the hell had happened. If one cog of this machine broke, everything would shut down after it. At this point, finding someone else to do the job would take too long, and if there was a personnel change, then Al P. would have to be taken out. He couldn't afford to have someone not on the team knowing his business. *More mess, goddamnit.*

Casey replied to Champa, saying he wanted to meet with him in forty-five minutes at the diner down the street from his pad. Casey showered and walked a couple blocks to Cafe de Carlito. The diner was a little hole in the wall that was always packed with secretaries and the like jonesing for their five-dollar lattes. Some of those bitches were getting downright irate, waiting for their shit. *Man, what a great racket,* Casey thought. *Just as addictive as coke, but more expensive, and legal to boot.*

Champa walked up to Casey and eyed the line of ladies at the to-go counter. "Man, these broads love that java."

"Yeah, I was just thinkin' the same thing. C'mon, let's walk." When they were away from the diner, Casey continued. "What the fuck's goin' on with your man?"

"He got pulled over last night, and the cops ran his shit. He had a warrant 'cause of back child support—" Champa's phone interrupted him, and he looked at the screen. "Hold up, it's Alejandro.

"Whassup, man, tell me somethin'. . . . Uh-huh, you shittin' me? . . . Seventeen Gs for child support? . . . How long was he in arrears for? . . . *How* many kids? . . . Okay, so if he pays that off, is he good? Okay, hold on a sec." Champa held the phone to his chest and looked at Casey. "Okay, the nigga got pulled over late last night, the pigs ran his license and saw that it wasn't valid 'cause he owes back child support to the tune of—"

Casey held up his hand. "—Seventeen Gs, yeah, I got that part. Tell him he'll have the bread in an hour, ask him when he'll be out."

"Alejandro, yeah, okay, spring that nigga, you'll have that paper within the hour, but I need him sprung now. . . ." Champa nodded as he listened. "Okay . . . so by two, then. . . . My man, thank you—oh, hey, have him call me when he's on the street. . . . Do not forget to tell him to reach out. . . . Later."

Champa hung up the phone and said, "Dig this—that nigga's got fourteen fuckin' kids!"

"So when he's not shootin' dice and losin', he's tappin' ass and skippin' out on support payments, that's great." Casey shot a disapproving look at Champa. "What else don't we know about this cat, Champa?"

Champa winced, knowin' he was on the hot seat. "Truthfully, I think he's cool. It's just one of the things that you gotta charge to the game."

Casey said, "Oh, this shit gonna get charged, believe that. When you see him, you let him know his poon-chasing ass is now in debt to me, and from here on out, I want no more drama."

"Okay, cool, I got it, Crush, and it will be handled. You want me to reach out to Shin and have him hustle down to Alejandro's with the loot?"

"Yeah, have him meet me at the office. He ain't gonna have enough cash on him."

The guys split up and met up at the office fifteen minutes later. Casey got there first and opened up the safe. The biometric safe was as high tech as they came. Opening it required not only a combination, but Casey putting his finger on a biometric reader. Inside the safe was just under $2.3 million in cash, a couple of 9 millimeters, a grenade, two untraceable cell phones, and the best fake passports money could buy—one for him and one for Carla. The grenade had been intended for Rono's punk ass, but chokin' that nigga out had been a better idea than blowing him to pieces.

Casey pulled out twenty Gs, stuffed it in a manila envelope, and tossed it on his desk. He looked in the safe one last time before closing it, staring at the rest of the money. A lotta cats in his situation would have taken all the money and the passports and gotten the fuck out while they could, but that wasn't his style.

Casey's cell buzzed, letting him know Shin was waiting. He closed the safe, picked up the envelope, and opened the door to let Shin enter.

Casey tossed him the envelope. "Okay, inside is twenty large, that'll cover Al P.'s bullshit and put some money in Alejandro's pocket for his trouble. Get down there quick and wait for him to be sprung. Actually, you know what, wait for him at Laselle's, it's an ice cream spot on Morris Avenue, around the corner from the courthouse. I don't need anyone makin' a connection between you and him. And make sure he brings what he needs for the meeting."

"You got it—what'd he get busted for?"

"For bein' a dumb-ass. Now, go."

Shin tucked the money in the breast pocket of his jacket and bounced. Casey walked to the lobby as Champa showed up. He told him to reach out to Jacob and let him know they'd be there around two. He figured that would be enough time for Al to get what he needed for the meeting and be there with time to spare.

Champa got a buzz from Al while Casey and he were eating lunch. Casey overheard Al say he was free, but before he could say anything else, Champa told him to go to Morris Avenue and look for Shin's G-Wagen. Al started to jabber with excuses about what had happened, but Champa cut him off by saying, "Kill game, nigga!" and hung up.

Champa glanced at Casey and said, "You'd think *he'd* know not to say shit on the goddamn phone."

"Right now, I'm thinkin' a lotta things 'bout this cat—none of 'em good." Casey chewed his food and gave Champa the red-eye.

"I know, I know. If the nigga ain't amazing at the meeting today, I will gladly take care of it."

Casey grunted and kept eating. His phone buzzed a minute later with a message from Shin that Al P. and he were in motion and would be at Jacob's spot at 2 P.M. Shin knew enough not to talk with Al on the ride over and to wait in the car until told otherwise.

At ten after two, Casey's black Escalade pulled up in front of Jacob's spot. Champa asked Casey to give him a minute. Champa got out of the Escalade, walked over to Shin's side of the car, said some words. After a moment, Shin got out and Champa got in. Casey rolled down the window in time to hear Champa go into a fuckin' tirade.

"Nigga, what the fuck you doin', havin' fourteen muthafuckin' kids? You think you some kinda muthafuckin' pimp! You're no goddamn pimp! Fourteen kids, goddamnit! what the fuck *is that about? Nigga, you betta pray your goddamn tech is the fliest shit Crush has ever seen! That seventeen Gs is coming out your end, you fuckin' feel me? Tell me why I shouldn't just fuckin' shoot you right now, huh!"*

Casey and Shin started laughing as they listened to Champa go totally berserk on Al P. Across the street, the Rastafarians at the restaurant were starting to take notice; Casey gave his horn a quick tap so Champa would cool it.

A second later, Champa got out of the car, so worked up that tiny beads of sweat had formed on his forehead. Then Al got out of the car, visibly shaken and walking like he'd just been sucker-punched in the face. Casey told Shin to stay on the street and keep an eye out.

Al composed himself and walked up to Casey sheepishly, staring at the ground. "Look, Casey, I'm sorry ya had to bail my ass out—I swear I was gonna make it right, but they popped me 'fore I could, thasall."

Casey stared through the other man, purposely speaking in a low voice so Al would have to strain to hear him. "This ain't no bullshit. This is some high-stakes shit we're doing, and if anyone gets wise to it before we pull it off, then we're all dead men. The only reason you still breathing is 'cause you talked a good game. Now you better be muthafuckin' able to back it up."

Not waiting for a response, Casey turned and walked to the building, the guys falling in behind him. When they got to Jacob's door, like clockwork he opened it before they could knock. Jacob looked Al up and down, but before he could say anything, Champa held up a hand. "Don't sweat it."

They all walked in except for Al, who was told to wait in the hall. The apartment was freezing, a necessity to keep the machines running efficiently. Jacob looked like he hadn't slept for a couple days. For the next hour, he ran down everything that he had accomplished; the voice capture and recognition, the data scan, everything was set and ready to be tested. The app that allowed Casey to see how close targets were to him was up and running as well.

Casey looked around the room, every inch of which was crammed with computers and monitors. "Is all this gear gonna make your electric bill spike and raise any suspicions?"

"Normally it would, but I've already hacked into my meter to make sure my usage doesn't register."

At least one of these niggas got their shit together. Casey was more and more impressed by Jacob's thoroughness, but he knew everyone had an Achilles' heel, so what was this guy's?

"Good. Okay, now what about tapping into squad cars?"

Jacob smiled, turned to his keyboard and typed furiously, then pointed to the forty-two-inch LED monitor on the wall. Its blue screen came to life and showed a video of a cruiser going down a street; in the corner of the monitor was a map with a red dot moving along Bronxwood Avenue.

"This is real-time, in the Bronx."

Casey smiled as he looked at the monitor, recognizing the familiar sites of the avenue buzz by—the food plaza, the meat market, and the small apartment buildings. He couldn't believe it, his plan was actually coming together.

Champa started laughing uncontrollably. "Oh shit, nigga, this is fuckin' brilliant, I can't believe what I'm seeing."

Casey was impressed with how clear the picture was as well. He turned to Jacob. "Well done, my man, but what about getting into the onboard computer and the DVR?"

"The DVR's easy—check this out." Jacob punched in a bunch of commands, and a file list popped up in a separate window.

"Can we see the video?" Casey asked.

"Yes, but it may not be a good idea. I can't verify that when I hack into the system and play something that it won't also play inside the squad car as well. The same goes for the computer, I'm afraid."

"So you need to log in when both guys are out of the car."

"Pretty much, I can tell when they leave the car because the video is always running. The good news is that I have learned how the computer and its applications work just by watching the officers all day. They've given me my own live tutorial."

Casey nodded with satisfaction. "Okay, tight, we'll get more into this later—for now, shut it down. Champa, get Al in here."

Champa walked out into the hallway, grabbed Al, and brought him back inside. Introductions were made and then everyone got down to business. Casey had the five phones that Al had brought loaded with the software and tested to make sure that they could be hacked. The process of loading the software was very smooth, just like Al said. He then tied those phones to Jacob's server so all the e-mails, text messages, phone logs, and conversations were constantly saved.

Casey grabbed two of the phones and had Champa dial the numbers. For the next twenty minutes, they had a conversation to test the voice-recognition software. As they talked, they could see the computer transcribing their conversation in almost real time. It highlighted key words in their conversation; then, two minutes after, Jacob's in-box pinged with an alert that included the text and a link to the audio. They ran more tests on the phones and Jacob's system for the next two hours and found quite a few minor bugs, all of which Jacob fixed on the spot. Even with those glitches, the system's speed and accuracy were incredibly impressive.

While they were finishing up the tests, Casey got a text from Shin: *I'm really hungry, let's get some Armenian food now.*

Casey looked up at Champa, and the room fell silent.

"It's game time. Alek Petrosian's at Marat's."

8

Casey opened the door and told Champa to step outside with him. "I'ma head down there with Shin. You stay here and keep shit on track." Casey picked up one of the phones Al P. had brought and held it up. "I'm takin' one of these phones so you can hear what's goin' on."

He turned to go downstairs, but Champa stopped him. "Hold up, Crush. What if shit goes down? You gonna need backup."

"Nothing's goin' down—he don't know me from Adam. 'Sides, it's a crowded restaurant."

"I still think I should roll with you, dawg."

"Look, I need you here handlin' shit. I'll call you from the car in two seconds." Casey quickly buzzed down the four flights of stairs and hit the door. He jogged across the street and got in Shin's G-Wagen. "Let's go."

Shin punched the gas and they were off. Pulling out his baby 9 millimeter from his front pocket, Casey checked that it was loaded and ready for action. Shin glanced over and raised his eyebrows. "Damn, you expectin' some drama, Crush? Do I need to call backup?"

"I don't know what to expect, but I always wanna be prepared, no exceptions."

"Okay, cool, so no backup, then?"

"We don't got time. . . . Does your guy in the kitchen have a piece?"

"Fo sho."

"Okay, between the three of us, we should be fine, but I don't think it's gonna get hot."

Casey put his Kahr PM9 away, grabbed the new cell phone, and dialed Champa, who picked up on the first ring. "Did you get all that shit we were sayin'?"

"Yeah, about the guy in the kitchen and backup and all that other stuff?"

"Exactly."

"I also think Shin's got a point, man."

"Champa, I'm not gonna debate this. . . . Did it transcribe the call, too?"

"Yeah, it did everything it was supposed to."

"Cool, tell Jacob when we have the targets locked, I'm gonna want a report detailing where they at 24/7, the names of their wives, girlfriends, kids, where they eat, and their addresses, all that shit."

"Yeah, he already knows—he's watchin' the computer transcribe everything you and me're sayin'."

Casey smiled hard—so far, so good. "Tight. Give him Alejandro's list of names and have him start getting pictures and as much info as he can on every one of those guys. I want a full report by tomorrow afternoon."

"Okay, anything else?"

"Nah, that's it for now. I'm gonna kill this phone till we get there. I'm out." He powered the phone down and turned to Shin. "How long till we get there?"

"'Bout forty minutes. So, what's the plan?"

Casey calmly sat back in his seat and chuckled. "That's a good question. I think we just roll up into that joint, take a seat, order, and look for the right opening."

Shin looked concerned. "Uh, okay."

"What?"

The driver rolled a shoulder. "I don't know, man, you always the guy with a plan. I mean, look at all this high-tech computer and phone shit, you know, but now we goin' in with no backup or any kinda plan. . . . Don't get me wrong, dawg—I roll witchu whenever, wherever, I'm just sayin' . . ."

Casey knew Shin was right, and even agreed with him—he never liked goin' into a situation without a definitive plan of action, either. "I hear you, man, but it's not like I got a lot of time or options. Sometimes a nigga just needs to roll in blind and trust that he'll see an opportunity and make that shit work. If a nigga don't know how to think on his feet, well, then he's a dead man walkin' already."

Shin took it in like a student at the feet of the master. "That's a jewel."

"Trust me, when I'm in it, I will handle the shit perfect, ya feel me?"

"Solid."

As they turned the corner, they hit a morass of gridlocked traffic. *Shit.* Shin tried the side streets, but it still took them a little over an hour to get to Marat's. They parked around the corner and walked fast to the restaurant. About fifty feet away, they saw Alek Petrosian exiting the front door, flanked by a pair of bodyguards.

Damn, too late. Casey instinctively slowed his walk down so he could observe and figure out a course of action.

Petrosian looked to be about six feet tall and in good shape; Casey guessed he was in his late thirties or early forties. He had shoulder-length jet-black hair brushed straight back and wore a custom-tailored charcoal gray suit. He was low-key but confident, walking into the street like he knew he owned it. His two apes wore off-the-rack suits and were a pale imitation of their boss. As one of them opened the door of his ride, Casey saw a little boy walking next to Petrosian, holding his hand.

He's got a kid? The boy looked to be about nine years old and had black hair like his father. The two were laughing as they got into the back of a Rolls-Royce Phantom. To any onlookers, Alek appeared to be a loving father taking his son out for a bite, not a notorious criminal who dealt in heroin and sex slavery. The car was badass—it had twenty-two-inch custom rims; a fly, black-and-silver two-tone paint job; and the lights were smoked out. The muscle rollin' with Petrosian got in the front seats, and two seconds later, the car was off.

"Shit, back to square one," Shin said as he watched the car turn the corner.

"You think so?" Casey asked with a grin.

"Huh? You mean you don't?"

"You see his ride?"

"Yeah . . . pretty fly, so?"

"Only one guy does that kind of work in this city . . . Hans Von Ettensberg."

Casey turned and started walking back to Shin's car, pleased that luck was on his side for once. He pulled out his cell, fired it up, and called Champa. "Yo, text me Hans's math."

"A'ight, what happened?"

"We caught a lucky break, I'll tell ya 'bout it later. What's goin' on over there?"

"We wrappin' up, it looks good."

"Is Al's tech flawless?"

"Yeah, man, it's solid."

"A'ight, I'm gonna swoop by there and get my whip. I'll talk at you in the A.M., Shin will drop you guys off, I'm out."

A moment later, Casey's phone buzzed with the contact info for his old friend Hans. He dialed the number and listened to the phone ring a few times, thinking he was gonna get voice mail, but then a man with a thick German accent picked up, *"Hallo,* this is Hans."

"What up, Hans—"

The other man interrupted him. "Crush Casey! Maaaaan, a blast from my past. What is up, man? I heard from Champa you were out."

"Thas right, how you doin', playa?"

"I am good, man, but I am about to sit down to dinner with the family right now. Do you have time tomorrow to come by and see my place? I can text you the address. This is a cell phone right?"

"Yeah, around ten A.M. cool?"

"Perfect. I'm looking forward to it, Crush."

"Me, too. See you tomorrow." Casey hung up while Shin dodged potholes, driving back to Jacob's place.

Hans was from Stuttgart, and was the number-one guy on the East Coast when it came to pimpin' out cars. There wasn't a pro athlete, rock star, or boss baller that didn't take their cars to him to get 'em customized with a new interior, a paint job, sounds, and rims. Certain customers, like Champa, got things that weren't on the menu, like the concealed 9 millimeter hiding place in the dash.

Back when Casey had first met Hans, it was a totally different story. The two had run a chop shop for years back in the day. They had an efficient setup: Hans and he would go to salvage auctions and buy twenty vehicles over a few weeks. These cars were deemed "totaled" by insurance companies, but their titles and VIN numbers were intact. They would stash those cars in a rented warehouse, and then go out and steal similar makes and models. Hans and his German buddies would rivet new VIN numbers to the dash and replace the secondary VIN on the car's firewall, take the safety sticker off the doorjamb, give it a new coat of paint, and spruce up the interior as needed. Then they would take a picture of each one and e-mail the jpegs to a guy in the Czech Republic who would find buyers who'd pay a premium for American cars. Having the proper paperwork and VIN numbers was a necessity for getting them through customs. Once they got word that all the cars had been sold, Casey would load them into cargo containers and ship them overseas. On average, Hans's crew could turn around three to five cars a week. Between the two of them, they were pulling down about $400K every forty-five days. As a side business, Hans would pimp out the rides for everyone in the crew. The man was a master, a true artist; his shit was second to none. It was just one of the many vibrant businesses that Casey had overseen before he was betrayed by Rono.

With less traffic on the street, they pulled up behind Casey's SUV at the back of Jacob's building in thirty minutes. Casey told Shin to hold tight, and that Al P. and Champa would be down in a minute.

He got out and walked to his car, where he noticed two men with dreads down to their waist sitting on the front of his Escalade, smoking trees. *What in the fuck is this shit?* He hit his alarm button on the key fob, the loud shrieking of the Klaxon startling the two men.

They jumped off the hood, pissed, and turned to glare at Casey. "Hey, mon, what the fook you doin'?"

Casey could tell their Jamaican accents were fake and rolled his eyes. *What a goddamn joke.* He dead-eyed the two men. "If I catch you dumb niggas messin' around my shit again, I'll put a cap in yo' ass, now get to steppin'."

Both men were about the same build as Casey, reeked of weed, and had bloodshot eyes. One stepped into his face and was about to say something when Casey snap-punched him in the throat. The wannabe Rastafarian fell to his knees, grabbing his throat and gasping for breath.

"Whassa matter—cat got your tongue, dumbass?"

His partner came at Casey like a shot, hauling off and taking a roundhouse swing at him. Casey calmly leaned back and hit him with two quick jabs and a powerful left hook to the side of his dome. The guy stood up for a half second, wobbling like he was on ice skates; then Casey hit him with a direct shot to the nose that knocked him flat on his ass. Casey shook his wrist to cast off the needles of pain that threaded up his arm.

Seeing this go down, Shin ran up behind the other dude and grabbed him by his long dreads. He dragged the squealing man around the corner and jolly-stomped his ass in the alley.

Casey looked menacingly at the dude whose bell he'd just rung and slowly walked over to him while he struggled to get up. Casey was too quick for him, and gave him a boot to the head. He wasn't even breathing hard, but he was exhilarated and enjoying the rush. He pulled the ganja man up to his feet and repeatedly punished the dude with blows to his head and body with the skill of a boxer. Casey heard the dude's ribs crack like dry wood when he pistoned two strong shots to his opponent's breadbasket. He stepped back and let the dude fall to the ground and curl up into a ball. Now Casey was sweating and breathing harder. He heard Al P. and Champa talking when they came around the corner of the building. The two saw that shit was being taken care of and quickly jogged over, but gave Casey his space.

"What the hell happened? Who's this nigga?" Champa asked.

Still a little winded from his impromptu workout, Casey ignored the question and wiped his brow. "Gimme your knife, Champa."

His man reached into his back pocket and pulled out a razor-sharp five-inch blade with a black rubber handle. Al P. put his hands on the top of his head and turned away, not wanting to see what was gonna happen next.

"Think this through, brotha?" Champa said as he handed the blade over.

The Rasta looked wild-eyed at Casey with eyes as big as saucers and quickly started to beg for his life, his voice losing its fake accent.

"Shut up." Casey kicked him in the chest, then flipped him over on his stomach.

He pressed his knee into his back, and the dude started squirming and yelping. "Come on, man, please don't do this, gimme a chance, brotha, please—"

"You ain't no brotha a' mine." Casey snapped the blade open with a flick of his wrist and grabbed a fistful of dreads in his other hand. He started hacking at the tangled knot, and one by one they came loose. That humiliated Rasta wailed like he was getting castrated.

Champa let out a *"Daaayum!"* and started laughing while Al P. shook his head, obviously freaked out.

Grabbing the last bit of locks, Casey set them free with one more swipe. He tossed them aside, closed the knife, and got up, wiping the sweat off his forehead with his shirtsleeve. He tossed the blade to Champa, pulled up the dude—who was crying like a bitch— and pushed him hard against the wall.

He got an inch from the sobbing man's face and said, "Now, look here, nigga, when someone asks what the fuck happened to you, you tell them it was Jah nigga known as Crush Casey, and he's back and not takin' shit from nobody!" And with that, Casey cocked back his arm, rocketed another shot to the man's ribs, and let him crumple to the ground.

Shin came around the corner, his shirt wet with sweat from the exercise he'd just had. He gave a fist pound to Champa and then saw the dreads scattered all over the ground and looked at Champa. "Damn, I shoulda thought of that!"

Champa laughed. "Well, youngblood, that's one reason why you ain't the boss, now, ain't it?"

Casey composed himself and addressed the guys. "We need to scatter. Shin, take these guys where they gotta go. Champa, I'll connect with you tomorrow afternoon." Casey leaned against his SUV and shot a hard look at Al P. "You delivered today, nigga, but that don't mean you still can't get your own haircut. No more fuck-ups, you got it?"

Al nodded in agreement and said, "I got it, Crush, I got it."

Champa just laughed; Casey knew he loved this type of gangsta shit.

Casey got in his Escalade, turned the motor over, and headed home. His knuckles throbbed from the pummeling he'd just delivered, but it felt familiar and it felt good. He was glad Al P. had witnessed that beatdown, too; it was insurance that the nigga would stay focused and wouldn't fuck up again.

Casey turned off the radio and drove home in silence with the windows down. He knew he'd sleep well tonight, and he did.

9

At 9:30 A.M., Casey was on the Cross Bronx Expressway going to see Hans. Usually a rat's nest, the CBE wasn't too bad this morning. From there he took the West Side Highway, and was at Hans's showroom in thirty minutes.

His old friend's place was on the bottom floor of the new Chang Electronics building, a fifty-five-story skyscraper with a design that seemed to be inspired by the Apple Store. *Damn, Hans, you done come up in the world.*

Casey parked his car in front and walked inside. The showroom was a playa's paradise: at least ten thousand square feet of luxury rides, all blessed with Hans's customized touch. When Casey walked in, he was greeted by a stunning Asian woman fitted to the nines in a tailored suit that made all her curves pop. "Welcome to CEC, how may I be of assistance, sir?"

"I'm here to see Hans. My name is Marcus Casey."

"Indeed, we are expecting you, sir. If you will excuse me for a moment. Please take a look at our portfolio and let me know if you see anything you like." The Asian beauty disappeared into the back. Casey strolled around, admiring the custom cars. He estimated there had to be at least ten million dollars' worth of inventory here, and was happy that Hans had come up so large. *Shee-it, maybe he's got the right idea here—there's a truckload of money to be made on the up-and-up.*

The woman reappeared a minute later. "Hans will be with you in a moment. May I park your car in our garage during your visit?"

Casey thought that was a bit odd, but wasn't one to refuse the hospitality, and he handed her the keys. A moment later, a thin man with white-blond hair, a pin-striped suit, and a big smile emerged from the back with his arms out stretched.

"Maaaan, this cannot be Crush Casey I'm looking at!"

The two men did their gangsta hug and shot the shit for twenty minutes while touring the showroom. Hans was knee-deep in Bentleys, Benzes, Ferraris, and even a Bugatti. Hans showed Casey the custom jobs he'd done in loving detail, speaking of each car like it had a personality and mind of its own.

After the tour, they stepped into Hans's office on the second floor. His space was the epitome of style, containing a sleek, black glass desk with a Herman Miller Aeron chair. A Bang & Olufsen stereo system hung on the wall, putting out classical music at low volume, and the room was filled with modern chrome and leather Italian furniture. On his desk was a picture of a different, even more beautiful, Asian woman with two little kids, set in a gold Cartier frame.

Casey admired it before looking at Hans again. "You a family man now?"

Hans nodded, beaming with pride. "Absolutely. Those are my twins, Sacha and Henrich, and my wife, Sabrina. Her father is the chairman of Chang Electronics and owns this building."

"Is that right? By the looks of this place, that's one caked-out dude."

"You have no idea, my friend. It is nuts—private jets, homes in London, Hong Kong, Gstaad, and Anguilla."

"I'm happy for you, man."

"Yeah, it's crazy. Sabrina is an amazing lady. She is hip to my past, and doesn't trip about that. She actually works here, handling the accounting."

"Perfect."

"So you got a lady, Crush?"

"Yeah, you remember Carla Aquina?"

"Of course. I heard she's running the Astor Palace Hotel—that spot is incredible. Man, I have not seen her in years. We should all go to dinner next week, man—you can meet Sabrina as well."

"Definitely, that's sounds tight."

"You want something to drink? We have everything."

Casey declined, and Hans motioned for him to take a seat on the couch. "Having a lady who knows your past and is still down with you is a rare combination."

Casey reflected on his own lady for a moment before nodding. "You know it."

Hans shifted on the butter-soft leather. "Speaking of the past . . . that shit with Rono was pretty fucked up. I am glad that bastard is in the dirt. You know I never liked him."

"Yeah, well, he's just a bad memory now. Did he keep the chop shop goin' after I landed in the joint?"

"Nah, after you went down, I closed the warehouse down and bounced to Europe for a few years. I heard he was looking for me and was pissed, but I was not going to work with that dude. That's the time I met Sabrina. Eventually, we returned to the city and I opened up a small spot customizing cars and built the business up from there."

"So, you one hundred percent legit now?"

Hans gave Casey a wry smile. "You are asking me that because of my conversation with Champa last week?"

A frown passed across Casey's face, but he smoothed his features quick. "Nah, I'm not hip."

"Okay, well, I will leave it up to him to talk about it."

Casey was curious, but he let that shit slide; he had a different agenda anyway. "I need to talk to you about one of your customers, a guy called Alek Petrosian. I was gonna ask you for an introduction, but it looks like you got too much at stake." Casey pointed to the family picture.

Hans digested what Casey said before carefully replying. "I do know Petrosian, and you are right, I have far too much to lose to do what you would like. Word on the street is that he is one ruthless motherfucker, pushing a lot of H, among other things."

"So how do I get at him?"

Hans thought for a second. "As it so happens, I am doing a car for him now, an S-Class Mercedes. It is going to be ready later today. Could you come back at five P.M.?"

"Sure."

"Okay, come by a few minutes early, and we can arrange it like you just happened to be here at the same time as him."

"Thanks, Hans, I appreciate that."

"Of course." The dapper German's cell chimed, and he glanced at it. "Unfortunately, I am afraid I have another appointment in a few minutes."

"No worries, man."

Hans rose. "Come on, I will walk you out."

They took his private elevator and walked through the showroom to the garage in the back, where Casey spied his SUV with brand-new twenty-three-inch rims on it. Hans held out his fist for a dap, which Casey enthusiastically pounded. "Consider it a welcome-home present, my friend. You have been missed."

"Shit, that looks tight, man, thank you."

"You got it. I also had them smoke out all the lights as well."

"I can see that, it all looks dope."

Hans was pleased with his crew's quick work, nodding at them with a smile. "So, when you return this evening, just park in this garage, not on the street. I will see you a little before five P.M., right?"

Casey nodded, said good-bye, and rolled out to the Urban Victory offices. On the way, his phone chimed with a call from Sean E

Sean. "Whassup, playa? I'm reaching out to see if you got a minute to chop it up?"

"Yeah, no sweat, where you at?"

"I'm on the water on my boat at the Stanton Marina, just south of Pelham Bay Park."

"Boat?"

"Yeah, man, you wanna come by and see my new shit?"

"Fo sho. Text me the address, and I'll see you in an hour or less."

Casey got the address, punched it into his GPS, and headed out to the marina. He'd been friends with Sean since elementary school. Casey actually stayed with Sean and his family for a few days after his father had been killed. Sean's mother was desperate to adopt Casey, but the family was living hand to mouth as it was, and his pops wouldn't hear of it. When Casey went to juvie, the two boys had lost touch, but when he got out, they'd picked up where they left off and got into business. By that time, Sean was a master thief who could boost anything from machine guns to microchips. When Casey had checked into Attica, 99 percent of the shit in his apartment, even the sharks in his fish tank, was hot thanks to his man. Sean E Sean had done a couple of bids himself, but nothing too serious. He was also one of the very few guys who'd written to Casey in the joint, and those lifelines and occasional care packages meant a lot to a brotha.

Exiting off the freeway, Casey drove through the sleepy residential area to the marina and parked next to Sean's white Panamera Turbo sedan. The marina was pretty small, only about a hundred boats, but Casey knew instantly which boat was Sean's: It was a dark blue fifty-two-footer that had FLYLIFE4EVER on the back. Casey walked the dock maze until he reached the boat and hollered for Sean. He came topside wearing a gray Powered by Hate sweatshirt, blue jeans, and a black Seattle Mariners cap.

"What's up, man, come aboard."

"Man, this is some pimpin' right here. Da-yamn!"

Sean was very proud of his new toy and toured Casey around the zesty Sea Ray 520 Sedan Bridge. It was very plush, with a full kitchen, three bedrooms, and a living room with a forty-two-inch LED flat screen. Casey was more a car guy than a boat guy, but being on board and seeing Sean's new float was givin' him the itch to get one himself.

"How much you drop on this, man?"

Sean smiled and said, "New, you looking at one-point-three, but I only paid . . . nothin'!"

"You boosted this thing, nigga? *Da-yamn!*"

Sean had a shit-eatin' grin on his face. "Nah, man, believe it or not, I own it clean. But there's a story behind it."

"*Of course!*" said Casey, laughing.

Sean poured two tumblers of OG XO for them, and the two men sat on the rear deck as Casey got filled in. "So, 'bout three years ago, I'm at Jon Jon the Jeweler's one day, and this fat-cat stockbroker walks in—he's worth a whole shitloada chedda, at least fifty mil easy. He says he's got some diamonds to sell and pulls out a little bag with about twenty-five stones that are two to three carats apiece. Jon Jon asks him where he got the rocks, and the dude's like 'none of your business,' and they go back and forth for about forty minutes. Finally, Jon Jon says, 'I ain't touchin' it, I don't know you, blah blah, blah,' you know how he gets, right, super-paranoid. Anyway, I peep the stones and they're pretty decent quality, so I figure the retail for each one is thirty to sixty grand. So I tell him he can sell the stones to me and I'll give him two hundred fifty K. He whines and moans, and I say, 'Okay, fuck it—three hundred, take it or leave it.' We do the deal, I unload 'em a week later for five hundred K. A few months later, I get another call from the dude, same situation. This guy ends up calling me every few months with stones, and we become cool. One day, we meet up and he gets tipsy and spills that he's givin' inside stock tips to a couple of guys and to keep his trail clean, he gets paid with diamonds."

"Man, that white-collar crime shit is something, but where's the boat come into it?" Casey asked.

"*Aha*, that's where it goes from white-collar crime to the shit *we* do. 'Bout a month and a half ago, he calls me up all panicked and tells me he needs to meet with me right away. I'm thinking, *This nigga got his ass busted and he's gonna try and take me down with him*, so I say, 'Nice knowin' ya, see ya.' He then calls me nonstop day and night till finally I say fuck it and go meet him. When I meet him, he tells me that he and his wife are getting a divorce—I guess she found out he was fuckin' some other broad, whatever—and he wants me to boost his art collection that's worth about nine mil or sumthin'. So I'm thinking it's like fifty paintings, but it turns out that it's only three! I'm like, 'Okay, I can manage that.' The plan was I go in, snatch the paintings, take them to *this* boat, drive it to another marina, and then a week later when shit is calm, I get the final payment. So he offers me five hundred K to do the job, I'm like, *What! This is going to be a helluva pay day!* Anyway, I get him up to a mil, and we make the deal and he gets me fifty percent up front."

Casey laughed as he heard this story; only Sean E Sean would be involved in a crazy deal like this. "Hold up, hold up—since when do you know shit about boats? Also, wouldn't his wife be suspicious and have the cops check this ride out?"

"His wife didn't even know he *had* a boat! This was his lay-up spot that he bought with some of the diamond money. Anyway, when I knew I was gonna do this, I went and took lessons for a week on how to drive this monster. This shit's actually easier than driving a car, but it does take some practice. So this is what happened: He tells me what alarm he has and I reach out to Zell—you remember crazy Zell, right?"

"Yeah, short brotha with a bad eye."

"Exactly, so I do a deal with Zell to disable it and help me out. So fast-forward a week later, Zell and I go up there, ski masks on, wearing all black and shit. We go straight to the alarm box, Zell does his magic, and it's all good. I break the glass on the back door, no alarm sounds off. So far, so good. We run to the rooms where the paintings are and start bagging 'em up. We're about to leave, and Zell's like, 'Yo, man—let's go check out the other rooms upstairs.' I tell him, 'No, we got what we want, we gotta bounce.' The muthafucka starts arguing with me right then and there, 'You ain't the boss of me' type a shit. I swear to God, I wanted to shoot him on the spot."

Casey nodded, totally into the whole scene—he loved hearing good crime stories, and few were better than Sean at telling them.

"So Zell finally relaxes and tells me, 'Okay, but at least let's check out the other rooms downstairs, we don't have to go upstairs.' *Stupidly*, I said, 'Okay, fine.' I take the paintings to the back door and we walk around. This place is fucking huge, like a goddamn castle and shit. We walk around, just checkin' out the rooms, and are about to leave when Zell says, 'Hold up, what's this?' and opens a door. The biggest fucking dog I *ever* saw in my life comes straight for me, jumps on my ass, and sinks his teeth into my leg. I'm screamin' my ass off, tryin' to wrestle this beast off me while Zell has his piece out, trying to aim and get a shot off . . . *in the fucking dark!* I'm screamin', *'Don't shoot, don't shoot!'* so Zell comes up and smacks the dog in the head with his piece and knocks the fucker out. I'm lying there, bleedin' all over the place, I get up and hobble to the back door, and we get out. My leg's killin' me, so we stop and get that taken care of by the doc Big Rich always uses. He gives me twelve stitches, then I leave solo to get to the boat, high as a muthafuckin' kite on painkillers. I woke up the next A.M. with my leg on fuckin' fire, go topside, and realize I'm in the other marina. Now, trip off this: *I don't even remember driving the boat there*, that's how fucked up I was, dude."

Sean lifted his right pant leg and Casey could still see his leg had been mangled bad. Casey acknowledged his war wound with a nod. "Jesus, what a fucking nightmare."

"Tell me about it. *That's* what my dumb ass gets for not following the plan."

"Yup, that shit looks like it was painful."

"True dat. So, a week passes, I'm hobblin' around like a god-damn cripple, and the dude shows up. He's pissed about the dog—that's not dead, by the way—and asks what the fuck happened. I tell him that somehow the dog got out and why the fuck didn't he tell me about the fucking dog in the first goddamn place? I tell him I may never walk right again, which is total bullshit, and that I got a good mind to take his money and throw the damn paintings in the ocean. That calmed that nigga down quick and he hands over the briefcase with the five hundred K. I tell him I need compensation for my muthafuckin' pain and suffering and shit. And then we go into negotiating mode. Meanwhile, he's looking at my fucked-up leg while tryin' to nickel-and-dime me. So I'm thinkin', *Goddamn, I want this boat. I been on it for a week, I took it out a few times, and I'm really liking it.* He starts complaining, and I tell him I know the paintings are insured, so it's not like he didn't just make nine fuckin' million to buy another goddamn boat, and he's still got the paintings. That woke his ass up, and long story short, that's how I got my boat."

"Woooow, that's straight comedy, dude. Incredible."

"What can I say?" Sean smiled, held up his hands and went to the fridge, got a Heineken, and offered one to Casey, who accepted.

"This a pretty fly setup, though," Casey said after a sip.

"Ain't it, though? It keeps my hood close, but not too close, and in case I need to bail out, a muthafucka's gotta get on a boat just to come get me."

"That's pretty smart." Casey leaned back on the couch. "So, what's on your mind? I know you didn't call me down here just to see your floatin' crib?"

Sean E Sean rolled a shoulder. "I wanted to see you, man. I mean, it's been more than a minute. Last time we hung out, we were both much younger men."

"Uh-huh, and . . ."

Sean smiled and let go of the pretense. "Straight up—why you doing all this, Crush? I mean, I know what you done told everyone and all, but really, what's up? The Crush Casey I knew back in the day didn't have partners, he had soldiers."

Casey looked at his old friend for a minute. Time had changed both of them, but some things remained the same. Sean always could put words to what was unspoken.

"What I said at the meeting was the truth, but . . . it wasn't the motivation or the complete picture. Not that it's relevant to everyone, but that's a fact."

Sean nodded and waited.

"You remember when my mom and dad passed and your mom took me in? Well, at that point something happened to me. I realized I was alone, and I always would be, even if I had people around me. At that point, I stopped giving a fuck, went into overdrive, and hustled my ass off to pull together the Vice Kings. Then later, Antonio was born and I thought I could keep rollin' the way I was without any ramifications, then I landed in the joint and . . ."

". . . then Antonio died. I'm really sorry 'bout that man, I couldn't believe it," Sean said, spilling a little beer in honor of the boy.

"Yeah, well, I was pretty fucked up. I was a nigga in crisis, that's for damn sure. Anyway, I got some direction in the joint from Mack D—"

"Triple OG, Mack D?"

"Yeah, he laced me with some good game, and I decided when I got out that I'd handle my business differently. I'd still hustle, but take out cats doin' that foul shit."

Sean studied Casey for a few seconds. "Interesting. What do you define as 'foul'?"

"Slanging hard shit and sex slavery, stuff like that."

Sean looked at Casey cockeyed. "So, by your definition, Mack would be on your takeout list?"

"That's true, but between you and me, once this is all set up and working, he's given me his word he's gonna be out of that game."

"If anyone could make that happen, it'd be you, but I'll havta see it to believe it."

"Yeah, well, it all speaks to my grand plan. The cats that I went to first were dudes that knew me from back in the day and are ballin'."

"I hear ya, it's a goddamn good crew."

Champa was waiting for Casey when he got back. They went into the office and sat down.

"I saw Hans today at his new spot," Casey said.

"Off the hook, right?"

"Crazy, he came up big-time. Anyway, he asked me about a conversation you guys had recently."

"Right, he tipped me to a potential heist I been investigatin'."

"Is that the same one you'd mentioned a couple days ago?"

"Yeah, it's a shipment of twelve high-end cars coming in from Italy worth about ten mil."

Casey whistled. "Damn, why so much? Who they belong to?"

"An Italian billionaire, Salvatore Mariano. A lot of the cars are collectibles, so they ain't your average whips."

"Okay, what's your idea on how to pull it off?"

"The cars land here in two weeks. I was thinking we hijack the transport trucks once shipment's been offloaded and has left the docks."

"How many transports we talkin' 'bout?"

"Probably two, maybe three—my man at the docks is finding out for me."

Casey rubbed his chin. It was a big job that would involve a lot of coordination and risk. "Whatchu know 'bout the owner?"

"He's made most of his money in the last ten years in natural gas. He dropped fifty-five million for a big-ass, nine-acre crib in the Hamptons that's gonna be his vacation spot when he comes Stateside."

Casey leaned back in his chair, thinking it over. Something about the job didn't seem right. *Why bring all your whips to a place you only gonna be at for a short period of time? A guy worth that much money gets ripped off, there's bound to be a lotta heat.* He could tell by Champa's face that he was amped about the job, though. "Okay, when'll you have all the details ready on this?"

"I'll have complete shipping company info as well as the transport times and all other details in the next couple days."

"If this comes off, it'll be good for the crew. Any ideas on how we move these cars? We won't be able to ship 'em anywhere, and since they're unique, they'll be extremely high profile."

"Hans already has a buyer lined up—a Chinese Internet mogul. All we gotta do is deliver the cars to him somewhere in the U.S., then it's on him how he gets 'em home."

"How's the money handled?"

"Cash money, brotha!"

"Damn, nigga, this sounds a little too good to be true."

"I'm goin' off Hans on this one, I guess he knows this guy through his wife's family and you know they straight ballin' over there."

"Okay, what's he want from this?"

"Five percent, he says he doesn't wanna get in the middle, he'll give me the cat's info and when it's all done, we give him his taste."

Casey looked at his watch. He needed to bounce back to Hans's spot to "bump" into Petrosian. "Looks like you got it under control. Get that info in hand, and let's build on this later."

Casey hit the streets to connect with Hans. Having him drop this car job in his lap was a good look, but it was also very risky. Still, Hans was his man, and Crush knew the German would never go left on him.

Traffic was always a bitch at this time of day, so Casey was glad he'd allowed plenty of time to get there. He pulled into the garage around back and headed to Hans's office. As he walked down the hallway, he heard a stranger with a thick accent talking. *Shit, dude's in there now—fuck it.*

Casey whipped out his cell and walked in, pretending like he was talking into it. He looked at the two guys and said, "Oh, sorry," then turned to walk back out the door.

Hans was quick enough to realize his cue. "Hey, Crush, it's cool, come on in."

Casey gave Hans a dap while he was introduced to Petrosian. The Armenian was dressed like he'd just come from a board meeting. He wore a three-piece slate gray Zegna suit, a diamond pavéed Rolex Daytona, and sported a lone emerald ring on his manicured hands. His goons weren't with him, but Casey could tell from the cut of his suit that he was strapped with a shoulder holster as well.

"Alek, this is a friend of mine—"

"Crush Casey, I know who you are."

Casey gave him a look and paused before replying. "How's that?"

Before Alek could answer, Hans nodded at an employee at the doorway before interrupting them. "Pardon me, gentlemen, there is a small matter I must attend to," he said, and left.

Petrosian smiled thinly. "The news of your 'alleged' former partner Rono's demise was quite the talk on the street. Word is that he got a bit choked up as he went out."

Casey nodded once; this guy was well informed, chose his words carefully, and was confident but not arrogant. *Definitely not your average street cat or flash-in-the-pan Eurotrash.* "I, of course, had nothing to do with that."

"Of course . . . I also hear that you have been forming quite a few alliances since your return to the fair city."

Now, how the fuck does he know that! The Armenian had Casey's full attention. He'd known word would eventually get out about his syndicate—he just didn't expect it to be this fast.

"Well, there is power in friendships."

"Indeed, but in war, numbers alone confer no advantage."

Casey recognized the Sun Tzu quote and countered with his own: "True, 'Invincibility lies in the defense; the possibility of victory in the attack.' And as a result, for men like us, our greatest asset is our alliances to ensure both these things."

Petrosian smiled again, this time with a shade more warmth. "It would seem we read the same books."

"We also have reputations that precede us. From what I hear, you move some weight, as well as some other shit."

Petrosian shrugged his worsted-draped shoulders. "There are a lot of rumors out there."

Casey nodded in agreement—they were both on the same page, and he was sure Petrosian knew what time it was. The time for bullshitting was over. "I'm building something big, an organization where the power is greater than the sum of its parts."

"I give orders, I don't take them, Mr. Casey."

"Spoken like a true leader. I'm not looking to be the center of the wheel, just the chain that makes it more efficient."

Alek raised an eyebrow. "Men who have power always desire more—it is in their nature."

"You talk an interesting game, however, I have business to tend to, so I gotta go. Let's connect on Monday in the A.M. if you're free," Casey said.

"Sure, why not? At the very least, it will be an interesting conversation."

The men exchanged cell numbers and walked out on the floor. Alek went out the front and Casey went over to speak to Hans, who was talking to one of his employees and dismissed the man with a flick of his wrist when he saw Casey approach.

"Well—?"

"Well, I was sure surprised when I walked in and saw the dude standin' right there."

"He came by early, he's a car freak and impatient, like many of my clients."

"I figured as much," Casey said.

Hans turned and called out to one of his salesmen. "Has Mr. Petrosian settled his account?"

"Yes, sir, he just left."

"Good, I will be in my office and do not wish to be disturbed."

Hans led Casey back to his office, where he locked the door behind him. Casey sat down in the plush leather chair this time, while Hans deposited himself on the bright red couch.

"So, Champa told me an interesting story about some cars coming in next week."

"It is a nice payday if you can pull it off, Crush."

"True, but doesn't it seem a little odd that this guy is bringing all his cars here just to have them at his summer crib?"

"The filthy rich are very different from you and me, my friend. I have seen much crazier stuff than that. These guys have so much money, they don't know what to do with it."

"Do you know this mark well, is he mob-connected at all?"

"Salvatore Mariano? No, never met him. As far as I know, he's not connected, but who can tell nowadays?"

Casey was satisfied with Hans's answers. In the end, he knew that the German simply wanted his 5 percent, and would never cross him up. Friend or not, nobody fucked with Casey without thinking there would be hell to pay afterwards.

"So, how tight are you with Petrosian?"

"Not at all. In the last three years, I have done four cars for him, but that is it. I do not socialize with the man; it is just business. He definitely does not know about my past with you."

"He may know more than you think—this guy has good intel and isn't sloppy."

"You think he knew your being here was not a coincidence?"

"I'm sure he figured it out—guys in our line of work generally don't believe in coincidences—but whatever. I'ma keep you out of any shit, so don't worry 'bout it."

Casey knew Hans may have been out of the game, but he still

liked playing from a safe distance, high-bling, legit shop notwith-standing. That's why he'd turned Champa on to the car job.

"What can you tell me about the buyer?"

"I met him about three years ago with Sabrina on a trip we took to China. He is one of the biggest guys in the Internet over there, and he is a serious car nut. The guy has his own private track in the middle of a forest on the mainland."

"Da-yamn!"

"While we were there, he took Sabrina and me out to it via he-licopter. It is fifteen square miles of private tarmac, eight miles of it straight. He has an insane crib in the middle of it and invites friends out to drive his collection of cars. Dude, I was in heaven. He has this warehouse that has the capacity to hold two hundred cars, and has four full-time mechanics."

"Why doesn't he just buy the cars he wants?"

"Well, a lot of these cars you cannot buy on the market anymore, or it would take a while to get because people never sell them. Look, he is very rich and very impatient, so he figures out a way to get what he wants—legally or otherwise—when he wants it."

Casey shot the shit with him for a few more minutes, then bounced back to his crib.

When he got there, he thought he noticed some guys in a van checking him out, but it took off right away. At first he thought it was the cops, but what if they were Petrosian's guys?

Casey made a mental note to be more aware of his surroundings—fucking with this Armenian guy could be tricky, even terminally so.

10

That weekend, Casey hit the streets while waiting for the call from Petrosian. It was still important to be seen and heard amongst his guys so they were reminded that he was back and rollin'.

On Monday, Casey got a call from Petrosian around noon.

"You know where Davilla Bar and Grill is?"

"Yeah, on Crescent."

"Why don't you meet me there in thirty."

"Yeah, I can do that, peace," Casey replied, and then hung up the phone.

The Davilla Bar and Grill was next to Romano's Social Club, a known hangout for guys in the "family." Casey didn't think the Armenian was connected with the mob, but anything was possible. Normally, he would have reached out to Shin and Champa, as having some backup on the street was always a good idea. But they were out on Long Island, talking to a dude that worked on the docks where the cars were coming in. *Fuck it, I'll go solo—probably better, anyway.*

Casey put on a shoulder holster and grabbed a Glock 19 that held seventeen rounds, more than enough if shit went down. He felt like he was being a little paranoid, but better that than dead. He put his jacket on and headed out the door.

When he arrived at the restaurant, he saw Alek sitting outside at a table by himself with his two Armenian goons at a separate table. Petrosian's black Rolls was parked in front, and it seemed like everyone who walked by stopped to admire it.

Casey parked his Escalade in a lot across the street and walked to the restaurant. The two goons got up with hard looks on their faces and met Casey. "We're gonna need to pat you down."

Casey smirked as he opened his jacket to show them his piece. "Don't bother, I'm packin', but I don't plan on killin' your boss or lettin' you two hold my piece."

Caught off guard by Casey's frankness, the pair turned to their boss for instructions.

Petrosian witnessed all this go down and laughed. "Let him through. I'm sure Mr. Casey has bigger plans for today."

Casey sat down at the table while the other two men took their positions and put on their ill-fitting masks of intimidation. Alek waved the waitress over, and a pretty sista in a tight-fitting outfit came over and asked if she could take Casey's drink order. He smiled at the young woman, who looked to be about nineteen, and ordered a soft drink.

Once she was gone, Casey took off his sunglasses and started immediately talking about his plan for a unified crew that would eventually run all the boroughs. "If there is no cooperation and con-solidation, then there will be limited success. A strategic alliance means we'd all be less vulnerable and more powerful."

Alek stared at him, his gaze level. "Like I said before: I give orders, I don't take them, and this sounds like you would want me to answer to you. That is never gonna happen."

"In that respect, you're no different than any of the other top cats I'm dealing with. Everyone's down with this 'cause it means more paper and less drama from the cops. If we don't run this shit like a military operation, then it's just a matter of time before we get taken down."

"I understand what you are saying, and what you believe. I happen to think that it is precisely our lack of unity that makes it harder for the cops to take us down. By not being centralized, they have to deal with guerrilla operations, striking when and where any of us choose. We make them play *our* game."

"I get that and respect it, but they have unlimited resources and will *never* stop. My point being that if you look at campaigns where guerrilla warfare has worked, it's only been in foreign territories where the invading army was burning too many resources for too few results, and public support evaporated. That's not what we're dealing with here."

Alek nodded. "A valid point, but an organization like you are suggesting creates many links of varying strengths. If one goes, it could take the entire chain with it. A smaller group is always harder to target, let alone hit."

"No doubt, however, our nature is to grow our businesses, thus we become bigger targets."

The waitress politely interrupted their debate to deliver their drinks—Alek was drinking something clear and odorless—and took their orders. After she left, Casey sat quietly for a beat, drinking his soda before speaking. "I know you see the value in this, and I feel like you're just makin' sure that it's been well thought out . . . or maybe you have questions about my abilities to pull it off?"

Alek stared at Casey for several seconds before picking his cell phone off the table and holding it up. "Communication—good communication—is hard to come by. A lot of those guys aren't known for that." He set the phone back on the table and leaned forward. "I know all about you, *Crush* Casey. And although I have no doubt of your ability to be heard and respected, I'm not so sure about whether these other cats truly understand or care that their going rogue will fuck shit up and take everyone down."

Casey felt a glimmer of hope. *If I can just keep him thinking about it, I can bring him around.* "If everything is compartmentalized, that won't happen. On the big jobs there will be that risk, but again, for men like us, there's risk in livin' every day. My point is that everyone's day-to-day shit is still their own concern. They just have to go about it and not cause any drama, that's all."

Alek shook his head. "I'm not feeling it, man. I'm seeing where you're coming from, but I'm not feeling your plan. Look, you're obviously a smart cat, and it took some serious brainpower to come up with this, and some serious balls to get it to where it's at now. But the truth—and you should know this better than anyone—is that it takes only one person to go left and you end up either dead, or doing time in Attica."

Casey showed no emotion at the Attica remark, aware that the Armenian had said it as a reference to Rono fuckin' him over and sendin' him to jail for twenty years. He leaned back in his chair. In that moment, he didn't see how he could get Petrosian to play ball, let alone stop his lucrative operations of selling heroin and sex-trafficking.

Casey's train of thought was derailed when, as their waitress came to the table with their food, chaos exploded.

A white van barreled down the street and slammed on its brakes to stop in front of Davilla's. Its side door slid open, and three men wearing coveralls and black masks and carrying automatic weapons jumped out and began shooting.

Casey saw the waitress catch a blast across her chest. Instinctively, he hit the ground, rolled, and drew his piece from his shoulder holster in one fluid movement. With no place to take cover, his options were either to return fire or run. He stayed low, aimed at the closest gunman, and started letting off shots. He tagged the first guy three times in the chest, making him stagger and fall back into the van. However, the shooter regained his composure, stood up again, and kept firing.

What the fuck? Casey quickly realized they were all wearing bulletproof vests. Just then, one of Petrosian's goons fell next to him in a bloody heap. He saw the Armenian scrambling, keeping cool, and squeezing off aimed rounds. The rest of the customers, on the other hand, were screaming and were either running away or curled up on the ground, frozen in fear. Glasses exploded above him, raining down liquid and shards of glass.

Casey screamed, *"They're wearing vests!"* He grabbed the gun from Petrosian's fallen man and rolled left, firing both guns as he went to keep the gunners' heads down. As he rolled onto his stomach, he nailed the first guy in the head. The driver of the van wasn't visible; he was probably taking cover. The second hit man had been shot in the leg, and he hobbled into the van while the third one tried to hunt down Petrosian. Casey carefully aimed and took him out with a shot to the head, while Petrosian nailed the other guy in the neck with two bullets, turning him into a human fountain.

There was the sound of whimpering and crying from the back of the restaurant, but other than that, silence reigned. Petrosian's other guy had also been shot; he wasn't dead, but was bleeding so heavily, it would only be a matter of seconds. Casey and Petrosian exchanged looks and checked themselves; neither had been hit.

"Did you get the driver?" Casey asked.

"I don't think so. That motherfucker is probably still in the van?"

"Okay, I'll get to the passenger side and open the door, you draw down on the nigga."

Alek nodded, and the two men jumped up and ran to the van twenty feet away, stepping over people, tables, and chairs. They passed the side open door, but didn't see anything inside.

Casey knelt and grabbed the passenger door handle and gave Alek a head nod that the Armenian returned as he lifted his pistol on the ready. Casey swung the door open, and with four rapid shots, Petrosian blasted the driver, who was huddled down in the well of the passenger seat. Alek reached in and pulled off the black ski mask to reveal a woman's face.

Casey looked in and was surprised and said, "Do you know her?"

"No, do you?"

"Nah."

They did the same drill on the other three, and neither of them recognized anyone on the hit team. In the distance, they heard the sound of cop cars with their sirens screaming. Petrosian's car was littered with bullet holes, and one of the front tires had been blown out.

Casey holstered his piece and put the other gun in his waistband. "I'm gettin' the fuck out of here, you comin'?" Not waiting for an answer, Casey ran across the street to his Escalade, with Petrosian following. He started the car and punched it, driving through the alley on the side of Davilla's, then turning onto 187th Street. After three blocks, he glanced in his rearview: Nobody was in pursuit. Casey slowed down to blend with the light afternoon traffic and asked, "So, who the fuck's trying to take you out?"

"Me? Why do you think *I* was the target?"

Casey turned and looked at him like he was crazy. "'Cause I'm fresh out the fuckin' pen, and the only nigga I know that wants me dead is six feet unda."

Petrosian shot him back the same look and said, "Says the man who's trying to put all of the gangs in NYC under his thumb. I'm sure you've made your share of enemies, Casey, especially given your rep. Regardless, I got two dead men and my shit is all shot up in front of that fuckin' joint."

Petrosian was talking while he was checking his pockets looking for his cell phone. "*Fuck!* I left my phone at the goddamn restaurant. *Shit!*"

Casey clucked his tongue. "That's gonna put you at the scene of the crime. At least with your car, you coulda said your guys had taken it to get washed or some shit."

"*Motherfucker,* I'm totally fucked!"

Casey let that thought sink into the other man's brain before he said, "Not really."

Petrosian narrowed his eyes at him in disbelief. "How the hell you figure that?"

At the next red light, Casey reached into his pocket, pulled out Petrosian's phone, and handed it to him. At first, Petrosian thought he might be grabbing his piece and started to react, but he relaxed when he saw what the other man was holding.

"Easy . . . some cats know how to think on their feet, thasall."

Petrosian nodded, obviously impressed and relieved. Casey had just saved his ass a lot of unwanted heat, and the Armenian knew it. "Okay, so I owe you one."

"You sure do. Did you see any security cameras at that spot? If there was, we're both fuckin' done, phone or no phone," Casey said.

"There weren't any. I don't go places where there are cameras if I can help it."

"Smart. So, where am I taking you?"

"St. James Park, my son's at basketball practice, and I want to make sure he's okay."

Casey steered the SUV in that direction and punched it while Alek called one of his boys and instructed him to bring another one of his whips to the park, pronto. They arrived at the park in ten minutes and pulled up next to the basketball courts. There were a bunch of little kids on the court running drills as the coach blew his whistle. Petrosian got out of the car and jogged to the fence, surveying the area while keeping a hand close to his piece. Casey stayed in the SUV, figuring he'd let him draw fire if there was gonna be any. When he felt the coast was clear, Casey walked over as well. As the practice broke up, Alek called out to his kid in Armenian. Surprised, Alek's boy ran around the fence to meet him, giving him a big hug.

"Hi, Dad, what are you doing here?"

"I just came by to catch a bit of your practice, Ara. Looks like you're doing great!"

"Yeah, and you know what? Coach says he wants me to start the next game!"

"Man, that's fantastic! Go get dressed, and we'll celebrate with some ice cream!"

His son gave a huge smile and screamed, "Ahhh, yeah!" and then ran back with his friends.

Petrosian turned back to Crush with a relieved look on his face. "How many kids do you have?"

"None," replied Casey, wondering if the Armenian was fucking with him, or if he was really clueless that he'd had a kid.

Petrosian regarded him with confusion. "Really? Shit, man, that's the key to your legacy. My son is my world—one day, he'll have it all."

"Is that right, your life, too?"

Petrosian looked at Crush and chuckled. "Of course."

A black Mercedes S600 pulled up, and two more burly men stepped out and stood by the car.

"Your ride's here. Look, just think about what I said, and let's touch base when you got a minute."

"You got it. And Crush—I appreciate you having my back today."

"I hear ya . . . in a minute."

Casey walked back to his Escalade and got in. As he headed out, he saw Petrosian's kid in a school uniform run to his dad and give him another big hug. He could tell they had a great relationship. Casey couldn't help but think about his own boy, and the similarities between him and this man.

He got out his phone and speed-dialed Champa. "Where you guys at?"

"Comin' back from Strong Island. Should be local in about thirty."

"Cool, meet me at the spot. I want to tell you about the surprise party."

Champa knew that was code for some shit jumping off. "What? Who threw that?"

"That's a good question. We can discuss the festivities when you get there." Casey weaved through traffic and was at the Urban Victory offices twenty minutes later. When he walked out, he hollered to Joe Pica that he needed to speak with him. They walked into the conference room, and Casey instructed him to shut the door.

"You got any new guys working here?"

"Nah, just the same people for the last three months."

"Keep it that way—no new people until I say it's cool."

"Okay, is everything good? Is there anything I should know about?"

"Everything's good, don't sweat it, I just want to be cautious. Speakin' on that, call someone and have them put a camera and a buzzer on the front door."

Joe looked like he wanted to ask a bunch of questions, but knew enough not to, and to just follow orders. "Okay, cool, whatever you say, Casey."

"Good man."

Casey reached into his pocket and pulled out a knot of cash. Counting off six hundred dollars, he handed it to Joe. "Make sure that happens today, and let me know when it's done."

A few minutes later, Champa and Shin got there and the guys went back to Casey's private office. Casey flipped on the TVs and tuned in to two different news channels to see if the story had popped yet.

"Man, what the fuck happened? I didn't even know you were meeting the dude today!" said Champa.

"Yeah, I didn't get much notice and said fuck it and met the nigga straight up."

"So who tried to dust this guy, what happened?"

Casey ran down the story in detail. "Because Davilla's is right next to Romano's Social Club, the police'll probably think it's mob-related or some shit. Personally, I bet it's gotta be someone that has beef with this dude. How they found out where we were so quick makes me think that maybe he has a sucka in his crew."

Champa looked at Shin and asked, "Does he have active beef with anyone right now?"

Shin digested that question for a moment and said, "Nah, for the most part, he keeps things mellow."

"Well, somebody wants that nigga dead bad," said Champa.

"And he would've been, but his dudes were sitting in front of us and caught most of the lead. Both those niggas was dead as fuck when we got gone."

Casey got a text from Carla, asking him what his plans were for that night. He texted her back that he just wanted to kick it at his crib. She replied to say she could grab some steaks and meet him at his place at 7 P.M. While they were texting back and forth, Shin said, "It's on the news, check it out."

Casey set down his phone, grabbed the remote, and turned up the volume. The square, white reporter was standing in front of yellow tape, facing the camera. Behind him was the restaurant, with overturned tables, the windows shot out, and glass all over the ground. Milling about in the background were cops doin' what they do.

"... *About an hour ago, a van filled with gunmen pulled up and opened fire on this normally quiet restaurant. When police arrived at the scene, they found four gunmen dead, along with five of the restaurant's patrons killed, and three critically wounded. Witnesses at the scene say that at least two of the patrons fired back and killed the gunmen. Police said they found multiple guns on the scene, including several automatic weapons. We asked the police if the incident was related to organized crime figures, and they said it appears that way, but they could not say so for sure. That's all we have for now, but we will continue to follow the story as it develops. . . .*"

"Oh shit, that's the nigga's car we saw at Marat's." Shin pointed to Petrosian's car on the TV screen.

"Yeah, he's gonna have to tap-dance and deny like a muthafucka to keep the pigs off his back. Shin, I want you to have Jacob dig up as much stuff on this guy as possible. When I met him, he seemed to know a whole helluva lot about what I was doing, so I don't know if he was just listening to street chatter and gettin' lucky, or maybe we got a mole in our midst."

"I'm on it, I'll see what I can find out," Shin said.

"Okay, enough of my drama. What happened in Long Island?"

Champa ran it down. "We went and saw my man, who's a security guard there. He gave us the specific time the boat's docking with the cars and the transport company info as well. He said that a pickup time hadn't been set up for the cars to be unloaded, 'cause they never know how long customs'll take. He guessed the cars would leave the docks within a couple days after they land."

"See if we have any natural inroads to the transport company so we can get more intel on them. If we don't, get one of Big Rich's girls and have her use her ways to get info from one of the truckers."

Champa laughed. "That's some Mata Hari shit right there, boy."

"So, are we all set with Jacob and Al P.? I mean are we ready to spring into action?"

"Yeah, totally."

"Good, now we need to figure out how to get at these guys so Al can load that program on their phones. Find out if there's a local bar where most of them hang out at. If that doesn't come through, then I'll think of something else. But we need to get this shit up and rollin'. Champa, get Jacob on the phone."

While Champa pulled out his celly and dialed, Casey turned to Shin. "You have our guys still posted up outside his crib to make sure everything's cool?"

"Yeah, they know to text me every time he leaves and tell me where he goes, but so far he hasn't moved once."

"Any fallout from that shit that went down Friday night with those wannabe Rastas?"

"Nothing yet."

Champa handed the phone to Casey and said, "It's Jacob."

"What's up, man—you got photos and a report for me?"

"Yeah, I got gang of info on 'em all. Are you coming over here or do you want me to e-mail it?"

"Is that safe?"

"To e-mail, yeah, I'll encrypt it with a password that will only be able to be used once."

"Okay, I'ma hand you to Champa and he's gonna tell you where to send it."

Champa took the phone and gave him an e-mail address, and wrote down the password. Two minutes later, when Champa checked his account on Casey's computer, the file appeared. It was about sixty pages long, so Casey had Champa print it. Casey and the guys reviewed the incredibly organized report; it had photos, copies of each man's driver's license, what kind of cars they had, newspaper clippings, who was partners with who, as well as other miscellaneous information.

"Man, this is fuckin' thorough!" said Champa.

For the next two hours, they all went over the files, seeing who lived close to each other, what were the similarities among them all, and plotting how to put those muthafuckas on blast when the time came.

Casey stood over his desk and looked at the files and said, "Catching these guys on the street is gonna be tough, but if we just snare one, the others'll fall into place."

"How do you mean, Case?" Shin asked.

"Well, once we get one and listen to all his conversations, then we'll have ears to pick up everything that's said and we'll piece that together to see how to trap the others. We're gonna have to adjust the plan a little bit."

"How so?" asked Champa.

"I was thinking about it last night. We gonna have to have different messages pop up on their cells; otherwise, it will seem like too much of a coincidence. It needs to be a message that's some kind of battery alert that says, 'You have 20 percent battery life' or 'Your phone is roaming.' Something they wouldn't talk about. The fake liquor ad is cool, but it's too out of the ordinary *and* it's dependent on them being in or walking by a bar. It's just not stealth enough."

"Okay, I'll tell Al to get that ready," said Champa.

"I know he can tell what type of phone it is before he sends the message, so make sure the messages match up with the same look each phones uses."

Casey looked at his watch; it was 6:45 P.M. He sent the guys on their way, gathered up the notes on the report, and jetted.

On his way home, he reviewed the afternoon's events in his head. He remembered he had seen what he thought was the same van when he left Hans's spot. If they were after him, they could have caught him that morning, so he surmised that the hit was definitely for Petrosian. *But how'd they know where and when to strike?* He went over different scenarios in his head but nothing was clicking. Then it hit him like a sledgehammer. . . . *Oh shit. Fucking Lomax.*

He pulled his SUV into the parking garage, turned off the motor, and sat there for a minute, thinking about the prospect of Lomax having some other parolee trying to take out Petrosian at the same time. It was entirely possible that the PO had doubled down, as insurance to get the job done. Lomax came off as an impatient guy, so it made total sense. The more he thought about it, the more pissed he got, 'cause if it was true, that shit had almost got his ass killed. On the other hand, it was very smart, and Casey grudgingly gave the PO his props for trying to cover all his bases. Now that crew was dead. *Damn, this shit is getting complicated!*

Casey got out of his car and took the elevator up to his place. Before he hit the door, he smelled the food cooking, the scent making his mouth water. He walked inside and found Carla in pink booty shorts, barefoot, and with cooking mitts on her hands, whipping up a feast.

She turned around and gave him a big smile and a kiss. "I hope you hungry, baby."

He looked Carla up and down and said, "Yeah, baby, Daddy's really hungry fo sumthin'."

She giggled at that; then her expression turned serious as she took him in. "You're a mess, you know that? What happened?"

Casey thought he'd cleaned himself up satisfactorily at the office, but apparently not. He took off his jacket and tossed it in the bedroom, then sat down at the table. "Things got a bit messy at lunch. Whatcha cookin'?"

"Our chef at the hotel gave me this recipe, so I got my fingers crossed that it came out okay."

"It smells great, baby."

Casey helped her bring everything to the dining room. A few minutes later, they both cut into their steaks and took a bite and looked at each other while chewing.

"Da-yamn . . . *that's* amazing," said Casey after he'd swallowed.

"Good, huh?"

"Real good."

"So, how was your day? Anything interesting happen?"

Casey chewed his food and didn't make eye contact when he answered. "It was cool—man, this is good."

Later on that evening, Casey and Carla were in bed watching the news when the story of the shoot-out at the restaurant came on. Casey listened intently, hearing basically the same story that was reported earlier. He turned the TV off and saw Carla giving him a strange look. "What's up?"

"Nothin', baby."

She eyeballed him, but kept her cool. "Crush, are you ever gonna tell me what's really going on?"

Casey'd already had a bitch of a day, and sure as hell didn't want to get into it at that moment. "Now, why would you want that burden?"

She stared at him like he was a damn fool. "'Cause news stories like that pop up and I see how you react, I think to myself, *Holy shit, did my man almost get his ass shot off today?*"

Casey sat upright. "And, hypothetically speaking, how's knowing that something like that went down and I tellin' you about it gonna make you feel?"

"It's gonna make me feel like you trust me, Casey."

She looked at him and he saw that she wasn't pissed; she was concerned. Casey hadn't expected that answer, so he lowered his eyes and took in those words. After a few seconds, he looked up at her and relaxed his body and said, "I had a meeting with this dude today. He's smart, he has his shit together, and he's ballin' hardcore. He's also got a boy, and from what I can tell, he seems like a good father."

Carla sat still, careful not to break the silence.

"Carla, that was me twenty years ago. It's like this guy's a muthafuckin' mirror image of me from back in the day. Even his kid seems like Antonio. Now, the problem is I got a parole officer that wants me to take him out, but I think about this kid, and I think about Antonio, and I got a problem with that. All the options I have are either fucked up or long shots at best. The best option—and the least likely to happen—is getting this dude to agree to join this alliance I set up and let go of the parts of his business that are problematic. Then maybe—just maybe—my PO won't have such a hard-on for this guy."

He could tell by Carla's face that he'd just blown her mind, but he could also tell that his relationship with her was about to hit a new level. Either that, or it was gonna be over in the next few minutes. He felt a bit fucked up about being so transparent, but if this relationship was gonna last, he'd have to let her into his world.

"I mean, how long is Antonio's death gonna haunt me like this? I walk by playgrounds or parks and see kids laughin' and playin' and see what I fucked up. On top of that, I see parents with their kids, and I don't know if I could do that yet—or ever—and I know you want that. I want to give you everything, baby, but my head's just not there yet."

Carla scooted closer and kissed him on the cheek. "You know,

Crush, we just gotta do the best we can and accept the results. It's when we get attached to a desired outcome before it happens that we get all fucked up. As far as your son, if you don't forgive yourself, you're never gonna have peace." Carla sat up and studied his face. "Can you do that? Can you forgive yourself?"

Casey contemplated her sage advice and it made sense. He didn't have an answer for her right away, and she was cool with that. Casey's quest to control everything, even his emotions, was sometimes a virtue and sometimes a curse.

He turned off the night table light and pulled her close. And in the dark he said, "Thanks, baby."

11

Casey was at the Urban Victory offices bright and early the next morning. Every detective's dossier was spread out in front of him, each with red marks all over it where he'd made notes. He went over the files again for a few hours, making sure he had a firm grasp on all the information, as well as figuring out which ones to target first. Most of these guys were in their mid-thirties to late fifties and had families. Out of the twenty-two detectives, not including Fordham, Casey narrowed down his targets to seven guys living in Manhattan. His reasoning was that it would be easier and less conspicuous to tail these guys in the city as opposed to other ones that lived in the burbs. Casey called Champa and Shin and told them to pick up Al P. and meet him at Jacob's ASAP.

The guys arrived within ten minutes, and when everyone was settled, Casey opened the meeting. "Okay, I figured how we gonna handle this shit. We gonna have to break up into two teams. Team One'll be Al P. and me, and Team Two is Champa and Shin. Al, I'm gonna need you to show Champa and Shin how to load messages on these detectives' phones."

Casey went over to a map on the wall with all the detectives' addresses marked with pushpins. "Seven of the detectives live in

Manhattan, the rest live in Queens and Brooklyn. We gonna target the Manhattan guys first, 'cause we'll have the city as cover. Al, how close do the guys need to be to connect to the other phones, and what'll they need to do?"

Al raised his eyebrows and replied, "They'll need to be within twenty-five feet of the target—the closer, the better. Once they're within range, they're gonna have to make sure they select the right phone, determine the make and model, then upload the correct message."

Champa looked at Casey. "Sounds a bit complicated. How long'll all that take?"

Al replied, "It's gonna seem like forever, but the reality is that it won't be more than a minute. You're gonna scan the area for their phone, and once you find it, you upload the app based on what type it is."

Casey saw that Shin and Champa looked a bit hesitant, given that they'd never tried this tech out before. "Don't sweat it, guys. We're gonna do a lotta practice runs on this, and by tomorrow A.M., you'll have it nailed. Besides, there's only one thing that can trip us up."

"What's that?" said Shin.

"If they don't have their Bluetooth turned on, then we're gonna have to go to Plan B, which will be trickier."

Casey could tell that Champa had already figured out Plan B. "Da-yamn, nigga, please tell me you're not suggestin' that we boost their phone, load the program, then give it back to 'em?"

Casey sat back silently so that this concept sank in with everyone. The room was pretty quiet until Shin broke the silence. "Casey . . . well, if we do that on the fly, shit, it's just—really risky, man. I mean, boosting's never been my thing."

"Look, we're not gonna just do it 'on the fly.' We'll see what happens tomorrow, and go from there."

The guys in the room breathed a slight sigh of relief. Casey liked dropping bombs like this every so often—it kept everyone on their toes and focused.

He continued. "We're gonna target guys in the early A.M., around seven fifteen, when they'll be leaving for their shift, and then at four P.M., when they get off. The only way we're gonna know that we've nailed a target is when Jacob starts seeing info pop up on the computer."

Champa jumped in. "How do we know they'll be workin' the eight-to-four shift and not the four-to-twelve?"

"We don't, but given that they're all pretty senior guys, chances are they have the A.M. shift."

Casey turned to Jacob. "The minute you see one of our targets get activated, I want you to run the phone through its paces to make sure it works okay. Once you're satisfied, let us know."

"That's cool, just text me a heads-up, and I'll be watching for it," Jacob said.

"No problem. Okay, Champa, you definitely gonna need to get a more low-profile ride for these maneuvers."

"Not a problem—my girl has a Lincoln with tinted windows I can use," Champa replied.

"All of you need to be wearin' sunglasses and hats anytime you're tailin' one of these cats—we want this as covert as possible. A'ight, Al, show Shin and Champa how to tag these phones, then we gonna run some trials."

Al P. got up and went through the process a bunch of times with the guys to make sure there were no hiccups. Then they hit the streets and did some run-throughs with Casey holding a target phone. After an hour of that, they started picking random targets. Al P. was pretty quick when it came to the whole process, Shin picked it up pretty fast, but Champa was pathetic, to say the least. Tech just wasn't that nigga's forte. Whenever they'd tag someone, they reached out to Jacob and gave him the heads-up, and he'd confirm their success a few minutes later.

Shin tagged a heavyset kid and dialed Jacob. "I got someone, you see anything?"

After thirty seconds, Jacob said, "Yeah, I got him on the grid, he's on Walton Avenue heading towards 172nd."

Casey looked at Shin and Al P. and said, "I want you to tag up as many people as possible in the next couple hours, at least thirty. I wanna make sure our system can handle it."

For the next three hours, the guys went hard at it, tagging people under every circumstance. They even tagged people while they were driving next to them, or riding the subway.

Casey reached out to Jacob: "How many targets we up to?"

"Lemme see . . ." Casey could hear him counting them off. "Eighteen, nineteen, twenty . . . twenty-six, twenty-seven, twenty-nine . . . thirty-two, thirty-three, thirty-four. Okay, there's thirty-four targets active."

"Okay, bet." Casey pulled the guys in. "Come on, we're heading back to Jacob's. If you can hit anyone up on the way, do it. I wanna push this shit as far as possible."

On the drive back, Shin and Al P. were targeting people like they were playing a video game. When they got to Jacob's, they went up the stairs and walked into their own command center. Everyone was pretty pumped up to see this shit in action.

Jacob sat in front of six forty-two-inch monitors, his fingers a blur on his keyboard, as well as controlling other monitors using verbal commands with a Bluetooth earpiece. Every monitor had a ton of open windows with conversations being transcribed, as well as maps with red, green, and blue dots representing the targets. The guys stood there transfixed by what they'd accomplished.

Champa was the first to speak. "That is some incredible shit right there, I got about six broads I need to unleash this shit on." Everyone in the room laughed, probably because they were all thinking the same thing.

Casey looked at all the words for all the conversations being transcribed out by the voice-recognition software. As alerts went off, passages would be highlighted. *Fuckin' amazin'* . . . On one of the monitors was a map of the Bronx, covered in all three colors of dots, some moving and some stationary.

"What do the red, green, and blue dots represent?" Casey asked.

"Red dots are people who aren't speaking on their phones, green ones are having conversations, and the blue dots are cameras I can tap into."

"Let's activate one of those red dots and make their phone a live mic. Pick one near a video camera, and let's see if we can get a visual."

Jacob took the cursor and clicked on one of the red dots near Claremont Park. The dot turned green, and seconds later there was audio. Casey could tell the person was near the playground by the background noise of kids laughing and yelling. Jacob then clicked on the blue dot to get a visual. The men all saw kids playing on swings and running around; the picture was pretty clear. They then heard two women talking.

"—I tol' the nigga to get outta here with that bullshit, he thinks he can come over and get some of this pussy, nigga, please!"

"That's right. Then what he say?"

"He tried to tell me he was late with my child support 'cause he got 'laid off.' But I know the nigga's selling weed on the side, so he ain't broke."

On the monitor, Champa pointed to two sistas on a park bench. "Can you zoom in on them?"

Jacob placed his cursor on the women and pressed the down key on his keyboard. "This is just a virtual zoom. It'll work pretty good, but the closer it gets, the worse the picture resolution will be."

The women on the video kept talking, completely unaware they had a rapt audience twelve blocks away.

"Mmmm hmm—"

"Then I tol' him I was gonna call Child Services, and he started screaming and shit, saying, 'Bitch, why you got to go there, a nigga's doing the best he can—'"

Casey looked at Al P. "Lemme guess—this is one of yo bitches we just tapped into?"

Shin, Champa, and even Al P. all started laughing their asses off. Al P. was probably laughing 'cause he was glad his tech was working. Casey told Jacob to bring up the transcript of the conversation. When they looked at it, the computer was able to decipher about 50 percent of the conversation from the park, but on the phone calls they were tappin', it showed 95 percent accuracy.

Jacob turned to Casey and said, "When you got so much background noise, it's gonna make it really hard for the computer to get better than that. If they were in a quieter place, the transcription quality would increase dramatically."

"You want to get some of the guys to monitor the live conversations, Case?" Shin asked.

"Nah, it's too risky to let anyone else know what we doing and where we doing it at. We'll just let the computer do the best it can, and if it isn't workin' out, we'll have to address it later." They went through everyone's phones to listen to voice mails and look at e-mails and texts. Everything was tight. The whole setup was very impressive.

Champa sat back on the couch and said, "Man, the pigs are gonna be so fucked up, they don't stand a chance."

"Let's not get too confident—there's still plenty of things that can go wrong this early in the game," Casey said. He sat in the chair next to Champa, his eyes still on the various flows of information. He watched the monitors for another minute, then turned to Al. "If we turn their phone into a live mic, how long will the battery last?"

"On most phones, you're talking six to seven hours," Al said.

Casey ran through the list in his head. "Okay, Jacob, I want you to let this run for another few hours and monitor it. Once you're completely satisfied, you can delete these people."

Al spoke up: "Before you do that, you oughta know that the last person I tagged was a cop. We should listen to him."

Shin looked at Al sidelong. "Damn, nigga, why didn't you say so?"

Al P. shrugged. "If it didn't work for any reason, I didn't wanna call attention to the fact that I'd tagged a pig."

Jacob got on his keyboard and sorted the targets by the time they were tagged and zeroed in on the cop's phone. By the sound of it, the two cops were in their squad car.

"—can you believe this little black bastard?"

"Whaddaya expect from a piece of shit like that? The bottom line is he's gonna get what he deserves. He may not have been guilty today, but he was sure as hell guilty some other day." The cop then addressed the suspect: "Ya see this, this little Baggie of coke is gonna lock you away for a nice little bit."

Casey and the guys could hear that some kid was in the backseat of the car, his voice cracking as he pleaded with the cops. "Come on, man, please! I didn't do nuthin, don't do this, man, this'll be my third strike, come on, please! Why you wanna frame me man, I didn't do nuthin'!"

Casey looked at Jacob. "Can you tap into this cruiser's video to get a visual?"

Jacob's fingers flew over the keyboard. "The visual will either be the guy in the back or out the front windshield, it may pop up on their screens, alert them that someone is—"

"I don't give a fuck. I wanna see the guy in the back."

Jacob looked at his monitor and said, "There are thirty-two cars out right now, so I just gotta match up the location with the NYPD computers." Jacob started going through the online map while everyone listened to what was happening.

"Look, boy, it's not my problem that you got two strikes. We both know you been doing dirt, so shut the fuck up and enjoy the scenery, 'cause you ain't never gonna see the outside again."

Casey could hear the cop go on the radio and call in that they were bringing in a drug dealer they'd just busted.

"Four Seven Adam to Central."

"Four Seven Adam, go," said a woman on the radio speaker.

"One under for possession to the Forty-seventh Precinct."

"Yo, fuck that, you know that's bullshit! Why you doing this? Come on, man, I got a kid!"

When Casey heard that, his fist clenched, and the desire for revenge exploded inside him. The whole room knew this BS went on every damn day, but it was still a bitter pill to swallow.

Jacob screamed, *"I got it!* I got it."

Everyone focused on the screen: the video was black-and-white and showed the back of the car, where a black kid was cuffed and writhing on the cruiser's seat.

"Fuck you and shut up! Everyone's got kids. I tell ya what, when your boy's old enough, we'll bust him, too, so yous could be in the joint together. What's his name, I can put him on my list."

His partner started laughing his ass off. "Dayton, you're one cruel sonofabitch. Oh shit, you're gonna give this nigga a heart attack."

The kid in the backseat lost his mind when he heard this and started screaming. *"Please, man—I was just hanging out! I'm sorry, I ran 'cause I was scared! Come on, don't do this!"*

"It's a little too late for that, your kind needs to see that they can't outrun us *ever!*"

The kid became enraged and was bucking in the backseat, trying to get free as he screamed, *"You know what, fuck you, fuck both a you! Y'all a bunch a cracker faggots!"* Then the kid started spitting through the metal partition.

Casey and the guys watched this all go down. Casey said, "Damn, this nigga's gonna get dug out for that, damn!"

Both cops started screaming once they felt his spit hit the back of their necks. *"Hey, hey, hey! Stop that, goddamnit! Bellamy, pull over in that alley now!"*

The guys heard the car screech to a halt and one of the doors open and heard one of the officers scream at the other. *"Dayton, what the fuck you doing don't be stupid, man!"*

Bellamy didn't respond; the guys could hear the back door open and see the cop's prey start pleading for mercy. The video showed the kid on his back, frantically shaking his head back and forth, his feet up toward the door.

"Come on, man, what the fuck, just let me be, man, don't kill me, man!"

The guys couldn't see the officer, but they heard his demonic voice calmly say, "I ain't gonna kill you, nigga, I'm just gonna give you a little electroshock therapy."

The suspect started jerking around like crazy, obviously scared out of his mind. He pleaded with the officer, but to no avail. *"Don't Tase me, please don't Tase me!"*

The next thing they saw was his body jerk; then he started screaming over the snap and crackle of the Taser hitting its target again and again as the officer administered his punishment. Casey and the guys tensed up when they heard that sound. They were all pissed and swearing at the screen.

The officer stopped after a minute, and his cruel voice said, "You feelin' pretty badass now, boy? Huh? Dumb motherfucker."

The officer blasted that poor dude again, laughing like he was a kid seeing a funny cartoon, until his partner screamed at him. *"Bellamy, enough! You're gonna give that bastard a fuckin' heart attack!"*

"Okay, okay . . . Ahhh shit, would you look at that? This nigger just pissed himself! Goddamnit, what a mess!"

His partner was heated and said, "Just get in the car, Bellamy, fuck!"

The guys could see the suspect going through hell; he was groaning and delirious from his torture.

"Got anything else smart you wanna say? . . . I didn't think so." After the cop said that, he chuckled, then started laughing hard.

His partner said, "What the fuck's so funny—you coulda killed him and then what?"

His partner responded, trying to catch his breath. "That's one fried chicken," and then they both burst out laughing.

Champa was seething and looked like he was about to explode. "Yo, we need to go handle those muthafuckas, Crush."

Casey looked at Champa and everyone in the room; like him, they were all very pissed off and shaken by what they'd heard and seen. He calmly took a deep breath, then exhaled and said, "These muthafuckas are gonna get theirs, and my man that's been fucked over's gonna get justice *and* get paid, believe that. But we got a lot bigger fish to fry, and we can't tip our hand yet. I know it's fucked up . . . but now is not the time. I guarantee, though, that we gonna put a lot of these muthafuckas on front street and hang 'em high."

The guys were all silent. Crush knew they realized he was right, but it sucked seeing a brotha get fucked over like that right in front of their eyes, and not be able to do a goddamn thing about it. They'd all experienced police brutality, and knew what it was like to feel powerless and terrorized.

Casey broke the silence. "Champa, reach out to Alejandro and tell him he's got a pro bono case he has to take, this brotha needs to be represented. Also, tell him to assume whatever he's saying is no bullshit and leave it at that. When we leak this tape, Alejandro will be kissin' my ass for putting him in place. This guy's gonna have a helluva lawsuit and get laced with millions by the time we're done."

Champa nodded and dialed the mouthpiece to let him know his services were needed.

Casey addressed everyone in the room. "This is a good object lesson. Always, always, keep this in mind as you go about doin' our business. These muthafuckas are gangstas in blue with badges, and if this shit gets out before we're ready, we're dead. Okay, Jacob, delete everyone we tagged today *except* for this pig. Burn the audio and video to a DVD—I wanna make this look slick for TV. Get pictures of everyone so when we don't have video, we have their faces on the screen with their badge numbers. Also, have the text of what they sayin' transcribed on the bottom of the screen so there's no mistaking who's sayin' what."

Casey stood in front of everyone, amped to the max. He knew his plan would work; it was just a matter of making sure the flow and quality of the intel were tight and quick. "Today was a good day, and in more ways than one, 'cause it showed the power we have. There's a lot of shit that could go wrong, but there's a lot that can go right, too, so be on your game at all times. Remember, this is a complicated puzzle, and we can't afford to have a single piece missing. Also, I know there will be a temptation to speak out on this shit, but we cannot, at all costs. If it gets out too soon, it'll fuck everything up. It's just a matter of time before the pigs figure shit out, and they *will* figure it out, hopefully only after we put them on blast. But until that happens, we need to keep this on the DL. Okay, now, for tomorrow . . ."

Casey pulled out a folder and laid out seven photos of the detectives. On the bottom of each photo was a home address. Casey separated four of the photos into a group.

"These four live in Lower Manhattan in an eight-block radius from each other. Two actually live in the same building." Casey pointed to a picture of a heavyset bald white male and another white guy that was also heavyset but had a crew cut and mustache. Casey's phone buzzed, but he ignored it and kept talking. "Tomorrow at seven A.M. sharp, Al, you and I are gonna be in front of that building. I'll be in the Escalade, but you'll be on the street. Hopefully these guys will leave together so we can double down and nail them both. You're gonna need to stagger when you hit their phone up, though."

Al cleared his throat. "I'll do a roaming message on one and low-battery message on the other. Both messages'll have a dismiss button that will activate the loading of the app."

Casey nodded and continued. "I'm gonna be close by, so right after we get these guys, we'll buzz to the next target." He pointed to Al. "You and I are gonna have a total of four targets, and Shin and Champa are gonna have three. For us to get all these guys in the A.M.'ll be a stretch, but once we got 'em, the others will fall into place."

Champa nodded. "Right, 'cause once we have one, we'll be able to track where he's at and just go to his location and tag his partner."

"Exactly," said Casey. "Okay, Al, tomorrow morning I'm comin' to get you early, so be on point. I'm gonna stay in the car 'cause one of these guys may recognize me. Champa, I suggest you do the same. Anyone got any questions?" Everyone looked around at each other and said nothing.

"Okay, cool. Before we go, Jacob, plug in these addresses into Google Maps and print out where they are and what they look like so we can recognize them." While Jacob was doing that, Casey checked his phone and saw a text from Petrosian asking if he could meet tomorrow. Casey texted him to say tomorrow was no good, but the day after in the evening was cool. Petrosian hit him back right away and confirmed and said he would reach out to him at that time. Casey slipped his phone back into his pocket while Jacob distributed the maps and photos.

"Okay, I'm out. See y'all tomorrow."

That night, Casey didn't really sleep all that well, but he did get some shut-eye. What happened the next morning would determine a lot of things. There were many unknowns—like, what if these guys didn't have their Bluetooth activated, or maybe they had special security on their phones. He also knew hunting these cops could take a couple weeks. When he got up, he shook those thoughts out of his head and got ready. *What will be, will be.*

He got to Al's fifteen minutes early. Al lived on Mulford Avenue, not far from St. Teresa's Avenue, in a three-story apartment building in a quiet residential area. Casey dialed him and in less than two minutes Al was in the car.

"Nigga, where's your hat and sunglasses?"

"*Shit!* Gimme a minute." Al hopped out of the car and hustled back to get his shit.

When he returned, Casey looked at him. "I need your eye on the ball, man. Is your head on straight?"

"Yeah, I'm good, man. I got everything I need."

Casey popped his car into gear and headed for the Lower East Side. Forty minutes later, they pulled up in front of a six-story brownstone sandwiched between a Chinese restaurant and a deli, and waited. Casey reached out to Champa and asked how it was goin'. He said there was a lot of foot traffic, but so far they had nothing. Al asked if maybe they should try another target, but Casey vetoed that. Fifteen minutes later, the two detectives exited the building and started walking down the street. Al put on his glasses and headed out the door. It took him a few seconds to catch up to the guys, and when he did, Casey watched him go into motion. Al pulled out his phone and started messin' with it. A moment later, the bearded detective pulled out his phone and looked at it, tapped the screen, and kept walking.

Casey called Jacob: "You getting anything yet?"

"Nope . . . wait—yes, I got it."

"Okay, tag that as the guy with the mustache."

"Done, I see everything on his phone. . . ."

From his vantage point, Casey saw Al workin' his phone again.

"I got another one, Casey," Jacob said.

"Cool, that's gotta be Shin. Al's still working on number two."

"There it goes, I got a third one."

Al turned around and waited for the all-good signal; Casey flashed his hazards and Al headed back. Casey already had the car running when Al jumped inside.

"Good work, man, we got 'em both, and Shin nailed his target, too."

Casey pulled into traffic and drove six blocks to the next detective's location. When they pulled up, he was walking out of the building.

"There he goes!" Casey pointed to a light-skinned brotha wearing a dark gray suit.

"I see 'em. . . ." Al got out of the car and took four steps and dropped his phone. It hit the ground and busted, pieces goin' in all different directions as he ran to grab them. *Shit!* Casey slumped lower in his seat, watching as Al put the phone back together and checked it while he was in pursuit. It was obvious the cell wasn't working. Al kept following his target, putting the busted phone in his back pocket, pulling out another, and getting to work.

I don't believe it, this nigga actually had a backup plan—fuckin' amazing. Casey dialed in Jacob. "Anything yet?"

"Not yet."

"Did Shin tag anyone else?"

"Nope . . . Okay, here we go, are you on Clinton Street near Stanton?"

"Yeah, I'll call you back." Casey hung up and flashed his hazards and Al jogged back to him. "Man, I thought you were done when you dropped that shit."

Al laughed and said, "That was, uh, quite unfortunate. I'm glad I brought a backup." He pulled out the broken phone and started trying to fix it while Casey drove to the next destination. It took them fifteen minutes to get eight blocks because of a traffic snarl, and by that time, Al had dissassembled and put the broken phone back together again. The guys waited twenty-five minutes in front of the building, laying in for their last detective. Finally Casey said, "I think we missed him."

Al replied, "I don't—I think he's pulling out of the garage in that brown Ford."

Casey looked back and couldn't really see anything. "Are you sure?"

"Yeah that's him, white dude with black hair and glasses."

The four-door brown Ford passed by, and Casey pulled out to tail it. Al had the phone in his hand, doing his magic. "You got his phone?" said Casey.

"Not yet . . . keep on him."

They followed the detective for nine blocks before Al was able to tag him, but they got him.

Casey reached out to Shin, who said they'd got two of their three targets.

"Cool, okay, let's meet back at Jacob's pronto."

When they got back to Jacob's pad, they were all pretty proud of the job they'd pulled off and were anticipating how it was gonna pay off. Jacob was busy at the keyboard, organizing the information while his computer pinged nonstop with alerts. Casey sat on the couch and enjoyed the moment; he wished he could share this with Carla, but it was too risky.

The celebration was short-lived, however. Jacob swung around in his chair with a very worried look on his face and panic in his voice. *"Casey!"*

Casey recognized that something was wrong and said loudly, *"Everyone shut up now!"*

The room fell silent and he leaned forward and looked at Jacob and said, "Go."

"I just ran through some of the detectives' e-mails and texts, and at noon today they're running a sting to take down Micky Benzo."

12

Casey looked at his watch. It was 9:14 A.M. on the dot. The whole room was in shock; everybody turned to him to see what he'd say. Intense situations like these were never a problem for him, however. He just calmly looked at Jacob and said, "Read the e-mail."

"The header says, 'Mercedes Operation,' and it was sent at seven A.M. this morning."

There will be a meeting at 10 A.M. today at Puzzle Towers to discuss protocol and procedure with the 28th Precinct. The 28th will be providing six patrol units that will be stationed three blocks away and will go to the scene when called. Our units will contain fourteen detectives: two will be located in the building for the meet in room 312, one will be at the front desk, five will be across the hall at the monitoring station in room 318, and the other six will be on the street. The subject Micky Bentson, aka Mick Benzo, is a black male, 5′8″, and is expecting to purchase 5 kilos of cocaine. He will be accompanied by John Jackson, aka JJ, a black male, 5′11″. The meet is set for today at noon at the Harlem Central Hotel on 1815 Park Ave. at 125th. When the subjects' purchase is confirmed they will be immediately arrested and separated into different rooms. John Jackson will be taken to room 318 and be debriefed and then be taken to Central Booking and then be released. John Jackson has informed us that there will also be at least two men waiting in the car on the street. Those men should be arrested when the other men are apprehended; their identities are not yet known.

The e-mail continued on with other procedural information and detailed how the bust had been set up over the last month and a half. While it was being read aloud, Casey wondered if Mick's crib was bugged and recalled the conversation he'd had with him a few days earlier. *Shit, that would fuck up everything for sure.* Until they could sweep Mick's crib top to bottom, he wouldn't know for certain.

Jacob finished reading the message, and Casey started snapping out orders. "Shin, go to Mick's right now, quick fast. I'll call you in a minute. Actually, hold on—Jacob, print that e-mail." Jacob printed it and handed it to Casey, who gave it to Shin.

"Okay, go, I'll call and tell you the plan before you get there." Casey turned back to Jacob. "Scan all the e-mails for Mick's name and let me know what you turn up. When they're in that meeting at ten, activate their phones so we can listen in." Casey paced the room in silence, then stopped and looked up at Champa. "Who's John Jackson?"

"I'm not sure, but I think he fucks with Mick's sister."

"Christ, you're fuckin' kidding me! Call up Mick and tell him that Shin's rolling over to see him right now and that you need his opinion on something."

Champa speed-dialed his man, and it went to voice mail. "Voice mail, Case."

"Keep on him a few more times."

Champa tried him a couple more times and got nothing.

Casey called Shin to give him the knowledge. "Yo, Shin, we can't get Mick on the line, so I want you to hang a few blocks from his crib. His shit's probably already staked out, and I don't need them knowin' you exist."

"Okay, got it. Just hit me up when you know what you want me to do."

Casey hung up the phone and turned to Jacob. "You turn up any more info?"

"Yeah, that Jackson guy's been working on setting Mick up for the last six weeks. Looks like he got busted with some H and, rather than doing some time, made a deal to set up his brother-in-law."

"*Brother-in-law?*" Casey and Champa both said.

"Yeah, he's been married to Mick's sister for about four months; this is the arrest report and the e-mail breaking down the whole deal."

Casey read the report off the monitor. Jackson had been busted with eight ounces of heroin and was pulled over because he was driving erratically. During booking he'd tested positive for coke; when they searched the vehicle, the cops had found an ounce of cocaine and the heroin. When they questioned him, they told him he was looking at an A-1 Felony that carried a sentence of fifteen years to life. They then offered him a deal to get to his supplier. Jackson was quick to sell out his brother-in-law and took the deal. Three days after the arrest, he'd tried to back out of the deal, but they weren't having it. For the last four weeks, Jackson had told Bentson he'd coordinated this buy with a supposed Miami connection he had. Mick had taken it slow and done all the right things to make sure the guys were legit. Unfortunately, he'd looked everywhere for problems except at his own brother-in-law. Casey read all the e-mails about the bust for the next thirty minutes; then Champa's cell phone rang. It was Mick calling back.

"Put him on speaker and keep me out of it," Casey said.

Champa answered and hit speakerphone. "Whassup, black man?"

"I'm in these streets, tryin' to get paid and wonderin' why you blowin' up a nigga's phone?"

Champa rolled his eyes. "Ahh, it ain't nothin', man. My boy's gonna be in your hood, and I need your opinion on something."

"I ain't got time today, Champa, I'm runnin' hard out here."

"It's important, Mick, and it won't take but a sec."

"Dude, did you *not* hear me—?"

"Mick . . . please, I'm in the mix right now, and I need your help. It can't wait. I only need five minutes, my man's already in your hood."

There was silence on the other end of the line for several seconds. Casey hoped that for once Mick wouldn't be a pain in the ass.

"You killin' me with this shit, Champa."

"Your opinion's important to me, man. I will owe you on this. It ain't gonna be but a minute."

Casey and Champa heard Mick speak in the background. "JJ, go to 124th near Frederick Douglass, behind the Apollo."

The guys all looked at each other, realizing that Mick was rollin' with the one cat they hoped wouldn't be around. Mick came back on. "I'll be in a black Denali behind the Apollo on 124th. Have your man flash his hazards twice."

"Okay, cool, he'll be there in minutes."

"He better be, 'cause I'm only waiting five. Out." Mick hung up the phone.

Casey didn't have to tell Champa to get Shin and clue him in. Once Shin was on the line, he ran it all down and handed the phone to Crush.

"When you see him, call me on your burner and hand it to him. How close are you?"

"Three blocks away."

"When you get there, keep a lookout for the cops, he may be being tailed."

Two minutes later, Shin was on 124th. When he saw Mick's ride, he flashed his hazards as directed. "He ain't gettin' out the car, Case."

"Okay, go to him. Hand him the phone and tell him Champa wants talk to him."

Casey walked into Jacob's living room, where he couldn't be heard. On the phone, he could hear Shin walking and then the sound of an electric window going down.

"What the fuck's goin' on, Shin?"

"Hey, Mick, Champa wants to holler at you."

Casey heard the rustle of the phone being transferred. "Nigga, what is your fucking problem? I thought you wanted me to look at something," Mick said.

"It's Casey, be cool, and don't say my name. You probably in a car fulla people, and at *least* of one them you can't trust. Shin's got something to show you, so get out of the car nice and easy and walk back to his ride."

Mick played it cool. "Champa, I don't have time for this muthafuckin' bullshit, we coulda handled this later." Casey heard a door open and close as Mick kept talking. "You guys stay here and keep the engine runnin' while I handle this lightweight." He could hear the guys walking, then Mick said, "Okay, what the hell is all this shit?"

"Mick, it's important for you and everyone else that you keep your cool right now. Remember that plan I told you about a few days ago? Well, we put it into action this A.M. and found out you about to get taken out by the cops this afternoon. Ask Shin for the e-mail."

Casey heard Mick ask, "Gimme the e-mail?"

Casey could hear him reading the e-mail aloud under his breath, his tone turning more shocked as he kept reading. Mick didn't say anything for a few seconds. "Crush . . . you know this nigga's fuckin' married to my sister, right?"

"Yeah, I know. The thing is we got to think this through so he don't take you down. I know you probably wanna go rip the nigga's head right off his shoulders, and I understand that, but this is complicated and it needs to be dealt with in a slick way so the pigs don't get wise."

"I'm so fuckin' mad right now, I don't give a fuck."

Casey could tell that Mick was fuming and on the edge of goin' gangsta. "I got a plan, but it means you got to stay cool. My plan also keeps you out of the joint and makes your sister a widow without her thinkin' you had anything to do with it. You wanna hear it?"

"Shit, nigga, you writin' the script on this, so tell me what you got to say."

"Okay, good, so are the details on that e-mail correct as far as time and location?"

"Yeah."

"How were you gonna pay?"

"I got a safety deposit box around the corner at Banco Popular. After this, I was supposed to go in and fill my briefcase with the chedda."

"Okay, stick to that plan, you go in solo and do what you'd normally do, but don't take any money out. This way no one will be hip to what's goin' on."

"Okay, but what about JJ?"

"In a minute. Now, I want you to think hard 'bout this, Mick. Has JJ been in your office or anywhere in your crib in the last six weeks?"

Casey could hear Mick breathing on the other end of the line before he replied. "He's only been downstairs, but that's it, he usually waits out front to drive me wherever I need to go."

"Good, do you ever discuss your business with him?"

"Nah, I don't tell him shit. This deal was the only dirty thing we ever talked about."

"Okay, well, talkin' about doin' a crime don't mean shit. Once this is over, you gonna need to do a sweep of your cars and place and make sure there's no bugs."

"I'm thinking 'bout that already."

"As far as JJ, he's gonna have to have an accident today. What were you gonna do after the bank?"

"Head back to my place and lay low till the meeting."

Casey checked the time; it was 10 A.M. The meeting at Puzzle Towers was just getting started. He glanced into the other room and saw Jacob wearing headphones listening in while the other guys read the action on the monitors. He had less than two hours to take out JJ, and his brain was already working a mile a minute.

"Okay, at eleven, you tell him you wanna go early and that it's just gonna be you two. Tell 'em you don't need no backup, 'cause you don't think they'll try anything in the hotel. Besides, you don't want the other guys knowin' your business. As you're heading to the meeting, I want you to go down Park Avenue, and when you pass 127th, tell him the car's riding funny and make him pull over and check the front driver's-side tire."

"Okay, then what?"

"Then the nigga's gonna get clipped. I'll have a car tailing you, and when he gets out, then . . . ya know."

Mick was silent on the other end of the line. Casey heard cars going past on the street. He knew Mick was past being pissed, and was probably thinking about his soon-to-be-devastated sister. No matter what happened, Casey knew Mick was destined to lose big-time today—it was just a matter of what it was gonna be: his freedom or his sister's happiness. The silence on the other end told him Mick was coming to grips with that.

Mick's voice was low when he finally replied. "My sister's gonna be fucked up over this, man. This dumb muthafucka's only been married to her for less than six months."

"Mick, he's sellin' you out to save his ass, he's a sucka. Believe me, it's just a matter of time before he does your sister low, too. If you pass on this meet, they gonna pressure him to pull together another one or they'll have him plant some shit on you. The bottom line is they got an in to you, and they gonna use that to take you down." Casey knew Mick was working overtime to figure something out, but the clock was ticking, and there was only one way this could go down.

"Do they have kids, Mick?"

"Nah, I mean she does, but . . . not with him."

"That's good. Look, brotha, the ball's in your court. I'm sorry to be the guy who's bringin' this to you, but I wasn't about to let you get put in the cross. If you got a different fix or just wanna handle this yo'self, then that's cool. But the time to make that decision is right now."

Champa walked in the room, and Casey held up his free hand so he knew not to speak.

There was a long silence again before Mick replied. "You know what, dawg, I got this. It's my mess, I'ma clean it up my own self."

"Okay, I feel ya. Do you need anything from me?"

"Yeah, I need your man here to take two of my guys and keep 'em busy for a couple hours."

"Okay, done."

The next thing Casey heard was Mick issuing orders to his men. "A'ight, you two niggas are rollin' with Shin right now. Champa's dumb ass got himself in some lightweight drama, and he needs some backup. Whatever he says goes, I don't wanna hear from you until he says he done with you."

In the background, Casey could hear talking, but couldn't make out what was happening. He heard a couple of doors slamming and a car pulling away.

Shin got on the phone and said, "Hey, Crush . . . him and JJ just bounced."

"Okay, take those two guys to Urban Victory and have them wait in the lobby and don't tell 'em shit. After you do that, run down to the deli next to the hotel and wait for Al. While you're there, eat a slow lunch and tag up the detectives we don't got already."

"Bet."

Casey hung up and looked at Champ and said, "What's the latest?"

"The cops'll be at the Harlem Central Hotel at eleven A.M. They already got the room bugged and wired."

"Okay, I'ma send Al down there now. There's a deli next to the hotel he can lay up in and hijack these guys' phones."

"What about Mick?"

"He said he was gonna handle it."

"What's that mean?"

"No idea, but he had two of his guys jump in Shin's ride. He's taking them to the office now." Casey walked into the main room and told Al that he was gonna be stationed at the deli next to the hotel and to tag up as many cops as possible.

For the next two hours, Champa and Casey monitored the correspondence and conversations of the detectives on the sting operation. In that time, Al P., Shin, and Champa hijacked all the cops' phones except for two, bringing their total to twelve detectives out of the twenty-three they'd targeted.

Casey could tell by the conversation that the pigs were hyped about landing a big fish. In going through the e-mails, he also found out, to his relief, that they'd been unsuccessful in placing a bug in Mick's place. Listening to the conversations of the detectives gave Casey a lot of insight to the protocols and politics of the department. It was obvious there were two groups in the OCCB: those that were old-school buddies of Fordham's, and those that weren't. Fordham's inner circle got preferential work hours and seemed to get all the glory as well.

When noon rolled around and Mick didn't show, the cops kept their cool and waited. When it hit twelve thirty, one of the detectives called JJ's phone and got his voice mail. At 2 P.M., after repeated calls to JJ's phone and no sign of Mick showing up, the disappointed cops called it a day.

After they'd left, Casey rang Shin and told him to go back to Urban Victory and pick up the two dudes and drop them at Mick's house, then come to Jacob's with Al P. The cops surmised that somehow Mick had found out about the sting, probably because JJ had spilled the beans. They knew he had a habit and wasn't particularly dependable. They really couldn't do anything, as they didn't have any hard evidence, so they just put two officers on JJ's house and waited for him to get home.

For the rest of the day, the computers pulled information from the twelve detectives' cells and organized it. Based on that intel, it seemed like Casey was not on the OCCB radar. The Garcia brothers, Sean E Sean, and Big Rich were also not talked about.

The one person's name that did come up was Alek Petrosian. They suspected him to be involved in the restaurant shooting and had taken him in for questioning. Petrosian had lawyered up and denied that he was involved in any way. He said that his men had taken his car to get it washed and must have stopped to eat when everything went down. There were no witnesses that were willing to look at a lineup, and as far as physical evidence, all they had were dead bodies and bullet shells that had no prints on them. It didn't seem like the cops had really pressed Petrosian, which seemed strange. They could have kept him overnight, given that his car was there, but they didn't. There was even an e-mail from Fordham to the arresting detective saying that based on what he'd read, he didn't think Petrosian was at the scene and to cut him loose. Casey had too much info he needed to get through to ponder that, and just filed it in the back of his head.

Around 5 P.M., Casey was burnt out from looking at the bright computer screens. He took one last look at the monitors from a distance, watching the red and green dots of the detectives they were bugging. He cross-checked it with the map program on his phone and found it matched perfectly. The next stage of the plan was to get the rest of the detectives and, most important, Fordham's phone bugged, that way they'd have a complete picture of everything going down at the OCCB.

Telling Jacob to alert him if anything interesting popped up,

Casey rose and started for the door. On the way, he got a text from Shin that he and Al were around the corner. He told Champa and Jacob he was goin' out and asked Champa to step outside with him. Downstairs, they waited in Casey's Escalade for Shin's G-Wagen to show up.

"So, what's your best guess on Mick right now, Crush?"

Casey'd been pondering that same question on and off all day, and couldn't be 100 percent sure about any answer. He tilted his seat back a bit. "Well, he had the opportunity for me to handle it right in front of him . . . but he declined. That makes me think he was hesitant to do what he knew had to be done."

"You think he gave JJ a second chance?"

"It's possible, but I doubt it. I'm sure he did the math over and over and came out with the same answer every time. It's tough, you know, the nigga's his brother-in-law and all, but Mick's always been about the business first, you know that."

"True dat, I'm just hopin' JJ didn't get wise and get the jump on him."

"We'll know soon enough. I'm not gonna reach out to him till tomorrow, when shit has calmed down some. Here's Shin."

Casey flashed his lights and saw both him and Al P. get out of the G-Wagen and approach Casey's car window. He rolled the window down as they walked up. "Good work today, you got a total of twelve. I want you to work with Jacob and hunt the other ten down tonight and tomorrow. Once we get all of 'em, we'll target Fordham, and when we have him, we'll be good to go."

The guys nodded. Casey told Al to go upstairs and get to work on that with Jacob, then instructed Shin to get in the back of his ride. Shin hopped in and the guys twisted around to talk with him.

"Did you see Mick or JJ's ride at his crib?"

"Nah, nothing. You haven't heard from him?"

"Nope . . . how'd he look when you left him?" Champa asked.

"Like he'd been sucker-punched . . . afterwards, his boys that I took to the office was asking me twenty questions."

"And you said?"

"Shit . . . I tol' 'em if there was something worth knowing, then they'd know it and to hang tight till then."

"Mick'll be all right, he's a double OG—the man's been through his fair share of heavy shit. I've seen the nigga take two nine-millimeter slugs in the chest and kept swingin', it was like they was givin' him fuckin' vitamins."

"No shit?" Shin asked.

"Yeah, so don't worry about him. He will handle this shit, and when he's ready, he'll pop up and you won't even know anything went down. Okay, I'm out, I got a meeting with Petrosian tomorrow. Shin, I need you to monitor the airwaves and gather as much info as possible and report back to Champa and me on what you find out. I want you and Al P. on the street ASAP, taggin' the rest of the people we didn't get today."

Casey brought his Escalade to life while the guys got out and started walking to the building. He called Champa, who walked back to Casey's open window. "I know you been preoccupied, but when am I gonna hear the next report on that car job?"

"Tomorrow night, all the pieces are coming together nicely."

"Okay, that's good, we need to keep all these plates spinnin'. I'm out, brotha."

Casey looked in his rearview and pulled into traffic, taking twenty minutes to get home. When he got there, Mick was sitting in front of his building in his not-so-inconspicuous black-on-black Mercedes Benz S500. Casey was glad to see the man, but a bit pissed that he'd parked right in front of his crib. If anyone was following him, they'd make the connection and bring heat down on him. He pulled up to Mick and rolled his passenger window down.

"Hey, follow me into the garage and park next to me—it's too public out here."

Casey pressed a button on his visor, and the parking gate lifted and Mick followed him into the underground garage. When Mick got out, he gave Casey a fist bump and said, "Don't worry, I was careful not to be followed."

"Yeah, okay, let's keep it light till we get to my crib."

The men rode the elevator up. When it reached the lobby, the doors opened on a very frail, old white woman struggling with three bags of groceries. Both men instinctively stepped to her to help her with her bags.

"Oh, aren't you sweet! Thank you, boys."

She pressed the button for the twelfth floor. When the doors opened, the guys followed her to her door, took the groceries to her kitchen, and put the bags on the counter. As they were leaving, she stopped them and pulled out an impressive roll of money. Peeling off two dollars, she pressed a dollar bill into Casey's and Mick's palms. "I always believe in rewarding good service."

The guys thanked her politely, walked out into the hall, and pressed the up key to head to Casey's crib. Once the elevator doors had closed, Mick cracked, "If she only knew she'd just let a couple rattlesnakes into her apartment, she'da been guardin' that money a helluva lot more closely."

Casey grunted in agreement as the elevator doors opened; he liked that his neighbors were totally clueless about his past and his present. He put the key in his door, and the men went in and sat down in the living room. Casey tossed his keys on the side table and offered Mick a drink.

"Yeah, give me a double shot of whatever you got."

Casey walked to the bar and cracked open a bottle of Johnnie Walker Black Label, the smoky smell of the scotch filling his nose as he poured two glasses. Taking the bottle back with him, he handed one to Mick, sat down, and waited for him to speak.

Mick drained his glass in two swallows, and Casey gave him another shot. Mick leaned back into the couch and looked at the ceiling. "I owe you one, Case."

"Come on, man, homeys don't keep score like that."

"Just the same, I'd be on my way to servin' life or dead in a shoot-out if you hadn't tugged my coat today."

Casey dropped a shoulder. "That's what this alliance is all about: makin' paper and watchin' each other's back."

Mick sat silent for a minute, took another tug at his drink, then finished it off. Casey grabbed the bottle and gave him another, and then Mick recounted what happened after he left Shin.

"When I got back in the car, JJ was jittery as hell. He starts in on me right away, asking a lotta questions. I gave him a line about how Champa had fucked up some deal and there were some people hot with him and he needed a bunch of niggas nearby to make sure he was covered if shit went off. JJ seemed like he bought it, but the cat was still acting strange. I had him drive me around the corner to the bank and played everything out like the meeting was still goin' down. After that I told him drive to the Harlem Central Hotel. We talked about the deal on the way, and I asked him straight up was he sure this was the right maneuver? Did he really think these guys were cool, 'cause it wasn't too late to back out."

Mick stared at Casey for a long moment. "And the nigga looked me dead in my eyes and told me he knew these guys was cool. 'Sides, how would I look if I put my brother-in-law in a cross?" Mick was wringing his hands and shaking his head. "I couldn't believe that muthafacka had the balls to go there. Shit, it took everything I had not to pull my gat and put a cap in his fuckin' face right then and there. The only reason I had him around was 'cause my sister had begged me to give him a job and make sure the chump-ass didn't go back to usin'."

Mick took another slug of Johnnie Walker Black. "I had him pull a detour and take me to 157th and Malcolm X. JJ asked me where we were goin', and I said I wanted to pick up an AK 'cause I liked the idea of takin' the dope rather than payin' for it. I told him that both of us were gonna go in blazin' and jack that shit, old-school-gangsta style. Of course, he got real jumpy at that. He was beggin' and pleadin' with me not to shoot up the place. 'Please, Mick, that's not a good look, come on, man, let's just handle it businesslike, come on, big homey.' I kept winding that muthafucka up for a few, but finally I let him convince me to do the deal as planned. I told him he needed to chill out, then I baited the fool and asked if he wanted a little something for his nerves. He tried to play it off like he was clean and shit, but quickly agreed it was probably a good idea. I told him to drive by one of my dealers to score some China White. We pulled up to the spot, and dig this—I had his ass wait in the car and told him to 'keep a lookout for the cops'— what a fuckin' joke. I went in and scored a half gram of pure heroin."

Casey knew if a junkie shot pure heroin, he'd OD in less than five minutes.

"When I came back to the car, the dumbass already had his rig out, ready to go. I told him to chill out and had him drive around the corner and park in an alley next to a slum building." Mick described how JJ put the H in a dirty spoon with some water and heated it with a lighter so the shit melted cleanly. Then he got out a Q-tip, took the cotton off and put it in the spoon, then carefully stuck his needle into the cotton and pulled the plunger back.

Mick leaned forward and held his head in his hands and didn't look at Casey as he continued. "By now, the muthafucka was shakin' all over, he was jonesin' for that hit so bad. He tied some rubber around his arm and tried to make a vein pop, but that didn't work, so he tried the back of his hand, but had no luck. He tried the other arm and struck out there, too. This shit's goin' on for twenty minutes. During all this, I see his phone light up, and from the caller ID, I knew it was my sister. JJ just ignored that shit and went about his treasure hunt. He finally found a vein in his foot and stuck it in. He pulled back the plunger so a little trickle of blood invaded the mixture, and then slowly pushed that shit into his vein.

"I gotta be honest, man—at the last minute, I was tempted to smack it out of the nigga's hand and beat the shit out of him and ask him how he could do this to my sister. But I knew all I was doing by givin' him this hot shot was speeding up time. It wasn't a matter of 'if' with that muthafucka, but 'when' he'd OD. Within thirty seconds of banging the H, he nodded out, then his face turned gray and his lips turned blue, and five minutes later he was stone dead. I made sure I left no prints on anything, dumped his ass in the alley, and took off."

Both men sat there in silence for a minute. Casey looked at Mick as he stared off into space. "That's some heavy shit, Mick. Does your sister know yet?"

"Not yet, I figure the cops or someone will find him soon. She called me a few hours ago, asking me where he was at, and I told her he'd come by earlier, then split. I said I was pissed at him for not handlin' his business right and when I saw him again, we was gonna have words. She knows he's had problems and suspected that he might be using again, so this'll be a shock, but not a surprise. It's just so fucked up—the only reason I took him in was 'cause she asked me to, guess she figured her big brother could help keep his ass outta trouble."

Mick let out a long exhale; Casey knew his homey was waiting for the other shoe to drop. Once his sister found out, she'd be destroyed, and while Mick would be there for her, he'd also have to live every day of the rest of his life knowing that he'd been part of the cause of the pain she was feeling.

"Like I said, it's a fucked-up situation, man, and you did what you had to do. When he put you in the cross like that, he chose himself over you and his wife. Dope makes people do fucked-up shit, this ain't news to us, man."

Mick downed the rest of his drink and got up. Casey could tell by his face that he was good. "I'm done feeling sorry 'bout this shit. I warned her about this cat from the onset. He had his shot and he blew it. I just wanted to come over here and let you know shit was handled and that I appreciate you savin' this nigga's ass from the joint."

"Well, that's how us OGs get down, right?"

"Indeed."

Mick gave Casey a dap and walked out the door to the elevator. Before the door closed, Casey held it open. "Let's keep shit on the DL for a couple days, there's gonna be a lotta eyes on you. I'll have Shin swing by in a day or two to check up."

"Yeah, I agree. Thanks again, brotha."

"Ain't no thang." The doors shut and Casey walked back to his apartment and shut the door. He knew Mick was good, and ultimately would be fine. He was also glad he hadn't been the one to take JJ out; he already had enough blood on his hands for a lifetime, and didn't need any more.

He wondered how Carla would feel about that, and was immensely glad he wouldn't have to find out.

13

In the sleepy haze of the early morning, Casey woke up to the faint sound of traffic outside and Carla lying next to him. He vaguely remembered her coming in the previous night, and was glad she had. He moved close to her and enjoyed the feel of her soft body as she spooned close to him. They lay like that for a while, tangled together and half-awake.

As the sun broke through the curtains, Carla rolled her naked body over and lay on her back, eyes closed, with the long, wild curls of her hair framing her face. She could have easily passed for a woman in her late twenties. Likewise, there were few people that would believe that she had a twenty-year-old daughter. Casey remembered her telling him the story of being pregnant at sixteen.

That fateful morning started out great: When she got to school, she had been immediately called to the principal's office. Rather than his usual emotionless face, he was curiously all smiles that day. She walked into his cramped office that always reeked of stale cigarettes, but even more so today, and saw her math teacher, guidance counselor, and some guy with a camera all staring at her. They were all cheesed up. The principal told her that she had won the statewide math challenge. At first she didn't understand, but then remembered taking a test a few months earlier. Carla had always dreamed of being an engineer, and this award was one step closer to realizing it. Her chances of getting a scholarship had now increased dramatically. She knew her mother would be ecstatic. Everyone in the room clapped and smiled and told her she had done them proud. Her prize was a certificate and her picture in the paper alongside a tiny announcement.

After school, she went to a friend's house to celebrate, but got violently sick on the way. She told her friend that she had been super sensitive to smells like coffee, her books, and even her shampoo that morning. She'd felt like she was gonna gag all day long. She also said her boobs were super sore. Her friend stared at her just as confused as she was, then told her to hold on and ran out of the room. She returned with something in her hand, a pregnancy test, and explained how to use it.

Carla's heart started pounding as she slowly walked to the bathroom and took the test. Inside, she knew she was pregnant—she could just feel it—but she took the test anyway. She saw the results and felt like she was drowning. She walked slowly across the room as if she was moving underwater, sat on her friend's bed, and burst into tears. Having an abortion was possible, but out of the question. She was scared of doctors, and her mother would never allow it anyway. She tried to think what would be better, to tell her mom about the award first or second, but she knew it really didn't matter—she would be crushed either way. She knew her hopes of becoming an engineer were now remote; what good school would ever give a scholarship to a kid *with* a kid?

As expected, her mother was livid and made her life hell for the next few months, but all was forgiven when the baby was born. Her daughter arrived healthy and cute, as most kids do. Carla graduated high school with honors, then went to school for hotel management while her mother tended to her infant. Her timing was perfect, as the amount of hotels dramatically increased in New York in the 1990s. She quickly established herself as a smart and reliable employee at one of the city's most prestigious hotels. Her hard work over the many years of service and loyalty paid off when a couple years ago, she was made general manager. It wasn't the engineering gig she'd wanted, but it paid the bills and was a lucrative career. As for her daughter, she was in her first year of college at Brown studying, of all things, engineering.

Carla's eyes fluttered open and looked at Crush. It was a little after 7 A.M. Casey was usually up at six—twenty years of prison habits were hard to change—but today he'd given himself a break and slept in.

"What's up, baby?" Carla asked as she stretched her sexy body out for Casey to admire, her arms slowly reaching above her head like a cat.

"Just lookin' at you, baby. I didn't hear you come in last night."

Carla looked at him slyly. "You gonna report me for breakin' and enterin'?"

"Nah, I'ma handle this all by myself." Casey grinned, and Carla grinned back at him. They fooled around for a bit, then took a shower together. Afterwards, they went down the street to Tommy's Diner and ate a quick breakfast so Carla wouldn't be late for work. She went off to the hotel, and Casey stayed behind, milking his last cup of coffee.

On his phone was a text message from a number he didn't know. He'd missed receiving it while lathering up his lady in the shower.

You got a minute to talk today, if so St. James Park at 2 P.M. is good for me. A.P.

Casey assumed "A.P." meant Alek Petrosian, but it could have been Al P. using a burner. He typed back.

Who is this?

A moment later, Casey's phone rang with a call from the number. "Whassup?"

"It's me, can you meet then?"

Casey recognized Alek's voice. "Yeah, I'll be there. This your new number?"

"Not really, I'll tell you about that when I see you."

"A'ight, later." Casey thought the Armenian sounded a bit weird, but he wasn't alarmed or anything. Hell, a lotta playas, himself included, were very cautious about what they said on cell phones. He polished off his lukewarm coffee, tossed some bills on the table, and jetted to the Urban Victory office.

On the way, he reached out to Champa to meet him there. He thought about bringing Shin or Champa to the Petrosian meeting, but figured it was better to go solo. He liked that Petrosian rolled with goons and he didn't, and knew Petrosian was perceptive enough to see this distinction between them.

On the street, Casey gave the impression of someone who feared no man and no situation, his confidence was evident, but he wasn't arrogant. To those who couldn't see the subtle distinctions, the two men would seem identical, but they weren't: Casey was a man who had lost everything at one time, and Petrosian was a man who hadn't made that misstep, at least not yet. It was true that the Armenian was a bad muthafucka, no doubt, but his respect was demanded, whereas Casey's was commanded. Casey ruled through his words, not through force. That wasn't to say that he didn't stomp a nigga's ass when it was deserved; he just knew that in the end, it was more effective to reign through his intellect. All smart men knew that true power came through profound words and innovative ideas.

As a young man, he'd learned this lesson well from a "gentleman of leisure" named the General, aka the Sweet Man. The General had a stable of seven hos, some of whom worked in Casey's hood. He drove a champagne-colored Caddy with a custom Louis Vuitton interior, and was always in motion. Casey was fresh out of juvie when he and Big Rich were kicking it and approached the General one afternoon about the secret of getting women.

Gen sized them both up, smiling like a Cheshire cat. Tall, thin, and black as night, with his nails always manicured and his vines always tight, he was also a man who loved having an audience.

"Look here, young niggas, you wanna know the secret to gettin' a bitch? It's the same secret to having power over anyone, you dig? It's a skull game." Gen spoke in a conspiratorial whisper. "It's keeping a bitch's mind confused—you gotta hypnotize these broads. It's puttin' your sexual desire in refrigeration. You may wanna freak these bitches real bad, but you need to be able to walk away from that sweet pussy in an instant. You see, just like everyone else, a bitch respects strength, and delights in gettin' over on a nigga. If she knows that she can dangle her snatch and you come runnin', then you're through, my friend. It's the same in business: Nobody gives money to someone desperate or who wants it too bad. Money makes money, and desperate money *never* wins. You got to be able to pimp yo'self and yo ideas before you pimp anyone else. You got to cop 'n' blow all day long, keep your pimp hand strong, be sweet one moment and sour the next, keep *everyone* guessin'. Keep them hos befuddled, bewitched, entranced, and beguiled, and they will hump for a nigga night and day till they can't feel their own pussy!"

Casey remembered him and Rich being mesmerized by the General's game, and for what it was worth, the General recognized future playas.

At the end of his speech, General looked at them and said, "How much scratch you niggas got in your pockets?"

Casey and Rich dug into their pockets and came up with forty-five bucks. Snorting in disgust, the General held out his bejeweled hand for their bread. He counted it with a quick flick of his fingers, then ripped the money up into small pieces, threw it in the air, and let it rain down on him. "Remember, young niggas, the game's to be sold *not* told—now let's see what you *really* got."

Casey smiled as he pulled into the Urban Victory garage and headed upstairs. He'd had many teachers in his life that had dropped jewels on him, but none had been as colorful as the General. He dialed up Rich as he was ridin' up the elevator.

Rich picked up and Casey said, "Whassup, pimpin'?"

Rich chuckled. "Aw shit, nigga, just tryin' to keep these hos in check and my Gators shiny, whas doin'?"

"I was thinkin' about that time back in the day when the General dropped that jewel on us about the game."

Rich laughed. "Yeah, he was somethin' else. I remember him tellin' us in his deep-ass voice, 'You know you niggas is cut for this,' and then askin' me how my sister was doing and was she eighteen yet?"

Casey cracked up at that. "Oh shit, that nigga was crazy! You remember when we saw him beatin' on one of his broads in front of the hair salon? His fist and curlers were flyin' all over the goddamn place! I'd never seen anything like it."

Rich was laughing even harder now. "Ahh man, now thas some hood shit right there."

Casey caught his breath and said, "Whatever happened to him anyway, where's he at?"

Rich sighed. "I guess you wouldn'a heard, but a few years after you went down, he started hittin' that pipe. He lost all his broads, then had a heart attack and died."

"Damn, no shit?"

"No shit, brotha, the game is cold."

"Damn, well, rest in peace, General."

"Fo sho, fo sho. Anyway, what else is good? I heard from Shin you got something jumping next week and wanna do a powwow."

Casey got out of the elevator but stayed out of the office to finish his conversation. "Yeah, I got an update and some other things to discuss. I'm thinking Tuesday same spot around seven in the P.M., but Shin or Champ'll confirm that with ya."

"Okay, movin'," Big Rich said, and they both hung up.

Casey walked into the office with the General and his sad end still on his mind and noticed there was more than a bit of activity goin' on. Joe Pica and a few of his regular staff were around a desk, obviously planning something. Casey caught his eye and waved him over.

"What's up, Crush?" said Joe.

"You know, keepin' my hustle strong. What's all the action here about?"

"Oh, we're getting prepared for a lecture at PS 127 for a bunch of fourth- and fifth-graders."

"Oh, okay . . . that's where you talk to kids about the reality of crime, drugs, and doing time, right?"

"Yeah, we're going over there at eleven for about an hour and a half. You wanna roll with us?"

Casey cocked his head sideways at Joe and shot him a confused look. "Come again?"

"Come on, Case, it's not that long, and if you got the time, it could be a good look for us."

His initial thought was, *Hell no,* but he checked himself and thought it over for a second. He had to see Lomax Monday, and doing this shit was technically part of his job description. If anyone from the parole office did come sniffin' around, it would be good to have this on record. Casey checked his watch: it was a little after nine. He had to check with Jacob to see what intel he'd collected on the detectives, and then he had the 2 P.M. with Petrosian, so he had the time.

"Yeah, okay, just text me when you're ready and I'll meet you down in the garage."

"Cool, I think you'll be surprised," Joe said with a smile.

Casey grunted, then turned and walked to his office. Champa entered the lobby as the guys finished their conversation and followed him. "I need to rap with you about this car job."

"Okay, cool, what day does it go down?"

"Next Friday, 6 A.M," Champa said through an ear-to-ear smile.

"All right, I gotta handle some shit this A.M. and in the afternoon, so let's talk later. Have a seat. I'm callin' Jacob for an update."

Casey sat at his desk and dialed. He hated talking on the phone about sensitive shit, but didn't have the time to go down there. Jacob picked up the phone on the first ring.

"What's up, man? I'm callin' for an update, but before we speak on that, I gotta tech question for you. . . . If we did a video chat, is there any chance anyone could hack into it?"

"You mean is it secure?"

"Exactly."

"Yeah, it's secure. I could go into a long explanation why, but the short answer is yes." Jacob ran down to Casey how to set up his laptop so they could video chat, and a few minutes later, he was staring at Casey from the monitor.

Casey cracked a small smile, clearly impressed. For someone who'd been in the joint for twenty years, running messages with scraps of paper and ghetto code, this shit seemed space age.

"I'm glad we're doing this via video conference and not on the phone. From now on, when you're at your computer, if you want, you can just hit me up this way. I'm always here," Jacob said. "To be honest, given all the stuff we're doing with phones, my paranoia level's at a new high, so this is definitely my preferred method of communication."

Casey watched Jacob's crystal-clear picture on his monitor. *Goddamn, this is some real* Star Trek *shit.* "Okay, so first thing, is there anything immediate I need to know? You know, like a bust goin' down or some shit like that? If not, run down what you've found out about Petrosian."

"As far as the detectives go, it's all business as usual. There was a little talk about the failed sting with Mick Benzo, and about his brother-in-law OD'ing."

"What'd they say about his brother-in-law?"

"They were pissed he couldn't hold it together until after the bust and hoped Fordham wouldn't be too angry about it."

"Hmmm, okay, what else?"

"Al P. and Shin tagged everyone except for Fordham, and they've got a plan to get him today. The whole system's buzzing along just fine, and I'm tweaking it to make sure it's getting better every day. It's quite a piece of work," Jacob said, the pride in his voice evident.

"Damn straight it is. You done good, son," Casey said. "How many more targets do you think the system could track before it became overwhelmed?"

"Well, once we have Fordham, we'll be at twenty-three. . . . I'd say with our current technology, we could easily manage another, I don't know, maybe . . . seventy-five."

Casey was surprised, but Jacob's expression on the monitor told him the young man was serious. Champa went behind Casey and pulled up a chair to look at the screen as well.

"You sure? That's a hella lot of info to filter—isn't that too much to manage reliably?" Casey asked.

"Not really, the way I have built this, we could expand it even more if needed. I've created a hierarchy based off an algorithm I wrote that prioritizes the targets that meet our criteria most often and then sends me alerts based on the keywords we're looking for."

Champa frowned. "Say what?"

Before Jacob could respond, Casey said, "Okay, I translate that to mean you don't have to physically monitor these guys as much as you normally would, because you tweaked the computer to do it for you based on how the computer profiles them."

Clearly lost by all this tech talk, Champa returned to the couch and sat down.

Jacob nodded. "Exaaaactly. The really cool thing is that the more information I get, the more sophisticated and accurate the computer's scans become because it grows the computer's information database that it draws on to make decisions exponentially."

Casey leaned back in his Herman Miller chair and contemplated this. *This hacking shit is fuckin' incredible—I could easily get addicted.* He glanced at Champa, who was texting on his phone, and snapped his fingers for him to pay attention. He looked at the computer screen and said, "Jacob, I want you to let Champa know when that cop we tagged gets calls to respond to anything major. On those calls, there's bound to be a ton of cops."

Champa nodded. "Okay, I'm guessin' you'll want Al P. to go to the scene and tag as many as possible."

"Yup, detectives, too. The more ears we have, the better off we'll be. I wanna cover as much of the Bronx and Harlem as possible. I wanna know *everything* that goes down."

"Not a problem, Case. I assume you're cool if I have Champa buy more drives?"

"Hell yeah, let's expand this shit and see what we catch. I also want you to generate two daily reports: one that you'll send to me at ten A.M. and the other at ten P.M. Each one should only be two pages max, something I can scan that's organized real good so as I know what these cops're up to. If I want more details, I'll have you send it to me. Now, what you got on Petrosian?"

Casey saw Jacob quickly taking notes. He liked that. He could tell the man was gonna be an incredibly valuable asset for future operations. He could only imagine the loot they could make by tappin' in to the big players in the stock market.

"I hacked into the DMV and got his current address. It's in the Bronx—Fieldston, specifically."

Fieldston was about ten to fifteen minutes north of the center of the Bronx, with homes there ranging anywhere from $1.5 million to $6 million. Casey wasn't surprised that the guy had some cake. He listened as Jacob continued.

"He has a son, but no wife. My search of marriage, death, and birth certificates came up empty, don't know if he was married in the old country or what. I noticed on his driver's license that his full name is Alek Vyacheslav Petrosian II, so I did a Google search and found an article on his father. It might be wrong, but based on the dates and other information I cross-referenced, I'm pretty sure it's a match. Here it is."

He sent the link to it. Casey clicked on it and scanned through the foreign text until he came to a picture of a boy about fourteen years old, standing next to his mother and father. Petrosian's likeness to his father was spot on.

"Do you know what the article says?" Casey asked.

"Roughly. I ran it through a translation program, and I'm sending you that version right now. Basically, it's from an Eastern European business magazine and was written in July 1985. It was an obituary on Petrosian's father. The piece says he was a prominent oil man who was married to a Russian woman. It talked about his dominance in the region and how he frequently traveled throughout Russia, primarily the Ukraine and Armenia, brokering oil deals with the West. It said that he and his wife were killed in an auto accident while traveling in the Ukraine. They were survived by their son, who would be moving to London to live with a relative."

"Is that it?" Casey said.

"That's it because that's *all* that exists. I did a *very* extensive search. The only other thing that popped up is more recent. On a bunch of Armenian blogs, he's mentioned as the most likely suspect in murdering Luca Bagramian in a drive-by shooting. There's one post here that says, 'Luca was a true player and he'll be missed. Almost immediately after he got dusted I hear this new cat popped up and is running things, a guy named Petrosian. Anyone hip to this guy? Did he whack Luca?' Luca's name pops up on a lot of other message boards as a big-time dealer."

Champa jumped in: "Luca's the guy I knew. Stone-cold playa, lemme tell ya."

"Anything else, Jacob?" Casey asked.

"Nope, that's it. I'll start monitoring that one cop's cell for calls and let Champa and Al know, right?"

"Yeah, you do that, I'm out." Casey signed off and closed his computer. Turning to Champa, he asked, "What's up with these message boards and people snitchin'?"

"Welcome to the Information Age, son."

"That's some bullshit right there. Shit, I mean, who needs the cops when people on the street are anonymously putting you on blast!"

"Anyway, check it, let's talk about this car heist and how—," Champa began.

Casey's phone buzzed with a message from Joe: It was time to go to PS 127. He looked up at Champa. "We gonna have to handle this later, brotha. I gotta bounce."

14

The two men both took the elevator down to the garage, where Joe and two of his early intervention "experts" were waiting. Joe told the other two guys to go on ahead and that Casey and he would be there momentarily. Casey told Champa to make sure Al P. was on point and didn't drop the ball; then Joe and he got into the Escalade and headed down to PS 127.

On the drive there, Joe said that he would introduce Crush halfway through the presentation. He told him he should feel free to talk as long as he wanted to about how crime is not the way to go. As Casey listened, he thought about how he was gonna be a total hypocrite talking that shit to those kids. These kids would be about the same age as Antonio was when he'd gone into prison. Casey had given him the "don't do crime" speech, and look what good that had done.

He started to feel uneasy about the whole situation as they pulled into the school parking lot. But then Casey remembered one of Mack D's favorite quotes from Tolstoy: "I know which is the road that leads home and if I weave like a drunken man as I go down it that does not mean the road is the wrong one." Mack always liked to talk about everyone's unique path, and Casey guessed that this was his, even though he sometimes veered off it.

They went into the school's main entrance; it had been at least thirty years since Casey set foot inside one. Along with Joe and the other two cats, he walked down the halls wallpapered with the kids' artwork. Casey remembered his own son had brought art home at that age almost every day.

When they got to the principal's office, Joe went in and Casey and the guys waited outside the door for him to return. Casey kept looking around, thinking that it was ludicrous that this school had actually invited a bunch of criminals to speak to children.

Joe emerged with an older black woman who looked to be in her early sixties. She wore glasses and had a gold cross around her neck. Joe introduced everyone as she led them to the auditorium. Her name was Principal Parker. Casey could tell she was from the South by the slight twang in her speech.

"The kids will be coming in any moment. I—I just wanted to thank you all for coming here today. My brother is serving time in Georgia, and it was about these kids' ages that he started to go astray."

The men stayed silent, just nodding as she spoke.

Casey noticed the kids walking in; some were quiet, but most were clowning around and being loud and unruly. Teachers snapped at the troublemakers, and girls giggled at the boys getting into trouble. *Some things never change.* Eventually they all sat down, with the six teachers and the principal all leaning against the back wall, making sure none of the youngsters got out of line.

Joe gave a brief introduction and talked about his past; Casey could tell he had a well-rehearsed speech. The other two guys went and said their bit, both making good points about not getting into a life of crime. Unfortunately, the kids had probably heard this shit a thousand times, and seemed on the verge of passing out from boredom.

Last up was Casey, and for the first time in many years, he found he was actually a bit nervous. He inhaled, stepped forward, and looked at the faces of more than two hundred kids, all either black or Hispanic. Clearing his throat, Casey addressed the children, his deep voice making them all naturally sit at attention.

"Raise your hands if any of you have tried drugs or been tempted by a life of crime."

Not one hand went up. Quiet voices mumbled as the kids looked around to see if anyone had dared admit such a thing.

"That's interesting. . . . Now, I think some of you aren't being truthful with me. . . ." Casey walked down the front row, picked one kid and told him to stand up and move to the center of the room. He then walked down the left side aisle and asked two more kids to go to the front and stand next to the first kid.

His selection may have appeared very random, but it wasn't. He told the kids to turn and face the audience. The three were nervous, as were the teachers when he did this. Two of the kids were black and the other was Hispanic; they were all about nine or ten years old.

Casey stared at the boys for a few moments to increase the tension before speaking. "Have any of you ever seen me before?"

All the kids shook their heads and mumbled, "No."

Casey looked out at the audience. "One of these kids is just like the rest of you." He turned back to the first kid. "You rep the One Five Three Players, right?"

The boy was shocked and didn't say anything, but the answer was written all over his face. Casey looked at the rest of the audience. "If it wasn't true, he woulda denied it, right?"

The kids all chorused yes while the teachers in the back row fidgeted and exchanged worried looks.

Casey went to the next kid. "You like to get high, dontcha?" The boy was about to protest, but Casey held up his hand. "Ah-ah-ah . . . only answer if you're cool with me checkin' to see what's in your pockets right now." The kid closed his mouth and looked down at his sneakers.

By the time Casey got to the third kid, the whole audience of children and teachers was transfixed. For them, it was like Casey was a mind reader. The third boy refused to look at Casey and shifted his weight from one leg to another. Casey felt real bad for the kid; he could tell by the way he was acting that he had a pretty serious habit and was ashamed of himself. The boy's nose was red and runny, his face was pale, and the exposed skin on his arms was a pasty white. *Shit, this kid's on a tightrope already.*

Rather than expose the boy, Casey had the three of them go sit down as he turned to his audience again. "Now, unless I get some honesty, I can do this all day with every single one of you, so lemme ask again. . . . Raise your hands if you have tried drugs or been tempted by a life of crime."

More than three quarters of the auditorium raised their hands. The teachers and the principal in the back were visibly upset, but they stayed put.

"Okay, put your hands down. You see, wantin' to try drugs or do crime . . . that comes from ignorance, curiosity, and fear. Some of you have tried drugs 'cause someone close to you does drugs and you were curious and also didn't wanna be made fun of. . . . That's the 'curiosity and fear' part. And some of you think you wanna do crime because you want the money and think it's cool and you may think that doin' drugs won't hurt you. . . . Well, that's ignorance. I totally get that because that's why I did it—" Casey paused as he paced the room. He could feel the eyes of every person there on him. "—it's also why I went to jail for twenty years, and why my son was murdered."

The room was still and silent as Casey looked at the different children one by one. It was a heavy moment that he let play out for what seemed an eternity.

"You're looking at a man who lost twenty years of his life and a father who lost his son because of drugs and crime. Nobody wins in crime; everyone loses. And as far as drugs, they'll make you stupid and will make sure that you will never be happy or successful. Now, not doing drugs and crime is not enough to make you a success. If you want to be successful and happy, that will depend on your strength to be able to say no to drugs and crime *and* say yes to always educating your mind."

The teachers and principal started to relax; this was more familiar territory for them, as it was for the kids. Casey knew that, and knew he'd have to take it to another level if they were to get it.

"Now, I want all you kids to close your eyes and imagine this picture in your mind. Imagine that you do drugs or are involved in crime, and picture the look on your mother, father, and grandparents' faces when they find out. They're all shocked and angry at first, but they're also devastated and scared, and feel like they're bad parents, which makes them hate themselves and feel sad. Some of them are crying because they're so hurt and ashamed.

"Now imagine it's been a few years, and you've been doing those same things, and imagine the unhappiness it's caused your family and how it's hurt you. Because you do drugs, you do bad in school and don't graduate and can't get a decent job, or maybe because you do crime or drugs, you get thrown into juvenile hall. That's a prison for kids, and trust me . . . you *don't* want to go there. It's a real live nightmare."

Casey walked the roomful of kids through what their lives would be, painting a bleak and horrible picture that he knew all too well, having seen it happen to endless people he'd known growing up. He ended it by having them visualize a life where they steered clear of crime and drugs and stayed in school and worked hard. The picture he painted was realistic and very upbeat, and the kids reacted to it positively. When he was done, he told them to open their eyes.

"Now, if you take one thing away from this afternoon, it's this: What you just imagined about saying no to drugs and working hard and becoming productive members of society—" Casey made sure he caught the gaze of the three boys he'd singled out earlier. "—*every* one of you can achieve that. It's not too late."

The kids were relieved, and Casey knew his little exercise had had the desired effect. He turned and walked back to stand next to Joe and the other guys. Joe took over and led the kids in an uplifting chant, and then they all filed out of the room, much more subdued than when they'd entered.

As Casey watched them leave, he wondered what had just happened. It was weird—he hadn't planned for things to go that way—they just had. Originally he was just gonna say a few words and that was that, but then he'd remembered the therapist using visualization in the joint, and had decided to wing it and see what would happen.

With a shrug, he watched Joe speaking to the principal; then he turned and walked to Casey and said, "Jesus, Casey, that was really powerful. I've never seen anything like that. Usually when we do these things, we speak, then there's some rah-rah, and we leave and *hope* we made a difference."

"Is that right?" Casey asked.

"Except I *know* you made a difference today, man. You put a lot of those kids on the right path. That shit was amazing. How'd you know that kid was in a gang and the other one did drugs? And that whole visualization thing was, like—man, it was incredible."

"Cool, I'm glad it came off."

"Seriously, though, how did you know those kids were involved in that stuff?"

"The first kid had 'one five three players 4life' written in black ink on the side of his sneaker. Those guys like to use young kids as mules to transport their shit. Taggin' their shoe is the way they're identified. The other kid's front jeans pocket was well worn from the pipe he carried. As far as the last one, I know what someone who's strung out looks like. I didn't put him on blast, because I didn't think he'd handle it well. That boy's in pretty serious trouble—he's got a bad habit, his parents probably do as well."

"That's true, the principal told me they've called Children's Services in the past, but nuthin's been done about it."

Casey, Joe, and the other two guys walked out of the auditorium and into the principal's office. She was effusive with her praise, commending all of them on what they were doing. They all thanked her and were leaving the office when Principal Parker asked if she could have a word with Casey.

"I'll catch a ride back with my guys, Case," Joe said.

The principal offered him a seat as she sat down behind her desk. "Mr. Casey, what I saw today was nothing short of extraordinary. All of these kids are deemed 'at risk,' and as a result, for myself and my teachers to make an impression on them—well, it's challenging at best. We feel fortunate if we can connect with at least one or two kids per class and make a difference in their lives. Today, I watched you connect with all of them at once. . . . You have a powerful gift to inspire, Mr. Casey."

Her words rang true. He knew that when he spoke, people listened. He also knew that his life's path left a trail of death and destruction in its wake. Casey gave her a faint smile. "I appreciate your words, Principal Parker, and I'm glad your students have someone like you to watch over and guide them."

"Thank you. I do hope you continue doing this type of work. It's desperately needed, and you're great at it."

"I appreciate that, ma'am, and anywhere that Urban Victory asks me to speak, I will be there."

The principal smiled and shook Casey's hand as he left her office. He walked down the hallway and out of the building to his car. Before getting in, he turned to face the school, thinking about the kids inside. He wondered if anyone had ever gone to Antonio's school to speak about drugs and crime, and if it would have made a difference.

He also wondered if it was Petrosian's dope that had fucked up that one kid, or maybe it was Mick's.

. . .

Casey turned over the Escalade and headed across town. He checked his phone; it was just before one. *Back to reality.* He had enough time to eat and then go meet Petrosian.

He hustled toward St. James Park and stopped to grab a quick bite at a taco spot where Knightsbridge Road and Briggs Avenue intersected. While polishing off three tacos and some chips and salsa, Casey texted back and forth with everyone, getting updates on how things were goin'. With the help of Jacob, Al P. was taggin' cops left and right. Shin was meeting with the Garcia boys, making sure everything was good, and Champa was working on his heist plan.

Casey wiped his mouth, balled up his napkin, and was about to get up to leave the table when a fine, light-skinned sista in her late thirties approached and said, "I know this *ain't* Crush Casey."

He looked up and squinted at the woman, trying to remember her while the other brothers in the restaurant checked out her frame. She was a real dime piece, but Casey couldn't place her. *Did I nail this broad back in the day?*

"Oh no, you don't remember me? It's Charlene. I used to roll with that *loser* Rono." She rolled her eyes and put her hands on her hips when she said "loser." That was enough to kick his memory into gear: She was one of the many girls Rono used to fuck around with.

"Yeah—yeah, I remember you. You got an older sister named Tina. You were a nurse or something."

"That's right. I'm working at United Trucking now, tryin' to pay the bills to support me and my baby girl. Anyway, look at you lookin' fine out here on these streets. Whatcha been doin', hon?"

Casey peeped the time on his phone—he really needed to bounce and definitely didn't feel like talkin' to one of Rono's old hos. Everyone on the street knew his past history with the man, and after that sucka was taken out, there'd been a lot of chatter about "who did it."

"You know, I'm always in play, looking at a few things."

The girl laughed and said, "Same old Casey, keeping them cards close to his chest. So look, give a sista a call—it'd be nice to hang with a real brotha for a change."

She dug around in her purse and pulled out a pen and a piece of paper. She carefully wrote her number down and handed it to Casey. He took it and put it into his pocket. Her face got serious and she said, "I'ma keep it real, Crush—I always liked you, you were always cool with me. I thought that Rono shit was foul. I don't know your situation, but . . . I'm here, ya know, so reach out if ya feel me."

"Cool, it was nice bumpin' into you, Charlene. Tell your sister I said hello. I got to bounce to a meeting, but I'm sure we'll see each other around."

The woman's face showed that she was a bit deflated, but Casey handled it in a fly way so that she wouldn't be salty. He got up, gave her a squeeze and a kiss on the cheek, and rolled to St. James Park, which was two minutes away.

When he pulled up, he saw Petrosian's Benz and a fresh pair of goons. Casey parked behind him and got out of his whip. As he came over, Petrosian's two security guys gave him a hard look and moved to intercept. Casey hated guys like this, all muscle and no brains. *That's one reason the two previous guys are tits up in some cemetery.*

Petrosian saw him, said something in Armenian, and the guys stood down. Petrosian extended his hands and said, "Hello, Casey, thanks for meeting me on such short notice. Let's go over here."

Alek led Casey to a bench, where the two men sat while his son played basketball. "I have something coming up next week, a very big job, and I want you to be a part of it. I like your style, and given that I'm down a couple men because of that business at the restaurant, I could use a man with your skills."

Casey was more than a bit surprised by the offer, particularly given their last conversation. He stared at the Armenian. "So, you wanna form a partnership?"

"I wouldn't call it that. Let's say I'd like to hire you as an independent contractor."

Casey's criminal curiosity was piqued; it couldn't hurt to find out more about what Petrosian was up to, even though he wasn't interested. "Okay, so what's the job?"

"I'm afraid that I can't give you a lot of details today, but I can tell you that you'll walk away with a hundred K for two days' work."

Casey stared even harder at Petrosian in disbelief. He knew if he was offering him that much chedda, then he was making at least ten times that, maybe twenty. It also seemed strange that he'd need advice on anything unless it fell out of his regular domain of expertise. Or maybe it was all just an elaborate setup. "So, what do you need me to do on this job you can't tell me about?"

"I'd like you to look over the plan, tell me if you think I've left anything out, and then help me execute it." Alek talked to Casey while watching his son play ball.

Casey looked at him and said, "First, I can't commit to any deal until I know what it is. Second, I may need more time to review your plan, especially as it seems like it's a big job and there's a lot at stake. Third, I want to know where you're at with what we previously discussed."

"I won't be able to give you any details until Monday morning. As far as more time to review, this is time sensitive, so if you decided to do it, I'll need you to work within those parameters. Lastly, as far as your proposal, I need more time on that, and I want to know who else is down with this and your proposed details of how it would work."

Now Casey was the one staring at the kids playing ball. "Monday A.M. ain't gonna to work for me."

"Why not? The clock's ticking on this and there's a lot of bread on the table for both of us."

"Not that it's any of your business, but that's when I'm meeting my parole officer."

Petrosian took a beat before replying. "That's must cramp the style of a man like yourself."

"Yeah, well that's the way it is. There are certain consequences in this game. Eventually that silver ball always goes down that black hole, that is, unless you can rig it otherwise."

"And that's what you think you can do?" Petrosian asked.

"It's already started, and paying dividends. Look, I gotta bounce now, I'll hit you up on Monday after my meeting."

"That's going to be difficult."

"Why's that?"

"After that lunch we had, where I almost lost my phone, I've decided to just stick to burners."

"Ain't that gonna 'cramp your style'?"

Petrosian laughed at Casey's joke. "You let me worry about that—I'll figure out how to touch base with you. We can discuss more about the affiliation on Monday, as well as this other gig." Casey shrugged at this and was about to walk when Petrosian continued. "Look, I don't go offering cats I don't know that well to come in on jobs with me, so I hope that would mean something to you, right?"

Casey saw that Petrosian son's game was breaking up, and he didn't really want to be there when his kid came over. "I get what you're sayin'. But the bottom line for me is that I'm gonna need some kind of inclination this week fo sho, but right now I gotta dip."

Petrosian stood up and shook Casey's hand and said, "Agreed."

Casey reflected on his meeting with Petrosian as he drove back to the Urban Victory office. He'd planned to tap the Armenian's phone, but that now looked like it was out of the question. 'Sides, whenever he was around him, the guy always talked in Armenian to his crew, which would have meant getting translation software. That tech was great for reading an article but mediocre at best for long chunks of conversations filled with slang. That coupled with the fact that Petrosian's crew would always be flipping burners meant it would involve way too much manpower.

He wondered what the gig was; if it involved dope, that'd be a nonstarter for him. Ten minutes from the office, it started to rain hard. People quickly ran inside to escape getting wet as the fat drops pelted the ground. The way they reacted reminded him of how the people at the restaurant had scattered for cover when the bullets started flying. If only Petrosian had been killed at the restaurant, then all this shit would be over by now. *Course, if he was gonna be dead, I'd probably be tits up next to him right now.* He knew second-guessing that decision would get him nowhere, so he tossed it aside as he pulled in to the garage.

Shin was anxiously waiting for him up in the office; Casey could tell he had news. "Where's Champa at?" he asked as he waved his boy into the back.

Shin held his tongue until they were in Casey's secure office. "He said he'd be here in ten minutes. Crush, I tagged Fordham this afternoon."

"*Dope!* My man! How'd you swing that?"

"Jacob picked up a conversation from one of the detectives talkin' about meeting with him for lunch, so I staked out the spot and tagged his ass."

"Cool, very cool—"

"That's not all, Crush. . . . They dropped your name."

Casey sat down behind his desk and pondered this. He'd thought he was off their radar, but it looked like that was obviously not the case. "Run it down. Every last detail."

"Fordham met two of his senior detectives for lunch in Chinatown earlier this afternoon. They discussed a few different cases, one being Mick's failed drug bust, another the Petrosian shooting, and the last, Rono's murder. I went ahead and had Jacob edit down the conversation to keep only the parts I knew you'd be interested in. He's waiting on your call right now."

Casey flipped open his computer and reached out for a video chat with Jacob. The hacker's face popped up on the screen. Casey got straight to it.

"Play it."

Jacob typed on his keyboard, and then there was the sound of three men talking over Casey's speakers.

"—So, how exactly did the Micky Benzo bust get fucked up?" Fordham asked.

On the screen was also a transcript denoting who was saying what. The two detectives tried to double-talk him with excuses, but Fordham shut them down immediately.

"—For fuck's sakes, are you two serious with this bullshit! I thought I was working with detectives, not a bunch of fuckin' clowns. This was an easy one, handed to you on a goddamn platter, and you and your team blew it! You bet everything on a junkie, for chrissakes! What'd you think would happen?"

The two detectives were silent while Fordham muttered about the bullshit he had to put up with under his breath and ordered lunch from the waitress.

"Now, what about Crush Casey? What's he up to nowadays? I still can't believe you couldn't pop him on the Rono murder."

"Captain, there were no witnesses and no physical evidence. By the time we got there, it was a done deal, Rono was DOA, and if Casey was ever at the scene, he was long gone. We're still sniffing around, but so far nothing is coming up. If anybody on the streets knows anything, they aren't talkin'. You know Lomax is his PO, right?"

"No, I didn't, and why the fuck am I hearing this for the first time now?" Fordham was clearly agitated by this news.

"We didn't think it was a big deal, Cap—'sides, that beef with him was fifteen years ago."

"Not a big deal? Jesus Christ, this is why I do the thinking round here, and you guys just follow fucking orders—if you can even do that. Do you think *he* forgot about how we framed his ass with twenty-five large in his trunk? Christ, the only reason he still has a career is because Internal Affairs didn't have the balls to cut him loose. Which, incidentally, they would have if you two had listened to me and put a couple keys of coke in his trunk like I told you to. There's always plenty of ways to get that shit back out of the evidence locker once he'd been tossed off the force."

Casey couldn't believe what he was hearing. *Lomax was set up by his partner and two other detectives!* Finally, he had some leverage with his PO. He didn't know how he was gonna use it, but rest assured, he knew he would.

"The last thing I want is to be anywhere near that guy, *or* to have him come nosing around our business," Fordham said. "He's in Parole, let him fuckin' die there."

The other detectives agreed, and in the background Casey could hear the waitress ask if they wanted anything else. When she left, they continued with their business.

"Back to Crush Casey—do you want us to put a guy on him?" one of the detectives asked.

"No, not now, maybe later. We can't spare the manpower, and what's it gonna get us right now anyway? That motherfucker knows how to keep his nose looking clean, at least."

"Okay, what about Petrosian?"

"You two keep a close eye on him yourselves—I don't want the other detectives around him. If we play our cards right, we'll be able to cash in when he moves his next load of heroin."

Casey pressed his fingers together and stared off into space for a moment; then he turned and looked at Jacob, contemplating the fabric of the plan he was gonna unleash on Fordham. *This cat has ruined too many lives to count.* Casey knew he would take him out; he just hadn't figured out all the details yet.

Casey's phone buzzed that Champa had arrived, and Shin let him in. He had Jacob play the audio back so he could be up to date on everything.

"Damn, we got a lot of balls in the air," Champa said.

"Yeah, but only because we got more intel. In the past, we woulda been blissfully unaware of what was up until shit happened. Time was, that woulda meant Mick Benzo'd be staring down a life sentence. Now we know everything that's gonna happen *before* it happens and can react accordingly. It's more work, but it keeps us ahead of the game."

Shinzo and Champa both nodded as Casey kept talking.

"I'm already seeing us expand this even further, into areas where there's a lot less risk and a whole shitload more paper to be made. No more hittin' licks in the street, just sittin' behind a computer, makin' loot."

"So, what's that look like?" Shin asked.

"It looks like Wall Street, brotha. That's where the real paper is, and where the right information at the right time can make you Warren Buffett money. All those corporate cats are criminals in three-piece suits—trust me on that. Part of their game's knowing they gonna get busted eventually, but makin' enough money off their shit that it don't matter. Very rarely do you see a big executive get put behind bars unless the level of fraud is massive."

"Hell, yeah, look at the mortgage meltdown. Hundreds of billions lost, and not *one* CEO indicted for it," Shin said.

Casey nodded. "That's right, now you feelin' me. Or take the drug companies, for instance. They release a new drug and it's on the market for years, it fucks people up and they get busted for that *and* they know that shit is bad but they sellin' it anyway and what happens? They pay a fine of five hundred million! Meanwhile, the drug's already made 'em three billion profit even after R and D costs, and the payoff's covered by their insurance."

"Like that shit that Erin Brockovich broad uncovered," Champa said.

"Exactly. Those are the cats I wanna target. If we play it right, we'll be caked out and the only thing that'll get us crossed up is if we get greedy and take unnecessary risks."

"Yeah, but how we gonna get close to cats like that?" Shin asked.

"That's the easy part. Regardless of how loaded these guys are, they can never resist a fine bitch. That's the army we need to start recruiting for."

"That'll be my job," Champa said, cracking him and everyone else up.

"Speakin' of jobs, don't we got a car heist to plan?" Casey said as he took his feet off his desk.

Champa stood up and said, "Indeed, my brotha. You got time tomorrow for me to walk you through it step by step? It'll mean takin' a little road trip."

"Hell yeah, how long's it gonna take?"

"Four or five hours tops."

"Okay, let's all meet here at ten A.M. sharp."

With that, the guys all went their separate ways. On his way home, Casey thought about how impressed he was at the way things were lining up. He'd assembled a crew that was head and shoulders above everyone out there.

He still felt cautious, though, because there were a lot more moving pieces on a much larger board than he was used to. He was also putting a lot of trust in Al P. and Jacob. Those guys hadn't been battle-tested, so the first sign of heat would be a true indication of just how down they really were. It was a gamble, but one that he felt he had to take. And then there was the unknown, the chaos that invariably got tossed into life when things seemed to be rolling along perfectly. Casey was patiently waiting for that other shoe to drop.

15

The next morning, Casey reached out to the guys at the last minute and switched the meeting place from the office to Kimchi's Korean Deli. He'd had enough of routine in the joint and didn't want to stay in old habits on the outside. Plus, it would confuse anyone who still might be keepin' tabs on him and his crew.

The guys all rolled up about the same time and walked into the deli and went straight to the back room.

"Okay, Champa, run it down," Casey said.

Champa took off his jacket, tossed it aside, and pulled a map out of the back pocket of his jeans and unfolded it. Written in red at various places were the numbers *1, 2, 3,* and *4*.

"Here's how we gonna do it. Number one's the pier, number two's where we hijack the trucks, number three's where we drive the trucks to and stash the cars, and number four's where we dump the trucks. I got my boy at Port Authority who is gonna tell me twelve hours before the cars arrive; right now they are scheduled for next Thursday, but he's gonna confirm that. The stash spot is a warehouse in Brooklyn and will take about five to ten minutes to get there. Once we hijack the trucks, we'll need to hook the trailers up to our trucks. It's too risky to roll with their trucks, 'cause they got tracking devices that enable the company to pinpoint exactly where we are. The transports will all take different routes. Although the original destination for these cars was the Hamptons, we should assume that they'll be missed soon after we jack them. Once we unload the cars, we'll need to dump the trailers."

Casey sat and listened until Champa was done running the plan down and started to run down questions.

"So, if I understand this right, the plan is to jack these trucks around seven A.M. as they pass through Brooklyn on the Belt Parkway, pull 'em over, switch trailers, and then drive them through Brooklyn, unload 'em, and stash the trucks at a different location."

When Champa heard the plan back, Casey could tell by his expression that he realized it still needed some work. Casey knew he'd been working hard on it and didn't want to burst his bubble by poking holes, but the fact was, it needed a lot of work if it was gonna work at all.

"Okay, we gonna build on your plan to make sure we don't take any unnecessary chances. For example, when we jump these trucks, the drivers may have time to radio for help. If they do, we are fucked. Also, the time it will take to park and switch trailers on two trucks is gonna take longer than we have. So what I propose is you find out which trucking company is being used; then we need to find someone on the inside or hack into their computers to see what trucks are assigned to do the pickup. Once we do that, we'll need to rig a device that will knock out their communication and tracking systems. The other issue we have is the drivers' cell phones. We gonna need to figure how to knock those out as well."

Champa listened to everything Casey said, agreed with it, and said he'd talk to Al P. about the communication problems. Afterwards, they got into Shin's G-Wagen and hit the streets to check out the different locations. The last one was the warehouse in Brooklyn. It was on Alabama Avenue, an industrial street that didn't seem to have a lot of traffic. The buildings around it were also warehouses. It was perfect, at least from the outside. Inside was five thousand square feet of nothing and glazed windows so prying eyes couldn't see inside. Champa said the owner was willing to do a cash deal, no questions asked. Satisfied, the guys jumped back in Shin's whip and headed back to Kimchi's to pick up their cars.

On the ride home, a troubling thought crossed Casey's mind: What if Hans's Asian connection decided he didn't want the cars or didn't come up with the right scratch, then what? Casey would be stuck with twelve mostly one-of-a-kind high-end sports cars. Getting rid of 'em would be a bitch 'cause they were hot, expensive, and problematic to transport. The only thing Casey could think of was to make Hans's connection pay a 50 percent deposit now and demand the rest when they handed over the cars.

Casey broke it down to Champa and Shin, both of whom agreed with his logic. He then called Hans to set up the arrangement. Hans picked up on the first ring, as if he'd been waiting for Casey's call.

"Hallo, Casey, how are you, man?"

"I'm good, Hans. I'm callin' to see if you and your lady would like to have dinner tonight or this weekend with Carla and myself."

"Absolutely, let me talk to Sabrina, she is right here." Casey heard muffled voices; then Hans jumped back on the phone. "Okay, I guess we have a school thing tonight, but Saturday is good, what time and where?"

"Let's say Casa de Honduras at eight P.M.?"

"That is perfect—Sabrina and I love that place and I haven't seen the Garcias in a while."

Casey hung up the phone and dialed Carla as well as the Garcia brothers, to let them know the plan. At some point during the evening, Casey would find a private moment and broach the subject with Hans. Getting five million in a few days was gonna be a task, so a lot was riding on Hans and the strength of his connection.

The guys pulled up to Kimchi's and got out of Shin's G-Wagen. Casey recapped what he needed from Champa, and he agreed to have the intel to him by Monday at the latest. Casey knew he would be hustlin' all weekend to make that happen.

The next evening, Carla met Casey at his place in a short white miniskirt and a sexy, off-the-shoulder top, ready to go to dinner. *Flawless as always.*

On their way to the restaurant, Casey told Carla he'd need her to distract Hans's wife and go to the ladies' room so Hans and he could have a private conversation. She knew not to ask questions and just smiled and said, "Okay, baby."

They pulled up to the restaurant, which was packed, and squeezed through the crowd to the front, where Big E was directing traffic.

"*Fam!* What's up, baby?"

"What up, E? You got a table, we got Hans and his wife meeting us."

E leaned in close to Casey and asked if he wanted to use the private room in the back or was the main room cool. Casey told him the private room would definitely be preferred. Hans and his wife showed up right after, and E led them all back through the bustle of the crowded restaurant.

The private room was off to one side of the kitchen, and was strictly for VIPs, which was whoever Mama Garcia felt was deserving. It was small, about ten by ten, and had a single, round table in the middle. On the walls were pictures of the Garcia family through the years, lit by an ornate chandelier.

Before sitting down, Carla took a look at the photos and started laughing. "Baby, is this you?" Carla pointed to a picture of Big E and Mama Garcia, both looking much thinner, Hen Gee in a Kango, an older man, and Casey with a mustache.

Casey inspected the picture with everyone else and laughed. "That's old school, fo sho. We took that picture at Mr. and Mrs.

Garcia's twenty-fifth wedding anniversary party. That's Mr. Garcia—rest in peace—standing next to me."

After everyone had their look at the photo, they all sat down. A waiter walked in with an ice bucket and opened a bottle of Perrier-Jouët Champagne, 1999 vintage. Hans held up the glass and looked at Casey and Carla. "If I may, a toast: To Crush Casey, a man who knows too many of my secrets to be anything but my friend!"

The whole table laughed because it was both funny and true. The rest of the evening was spent telling old stories and having the ladies getting acquainted. Hans's wife was sophisticated, educated, and obviously very dedicated and in love with her husband.

After the main course, Casey gave Carla's leg a squeeze and she asked Sabrina if she wanted to join her in the ladies' room. The girls got up, and once they were gone, Casey got down to business with Hans.

"I need to talk to you about this job—we're fine-tunin' everything and it's all lookin' good, there's just one last thing that needs handlin'," Casey said.

"A deposit?"

"Exactly, can you get five mil from your guy before we pull this heist? The last thing I want is to have a buyer that knows I'm in a spot and then tries to get clever."

"I spoke to him a couple days ago and told him that this situation may arise. I vouched for you, and he said he would send the money via courier to me."

"And—?

"And nothing has shown up and he is not returning my calls."

"Okay, so you think he's gonna go left, I need to know by— Hold up."

Casey heard the girls coming back; he also saw Big E and waved him in. "Hey, brotha, do me a favor and keep the ladies occupied in the kitchen for a few minutes?"

"No sweat." E walked out and told the ladies that he had desserts he needed them to puruse. The women happily followed in his huge wake.

Hans leaned in and replied in a low voice, "There could be a lot of reasons—last time I spoke, he said he had some problems with the government over there, but it did not sound serious. The bottom line is that I know he really wants those cars."

"Are you sayin' I should roll the dice?"

"I cannot tell you that for sure—I know this guy and think he is straight up, but as we both know, shit happens." Hans pulled out his BlackBerry. "Tell you what, let me text him right now and tell him I need to know when the money will be here and if it is not here by—what?—Tuesday P.M., then it is a no-go?"

"That's too late for me, Hans. I need to call in the crew and set this job up so that it goes smooth. Also, if I call off the job at the last minute, I'ma look like an amateur."

"Yes, I see what you mean. So then, what is the deadline, Monday P.M.?"

"Well, if it's Monday night, it might as well be Tuesday nine A.M., but no later than that."

Hans started to text as the girls came in with Hen and Big E. "I hope y'all still got your appetites, as these ladies are 'bout to load you up," Hen said.

"Bring it, man, I'm ready. So where's Mom at?" asked Casey.

"Her arthritis was kickin' up, so she went home a couple hours ago. She'll be fine, she just needs to take the meds, thas all."

A waiter walked in with a huge tray of desserts, and Casey, Hans, and the ladies dived in. Hans covertly slid his phone over for Casey to approve the message; Casey read it and nodded.

On the ride home, Carla was curled up on her seat, a big smile on her face as she watched Casey navigate the late-evening traffic.

"What you smiling 'bout, baby?" he asked.

"I was thinking about my conversation I had with Sabrina when we were in the ladies' room."

"She seems real cool, and a good fit for Hans."

"Yeah, she's whip-smart. In the bathroom, she told me that she knew the first moment they met that he was the guy for her. She thought that her dad might trip, so she let it be known that he was gonna be her future husband, no matter what."

"Wow, that's big. You know her pops is crazy rich, right?"

"She didn't speak on that directly, but I could tell. I've seen enough sophisticated ladies at the hotel to know she came from money." Carla paused and said, "She also said she could tell that you and I were a perfect fit." Carla giggled when she said that.

Casey smiled and gazed back at her. "Like I said, a smart lady."

Casey didn't hear from Hans on Sunday, which was a bad sign. On Monday morning, he reached out to get a status report, kicking it around his crib until it was time to leave for his meeting with Lomax, which he wasn't looking forward to. He knew the PO was gonna give him shit 'cause Petrosian was still breathing. Someone like Lomax was clueless as to how the streets worked. He thought that just because he dealt with cons all day that he had an understanding of how they operated. But unless you're in it, you don't know shit. It reminded Casey of sports broadcasters that spoke with such authority about a game they'd never played.

Eleven thirty A.M. rolled around, and there was still no word from Hans. Annoyed, he went downstairs to catch a cab to the parole office.

On the street, Casey eyed a late-model sedan idling at the curb and guessed it was a gypsy cab. He put his two fingers in his mouth and whistled to get the driver's attention. He hated taking the regular cabs because their backseats felt like a cell—also, he didn't care for the constantly blaring TVs they all seemed to have nowadays. The car pulled up and Casey got in the back and was instantly hit by the overpowering smell of air freshener.

He gave the driver the address and sat back for what he knew would be a twenty-minute drive. Casey could tell the guy was Haitian from the flag hanging off his rearview mirror. In his mid-fifties, he also had a slight accent and was missing a few teeth from his grille. As they drove, Casey noticed the driver kept looking at him in the rearview.

"What is it, dude, why you eyeballin' me?"

The cabbie gave him a semi toothless grin and replied, "Because I'm rememberin' Crush Casey from back in de day when I worked at Casa de Honduras."

Casey looked harder at the dude for a second, but still couldn't place the face. "You worked for the Garcia family doin' what?"

"I was a waiter dere for a few years, till Mama Garcia fired me because she said I was eatin' too much."

Casey laughed at this, knowing the guy was for real. Mama Garcia was temperamental at best with her employees. On more than one occasion, Hen had run after an employee to get 'em to come back because she'd fired 'em on a whim. "I was actually there Saturday night. So what's your name and how long you been driving?"

"Webster, I've been driving for about eight years."

"Wow, that's a minute—I'm impressed you still breathing. I know a lotta you guys run into serious drama in this game."

"Mon, you ain't kiddin'! Get this—I got robbed at the end of my shift two weeks ago by some bitch who was pregnant! She pulled out a piece and held it to the back of my neck and told my ass to 'pay or get sprayed'!"

"Damn, how much she take you for?"

"Eighty bucks, *and* she stole the car!"

"That's not a lot of scratch. How much you make a day on average?"

"Shit, on a good day, *maybe* a hundred bucks—on a bad day, twenty-five. I work twelve hours a day, six days a week. It's fucked up, but I don' have a lotta options."

"So how many times you been robbed?"

"Since I started doing this, five times. I thought about installing a bulletproof partition, but I can't afford the three hundred fifty dollars. The time before that pregnant bitch was different, though. This dude pulled a knife on me and I slammed on the brakes, he fell off balance and I jump out the car and radioed in an emergency. The sonofabitch gets out to run and I grab a brick and hit him in da head. He falls to the ground and then we start to tussle. Two minutes later, seven other drivers show up with bats and block off the street so the cops can't get in. Maaaahn, dat shit was crazy."

"That's no joke, did he survive?"

"Yah, he was fucked up fo sho, but he lived. The cops busted his ass for assault and for the weed he was carrying. We all got took in, but got off 'cause they couldn't build a case with no witness willing to come forward."

The Lincoln Town Car pulled up to Casey's destination and he got out. The driver said the fare was twenty-two bones and Casey laced him with a hundred-dollar bill. The Haitian cheered up at that and thanked him profusely. Casey took his card and said he'd call him when he needed another ride. He knew if he ever did call, the dude would be there quick fast and no questions would be asked.

Casey walked into the main lobby of the Bronx County Hall of Justice, went through the metal detector, then took the elevator to the fourth floor. The ten-story building housed a bunch of Criminal Court rooms, the Department of Corrections and Probation, the District Attorney, and Lomax.

Casey walked into the lobby of the probation office and sat and waited with all the other cons. An hour later, he was called to see Lomax. When he finally saw him, the PO was sitting on his bloated ass behind his desk, unwrapping his regular corned beef sandwich.

Lomax was always eating something. He ran through the standard interview, then told Casey to close the door.

"So, how you enjoying your life of leisure, Mr. Casey?"

Casey knew that was a question that was not meant to be answered, and just sat there with no emotion on his face.

"One of your fellow criminals, Alek Petrosian, got into a bit of a dustup at a local café last week. A restaurant and his Rolls got shot up, along with quite a few innocent bystanders, but he claimed he wasn't at the scene. Now, what do you think about that?" Lomax tossed an eight-by-ten of the crime scene in front of Casey.

"I would say he's lucky that the *impatient* person who ordered the hit enlisted incompetent people."

Lomax glared at Casey as he swallowed a bite of his sandwich. "Well, if his 'luck' doesn't run out ASAP, some other people are gonna regret it."

Lomax pulled out two more eight-by-tens; this time it was a photo of two white guys. "He's suspected of killing these two cops, as well as these characters late last night."

Casey looked at the second photo and recognized the shot-up bodies of Ernesto and Rodrigo from Big Rich's crew. *Shit!* Casey's mind raced. He was pretty certain Rich didn't know about this yet; otherwise, he would have gotten a call. He also wasn't sure any of these murders could even be pinned on Petrosian. Rodrigo and Ernesto were always steppin' on someone's toes, and as far as the dead cops—well, who gave a shit? Casey's hunch was this was Lomax's way of trying to stir the pot and manipulate the situation.

"So he's suspected of all this, but you don't know for sure. Sounds like a lot of guessin' goin' on. Who knows, maybe this cat's only local for a minute and is gonna be on the move soon."

Lomax's flushed face grew even redder as he stuffed it with the sandwich. Beads of sweat appeared on his brow. "He's responsible for fifty percent of the heroin coming into this city—he's not plannin' on leaving town! He needs to be stopped, and if he's not, there will be repercussions, I guarantee you that—"

In the middle of his tirade, he really started sweating profusely, then clutched his chest and gasped for breath. Casey stood and watched the man struggle, at first thinking that he was choking, but then realizing he was probably having a heart attack.

He opened the office door and called for help, and the tiny room quickly filled with officers. One of the officers shouted for someone to call 911, while Lomax flopped around like a fish out of water. Another slammed Casey against the wall and cuffed him and started screaming at him for an explanation. Casey kept cool and denied doing anything wrong, but it didn't seem to be convincing the cops. One of them told Lomax that help was on the way and asked him if he had been attacked. Through his gasps, Lomax said no. Casey breathed a sigh of relief at that, but they still kept him gaffled up in metal bracelets.

The paramedics rushed in and started tending to him. Lomax's face was as pale as a sheet, his lips were dry, and he was still gasping for air. One of the paramedics, a short white woman with a tremendously big ass, screamed that Lomax was choking. She grabbed his seat cushion, tucked it under his head, and flipped him on his left side. A clear fluid ran out of his mouth. She turned to one of the officers and asked if he had epilepsy. The cop raised his hands as if to say he didn't know as she flipped Lomax on his back. With the help of her partner, she put him on a gurney and quickly wheeled him out. As they did, Casey could hear the cons celebrating and clapping in the lobby when he passed by.

The remaining officer drilled Casey with a bunch of questions, but he just dummied up; he had nothing to say to them. One minute Lomax was interviewing him; the next minute he started convulsing. Reluctant but satisfied, the officer took off the cuffs, telling another one it was more likely Lomax was a victim of that shit he ate every day from that greasy spoon deli. He turned back to Casey and told him to beat it, which he gladly did.

Casey went through the waiting rooms and didn't wait for an

elevator, just jogged the four flights of stairs down to the lobby. He hit the street and turned left, but immediately heard a quick horn blast and looked up.

"You need a ride?" Petrosian was sitting in the back of his Benz with a smile on his face as one of his goons opened the door.

Casey looked at him sideways, wondering what the fuck this guy's game was. "What the fuck you doing here? Did you follow me?"

Petrosian held up both hands. "Hey, man, this ain't no drama. I'm just here to make your day. You told me yourself you'd be here, remember? I figured you were always game to talk business. If I'm wrong, I'll bounce."

Casey didn't like what he was seeing. First, all the Lomax drama, and now this muthafucka pops up, all smiles outta the blue. Petrosian must have known he wasn't packin' if he'd just walked out of the Bronx Parole Board office. It smelled like he was gonna be another casualty like his PO.

"I want to talk to you about that job, but not on the street in front of Cop Central." Casey wanted to wring his neck, but stayed cool. He'd rolled the dice, kickin' it solo with Petrosian in the past, but those days were over. "So get out of the car and walk with me."

Surprisingly, Petrosian did just that. They walked a block in silence to make sure they were clear, the Armenian's car shadowing them the whole way.

As they kept walking, Petrosian looked around and said in a hushed voice, "All right, here it is. I got a line on *literally* a boatload of exotic sports cars—an Italian billionaire's private collection—coming into the NY docks this week."

Casey stopped and stared at Petrosian, not believing what he'd just heard. After a beat, he kept walking and said, "Well, that is interesting."

Now it was Petrosian's turn to look at him funny. "How so?"

"Because I just happen to be stealin' those cars myself later this week."

"Bullshit!"

"No bull, my man. A dozen high-end sports cars belonging to Salvatore Mariano, coming in this week on Pier Seventy-eight. I've already got it all set up with my guys."

Both Casey and Petrosian stepped into an alley that was out of earshot of the passing foot traffic. Petrosian was deep in thought and not returning Casey's gaze. Casey broke the silence: "I'm not in the headspace to talk about this now, but it's obvious that we need to get into it."

"Yeah, of course. Let's meet tonight at Marat's, it's an—"

"Armenian restaurant in Queens, yeah, I know."

Petrosian's eyebrows shot up, and then he started laughing and broke the tension. "Okay, okay, let's say seven P.M. I don't want this to be a 'thing' between us."

"I agree, but you know I got an agenda."

"Yeah, well, let's see how this plays out."

Casey nodded and the men bumped fists. Petrosian stepped into his ride, but before it pulled away, he rolled down the window and said, "By the way, tough break about your parole officer. But I'm sure it will be nice not to have that headache anymore. See you tonight." He smiled at Casey as the car sped off.

What the fuck! This muthafucka is too goddamn slick. How the fuck did he get at Lomax, and how did he know he was my PO! Shit, what else does he know? Casey watched Petrosian's car disappear into traffic and went over his interview with Lomax. *He musta put something in that sandwich, but how would he know his habits so well to know where he ate and then put someone in place to poison his food?* It was the only plausible answer, but it would have meant some incredibly fast work on Petrosian's part, not to mention some pretty serious connects in the police department. It just didn't add up.

Casey didn't know how to feel about Petrosian's handiwork: Had the Armenian just done him a favor, or had he complicated things even more? Having Lomax dead was a double-edged sword, because the new PO would most certainly keep him on a shorter leash, doing spot checks and always being on his ass. On the other hand, he wouldn't have an agenda, so Casey would be off the hook when it came to Petrosian. Not that it mattered, 'cause the way things were looking, Casey guessed there was a showdown coming between Alek and him in the not-so-distant future. *What a fucking mess!*

Casey reached into his pocket for his cell. *Shit, still no message from Hans!* He speed-dialed Champa: "Meet me at the office—the shit just got complicated."

On the way to the office, Casey got a voice mail from his new PO. *Damn—so much for having room to breathe.*

"This is Officer Gleeson from the Department of Probation. I'm going to be taking over your case while Officer Lomax is in the hospital. Please report to the probation office next week on Wednesday at nine A.M. I'm also going to need you to call in and let me know that you got this message."

Casey listened to the message twice to make sure he got all the details. He was surprised that Lomax was still breathin'. *I guess that old bastard is harder to kill than Petrosian imagined.*

He called Officer Gleeson back, hoping he'd get voice mail, but didn't. Gleeson answered the phone sounding like he'd just woken up.

"This is Marcus Casey, I'm returning your call."

Casey was told to sit tight and put on hold for ten minutes.

"Okay, Mr. Casey, I got your file in front of me." Gleeson asked him to recount what had happened in Lomax's office, and Casey told him the truth about what went down. The PO seemed satisfied but suspicious. Typical cop shit.

"It says here that you work at Urban Victory, looks like there are no infractions on your sheet, and that he'd recommended you for early mail-in status for the first of next month, assuming there were no issues. So, if you keep your act on the straight and narrow,

I'll follow his lead, but if you screw up, I'll assume the worst. Are we clear?"

Casey hadn't expected such a positive report, especially based on the attitude Lomax always gave him. "Yeah, absolutely. So, is Officer Lomax gonna recover okay? Do they know what happened?"

"I'm not at liberty to discuss that. Good day, Mr. Casey."

Casey hung up the phone and immediately dialed Jacob. He told him to find out what hospital Lomax was in and what was wrong with him. He hoped Lomax had had the good sense to take that Saint Jude's medal home with him, or at least take it out of the evidence jacket. The last thing he needed was to have more loose ends in his life. If anyone found that and connected the dots, he'd be on his way back to Attica, and *that* was not an option.

16

Casey whipped into his garage and almost hit an old lady walking to the elevator. He held up his hands and gave her an apologetic look. The grandma shot a nasty face at him like he was a maniac, her expression quickly changing to fear when she saw Casey turn cold in response. He realized he needed to chill the fuck out. Shit was coming to a head and getting complicated. Paying close attention to all the details was his strength. Even so, today's events added another layer of difficulty that would have to be dealt with very carefully.

In the elevator, he got a call from Rich saying he had a big issue to discuss; from the edge in the man's voice, Casey could tell he needed a one-on-one. He told Rich to meet him at the office as soon as he could get there. Champa was in the lobby waiting for him, talking a mile a minute to somebody he had beef with, probably some broad.

Once they were in the secure office, Casey dropped his bomb on him: "Petrosian's hip to the cars coming in. He asked me to help him boost 'em."

Champa sprang to his feet and said, *"What? Are you kidding me? Oh, hell no! What the fuck, Crush?"*

Casey jumped up from his chair, pointed at Champa, and screamed, *"Calm the fuck down, Champa, I don't need you trippin'! I just went through a tornado of shit today! Fuck!"*

Champa cocked his head in disbelief and stood silent, then threw his hands in the air and stared at Casey. Casey was not the type to lose his cool. He collected himself, put both hands on his desk, and leaned forward. "Look . . . my PO had a heart attack right in front of me today. I was an inch away from being thrown back in the joint because they assumed I had something to do with it. Okay? Then I walk out of the building and fuckin' Petrosian's waiting for me, grinnin' like a muthafucka, askin' if I want a ride. Then he tells me about a 'car heist'—our heist!"

"And what'd you say?"

"I told him I was already doin' that job, and I wasn't gonna say anything more about it on the fuckin' street. Then the nigga lets me know *he* took out my PO."

"We shoulda taken Petrosian out, and 'cause we didn't, this is the consequence."

Casey glared at him. "Give me a fuckin' break, Champa. That woulda set into motion another series of events with even worse results. You can't just start laying niggas out whenever there's an issue. If that was the case, we'd be knee-deep in bodies."

Arms folded, Champa sat on the leather sofa and didn't say shit. Casey looked at him and dropped another nugget on him. "Oh, and it gets better. When I was in Lomax's office, he showed me a photo of two of Petrosian's alleged victims—Ernesto and Rodrigo."

Champa's face screwed up but he kept his cool. "Okay, well, that's a whole other issue that I'm sure'll be dealt with. But right now, my concern is what's gonna be done about this heist. There is a lot of paper riding on this job. Gigs like this don't come along every day."

"I told Petrosian I'd meet with him tonight to discuss it. I want you to roll with me, but you cannot make shit worse, Champa. You gotta be chill."

"Okay, I ain't gonna sweat the dude, but you're still not telling me how this is gonna work."

"Well, we only really have one option: cut him in for a piece."

"Oh, I knew that was comin'," Champa said, annoyed.

"Given his position and the time constraints and everything else we gotta do on this job, it's what needs to be done."

"And what if he ain't down with the piece he gets?"

"Then this gonna be an even bigger mess than it already is."

Both men sat without speaking, contemplating the situation. Casey had been up against some heavy and complicated shit in his life, including his twenty years in prison, but this took the cake. Something told him it was gonna get even more complicated, and the worst part was that he figured he was right.

Casey's phone buzzed as two text messages hit his phone. One was from Hans that said, *We're good.* The other was from Rich saying he was in the lobby. Casey told Champa to take Big Rich to the conference room, and not to let on that he knew about Ernesto and Rodrigo. There was no way and no time to explain his complicated relationship with Lomax.

Casey was about to call Hans when Shin called in and told him that he was at Jacob's. He said Jacob had picked up a lot of chatter from the detectives that Ernesto and Rodrigo had been killed.

"Case, they were also talking about you, Petrosian, and Big Rich. They think there's some kinda connection, and said they're gonna have units on all you guys."

"Fuck—do you know when they gonna start that shit?"

"Fordham said he wanted to have people in place first thing in the A.M."

"Okay, that's good intel. I got Rich here now, I'ma talk to him and see what he says and double back with you in a minute. In the meantime, monitor this shit close."

Casey knew if he was being watched, it meant he'd have to be careful with whom he was seen with. He also couldn't break curfew, or they would bust his ass for sure. That, coupled with a new

PO, meant the noose was drawing tighter around his neck. Everything seemed to be coming to a head; from here on out, there would be no room for fuckups.

Casey dialed Hans and got confirmation that the five million had arrived and was legit. *Finally, some good news.* The last thing he needed was for the money to be short or counterfeit. Hans assured him the loot was government grade A, and that he was anxious to get it out of his hands and into Casey's. That much cash would fill a large duffel bag and weigh about a hundred pounds. Casey's safe wasn't big enough to hold it, and it wasn't like he could deposit it in a bank. He knew the only option was to just keep it in his office cabinet. His office was damn near a safe anyway. He was pissed that he hadn't thought of this problem beforehand, and wasn't better prepared. Casey shook it off and went down the hall to see Big Rich.

When Casey walked into the room, Rich got up and gave him a dap. He had a serious look on his face, which didn't surprise Casey. Case figured it was best to let Rich speak his mind and then clue him in on what he knew.

"So I got a call this A.M. that Ernesto and Rodrigo were found shot up between two houses on Elsmere Place in Tremont. I don't know who or why but I'ma find out what the fuck went on out there."

"Were they doing a job for you and just fucked up?"

"Nah . . ."

"So what do you think happened, did they go rogue again?"

"Earlier that night they were drinking at a Puerto Rican spot a block away from where they were found. I had it checked out, and my guy said the bartender heard them bragging about how they were down with Crush Casey and were gonna be doing big things."

"What!"

"Yeah, now, that's why I'm here."

Casey rubbed his face and felt the stubble from his beard. He looked at Rich, then Champa. Having his name floatin' around the street like that was not cool. Rich had come to see him 'cause he knew it was something Casey'd be concerned about.

"What'd they know, Rich?"

"Nothin'. They didn't hear fuck-all from me about what we talked about. After that meeting, I scared the shit out of 'em and told 'em if they fucked up again, they'd be dead. I told 'em if it wasn't for you, they'd be in the joint right now getting fucked in the ass."

"Okay, I appreciate the heads-up. My guess is that they stepped on the wrong toes or were just running their mouths and somebody cashed their check. If anything else comes up on this, lemme know. Unfortunately, I know for a fact we gonna be under surveillance as a result of those two."

"Damn, Crush, this shit only happened—how you get that intel so quick?"

"We got some high-tech shit in play that's giving us a big advantage, I don't wanna say more than that right now, but Jacob's been a big help."

"Okay, cool, sorry about this shit with them knuckleheads. I'm glad things're working out with Jacob, he's a smart young brotha."

"It's all good, don't sweat it."

Big Rich headed out and Champa and Casey stayed behind in the conference room. Champa shut the door and looked at Casey, a concerned expression on his face. "I'm thinking those guys had been shooting off their mouths for a few days, and word got around to Petrosian—"

Already on the same page, Casey finished his thought. "—And then he found them and questioned them to see what info he could get. He didn't learn shit and couldn't let 'em keep breathin'."

"Why do I think this is gonna bring a lotta heat down?" Champa asked.

"'Cause it already has. Lomax said Petrosian was a suspect, that means the cops know something we don't."

"You think those guys went renegade and were slanging shit for Petrosian and he got hip to them being connected to you?"

"That's a possibility. Petrosian also has his ear close to the street, he always seems to know what's goin' on. Regardless, what I told Rich was the truth. Before I walked in here, Shin told me the detectives got Petrosian, me, and Rich on surveillance, starting in the A.M."

"So, is the meet with Petrosian still a go for tonight?"

"I don't have a choice—once they're on us, it's gonna be a bitch to try and shake 'em. I also can't tell Petrosian what I know, 'cause he'll wanna know where I get my info from." Casey looked at his watch: four fifteen. He had to get to Hans's, get the loot, get back to the office, and meet Petrosian at seven in Queens, and all this during traffic. Casey grabbed his keys and headed for the door.

"Come on, Champa, I want you to follow me to Hans's, we got a pickup we need to make."

"What's up?"

"Hans got the five mil in, I want you to shadow me there and back in case there's any drama."

During the drive, Casey called Shin and told him to meet him at Hans's and to stay close and to call Joe Pica and to make sure everyone was out of the office for the rest of the afternoon. He called Hans and told him he would back up into the garage and for him to toss the money in the backseat. The last thing Casey wanted to be was stationary while holding five million in cash.

After all the arrangements were made, Casey got Jacob on the line on one of his burner phones. "What's up, Jacob, any more news?"

"Nothing you don't already know, just a lotta confirmation on who's gonna be tailing you guys."

"That still on for the A.M.?"

"Yeah. Now, you know you'll be able to see where they're at 'cause you have that tracking device on your phone, right?"

"Yeah. Make sure you listen in on what they say while they're on me. What'd you find out about Lomax?"

Casey could hear the quick clicks of the keyboard rattling out a staccato rhythm. "Okay, Lomax is out of ICU at Bronx-Lebanon, he's in a regular room—let's see, 415, to be exact. His medical report said that they think he ingested some kind of pesticide. They put him on a ton of liquids to flush out his system. Damn, he weighs two eighty—that's a big guy."

"So, he ain't gonna die?"

"Nah, looks like he'll be fine. It says he may have some pulmonary damage, but they won't know for a month or so. He'll be at the hospital for at least another week."

"Okay, if anything changes, let me know."

Casey hung up the phone and turned the wheel quickly to dodge a nasty pothole. He was about twenty minutes from Hans's spot as the sun started dropping, and kept checking his rearview to make sure Champa was the only person following him. He got a call from Carla and thought about letting it go to voice mail, but if she didn't hear from him, she'd just keep calling, so he answered.

"Hey, baby, what's up?" Casey asked.

"Hi, I wanted to know what your plans were for tonight?"

"I'm running some errands, then I have a meeting, how about I call you when I get home?"

"Okay, is everything cool?"

"Yeah, baby, just dodgin' these potholes, these streets are a mess."

Carla seemed to buy it, and they ended their conversation. He didn't know how he was gonna keep her at arm's length for the next seventy-two hours. He didn't want her exposed to any potential drama—he had enough to worry about and didn't need to add her safety to the list.

Two minutes later, Casey was a few blocks from Hans's and dialed him. "Hey, man, I'm down the street. Stay on the phone, I'll let you know when I'm seconds from you."

"Okay, you got it."

"Also, if you got security cameras, turn 'em off now."

"Already done, my man."

"Cool, I'm turning down your street and backing in now."

Casey hung up the phone and backed in while Champa pulled his Aston Martin forward and blocked the small, two-way street so no traffic could get through. Stationed near the entrance of the garage was Shin's G-Wagen. Casey braked and unlocked the doors; Hans jogged out with a large duffel bag that looked heavy. He swung open the back door and tossed the bag on the backseat of the Escalade. Casey slowly pulled out of the garage and followed Shin back to the office with Champa right behind him. Casey checked the clock on the dash, 5:22 P.M. He was making good time, but it would still take forty-five minutes to an hour to get to the office. He could see Champa behind him as the cars crept through traffic; things sped up when they hit the West Side Highway. As soon as they pulled up to the office, Shin got out and took the elevator up to make sure everything was clear. Champa and Casey kept the cars running and stayed inside till Shin gave the signal. Once Champa got the okay from Shin, he got out and hit the elevator button, which opened immediately. Champa pulled his piece and held it out of view, and Casey got out of his Escalade and bailed in with the loot. On the ride up, both guys had their pieces out, ready for shit to go down. The doors opened and the guys got out. Shin had his Glock out and was holding the door. Casey walked by him through the door and went straight back to his office. Shin stayed by the elevator, and Champa stayed by Casey's office door to keep a lookout.

Casey put the black bag on the leather couch and unzipped it. He glanced at the screens and saw the guys all keeping watch. Inside were a lot of stacks with purple bands. Casey grabbed four of them and went to his desk. He selected four bills, one from each stack, and checked to make sure each was legit. They were. Casey zipped up the duffel and tossed it in the cabinet behind his desk. On the elevator ride down, he checked his watch, 6:35 P.M. Downstairs, he laid out the plan to the guys.

"Champa, you're gonna roll with me. Shin, I want you to grab a table, and if shit goes south, then start bustin'. I'ma take one of Al's phones and have Jacob patch it in the audio to you so you can listen in on everything."

"Do I need to call more guys?" Shin asked.

"Nah, if we do that, it will bring too much attention and tension. Petrosian ain't gonna try shit: he knows there'd be a full-scale war if he did, and he ain't prepared for that."

And with that, the guys got in their cars and headed for Marat's. They got there a little after seven, as did Petrosian. Casey was already at the secluded corner table, with his back against the wall, when Petrosian rolled up with one of his guys. Casey immediately recognized Petrosian's partner. It was the same guy with the scar that he'd seen at the parole office. Casey was too caught up in the moment to do the math, but he knew it would come to him.

Casey could tell that Petrosian was annoyed by the presence of Champa, and waited for him to speak on it. All the men sat down as a plump waitress wearing an outfit two sizes too small came over to take their order. Petrosian cut her off in midsentence and told her something in Armenian that made her disappear so fast, it was like she'd never even been there. He looked at Casey and Champa and in a low voice started what would be an eventful evening.

"Who the fuck's this guy, and what's he doing here?"

Casey stayed calm—that dramatic shit might work with some people, but it didn't do shit to him. He purposefully took a slow drink of his water and asked, "You mean you don't know?"

Petrosian didn't take the bait. Casey could have asked him the same question about the other guy, but he didn't, because it didn't matter. Everyone at the table was supposed to be there, and to start asking questions now would be stupid. Petrosian composed himself and sat back. Casey introduced everyone to Champa. And Petrosian introduced his man.

"This is Vladik, he's my go-to guy. Champa, you don't know him, but Casey does."

"In a manner of speaking, I do. We have mutual acquaintances," Casey said as he stared at Vladik's smug face.

There was a lot of tension in the air as the men all sized each other up. Casey hoped that Champa had his temper in check and wondered what the story was with Vladik. Obviously he'd been in the joint, and fate had paired him up with Lomax and him.

"Before we get into the business at hand, why don't you tug my coat about Lomax?" Out of the corner of his eye, Casey saw Shin sitting at a table on the other side of the restaurant, his Bluetooth glowing in his ear. Petrosian smiled, as did his partner. Alek turned around and snapped his fingers for the waitress, who came over quickly.

"Shall we order first?" Without waiting for an answer, Petrosian and his man ordered in Armenian.

Casey didn't bother looking at the menu. "We'll have the same."

Petrosian chuckled at this and nodded his approval. When the waitress left, he got back to business. "Let's just say the planets aligned in your favor and mine. That guy was a pain in the ass, not only to you, but to others as well. He had my man calling in a couple times a day, had him doing office visits every two days, and was doing curfew checks on a regular basis. I can't run a business with one of my guys getting that much attention, and I'm sure he was making your life difficult as well."

Casey frowned for a second. "Well, that wasn't my experience. Sounds like he had a special interest in what your man did."

"Yeah, well, he's no longer a problem for either one of us."

"You sure about that? Whoever you had handle it didn't cross the finish line, 'cause he ain't dead."

Champa chimed in: "Maybe if the same person that dusted my man Luca Bagramian had handled the job, it wouldn't have been fucked up."

Petrosian's face tightened, as did Vladik's. Casey showed no emotion, but was pissed that Champa had made a dumb crack like that. He knew the brotha was a hothead and had a lot invested in this job, but he wasn't helping things by talkin' shit. Casey kept the conversation flowing, knowing the situation could quickly disintegrate further.

"Anyway, we got other things that need sortin', seems like we both got our eyes on the same prize."

"It would appear so. I'm prepared to offer you twenty percent of the deal, but that's it," Petrosian said as he reached for his drink.

Before Casey could get a word in, Champa was off like a rocket. He leaned in and through clenched teeth said, "Nigga, are you crazy? This is *my* job, and if anyone's decidin' who gets what, it's us!"

Casey noticed Vladik slowly start to move his hands under the table and snapped, "Nigga, keep your hands on top of the table unless you intend to set shit off."

Petrosian looked at Vladik and said something low in Armenian that cooled him out and then smiled as he addressed Casey. "It looks like we got a potentially explosive situation here, but it also has the potential to make some big paper."

"Yeah, if we *all* keep our heads—" Casey shot a hard glance at Champa as he spoke. "—I think this can be worked out."

"Agreed."

"Our source tells us that the shipment is due to be unloaded at six A.M. this Thursday and then loaded onto two transports and taken to the Hamptons. We have all the logistics already worked out. My question is, do you have a buyer in place?"

Negotiations had always been a strong suit for Casey; he knew exactly how he was gonna maneuver Petrosian to get what he wanted. Now it was a battle of intellect. Petrosian's ego would force him to answer.

"Yeah, I got three million on the table guaranteed," the Armenian said confidently.

Casey hoped that Champa would stay still and not go renegade and start braggin'. At the same time, a new thought sprang into his head: *Why would a drug dealer all of a sudden become a heist man? On top of that, why would he sell twelve million dollars' worth of cars for only three million?* Regardless, Casey would use this to his advantage.

"Okay, so after it's all said and done, you're looking at a two-point-five-million-dollar take at best, right?" Not waiting for him to respond, Casey kept talking. "Now, given that we're all subject to whatever deal is done, we want assurances. Has your buyer given you a deposit?"

The Armenian leaned back in his chair. "No, but I'm not concerned, he's good for it."

"And are these cars supposed to be delivered to him in the U.S.?"

"Yeah."

Casey could tell that Petrosian was annoyed at being questioned, and was close to blowing his cool. If that happened, then everyone would lose. He was either lying about his deal, or he'd realized that he wasn't as prepared as he should have been. The latter made the most sense to Casey, as Alek had asked him to look over the heist to begin with. Casey realized that the Armenian was on the verge of being embarrassed in front of his lieutenant, and he needed to finesse this situation.

"I have a proposition I'd like you to consider. This job is quite complicated for a number of reasons. The first being that a lot of the cars are mostly one-of-a-kind, so selling them means finding a unique kind of buyer. This is only relevant if your buyer drops out. The second is there are GPS systems on the cargo trucks and cars. Those need to be quickly disabled, as this whole fleet will undoubtedly be tracked by the trucking company. This is no small feat. Those GPS systems work regardless if the truck is off or on. The third thing is delivery and payment."

The blond-haired waitress interrupted the flow of conversation. She and a busboy had two trays of food that they put in the middle of the table. Casey grabbed one of the large serving spoons and started helping himself. As he served up what looked like some kind of noodle casserole in a spicy red sauce, he grinned at Petrosian. "This ain't a Lomax special, is it?"

Petrosian cracked a smile and let out a chuckle. After the waitress split, Casey picked up where'd he left off. "I'm not saying you don't know all this, I'm just bringing it up to let you know that we know it, too."

"Okay, I still haven't heard your proposition, Casey."

"My proposition, Alek, is this: You get two-point-five million as your take from the cars, you don't have to sweat the details, and you and two of your men do the job with us. As far as delivery goes, that's my buyer's problem; we just take them to a warehouse and walk away. And you'll get paid within twenty-four hours after the cars are in the warehouse."

Petrosian tried to act nonplussed as he kept eating his food. Vladik was not so good at masking his reaction, and was noticeably sour. There was no way that Petrosian had his shit as tight as Casey and his crew. He was also offering him a guaranteed payout with less headache and no expense! If he turned his nose up on this deal, then either he didn't trust Casey, or there was something else going on.

Petrosian wiped his mouth and folded his napkin and responded to Casey. "How do I know I can trust you?"

"You don't, and you know you never would. None of us here are Boy Scouts. Everything we do has a calculated risk. When shit went down and lead flew, we showed what type of men we were. Now we uppin' the ante. This is a tight deal, and it can be the first of many. Now you know where my head's at—I'm about business 24/7—so it's time to break bread or fake dead."

Petrosian cut into his bloody steak and shoved a piece in his mouth while he contemplated Casey's words. "You talk a good game, Casey."

"I'm being straight with you, Alek. When it comes to this shit, I don't play games."

Despite Vladik's glower, Petrosian nodded. "Okay, I'm down. Now what?"

Anyone else might have relaxed once Petrosian had capitulated, but not Casey. He knew that the Armenian could flip the script at a moment's notice. "All right, here's how it's gonna go down: We'll all meet at five thirty A.M. Thursday at the warehouse where we gonna stash the cars. When we jack the transports, my two men'll ride in the trucks with the drivers and keep their eyes open for drama. I want to make one thing clear—this is a heist, not a murder. I don't want those drivers gettin' killed or fucked up."

Petrosian nodded again. "Understood. What next?"

"Next, you and I, riding together, follow the trucks to the warehouse. Once the cars are unloaded, your guys take the cabs and trailers to two different locations and stash them. My guys will shadow the transports and bring your men back here afterwards. Then all we gotta do is collect the delivery fee, and everyone gets their slice."

Petrosian peppered Casey with a lot of question on the details, and seemed satisfied with the answers. Casey didn't tell him he already had five million as a deposit or anything about the pickup; that would have been too much info for him to think on.

The men all got up, shook hands, and left the restaurant together; Casey saw Shin calling the waiter over for his bill. When they reached the street, Petrosian's S600 was waiting for him. He turned to Casey and said, "I'm sure we'll talk a lot in the next couple of days."

"Believe that," Casey replied.

Champa and Casey walked to his ride. Once they got in the Escalade, Crush turned to Champa. "I sure appreciate you not making a bad situation worse, nigga!"

"Yo, fuck that guy! I don't know why you cut him in for a piece anyway!"

"Are you fuckin' serious? You think he was gonna walk away from this job! If it wasn't for my connection to him, you can be as sure as shit on Thursday morning there woulda been a blowup. And then what, Champa? Did you ever think or plan for someone else trying to boost these cars? And what happens if Hans's China-man doesn't come through with the back end? At least this way we got a potential second buyer. I mean, shit, Champa, you my nigga and all, but sometimes you don't think before you talk, and this was a time when it really could have fucked *us*!"

"Okay, okay, okay, I hear what ya sayin'! I know you got shit locked down on all fronts, but fucking two-point-five million! Jesus Christ, man, you couldn't have offered the nigga one and a half and worked up from there?"

"Offering anything less would have made it a negotiation, and we supposed to be running this job in basically two days. I needed a quick yes on my terms. We don't have time to waste."

Champa had his arms folded across his chest. Through his window, Casey saw Shin outside, waiting to be waved in; he was smart enough to recognize that Champa and him were having words.

"So, how we splittin' this pie anyway?" Champa asked.

"Well, after Petrosian's take, we looking at seven mil 'cause we got Hans getting five hundred K. On top of that, Al P., Jacob, and other miscellaneous expenses is around a hundred K, so at the end of the day, that's six-point-nine mil. If we give Big Rich, Sean E Sean, Mick, and the Garcia boys a mil each, that takes us to two-point-nine. Then there's just Shin, you, and me left."

"So, what you thinking as far as Shin goes?"

"Well, he ain't a boss like the other guys, but he is in the inner circle and he's valuable. So, you tell me, Champa."

Champa chewed on his toothpick as he looked straight out the front window and then turned to Casey and said, "Shit, I'd say three hundred K. That's a lot of cheese for a cat that doesn't have the headaches we got."

"I think that's fair—then you and I both get one-point-three mil each."

Casey knew that was the way the splits had to be. His crew had to get equal shares for the plan to work, and Champa's extra piece was fair because he'd found the job and did most of the setup. "So we cool, nigga?"

"Yeah, we cool, man."

Casey held out his fist and Champa smiled and gave him a pound. "I can tell you spendin' that money in your head already."

Casey rolled down the window and told him Shin would take him back to the office. "I need to make curfew, so I got to hustle back to my crib. Call the guys, except for Rich, and have them meet up tomorrow."

"What about Rich?" Champa asked.

"He's gonna be under surveillance, and I don't need the pigs makin' the connection. Before the meet, you can go brief him on what's up."

"Okay, bet."

Casey made it home that night at 9:30 P.M. He didn't see any cops, so it was safe to assume he wouldn't be catchin' shit for being late. Getting thrown back in the joint for something as dumb as breakin' curfew was not a good look. Now that he had a new PO, he'd have to be a lot more careful.

In his darkened bedroom, Casey thought about the insanity of the current situation. Who was he to be Superman, cleaning up the streets? Drug dealin' and sex slavery were never gonna go away, and it was just a matter of time before he caught a bullet with his righteous bullshit. As far as Petrosian went, he knew that sooner or later that would come to a bloody conclusion that would result in him putting one more man in the dirt. That really didn't bother him. Casey knew his ticket was taking him to hell for all the shit he'd done or caused. It was the fate of Petrosian's kid that gnawed at him. Casey would be responsible for another kid growing up solo, no parents, no family. Another kid going into the system to get fucked around by bullshit foster parents, with the end result being another gangster on the street.

Casey sat up in bed and turned on the light. He reached for his phone to call Carla, but then just set it down. Talking to her would just confuse him more. After this job, he was gonna have to re-evaluate things. With the money he'd stashed and his take from this job, he'd have about three and a half mil. That was enough money to get lost and square up. He picked up his phone and sent a text to Carla and asked if she wanted to get breakfast at eight the next morning at the usual spot next to his building. She responded with only a smiley face. Casey stared at the glowing reply in the darkness.

What'd I do to deserve you, baby?

He didn't sleep much that night. There were tactics and logistics that he wanted to double- and triple-check. And like a seasoned chess player, he looked five moves ahead and strategized how to handle every possible scenario. When he was in the joint planning his revenge on Rono, he'd learned from Mack D the value of marrying tactics with a strategy.

"'Strategy without tactics is the slowest route to victory. Tactics without strategy is the noise before defeat.' Your lust for blood is gonna make *you* the loser if you don't have those two things working in harmony. If you want to pull a suicide mission, then just keep thinking the way you thinkin', brotha," Mack D had said.

Mack had that ability to crystallize complicated concepts in a way that made sense. He always fed quotes from wise men like Sun Tzu, Aristotle, and Seneca to Casey on a daily basis. There were days when the two men would just chop it up for hours on end about some esoteric shit. One of Mack's favorite subjects was dualism, which he defined as the power of the mind over the body. By accepting that the body was limited in strength and that the mind's power was limitless, he believed that the mind could always overpower any physical impediment. Casey was always a man who used a combination of his brainpower and his fist, but he knew to be truly powerful, he'd need to rely solely on his intellect. Champa was right that taking out Petrosian would solve that problem, but it would simultaneously create more problems.

It was times like these that it would have been good to bounce things off Mack, but with Attica being some four hours away, that wasn't gonna happen. Casey looked at the digital clock next to him and pulled himself out of bed. He took a quick, cold shower to wake up, and then hit the weights for a good ninety minutes, then showered again and got dressed. Checking the tracking app on his phone, he saw the dots of the detectives, two of which were on his street.

Shit, it's already started.

Casey called Champa and in a coded message let him know that he had "flies" on him. From here on out, his guys would need to keep their distance so no connections were made.

Casey pushed through the double doors of his building and turned left to head to the diner. Parked down the street was a brown Lincoln with two detectives that Casey recognized. He ignored them and kept walking to the diner. Across the street, Carla waved as she waited for cars to pass, then bounced over to him, giving him a deep kiss.

"What's up, baby?" Casey said as he gave her a squeeze.

"Lots. I got a big meeting with the owners today. Word is they're gonna open a sister hotel in Miami or L.A."

"Damn, woman, you gonna cut out on me?"

Carla laughed and snuggled close to him. "You sayin' you wouldn't follow me?"

"Look at you dodging the question," Casey said as they walked inside.

Casey steered Carla to a table by the window so he could keep an eye on the detectives. They both ordered and when the waitress left, Casey leaned forward and took her hand. "Maybe leaving town is a good idea."

"What are you talkin' about? Jesus, is something up?"

The waitress dropped off their two cups of coffee and said the rest of their order would be up in a few minutes. Casey waited for her to leave before replying. "Nah, I'm just evaluating shit and thinking a change in the near future could be fly—"

As Casey spoke he saw the detectives get out of their car and start walking toward the diner. *Fuck!* He knew they were probably gonna roll up on him and start shit-talking and freak Carla out. She could tell he was distracted and gave him a funny look.

"Listen, in about thirty seconds, two cops are gonna approach us. They don't have anything on me, it's just some cop bullshit. They're looking for us to react, so if you could be cool about 'em hasslin' us, that would be fly."

Carla stared at him for a long moment, and Casey wondered if she was gonna lose it right there, or simply get up and storm off. She took a deep breath and just nodded.

Casey gave her hand a long squeeze before letting go. "Thanks, boo."

The two cops pushed through the doors and came up to their table. Both men were white and looked to be in their fifties. One was short and balding and wore a stained tie; the other had red hair and a mustache. They each hooked a chair from the adjoining table, sat down in front of Casey and Carla, and smiled.

"So what's for breakfast, guys?"

Casey looked at the detective dead-on and showed no emotion. "Why, you treatin'?"

"Yeah, we got three meals a day at Attica, but then again, you already know that."

"Attica's in my past, and I ain't goin' back, so whatever you suspect, you can rest assured that you're mistaken."

"Is that right? You seem pretty confident. What would you say if we told you we know otherwise?"

"If you really did know otherwise, I'd already be in cuffs," Casey said as he dead-eyed the pair of detectives.

Carla sat back and watched the dialogue go back and forth like a tennis match and sipped her coffee, doing her best to remain calm. The detectives knew they were getting nowhere and started a new line of questioning.

"You know Big Rich, right?"

"Of course."

"You know he's in a lotta trouble?"

"Is that right?"

"Yeah, it seems someone's killing off his guys."

Casey didn't respond. He knew that when it came to cops, the shorter and more nondescript the answer, the better. These pigs didn't have shit on him. If they only knew the surprise party they were about to have come down on them, they'd lose their fuckin' minds.

"What about Ernesto Sanchez and Rodrigo Jimenez, Casey, you know them?"

"Can't say I do."

"Alek Petrosian?"

"Nope."

"I think you're a liar, Casey. I think you know all these guys, and you know exactly what's going on."

The other detective eyed Carla up and down like she was a piece of meat, another pathetic attempt to get a rise out of Casey. "Damn, honey, you're fine! What're you doing with this scumbag? You could do much better."

Carla looked at him but said nothing, just stared right through him. Both detectives sat back and looked at Casey for a few seconds, as if wondering what to do next.

"Okay, Casey, if your memory comes back, we'll only be a step away."

The two detectives got up from the table. The whole diner had taken notice of what had transpired, which meant Casey wouldn't be eating there again anytime soon. He watched as they left the diner while Carla sipped her coffee.

She gave him a look that he could not quite interpret. "Nothing going on, huh, just evaluatin'? You're too good for me to read, Casey, so why don't you just give me the brutal truth."

Casey could tell her emotional state was a combination of scared and pissed. He felt bad that she'd gotten caught up in his bullshit. "Yeah, well, I have told you more than most—"

"So I'm lucky, is that it? Are cops gonna be showing up at my work today? Wow, that's great, my bosses will just love that. Instead of being offered a promotion, maybe they'll just offer me the door? I guess I'll just be collateral damage, then, huh?" She was pissed and growing angrier as she spoke.

"The cops aren't gonna show up at your work, Carla. Look, I am a changed man, and you are gonna trust that either I am on the right path or that I'm not the guy for you. I called you because I wanted to talk about the future—our future."

"Oh, so suddenly now you're down with having a kid?" Carla asked sarcastically.

"Okay, I'm gonna bounce, since there's no talking to you right now. I hope you have a good meeting, and let's just talk when everyone ain't listenin' in and you're calm—" Casey started to rise from the table as he said this, but was cut off by Carla.

"Fuck you, Casey! You got me hanging by a string, you know you're my world and the one thing I want is you and a family, and you dump that talk in the middle of this drama!" She started to tear up as she spoke. "Now, because it's *difficult*, you wanna put a hold on the conversation. What is that, some of that Sun Tzu shit you like to say—'Retreat and return with superior firepower.' Isn't that what I heard you quote a couple days ago? Don't you fuckin' play me, nigga—I ain't the cops or one of those street hoods you roll with, either."

Casey reached across the table to take her hand, but she jerked it away and glared at him as she leaned back in her chair. *Christ— women!* She could have been a prosecutor or a cop, 'cause she was lightning quick when it came to dissecting any situation. It was almost like the more upset she got, the smarter she became. He admired her intelligence and sympathized about the way she was feeling, but resented that she didn't cut a nigga some slack. He calmly looked at her and in a hushed tone said, "If you want to go to my place and discuss it, then we can do that, but I'm not gonna discuss it here, Carla."

Carla quickly got up from the table, grabbed her purse, and stormed out. There was no sense in running after her; 'sides, that wasn't his style anyway. Casey put some cash on the table and walked out of the diner. He passed the two detectives, who'd witnessed the whole scene from their car, and were laughing at Casey. *Enjoy yourself while you can, muthafuckas.* He told himself that he had to put that drama out of his head. He went upstairs to his crib and reached out to Jacob via video chat.

"Hey, are the detectives tailin' your uncle yet?"

"Yeah, they're in front of his crib. I can tell him, right?"

"Yes, but don't let him know anything about how we're getting our intel. It's not that I don't trust him, I just don't want him to be distracted. Ya feel me on that?"

"I got it—he spoke to me yesterday and did some lightweight digging, but I kept shit quiet."

"Okay, good. Any more detective chatter I need to know about?"

"Nothing material. What I can say is that these guys love talking about their shakedowns and dirty dealings. They're their own crime syndicate—sellin' dope, taking payoffs, a whole bunch of shit."

"That's great, keep all that shit organized because we're gonna make that public in the next twenty-four hours. If you can get video on these guys doing it, that's even better."

"I'm on it, I don't have a ton of video, but I got enough."

"A'ight, when it's time to unleash this shit, I will let you know. Once we do, I'm sure they'll put two and two together and figure out what's goin' on, so when we get 'em we gotta get 'em good."

Casey closed the lid of his laptop. It was a little after 8:30 A.M. when he finished his conversation. Champa was gonna have all the guys at the office at one to discuss the plan and what each person's individual role would be. He went downstairs and drove to the office, making sure that the detectives had no problem tailing him. Once there, he told Joe that some detectives might be sniffing around and to not get freaked out. If they asked what his hours were, tell them ten to six, any other questions he should just go quiet.

In his office, Casey checked the money; there was a temptation to take that chedda and bounce, but he'd never do that. Still, it was hard to not think about it. Looking at his phone, he could tell the detectives were still outside. Casey peeked out of his window, spotted their car, and grimaced. He had to shake them for at least a couple hours; he needed at least that much time to pick Lomax's brain.

17

Casey called Webster and told him to pick him up at the Urban Victory office, but specifically in the alley, not in front. Webster agreed and said he'd be there in five minutes tops. Casey put on a jacket and a baseball cap and went out to tell Joe he was going out for the next two hours, and if the cops checked up on him to tell them that he went out to get supplies. Joe didn't question what Casey said; he just agreed.

Before he left, Casey checked his computer and saw his daily report from Jacob, which he printed and put in his coat pocket. Casey then took the elevator to the second floor, then took the stairs the rest of the way down. The stairs came out toward the back of the building, where deliveries were made. He hung back there and checked for Webster every so often. The air felt damp, like it was gonna rain again.

Getting to see Lomax undetected was gonna be dicey. There'd be security cameras, and he might have to check in at the front desk. Add to that the possibility of Lomax having a visitor when Casey showed up, or maybe just freaking out that one of his cons came in unannounced, made Casey a bit uneasy. Still, it was peculiar, but not illegal.

Casey looked out the door and saw Webster pull up. Checking his phone, he saw the detectives were still at the front of the building. He pulled his cap down, hit the street, and slid in the back of the gypsy cab.

"We're goin' to Bronx-Lebanon Hospital, you know where it is?"

"Yeah, of course."

"Good. Also, keep these maneuvers I'm doin' quiet. I don't want you speaking to anyone about my business. I'm gonna be in the hospital for an hour or so, so stay close by and I'll call you when I'm comin' out."

"Okay, Casey, anything else I should know?"

"Nah, just keep quiet, I'll be cool, and you'll be well paid."

"You got it, boss man."

Casey pulled out the report and started reviewing it. Jacob had done an excellent job of distilling the information to its essence. Of the twenty-three detectives, Jacob had caught all but six red-handed doing dirty shit. There was extortion, drug dealing, evidence tampering, payoffs, ticket fixing, just a ton of shit. It seemed like they all acted independently on a lot of their dirty work, but also collaborated on bigger shit as well. *Christ, they must be making a gang of loot.* Casey asked Webster if he had an iPod, which he did, and told him to put it on because he needed to make a private call.

Casey kept reviewing the report as he speed-dialed Jacob on one of his burners. "Hey, Jacob, I'm looking at all this shit—it's really thorough."

"Thanks. As far as all the cops we tagged, I have a separate report on each of them as well."

"Question, what are these icons next to these entries?"

"That denotes if the evidence is audio, e-mail, SMS, or video."

"Okay, that's what I thought. You got a lot of video, more than I expected."

"Yeah, I programmed the phones to link into a database of cameras so that when they're near them, they're automatically activated, so I capture video and audio."

"Jesus, dude, you're turnin' this into a fuckin' art form."

"Thanks. I've already organized it all and have the files ready to upload to YouTube. I also came up with a plan to spread these videos virally through all the popular social networks."

"I love it. So this is all untraceable, right?"

"Yeah, it's pretty cool. What I do is upload it to the cloud, then access it from random corporate networks all over the world that I hack into and use to start posting them."

Casey smiled as he listened to Jacob breaking it down and imagined the shit hitting the fan. He imagined the chief of police, mayor, and governor doing daily press conferences, trying to cover their asses.

"Fuckin' amazing, but instead of uploadin' it from random corporate networks, I want you to upload it from the cops', mayor's and governor's computers. Let 'em all wonder if they got a mole in their midst."

Jacob loved that tweak, and Casey could practically hear his brain working on how to execute it. He hung up the phone as they pulled up to the hospital.

Bronx-Lebanon had gotten quite a face-lift since Casey had been there last, well over twenty years ago. Even though it was now a top-of-the-line hospital, Casey still hated it; like all hospitals, it reminded him of too many bad times. He remembered going there to see his mom, tubes sticking out of her as she desperately fought for her life. And his father kneeling by her bed, praying for her to get better. As that bitter scene flashed in his mind, he clenched and released his fist. After his father died, he remembered thinking how God never answered his prayers or his father's. From then on, it wasn't that Casey didn't believe in God; he just thought it was pointless to put faith in anything but yourself.

Webster cruised up to the entrance, and Casey got out and walked through the double doors into the lobby. In front, next to the welcome desk, sat a cop reading a magazine while the two receptionists dealt with visitors. Casey blew right past them as if he owned the place and headed for the bank of elevators. The hospital had that antiseptic smell that brought back memories. His boy was born on the third floor of this joint. He recalled the first cry Antonio made when he'd greeted the outside world. At the time, it was a mixed feeling of amazement and vulnerability.

The doors pinged open on the second floor, and a crowd of people shuffled in and out of the elevator. That same exercise happened on the third floor as well. Casey looked down the hallway and briefly saw new parents and the parents-to-be mingling about. *Good luck, it's a fucked-up world to raise a kid in.*

When the doors opened on the fourth floor, Casey was the last to get out. He walked down the hall and hunted for room 415, finding it before he could really collect his thoughts. It was a single room. Casey stepped in unnoticed. On the bed, looking like a beached whale dressed in a hospital gown, lay Lomax, watching *Judge Judy.*

Lomax saw Casey and did a double take. Casey liked that. Lomax wasn't his usual cocky self for a change.

He turned off the TV, sat up with an effort, and addressed Casey in a weak voice. "What the fuck is this?"

Casey made sure his body language was nonthreatening as he approached his bed. He didn't want Lomax to have a real heart attack because of this surprise visit.

"We didn't finish our conversation the other day."

Lomax eyed Casey and said nothing. The tension was thick; the fact that Casey had rolled up on him was a ballsy move. Casey sat down on the chair adjacent to the bed, and Lomax snapped, "Don't get comfortable."

"Around you? I don't think that's possible. I didn't come here to play some game. I need some information."

"You got two seconds to get the fuck out of here before I call the nurses and have you thrown out."

"Fine with me. I just thought you might be interested in finding out who put you in here in the first place."

Lomax's face twisted up like he'd eaten something sour as Casey got up to leave. "What the fuck are you talking about? What'd you do now?"

"I know you were sweatin' someone pretty hard with your PO shit, and they got tired of it and tried to off you."

Lomax's eyes narrowed for a moment until the lightbulb in his head went off. "Vladik Hekimyan?"

Casey didn't want to confirm or deny his guess, at least not until they both had an understanding.

"You see, when you play someone close like that, and you disrupt their business, you have to assume that they will react."

"Sonofabitch. Do you know this for a fact?"

"Are you saying it don't add up?" Casey looked at him incredulously.

"Close the door."

Casey closed the door and sat back down.

"So what makes you think he actually did this, and what else do you—?"

"Hold on, Lomax, we need to get some things straight before we go down this road. Are you ready to cut the pretense shit and be straight with me?"

Lomax folded his thick arms across his chest and nodded. "Okay, no bullshit. What do you wanna know?" he asked.

"Where's my jewelry, my Saint Jude?"

"Ahh, so that's what this's about? You afraid it's going to get into the wrong hands or something? It's safe in my filing cabinet, so you can relax about that."

"When do I get it back?"

"Why? You feel like you need the powers of your Saint Jude's medal?"

"Is this the way it's gonna go?"

"Like I said, relax—you'll get it when I return. Is that what this was all about?"

"The crew in the van, that tried take out Petrosian at the Davilla, who were they, and are there more like them?"

"Who they were doesn't matter, and no, that was it—except for you, of course."

"What do you know about Vladik?"

"He's Petrosian's right-hand guy. He just finished a six-year sentence for a Class C Felony."

"What'd he do?"

"Sex with a minor. The girl was seventeen and from the Eastern Bloc, undoubtedly she worked for Petrosian. The judge gave him the max because the other charges didn't have strong enough evidence."

"You got any idea how big of a crew Petrosian's got?"

"Including himself and Vladik, maybe a total of eight guys. He's got a lot of contacts sprinkled throughout Armenia, Russia, and Czechoslovakia that he gets the girls and dope from."

"Is he part of a bigger syndicate?"

"It's hard to say—I don't have the same access as I used to have. Any information I've gotten has come in bits and pieces. But regardless, when you're in that part of the world, there's so much corruption, it's impossible to get solid intel. Are you worried about retribution?"

"I wouldn't say 'worried,' I just want to know what the whole story is. Why do you think he hasn't been busted yet?"

"I think he has someone on the inside keeping him one step ahead of everything."

"Any ideas?"

"My old partner and now the chief detective, John Fordham."

"And what do you know that supports that?"

"Because there was every reason to hold him after the shooting went down. His car was right in front of the restaurant, and two of his guys were dead. Fordham's office did little to nothing to investigate that incident."

"So maybe he's lazy?"

"Not a chance, he likes everyone to know who's boss. That means he puts you away or you work for him. I can't prove he's connected to Petrosian, but it adds up."

"So is your primary motivation Petrosian or Fordham?"

"Both!"

"Uh-huh. So why have you been feeding me info? Don't you have faith in the system?"

Lomax's face grew redder as he talked. "You mean the system that couldn't see someone was trying to frame me when I got busted down to being a parole officer? The way I see it there's the law and there's your own moral law, and sometimes those two don't match up."

Casey shook his head and laughed when he heard this. If he only knew what was in store for Fordham and his partners, he woulda sprang his fat ass out of that bed and done cartwheels.

"Damn, Lomax, you kinda sound like a criminal, you know that?"

"Look, when I was active, I bent the rules here and there, but I didn't break them, and look what it got me. I'm just fighting fire with fire here."

"I can dig that. But look, from here on out, this arrangement needs another level of transparency. Up to now, I've been the only one with something to lose, and as a result, that has put me in a situation I don't like. No more of the cryptic talk and clues. And I ain't 'working' for you. If you want me to do something, it's my decision."

"Okay, well, right now, you know what I know. And when I get back on my desk, which should be in about a week, that's the way it'll stay."

Casey didn't trust Lomax, so he didn't really invest too much in those words. The way things were heating up, Casey could be dead in a week. He was glad this shit was out in the open with Lomax and that his conversation hadn't set off a power struggle between them. Having someone on the inside would be an asset, but he knew Lomax would never be a friend and that their relationship would be tenuous most times. After all, he was still a cop. There was a light knock at the door, and a nurse stepped in to check on his vitals and to let him know lunch was gonna be served.

Casey took that as his cue to leave. "All right, I'm out of here."

"Hold on, Mr. Casey, how about telling me what the hell's going on?"

"All I can say is to keep an eye on your TV for the next couple days—if all goes well, it will all be very entertaining and gratifying."

"So much for transparency."

With a shrug, Casey let that slide and left the room. As he walked down the antiseptic hallway to the elevator, he dialed Webster to meet him in front. As things stood, Lomax was gonna be in Casey's life for close to the next three years. The only way that would change was if he put him up for review for discharge consideration. He wasn't gonna hold his breath for that, but once he put Fordham on blast, well, who knows what could happen?

Webster rolled up in front of the hospital, and Casey got in the backseat. He checked his phone to get a locale on the detectives that were following him. They were still in front of his office building, clueless that he was miles from there. He sent a text to Champa to make sure the crew used the back entrance to the building to make sure they wouldn't be spotted.

Back in his office, Casey prepared for the meeting and ran down the plan with Champa and Shin. The key was to keep Petrosian near Casey and his two guys near Shin and Champa. The less his crew had to deal with them, the better.

"Okay, instead of the Garcia boys running shotgun on these trucks, you guys'll do that. As far as Petrosian's guys go, I'll figure out how they fit in later. The other details all remain the same."

Casey looked up at the screen and saw some of the guys coming in. He sent Champa out to greet them and take them into the conference room while Shin hung back at Casey's request.

"Have a seat, brotha. I need to talk to you about something."

Shin sank into the leather sofa, and Casey took a seat opposite him. Shin had shown his stuff in a lot of ways, and Casey knew that if he kept following his lead, his future could be big.

"You been doing a good job out there, and you haven't been a headache."

"Thanks, Crush. I gotta say, watchin' you pull this together has been mind-blowing. Seein' the way you handle Al P. and Jacob, then gettin' all the big bosses to jump on board, man, this shit's incredible. I appreciate you rollin' the dice on a brotha."

"Cool, well, keep watchin' and learnin'. You're earnin' a good rep and stripes out there. Eventually you could be runnin' this whole thing one day."

"Fo sho, boss. I wanna learn as much as I can. I know there's a lotta pitfalls, and that shit can go left at the drop of a dime. I see how you're always looking for cracks in everything, and I do the same in my own way."

Casey looked at the monitor and saw that everyone was at the meeting and knew he had to wrap things up. "Okay, so this is a pop quiz for you. Knowin' what you know about this job, assume you're me and try and guess what I'ma break you off for this heist."

Shin didn't hesitate to answer, and Casey wasn't surprised. In his head, he had probably calculated what he hoped he would get a thousand times. "Two-fifty would be fair."

"Champa thinks different. He thinks you should get three hundred."

"That's tight, I appreciate it, man. You know I ain't gonna let you guys down."

"I know you ain't, Shin. Okay, let's roll into this meeting."

Casey walked into the crowded room, followed by Shin. He sat at the head of the mahogany table and kept quiet as he looked around at the men seated before him. He had known all these guys for at least thirty years. All were powerful men in their own right. All had experienced great triumph and great loss.

"I gotta lot to say, and I've put a lot of thought into it. I'm gonna lay it all out, and then take your questions. The job I've lined up takes place this Thursday at seven A.M. near the Port Authority shipyard in Jersey. It's the heist of twelve sports cars being imported from Italy. Most of them are one-of-a-kind. I have a buyer lined up, and I have a fifty percent deposit. If for some reason he does not pay on time, we keep the deposit and sell the cars to someone else. Once we jack the cars, we'll take 'em to a warehouse, where they'll be stored; after that the trucks and trailers will be ditched. The whole job will take less than four hours. I've got each one of you assigned to certain parts of this job that I'm gonna run through. Now, there is another cat on the job with two of his men. His name is Alek Petrosian. I will get into that later."

The guys exchanged looks with each other but kept quiet as Casey laid out his plan. This was not the first time any of them had rolled with Casey. His reputation was that he planned out everything to a T and would not tolerate anyone deviating from the plan unless he said it was okay.

Casey looked at Sean E Sean and started with him. "Sean, I need four detective badges with photo IDs. I'll give you the photos before you leave. I also need four Nissan Altimas with detective's lights."

"The badges and lights are easy, the cars are the trickier part. Do they all need to be the same color?"

"That'd be best, but if they're not, we can deal with that. Can you get those wheels on such short notice?"

"Yeah, I know how to make that happen."

Casey then turned his attention to the room and started laying out the whole plan in detail. The guys would all meet at 5 A.M. sharp at Urban Victory; from there they would head out in the stolen cars to a spot a couple miles past the shipyard and lie in wait for the trucks carrying the cars. They would pull the trucks over with their lights flashing, take the guys out of each truck, and tie them up in the backseat of one of the cars. Then the team would swarm the transports and disable the GPS systems on the cars and the trucks. Once that was handled, the trucks would be driven to a warehouse, unloaded, and the transports would be driven to different locations and dumped. Casey would have Shin, Mick, and the Garcia brothers hold down the warehouse until the cars were picked up. Once that handoff was made and the loot was collected, everyone would meet up at Urban Victory to collect their cut. Casey knew there were questions waiting to be asked, so he opened up the floor.

Mick got into it first. "What are we getting paid?"

"Each crew gets a million bucks when the final deal is made."

As expected, the whole crew reacted to this in a positive way.

Once the talk about the loot died down, Hen Gee caught Casey's eye.

"Yeah, Hen, what's your question?"

"A few things, this sounds tight and a helluva payday for a short amount of work, so we're appreciative of that. My questions are: How do we knock out the GPS? How do we stop the drivers from alerting dispatch or the cops that they've been pulled over, and finally, can you be more specific about the kind of cars?"

"All good questions. There are a dozen cars in total. Most of them you all'd be hip to, but there are some that are ultra-high-end and rare, like the Koenigsegg Trevita and CCXR, the Pagani Zonda Cinque Roadster, and my favorite, the Bugatti Veyron Super Sport."

There was a chorus of *ohh*s and *ahhh*s as he ran down the complete list. Casey watched all the guys, and knew more than one of them would be tempted to take a couple out for a test drive before they gave 'em up.

"As for stoppin' the drivers from droppin' a dime, we do that by jacking their phones and knocking them out remotely. I already got a man on that. As for killing the GPS, I'll let Champa take that one."

Champa stood up and put a twelve-by-twelve box on the table. He reached inside and pulled out what looked like a phone charger with an antenna on it and held it up. "This little gadget is called GPS Tracker Defense. It plugs into the cigarette lighter, has a fifteen-foot-radius, and will knock out the GPS system of any car. When we pull over the trucks, we'll put these on board, then go to the other cars and install them. I got the manifest for all the cars, and all the lighters work without the keys in the ignition. As an extra precaution, once we get to the warehouse, we will take out the GPS fuses to make sure we don't get tracked."

The room was clearly impressed as Champa started tossing the units to everyone in the room for inspection. Champa told the guys that he'd had all the units tested to make sure they worked, and they all checked out. Sean raised his hand and said, "Do you got four extra so I can put 'em in the four cars I'm boostin'?"

"Yeah, I got you on that. I also can show you where the GPS fuse'll be on those cars, too."

"This looks flawless, as always, Case. One thing, though . . . Who's this Petrosian guy? He's the same cat that's got the rep for sellin' H, right?" Hen Gee asked as he handed the GPS blocker to his brother to inspect.

"Yeah, it's the same dude. I been havin' conversations with him on some other business, and during those talks, he asked me to do this heist with him. Rather than walking away from this job or starting a war, I decided to give him a piece."

"I don't know 'bout everyone else," Sean said as he leaned forward in his chair, "but working with a dude I don't know who's got his kind of pedigree makes me a bit uneasy, Case."

"I agree. This all came down real quick, and that's the way the cards were dealt." Casey saw Mick was about to speak, and knew exactly what he was gonna say. He cut him off before he could say it. "Takin' him out ain't an option, 'cause his people know me and about the job. If that went down, there'd be retribution against me for sure. None of us need that kind of heat."

Casey felt the tension rise in the room. These guys didn't like newcomers, and he couldn't blame them. Most people had a level of discomfort that stopped them from moving forward at certain times in their life. Every time he'd encountered this, Casey had always pushed past that feeling; he had felt like this whole thing was fate. If he hadn't reached out to Petrosian, they would have surely met when the cars were stolen, and then what? There was something about this whole thing that felt like someone's master plan.

Mack D used to say he never believed in fate or God, for that matter. He often quoted G. K. Chesterton, saying, "I do not believe in a fate that falls on men however they act; but I do believe in a fate that falls on them unless they act." This was where he and Mack diverged. Casey argued that when he looked at his life, it had a consistent order that seemed to be too perfect to be random, as if it were preordained or written. Things that seemed like coincidence or accidents that he thought were of no relevance ended up having a massive effect on his life. And though he was an individual, it seemed like he was an instrument in a band that created a collective work that made sense out of what seemed like chaos.

"Fuck it, I'm down to roll with you on this, Crush. Shit, I'd be in the joint right now or dead if it hadn't been for you," Mick said.

"I second that," Sean said.

Casey looked at Hen and Big E as the brothers stared at each other. He knew Hen was down, but wouldn't move forward unless his brother was up for it. Those guys always acted as one, and today would be no different. If they didn't agree, it would set a bad precedent, and Casey's alliance might be dead before it really got off the ground. Big E looked at Casey and said, "So you trust that this Petrosian cat won't go left on us?"

Now was not the time for anything but the absolute truth. Casey stared back at Big E and gave it. "Nope."

Big E laughed and held up his hands. "Okay, fam, I'm down. Let's play this out."

With that, the guys went their separate ways. Big E hung back for a sec. He pulled Casey aside and asked, "You know you my dawg, right?"

"Shit, man, I get it. I respect that you got to do your due diligence."

"Okay, fam, we're in. Let's make this paper."

After the guys left, Casey met with Shin and Champa in his private office. Champa told him that he'd spoken to Rich that morning and clued him in on everything. The only thing left was to drop a dime on all the detectives. Casey was concerned about waiting too long or springing his surprise too soon. He needed Fordham and his guys incapacitated while the deal went down; otherwise, he was sure there'd be problems. He opened up his computer and initiated a video chat with Jacob. When his face popped up, Casey could tell there was something wrong with him.

"What the fuck's wrong with you, dude?"

"Man, I just started feeling like shit after lunch. I think I'm getting the flu."

"Are you sure it's not food poisoning? Please tell me you didn't order from that Jamaican restaurant downstairs?"

"Nah, I just heated up a can of corn chowder."

"Okay, well, look, I'm sorry you're feeling bad, but you know what's about to go down. So fill yourself up with whatever you need to make it through the next couple days. Your shit's critical at this point in the game. Remember, your uncle's ass is on the line as well."

"I won't let you down, Case. I had the drugstore deliver a bunch of stuff already. I'll be on point."

Casey had a real bad feeling about this. He had a lot of planes in the air, but his air traffic controller looked like he was going downhill quick. He couldn't spare Shin or Champa to go over there, and even if he could, he couldn't afford for them to get sick as well.

"How long'll it take to get everything we got on these detectives live?"

"Forty-five minutes from when I press the button."

"So what does that mean exactly?"

"All the videos will be uploaded to YouTube and other video-sharing sites, and all the major social networks'll be flooded with links and messages about the videos."

"So how long will it take for it to really take off and saturate the Net?"

"About two hours, if I time it right. Ideally, I'd want to upload right after people come back from lunch; that way, local news has time to cover it for their six P.M. broadcasts. I also have it set up to e-mail multiple people at all the major news outlets. I got it set so the news folks will have links to high-res footage."

"Okay, that's perfect, let's do that. The cops'll be scrambling like crazy to cover their asses and figure out how to respond. By the time Thursday A.M. rolls around, that whole outfit will be wondering what hit 'em. And mark my words, they'll all start turning on each other like rats."

For the next three hours, Casey got a rundown of all the evidence that was gonna be released on the Web. Anything that wasn't a slam dunk, he told Jacob to hold back on releasing. He wanted there to be no doubts whatsoever; it had to be an open-and-shut case of guilt. When they got to Fordham, the evidence they had on him framing Lomax and all his other dirty deeds was airtight. Casey wondered what impact it would have on Lomax's career and psyche. It would be justice and clear his name, but there was no remedy for the passing of lost time, or the memory of what had been done to him.

Casey looked at his watch—it was already 6:30 P.M., the day had sped by, and he still needed to speak to Hans.

"Champa, I need you to buzz down to Hans's spot and tell him the cars'll be ready by five P.M. Thursday at the latest. Find out when his Chinaman wants to pick them up and give us the cash."

"Okay, bet, then what? You want me to call you?"

"Nah, come by the crib. Tell Hans we're gonna hold these cars for his man until six A.M. on Friday, then look at other buyers if he don't come through with the rest of the payment."

Casey left the office and headed for home. As he pulled out of the garage, heavy rain drummed down on his SUV. He thought about reaching out to Carla, but didn't want the distraction—correction, he couldn't afford the distraction.

18

Casey went to the fridge, got some of Carla's leftovers, and sat in front of the TV to wait for Champa to come by. A little after 8 P.M., he got a text from Champa sayin' he was a block from his crib. Casey finished his grub, then heard Champa's familiar knock on the door. When he opened the door, the other man walked in, drenched.

"Jesus, it's pissin' down something fierce out there," Champa said, closing the door. "The forecast said it's gonna be that way the whole week. You think that's gonna affect the boat docking or this job?"

"Nah, it ain't like it's a hurricane. What'd you hear from Hans?" asked Casey.

"He reached out to his Chinaman, who said he was gonna pick up the rides at five P.M. in the afternoon on Thursday, then take 'em to the airport, where he's got a cargo plane waiting to transport them," Champa said as he took off his rain gear.

"Da-yamn, that's gonna be so major cake to fly them whips over to China. Did Hans confirm that the dude's gonna have the money all ready?"

"Yeah, it's all set. The actual guy won't be there, but one of his people'll be on deck. Hans said we'd get a picture of the guy later today."

"Okay, tell him that the cars'll be in the Bronx, but don't give him the exact location until an hour before pickup."

"You got it, man."

Champa split, and Casey hit the sack. Tomorrow at this time, the shit would have hit the fan, one way or another.

The next morning, Casey woke up to the sound of rolling thunder and rain pelting his bedroom window. He lay in bed quietly, thinking about how his son's mother had always loved the sound of rain. She believed it was purifying, and washed away the bad. She had been a good woman who bet on a bad man and paid the price. He contemplated whether Carla felt she had paid a price as well. He knew she'd see the news today, when everything went down, and wondered if she'd have any inkling that he was behind it. It would be nice to share that victory with her.

Glancing at his nightstand, Casey saw he'd forgot to plug in his phone last night, so he grabbed the cord and plugged it in. The phone came to life and started chiming like it was possessed. He picked it up and saw he had six text messages, all from Jacob. Casey quickly thumbed through the messages—the level of urgency in them made Casey realize something big was up. He got dressed, opened his laptop, and initiated a video chat. When Jacob appeared on the screen, he looked like the flu was getting the best of him, with pale skin and black circles under his eyes.

"Christ, you look like hell!"

"I'm fuckin' dyin' over here, Casey. I feel like it's getting worse. I was up all night puking my guts out."

"Jesus, dude, you gotta hold it together for another forty-eight hours or this whole operation's fucked. Lemme see if I can get a doctor to come see you."

"I appreciate that. I'm sorry about this, but that's not why I called you. Late last night, I picked up a phone conversation between Fordham and Petrosian."

"What?"

"Yeah, it was around midnight. They got some deal going—I don't know what, but it's obvious they're tied in together. Some of the conversation didn't make sense, but I can play it back now."

"Do that—hold on a sec." Casey ran to his dresser, snatched his headphones, and plugged them into the computer's audio jack—he wanted to hear this shit crystal clear. "Okay, go."

The first voice he heard was Fordham's. "Hello, this is Chief Sergeant Fordham."

"Can you talk?" The Armenian's distinctive voice came through loud and clear.

"Hold on."

In the background, Casey could hear noise like Fordham was walking through a bar and then onto the street. When he got back on, he was obviously hot.

"Why the fuck are you calling me? I sure as shit hope this isn't a number connected to you or your people."

"It's clean, you should know by now that I wouldn't make a mistake like that—"

"Save it, what do you want?"

"First, I appreciate that you got the heat off me on that shooting—"

"Get to the goddamn point."

"That guy Crush Casey got wind of the job and is taking it over."

"What the fuck! How the fuck did that happen?"

"He was already hip to it and had a big crew in place to take it down. If I'd challenged him, it would have meant war, which neither you nor I need right now. I agreed just to buy some time."

The only sound Casey could hear was the sound of cars whizzing by on the wet street. "Did you hear what I said?"

"I fuckin' heard it. I'm thinking, goddamnit," Fordham said brusquely. "Just take him out as soon as possible."

"That's your solution? Really?"

"Look, I leave it to you to handle this shit, so why are you making this my problem?"

"Can't you pick him up and hold him or frame him for something?"

"Okay, I'm done with this conversation, you gotta figure this one out yourself." Fordham hung up on Petrosian before the Armenian could reply.

Casey unplugged his headphones, his mind racing to figure out what the deal was between Fordham and Petrosian. Jacob was about to speak, but Casey held his hand up so that he could think. *Were those two guys partners on everything, or just this one job? How'd they get connected to each other?*

He guessed that ultimately it didn't matter. What did matter was that Casey could expect an attack from Petrosian. Then again, if Fordham was put on blast, he'd have no reason to ally with the Armenian. Taking Petrosian out at the job was too risky for both of them. If there was a showdown, it'd be at the warehouse, after the cars were unloaded. Crush's nature was to attack immediately, but with the heat on him and the job less than twenty hours away, it didn't make sense. *Well, at least Champa'll be happy to split another two-point-five mil—if we survive this.*

"Casey, there's more you need to hear."

"More conversation between those two?"

"No, between Fordham and one of the detectives following you. This conversation took place a little after one A.M. You'll recognize the first voice, that's Fordham."

Casey put his headphones back on to listen and watched Jacob type at a lethargic pace as he readied the clip. He looked like he was gonna pass out; then Casey heard Fordham's voice.

"We got a problem— Hello? Are you listening?"

"Yeah yeah, I'm here. What's up? What time is it?"

"That Armenian's let Crush Casey get the better of him. He's taking over that car heist, and you know what that means."

"Jesus. Okay, well, is he gonna handle it?"

"No, he's being a pussy and says there's no time."

"Okay, so what's the plan?"

"When he drives out of his building tomorrow, pull him over and plant a piece in his car. That'll be his third strike, then I won't ever have to deal with his black ass again."

Casey clenched his fists tightly, thinking how this sonofabitch was gonna burn. Now it was a race to see who could get the other man first.

The other detective laughed when he heard Fordham and remarked, "You got it—we will wait outside his garage, he usually leaves around nine A.M."

"Okay, call me as soon as he's in custody."

"What about his crew?"

"Once you cut a snake's head off, the rest of the body dies. That's what I'm betting on."

Jacob looked at Casey and said, "That's why I was burning up your phone. What are you gonna do?"

"I'm gonna have to lay low and out of sight until these videos hit, then hopefully these guys'll be knocked out of commission."

"And Petrosian?"

"I haven't figured that out yet, but I will. I gotta get outta here—call me if anything goes down. Just keep lookin' out, monitor things super-close. I'm gonna get a doctor to your place in the next coupla hours."

"Okay, cool, I appreciate that. I'm still set to let things fly at two. It's just a press of a button."

Casey closed his computer screen. It was 8:30 A.M. He grabbed his money and checked his phone—it didn't have much of a charge. *Shit, this is a perfect muthafuckin' storm.*

He dialed Big Rich and it just rang and rang, then went to voice mail. Rich was a night owl, and probably wouldn't be up for a few hours. Casey dialed Champa and let him know Jacob needed a doctor, and to go to Rich's, wake his ass up, and have his doctor friend roll to Jacob's place.

"Matter a fact, Champa, take the doctor to his house, but stay clear of that nigga. It's like he's got the bubonic plague or some shit."

"Okay, movin'!"

Casey didn't have time to brief him; he would do that later. He unplugged his phone and checked the map app to see how close the detectives were to being at his house. *Shit!* The flashing dots were already in front of his building. His building didn't have a back way out like his office, so that was not an option. He'd either have to hole up or make a run for it. The latter would be conspicuous, and would add even more insanity to this madness. Casey paced the floor, occasionally looking outside to check on the car below. Fat raindrops pelted against the window as Casey's brain went into overdrive. He had too much at stake to get fucked this close to the finish line. He went into his closet and got his Glock; he'd made up his mind long ago that there was no way in hell he'd go back to the joint. As he picked up his keys, he saw Webster's card next to him.

Oh shit, that's it! Casey grabbed it and dialed him on a burner phone. *Come on, come on . . .* "Webster!"

"Yeah, who dis?"

"It's Crush Casey. I need you and three of your other drivers at my place. You're gonna help me out of a jam. It ain't nothin' illegal. Are you down?"

"Hell yeah, mon, what ya need done?"

"I need four cars to box in a gray Lincoln in front of my building, and don't let them out for at least two minutes—no matter what. I'll lace everyone with some good bread later today."

"I'm down. Me and my guys can be der in less than twenty minutes."

"Cool, call me when y'all get here."

Casey's next call was to Shin. "I need you to get to my building hella fast and park a block away on the northeast corner and wait for me. How long will it take you to get here?"

"About a half hour with the rain."

"That's not gonna work. You need to be here in twenty minutes or less. When you arrive, I need you to keep the engine running and we'll switch cars."

"Okay, I'm in motion, what's goin' on?"

"The pigs are gonna try and arrest me."

"Oh shit!"

"Yeah, Jacob hipped me to it. When we switch cars, drive like you're goin' to the office. Let 'em pull you over. They'll be pissed that I'm not in the car; just tell 'em you picked it up 'cause you needed to borrow my ride. If they ask where I'm at, tell 'em I'm still in my apartment."

Casey went downstairs to the parking garage, pulled to the mouth of the garage, and waited for Webster's call. He checked his cell—his battery was weak, as was his signal. The next twenty minutes seemed like forever; then his phone lit up.

"Okay, we all in place, lemme know when to move in."

"Move in right now. Make sure a car's in front and back and the car on the driver side is real close so the driver can't get out. Have the drivers for the front and back park then bail out quick to the diner."

"Okay, lemme tell da guys and I'll call ya back."

Casey hung up and dialed Shin to get his ETA. "Where you at, brotha?"

"A couple of minutes away."

"Well, hurry the fuck up!"

"I'll be there in a second."

"Okay, when you see me, jump out."

Casey's knee bounced in anticipation as he waited for Webster's call; if this worked, it'd be a miracle. Staying out of sight for the rest of the day would be tough. If those guys weren't in deep shit by the time his curfew came around, things would get critical.

Casey's phone chimed with a *10 percent battery life* message; then Webster called.

"Hey, Casey, I see the car. I have a car in front of him and in back. I had my drivers do what ya said. When do you want me to pull in?"

The sound of the rain was so loud that Casey strained to hear him. It was really pouring now. He turned on his car and popped it into gear. "Pull up now and tell me when the car is completely blocked in. And stay on the phone until I say otherwise."

"Okay, two seconds . . . okay, I'm good. I'm in place."

Casey pulled out of the garage and then onto the street as if it were a normal day. The rain beat down hard on his hood as he hit daylight. The sidewalks were a sea of black umbrellas as people walked fast to their destinations. Casey heard the honking of the detective's car and in his rearview saw one of the detectives get out of the passenger side of the vehicle and run over to Webster's car. Casey was at a red light about a quarter block away when he heard the exchange between the two men.

"Move your car now!"

"I'm just waiting for my sista to come out. It won't be a second, mon."

"NYPD, motherfucker! Move your car now or go to jail, goddamnit!"

"Okay, okay, okay, sorry, I didn't know. I'll move it now."

Casey saw the detective getting soaked as he flashed his badge in Webster's face. The light turned green and he slowly turned the corner, then hit the gas. At the end of the block, he saw Shin's G-Wagen with the hazards flashing, with Shinzo standing outside. He was on him in seconds and slid to a stop, coming within an ass hair of rear-ending him.

Casey jumped out, ran past Shin without saying a word, and got into the driver's seat. Putting the Benz in gear, he pulled out and took a right. He went a block and a half, knew he wasn't being followed, and immediately called Shin.

"Where you at?"

"I'm a block away from you, goin' the opposite direction."

"Okay, they gonna be on you in seconds, and when they are, you know what to do, right?"

"Yeah, I'll just dummy up on their ass."

"Good man, I gotta stay footloose from these fools, so—"

"Hold up, dawg, I got a flashing light—they pulling me over."

"Okay, keep your phone on, I wanna listen."

Casey's windows on his Escalade were heavily tinted. That, coupled with the rain, meant the detectives would be clueless to who was actually in the SUV.

He heard the electric window go down, and the detective's angry voice next. *"Who the fuck are you? Where's Marcus Casey?"*

"Back at his apartment, I guess? I'm just borrowing his car. Do you need to see my license?"

"No, I don't need to see your fucking license! Get the fuck outta here!"

Casey heard the electric window going up and Shin laughing. "Crush, you hear that?"

"Yeah. Good lookin' out. Where are they now?"

"They just drove off."

"Okay, drive my shit to the office and wait for me there. Also, call Sean E Sean and find out when he's gonna have those cars and see if he needs any assistance."

"Okay, bet."

Casey's next call was to Jacob so he could eavesdrop on those detectives. Having all the phones bugged was like a Get Out of Jail Free card. He also needed to figure out where to lay up for the afternoon so the cops couldn't find him.

Jacob's phone rang and rang, then went to voice mail. He redialed and got voice mail again. He glanced at his watch—it was 9:30 A.M. on the nose. Maybe he wasn't answering 'cause Casey was using his burner phone and he didn't recognize the caller ID. He tried him again. Nothing. He dialed Champa—maybe the doctor was examining Jacob.

"Hey, you at Jacob's?"

"Nah, I'm still huntin' the doctor's ass down."

"What? Champa, that nigga's dyin' over there and he ain't pickin' up his phone! If he's outta commission, we're all fucked!"

"I know, I know, Case! I called the dude, and he was supposed to meet me, but he never showed. I'm goin' to his place now."

"Fuck! Call Rich and get a backup doc! If he don't have anyone, call the other guys and see if they do. I'm going over there now."

Casey tossed the phone on the passenger seat, whipped the G-Wagen around, and headed to Jacob's walk-up. With the rain and traffic, he figured he'd be there in a half hour. On the way over, he searched his brain for alternatives but came up empty. He had seen Jacob do his magic, but was totally clueless on how to operate the equipment, and it's not like he could call up some tech support to help him out.

Casey pulled in the alley of Jacob's building and surveyed the situation. He didn't see anyone suspicious, just the two guys Shin had watching the building. Casey got out and dodged raindrops as he ran to the front door. Once inside, he looked through the glass doors at Shin's guys and waved them over.

Two burly brothers got out of their rice burner and hustled over to the building's entryway. "Hey, Crush," the two men said in unison.

"Has anyone out of the norm been in this building in the last few hours? Think carefully before you say anything."

"Nobody new's been in or outta this spot this A.M. or last night."

"Okay, good. You guys're packing heat, right?"

"Yeah."

"Okay, I want one of you to hang in this doorway and the other to stay back in the car. If cops—and when I say cops, I mean in uniform or detectives—come in here, call me on this phone."

"Okay, no problem."

"Be prepared to take 'em out on my signal. And don't let me fuckin' down!"

The guys nodded, and Casey had them take down the burner's phone number. Then he ran up the four flights of stairs two at a time until he got to Jacob's floor. He was a bit winded and took a second to catch his breath before he started pounding on the door. No answer. He pulled out his phone and called and got voice mail again. *Fuck!* Casey took four steps back and charged the door with his shoulder. On impact, he could hear the wood splinter and feel the door give way under his force. The computers in the living room were alive with all sorts of activity, and alerts were going off like crazy. Casey called out for Jacob and heard nothing. He was torn between looking at the screens and looking for his man but knew finding Jacob was more important. He went to the bedroom, then checked the bathroom, then went to the hall bathroom. Two seconds before he reached the door, he smelled the stench of vomit, and that was where he found him, passed out in his own puke. He initially thought he might be dead—*shit, maybe he choked on his own vomit*—but when he flipped him over, he heard him moan. His face was pale and his shirt was soaked with sweat. Casey dropped to his knees and tried to revive him.

"Jacob, it's Casey! Wake up, man. Jacob, come on, brotha! Wake up, Jacob."

Casey shook him and slapped him in the face a few times, which did jack shit. He turned on the water and looked for a cup, but found nothing. He ran into the kitchen and found a glass, then ran back to the bathroom. He stepped back over Jacob's body and damn near busted his ass when he slid in the vomit. *Shit, that's all I need is to crack open my dome.* He filled the glass with cold water and threw it in Jacob's face. That brought him slightly around. Casey dropped to his knees and started talking to him.

"Jacob, wake up, man, come on. It's Casey! Wake up, Jacob!"

Jacob was slipping in and out of consciousness, but wasn't coming to. Grabbing his arm, Casey put it around his neck and stood up, careful not to slip and fall. Jacob's body felt like a furnace.

Casey carried him to his bed and laid him down on it. As he did, he heard Champa come through the front door and hollered to him. *"Champa, I'm in the bedroom!"*

Champa ran back with the doctor in tow. The doc was a light-skinned brotha, about six foot seven and incredibly thin. He looked to be about sixty-five and was wearing a rumpled suit. The doctor rushed to Jacob's side, opened his bag, and took his temperature. From the smell of it, he had already been tossing back a few that A.M. Casey shot a look at Champa, who just rolled his eyes and shook his head.

The doc took the thermometer out and reviewed it. He had a concerened look on his face as he turned to Casey and Champa. "This man has a temperature of 103. Can he be taken to the hospital?" The doc had obviously dealt with a lot of criminals, which was why he phrased his question as "can he" rather than saying "he should."

"No, he can't—he needs to be revived and ready to work ASAP," Casey said. As the words came out, he was very aware that he sounded like a total heartless prick. The lives of his crew were at stake; he would have said the same thing if Champa, Shin, or any of the other guys were lying there. That was the nature of the game, and everyone knew it. Nothing personal; that's just the way shit was.

"Okay, see if there are ziplock bags in the kitchen. If there are, fill four of them with ice. Also, set the thermostat to seventy degrees and get a big glass of water."

Casey and Champa booked it to the kitchen and started searching drawers and found some ziplock bags and started filling them up. "Champa, where'd you find this guy?"

"Exactly where you think I found him. He was on his way to being two sheets to the wind when I showed up. He was at McDermott's Pub with two boilermakers in front of him."

"Well, I guess we know why he ain't legit no more."

"Rich swears by this guy, drunk or sober. On the way here, I made him drink two cups of coffee."

"Well, he's the only hope we got—come on, let's get this in there."

The guys carried the ice packs into the room. The doc had an IV in Jacob's arm with the bag of solution hanging from a nail in the wall and was taking his blood pressure. Ghetto medicine at its best. Casey tried to avoid thinking about how absurd this mess was, but it was hard not to. He had a drunk doctor treating a Rastafarian computer nerd that held the key to framing the top detectives of the NYPD. *Can this shit get anymore ludicrous.*

The doc had taken off all of Jacob's clothes except for his boxers. He grabbed two of the ice packs and put them under each armpit, then took the other and gently put it on top of Jacob's head. He took the fourth ice pack, lifted up Jacob's boxers, and put it on his crotch. The guys instinctively recoiled at this and exchanged startled looks. The doc reached into his tattered black bag and pulled out a syringe and a small bottle of medicine.

"This should give your friend a bit of relief and some energy," he said as he started to draw back the medicine into the syringe, his hands a bit shaky.

"What is it, Doc?" Casey asked.

"It's a little cocktail I invented. . . . It works pretty good, unless there is an allergic reaction or something."

"Or something?" Casey asked incredulously.

The doc looked at Casey through bloodshot eyes. "Look, I'm under the impression there's two seconds on the clock and you need this man functional immediately, so I'm pushing the standard medical protocols. Am I incorrect?"

"Spare me the metaphors, Doc, and do what you gotta do."

The doc grabbed Jacob's arm, stuck the needle in, and administered his "cocktail." Champa and Casey were at the foot of the bed, watching Jacob. The clock next to him said 10:45. In three hours, Jacob was due to "press the button" that would release holy hell for the NYPD.

The doc took his temperature again and looked at the guys. "It's going down slightly. Let me have the water."

"How's he gonna be able to drink? He's passed out!" Champa exlaimed.

"It's not for him, it's for me. I'm still feeling a bit tipsy."

Casey was more than annoyed with this whole situation, but let it slide. He walked to the other side of the bed and crouched down; whatever Jacob had, he sure as fuck didn't want it.

"Two questions, Doc: How long till he's conscious? Also, is he contagious?"

"I'd say he should be somewhat alert in a half hour or so and able to function an hour after that. He's badly dehydrated, has low blood pressure, and he probably overdid the meds." The doc pointed to two empty bottles of over-the-counter flu remedies. "As far as contagious, you're okay. Just wash your hands with soap, *a lot*. That bathroom will need to be cleaned with bleach as well."

"So, what does he have?"

"My guess is the Norwalk virus, it causes viral gastroenteritis. He made things worse by overdoing it on the meds. That's why he passed out and threw up. I checked his skull, and he's also got a nasty bump and maybe a minor concussion."

Casey got up and went to the kitchen with Champa to wash his hands. Once there, Casey grabbed a bar of soap and turned to Champa. "I don't need to tell you how this whole ball of wax is hanging in the balance. If he doesn't come to, we might as well blow up the NYPD, 'cause that's the only way we're gonna survive this mess."

"Yeah, I've been thinking about that. Do you think Al P. knows enough about Jacob's tech to step in?"

"I doubt it, but call him up and get him over here, that's a good thought."

Champa dialed Al while Casey went in to check on Jacob. Casey could tell by the color of Jacob's face that he was in better shape. "He's lookin' better, the color in his face is returning."

"Yup, the temperature's coming down, too, and he's on his second bag of saline solution." The doctor shrugged. "He should be conscious any minute now, although he might be a bit useless."

Champa walked in and called Casey out of the room, then told him Al was ten minutes away. Casey walked over to the computers and looked at the screens. He could see conversations being transcribed from all the different phones. *All that activity, but no one to access it.*

Casey heard the doc call him from the other room. The guys walked in and saw Jacob semi-conscious. He was far from being able to do shit in his state. A few minutes later, they heard a hello from the living room; it was Al P. The guys called him back to the bedroom.

Al looked at Jacob, then at Casey and Champa, and was noticeably shocked. "Jesus! What happened to him? Is he gonna be all right?"

"Yeah, but we may be fucked unless you can figure out his tech. Come out here." Casey led him and Champa to the living room and out of earshot from the doc. Casey didn't trust the doc not to spill his business on a bender.

"You've been over here regularly, do you feel you know how to work this shit?" Casey looked at Al, who instantly knew what was at stake.

"Shit, I've watched him a hundred times and know how to go over the material, but if you're talking about putting it on the Net, I can't do that."

Casey looked at his watch; it was 11:30 A.M. Time was evaporating.

"Okay, Al, I want you and Champa to start goin' through the conversations from this morning till right now, and lemme know what's being said." Casey looked at Champa and continued his train of thought. "I'm gonna check on Jacob once more. He told me he had everything ready to launch, I just need him alert long enough to tell us how to do it."

He went into the bedroom and started peppering the doc with questions about his patient. But the bottom line was that he couldn't give Casey any kind of definitive answer on when Jacob would be in better shape. Casey looked out the bedroom window; it was still raining like mad. From the other room, he heard Champa call for him as the sound of rolling thunder filled the air.

"Case, you got to see this."

Casey walked out, closing the bedroom door behind him. He walked into the living room, where Al was wearing headphones and Champa was reading papers being spit out by the printer.

"Dude, five-oh is all over this shit! They're casting a net over the whole crew to find you. Mick, Rich, Sean E Sean, the Garcia brothers, and me!" Champa said.

"Exactly what do you mean?"

"I mean they're looking to pick everyone up for questioning."

"Fuck! I gotta unleash this video and audio now or we're all done!"

"Even that may not be enough," said Champa.

"*What?*"

"If they get some of the guys, they can hold them overnight and not charge 'em. If that happens, we'll lose out on this job. We need *all* our manpower free and clear."

"Call Sean and Mick and tell 'em to lay low. I'll call the Garcia boys and Rich."

In the next few minutes, Casey and Champa made calls to all the guys and told them to get into hiding fast, and if all went according to plan, shit would blow over tonight. Naturally, this sent a shock wave through the crew. There were a ton of questions from everybody, and no time to answer them. Casey and Champa just told them to sit tight and trust that all this drama would be worked out. After the calls went out, Casey went back to the bedroom to have a conversation with the doc.

"I need him up and conscious, Doc."

"I'm doing the best I can. I'm not a—"

"*Save that shit!* You need to start working overtime on this problem right now! Putting ice on his balls, giving him shots and IVs is not getting results! *Now, what else can be done?*"

Champa walked in the room when he heard the shouting and stood behind Casey, glaring at the doc. The doc was peering over his reading glasses and calmly looking at Casey. He then reached into his bag and pulled out something that looked like a long white pill about an inch and a half long.

"I hesitate doing this, as it may cause a seizure," the doc said as he took off his reading glasses.

As the doc spoke, Jacob started showing more signs of life.

Casey went to the side of his bed and started talking to him. "Jacob, it's Casey. I need you to wake up, brotha, it's game time, man. We need to do this right now, so I need you to pull it together, my man."

Jacob's eyes fluttered open and he started talking, but his words were all slurred. They couldn't make out what he was saying until he said, "My dick feels . . . frozen?"

The doc removed the bags from his crotch and under his arms. As he did, Jacob let out a yelp and twitched a little. He looked like he was waking up from a bad dream, but Casey could see his eyes focusing.

"Man, I feel totally stoned."

"Jacob, look at me, it's Crush. We need to set shit off *now*, you understand what I'm saying?" Crush was about a foot from his face, trying to get Jacob to look at him. He gave Champa a head jerk to come over. "Pick him up, we gonna take him into the living room." The guys locked their arms under Jacob's knees and behind his back and carried him into the other room while the doc held the IV bag over his head.

"Jacob, concentrate. Tell Al what to do. How does he launch everything?"

"Casey . . . I think I'm gonna throw up."

"Later, Jacob, right now you gotta tell Al how to launch every-thing," Casey said impatiently, his arms starting to burn from holding the hacker's big ass.

"Open . . . the hard drive . . . and go into the folder . . . called 'Surprise.'"

Al selected the hard drive and opened it, then double-clicked the folder called "Surprise." The folder opened, and a message popped up, demanding a password.

"What's the password, Jacob?"

His words slurring, Jacob gave the password: "90347G09753RE0372."

Al P. grabbed a pen, quickly wrote it down, then typed it in and hit the Enter key. An error tone promptly sounded, and a message popped up to confirm it hadn't been entered correctly. He tried it again and got the same result. This time the message told him he had one more chance, or the folder would be destroyed. Al was about to type it in again when Casey stopped him.

"Hold up." He turned to the hacker. "Jacob, that's not the pass-word. It's not working. I need you to concentrate, what's the pass-word?"

"Shit, uh . . . try it again, but you need to have caps lock on."

"Are you sure, Jacob? We only got one more shot at this," Casey said.

Jacob nodded and Casey told Al to try it. Al hit caps lock, reen-tered the password, and clicked Enter. The folder opened. There were two files in the folder; one was named "Launch"; the other, "Tracker." Casey and Champa laid Jacob on the couch and went back to the computer.

"Okay, double-click it, Al." Casey looked at his watch; it was 12:18 P.M.

Al double-clicked it, and a shitload of dialog boxes opened up all over the window with status bars. On top of the dialog boxes were the names of social Web sites, news sites, the governor's, mayor's, and police chief's names, as well as video-sharing sites. All the blue status bars were creeping along; then, minutes later, messages started popping up, saying that the specific files had been successfully uploaded. In total, eighteen files had been uploaded onto 234 Web sites.

Champa looked at Casey. "Is that it?"

Casey looked back at Jacob, who was passed out on the couch in his boxers, and then back at Champa. "Yeah, I think so. Al, open the 'Tracker' file."

When Al opened the file, it took up the whole screen and had columns that showed how many views what files were getting in real time. It also showed what news outlets were viewing it. The social network sites reacted first; it was initially slow, but a half hour later, it started picking up speed. An hour after that, it was on fire with over twenty-one thousand views. But so far, only two out of the twenty news sites had picked it up, which caused Casey a bit of concern. It was only 1:30 P.M., however, and he figured things should really pick up around 2 P.M.

Champa and the doc had moved Jacob back into the bedroom; then the doc left. He said that there was nothing left for him to do, and that Jacob should be noticeably better very soon. Case broke him off a G and made sure he understood to keep his trap shut about what he'd seen and heard or suffer the consequences.

After the doc left, Casey went back to monitoring things with Al P. The general dialogue they heard from the cops was that they couldn't find any of Casey's crew. On one call Casey listened to, he heard Fordham connect the dots and say that it seemed too coincidental that all these guys had disappeared at the same time. Because Petrosian no longer rocked a cell phone, Fordham had his guys looking for him as well.

A little after 2 P.M., just as Jacob had predicted, all hell broke loose. All the news sites had reviewed the material multiple times, and the cumulative views of the videos skyrocketed to well over a million. A half hour later, news Web sites started running stories about the videos, and then it broke on CNN. Casey, Champa, and Al sat transfixed in front of the TV as the network reported on the treasure trove of police corruption that had been released anonymously on the Internet:

"Good afternoon, this is Wilson Koster, with today's top stories. Eighteen shocking videos were released over the Internet earlier today, detailing widespread corruption in the New York City Police Department, mostly in the Organized Crime Control Bureau. The videos contained taped phone conversations and video of detectives bragging about their own criminal activity. The crimes they inadvertently confessed to range from ticket fixing, narcotic trafficking, and, in two cases, the murder of two people. Mentioned by name in some of these illegal dealings is Chief Sergeant John Fordham, currently in charge of the OCCB. So far, the mayor's office and the chief of police have declined to say anything except that these matters are currently under investigation. We're going to play some of the videos right now, but warn you that the language and some of the images can be quite harsh and disturbing. Also, please note we are still looking into the validity of these videos, but from what we can tell so far, they are legitimate, in several cases taken from the officers' own in-car cameras."

The network played three videos with commentary interspersed between each one. The first was of two detectives talking about killing a drug dealer and his girlfriend in Queens, the next was of Fordham talking about getting payoffs and framing Lomax, and the last one was of the two cops beating and Tasering a black kid they'd picked up. Casey stared at the screen with a satisfied smile. *Fuck you muthafucka, payback's a bitch!*

The guys channel-surfed other twenty-four-hour news networks that were covering the story as well. Casey had Al pull up the screen that tracked the locations of the detectives; they were all at Puzzle Towers. With that, he breathed a sigh of relief; he had those muthafuckas on the run.

Casey turned around and saw Jacob gingerly exit his room with a robe and slippers on. He looked a lot better, which wasn't saying much.

"You operational, man?"

"Yeah, barely." Jacob scratched his head as he noticed the news reports. "Do I remember correctly that you launched everything?"

"Take a look," Casey said as he pointed to the TV.

Jacob took a closer look at the TV and the computer screen and examined the stats.

"Whoa, this shit is taking off. We're trending huge on every network." Jacob motioned for Al to get up and got into his seat and started typing like mad. While Jacob got back in play, Casey called Shin.

"Shin, you been watching the news?"

"Yeah, insanely great, right? I told the guys to tune in but not to brag on the shit. 'Our anonymity is the only way we can keep breathin'.'"

"Good man, now hit up Sean E Sean and get a progress report."

"Did that. He's got the cars, badges, and lights. Three of the cars are tan, and one of 'em's white."

"Okay, bet. All the guys are cool, right?"

"Yeah, everyone's on deck."

Casey hung up and watched all the action unwind. At 6:30 P.M., the mayor and chief of police gave a press conference that was carried live on every network. Casey wished Mack D knew about this shit—he'd be laughing his ass off. Both the mayor and the police chief had serious looks on their faces. The mayor stepped to the podium first.

"Today a series of videos were released that show illegal behavior and recorded conversations about criminal activities by some detectives in the Organized Crime Control Bureau. This is extremely troubling, and I fully support the police chief as he launches a detailed investigation into these matters. This is something that I take very seriously, as does the police chief, and we will not rest until it is resolved."

Then the mayor turned the mic over to the police chief.

"As the mayor said, I have an investigation under way, and will personally see to it that justice is served. The New York City Police Department has men and women who do a great job for the city, and I think it's important that we all remember that, and not let the actions of a few taint the hard work and efforts of the majority of police officers. Those personnel in question have been put on immediate leave until the incidents of lawbreaking and misconduct can be fully investigated."

After their speeches, the mayor and police chief were asked a ton of questions by the rabid press pool.

"Do you know who submitted the videos and audio recordings, Mr. Mayor?"

"No, I do not, but it should be noted that what they did was illegal, and if caught, they will be prosecuted to the fullest extent of the law."

"Chief, how many officers have been put on mandatory leave?"

"In total, nineteen."

At this point, the mayor's press secretary stepped in and said there would be no more questions.

Casey told Jacob to turn down the volume of the TV and addressed the room. "Champa, find a handyman to fix this door ASAP. Al, I want you to stay here and monitor this shit for the next twenty-four hours with Jacob."

Before Casey left, he told Champa to have the guys meet him at the office at 8 P.M. for a final briefing.

19

When Casey walked into the room, all the guys rose and applauded. Everyone had shit-eatin' grins on and wanted to give props to the brotha who'd put the pigs on blast like no one had ever done or was able to do. Everyone in the hood was talking about how "the man" had been checkmated. It was the first time since the Rodney King scandal that someone had put the cops on front street, and it was sweet.

Casey sat at the head of the table and began to speak. "I appreciate that, guys. Pullin' that shit off took a lotta work and a bit a chedda, but as you can see, it paid off."

"Hell yeah, it did!" Mick said, making the rest of the room laugh.

"I don't know how long we'll be able to keep it up, but I can tell you that this high-tech shit is our future, and that ain't no joke. I gotta give major props to Champa and Shin—no man's a one-man show, and I'm no different."

All the men around the table nodded and looked at the other guys, giving them props. Then Casey got down to business and laid out the master plan for tomorrow's heist. At the end of it, he dropped his bomb: "After we stash the cars, we can definitely expect gunplay."

The whole room was taken aback. Everyone stared at Casey for a second; then they all started asking questions. Casey stayed silent, waiting for everyone to chill out, then broke down the conversation he'd heard between Fordham and Petrosian. "Now that Fordham's in the mix, that may negate the possibility of drama, but I ain't betting on that. I suggest we posse up to make sure it's an unfair fight. We will need to be covert because we don't want to draw attention."

Casey turned to Mick, who was stroking his goatee, deep in thought. Mick had the most muscle out of everyone in the crew because of the business he was in. He even had a few brothas that were ex-military.

"Mick, you got eight guys that can be on building tops and on the ground patrolling shit on the DL?"

"Without a doubt, I can have them scout it out tonight and get them posted up at first light," Mick said.

"I got a question, Case," Hen Gee said. "I'm looking at this whole thing from ten thousand feet up, and somethin' ain't sittin' right."

"Speak on it."

"Well, Petrosian ain't known for boostin', just slangin' shit and importin' girls, right? So why he doin' this all of a sudden? Just hear me out—he's already gettin' broke off about what he'd make, so why'd he try shit now? I mean, why risk getting himself and his crew shot? Why inherit the extra headache of selling and transporting the cars? It don't make sense."

The same thing had been gnawing at Casey as well, but as he listened to Hen Gee, a lightbulb went off in his head. "I'm onna same page, till now I didn't get it, either. I think this is about a lot more than just cars."

Big Rich read Casey's mind and blurted out, "This muthafucka's smugglin' dope in these rides!"

Casey nodded. "Yup, Mariano or somebody close to him has to be part of this as well. My guess is Alek's got someone in customs turning a blind eye. Maybe that's how Fordham is tied into all of this."

Casey's phone vibrated with a text message from Jacob, asking him to get back to him ASAP. "I want you guys to chop this up more, I got to talk to my intel man real quick."

Casey hustled down the hall and went into his office and initiated a video chat. Jacob popped up on the screen with Al P. in the background.

Al spoke first. "Crush, we noticed the phones weren't movin' anymore. We went and looked at the transcripts of what was goin' down. On top of the police chief losing his shit with those guys, he also had 'em turn in their badges, service revolvers, and phones!"

Casey sat back in his chair, stared at the screen, and digested this new information. In case there was any doubt, Jacob spelled it out. "Crush, we're blind to what these cats are doin' and sayin'."

The playing field was now level and the odds were even. This news was a mind fuck. In the past, Casey'd never known what the pigs were doin', but he'd quickly got used to knowin' everything and bein' able to plan accordingly. Now that that advantage was gone, he felt totally fucked.

Casey rocked back and forth in his office chair, thinking. "We got Fordham and everyone else's address, right?"

"Yeah?"

"Are there any cameras in Fordham's area we can tap into?"

Jacob started typing. "There's a camera in his garage . . . lobby . . . across the street in a laundrymat and . . . in the Sub King restaurant. Let me see if I can get access for his two building cameras."

"Al, I want you to go to his building and try and hijack his personal phone."

Al's head jerked back in surprise and he was about to protest before Casey cut him off. "Don't go pussy on me right now, Al. All I need you to do is go to his building, stand outside his apartment, and jack into his phone. With any luck, maybe some of his guys'll be there, and you can hijack their personal cells also."

"Casey, goddamn! I done everythin' you asked me to, and now you got me puttin' my head right in the muthafuckin' lion's mouth!" Al paced in the background, panic on his face. "I'm not like you and Champa, man. I don't do that balls-to-the-wall, high-wire shit for a livin'! What if he's got a doorman? How am I gonna get in? What if he comes out and catches me? I mean that mutha-fucka's gotta be stressed out, he'll kill a nigga in a second if he thinks he's being played. I can't do it man, it's too big of a—"

"Goddamnit, quit crying like a fuckin' stuck pig! When I tell you to do something, you fuckin' do it! Use your head, for Christ sakes! get fuckin' creative! I don't care how the fuck you do it, just get—it—done!"

Casey could tell both guys on the other end were scared shitless when he let go his fury. Casey knew Al had a point; sure, it was risky, but he hated excuses and defeatists. He also understood he needed to keep a cool head, or nothing would go according to plan. In fact, things would probably just get more chaotic. Composing himself, he went into crime mode to work the problem.

"Okay, this is what you'll do. Order some sandwiches for pickup from the Sub King. Then cross the street and tell the doorman you're making a delivery to Fordham's apartment. When you get to his floor, try and tag him up. If he comes out, pretend you're look-ing for the apartment next to his. After you lock in his phones, toss the sandwiches down the trash chute and get the fuck out of there."

Al sat and digested what Casey said before he responded. "Okay, that's a good plan, but what if—?"

"Just figure it out, Al—I gave you the plan, now it's on you. Don't fucking blow it. Oh, and after you're done, get back to Jacob's, I'ma need you there for the next twenty-four hours. Jacob, make sure you get him up to speed on your tech. In case you have a relapse, I need someone that can step into your shoes already on deck. Shin'll be there in ten minutes to take you to Fordham's, Al, so be waitin' out front."

Casey closed the lid of his computer so he wouldn't have to hear any more of Al's whining. Sending him in like that was precarious, but it was a card that needed to be played. Seeing him almost go to pieces didn't inspire a lot of confidence, and Casey didn't want him taking on this mission in a half-assed kind of way.

He texted Shin to come to his office. When his captain arrived, Casey laid out the situation and said that he needed him to make sure Al delivered. Unlike Al, Shin was gung ho. He also said that if for some reason Al was caught, it would be on Shin to handle the loose ends.

"I need some edification on 'handle the loose ends,' Crush."

"By no means can Al be arrested or taken in. If that happens, he'll be interrogated, and *we* can't trust that he wouldn't spill the beans. That guy tends to get jumpy, and when he does, he runs off at the mouth. Do you know what I'm saying?"

"Okay . . . wow."

"Shin, if he spills the beans, we *all* go down. He's not like you or Champa, he's an independent contractor. He's not loyal to the crew, and I cannot have any loose ends that might sink this ship."

"I hear ya, Crush, but I know he'll hold his water. I've been hanging with the dude through all this, and he respects and fears you. I know he wouldn't cross you—us, like that. Look, you the boss, and what you say goes. I just wanted to put that out there."

Casey respected Shin for speaking his mind. He didn't want any puppets or yes-men in his crew. In hindsight, he recognized that Rono was that type of cat who would always say yes and agree to everything while secretly talkin' shit out of earshot and simultaneously plotting to stab him in the back. Casey took a deep breath and let it out. He could either dominate or empower Shin; he chose the latter.

"Okay, Shin. It's your call. It's on your shoulders."

"Cool, I'll take his temperature as we drive there, and if I think he ain't truly down or if shit goes south, I'll do what needs to be done."

"Okay, move out, and call me on the burner after it's done."

The men bumped fists, and as Casey walked back to the conference room, he got another text, this one from Carla:

They offered me the gig in Miami. I need a change of scenery, so I'm taking it. Please give me my space. Don't make this harder than it already is. xoCarla.

Casey felt his stomach tighten as he read the text. Carla wasn't the type to play games; this wasn't a ploy to get attention, this was her saying good-bye, at least for a while. He didn't want to accept it, but he knew he was a hard sell under the best of circumstances. This time tomorrow, he could either be in jail or dead. He didn't regret getting involved with Carla; he just wished it could have worked out. Crime was his life, and like Mick's brother-in-law, he couldn't shake his addiction, no matter what the cost.

Casey slipped his cell in his pocket as he rose to walk into the conference room and let everyone know the latest development and his plan to deal with it. The news made a lot of the guys uneasy, and he reminded them that up until now this was the only time they'd ever had this type of intel. In the past, they'd always taken calculated risks and operated blind.

Sean E Sean sat back in his seat, pulled out the natty chew-stick from his mouth, and addressed everyone. "If shit goes down, then so be it. We all know how the game is played. Right now, my only concern is the rides—if they get shot up, there goes the loot from the Chinaman!"

"That's a good point, which is why Petrosian has to be handled when the trucks get to the warehouse, before the cars are unloaded," Casey said as he turned to Mick. "Mick, I'ma need your shooters to pop them from the rooftops military-style. Is that a problem?"

"Not at all, my cats can do it quick and easy. I'll just need to get them the descriptions."

"Okay, cool. I realize the degree of difficulty has just been raised on this gig, so if anyone's lookin' to back out, now's the time to speak up."

Casey looked at everyone's faces; none of the guys seemed anything but stone-cold confident.

"Okay, cool, then back to business. Everyone needs to meet at the warehouse at five A.M. tomorrow. Champa, I'ma need you to pick me up at my crib so I can roll with you. Mick, Hen, and E, go to Sean's spot and y'all drive the cars to the warehouse. From there, we'll bail out. Any questions?"

Casey surveyed the room and checked with each guy to make sure they were cool. This was by far the biggest job he'd ever pulled, the biggest payday, and with the most at stake. The meeting broke up, and everyone went their separate ways, knowing what had to be done. Casey pulled Champa aside and told him to be at his crib at 4:45 A.M. sharp.

When Casey got home, he was hoping that Carla would be there, but the place was empty. She was done. It was probably for the best; any kind of distraction right now was not a good thing. Casey kept waiting for Shin to call, but heard nothing until just after midnight, when his burner buzzed.

"What up?"

"No luck. We went there and he wasn't in his spot."

"Well, what the fuck happened?"

"We got here, and Al did everything according to plan. There was no doorman, so I went up, too, and peeped shit through the stairwell while he did his thing. He tried for twenty minutes, but came up empty. Either Fordham's out, or he doesn't have a phone on in that crib. We've been waiting outside for the last three hours. Shall we just lay up and see if he shows or leave in the A.M.?"

"Nah, go home. I need you and Al at the warehouse tomorrow at five A.M. Make sure he brings a piece with him and that he knows there might be drama."

Casey hung up the phone and looked out his window. Outside, it was still sprinkling. He set the alarm on his phone for 4 A.M. and tried to get some kind of sleep.

Casey woke up a minute before his alarm would have gone off. Grabbing his phone, he canceled the alert. He hated the annoying sound—it reminded him of the alarms in the joint. Anxious to get shit started, he jumped out of bed. He was always a little hyped on game day.

He took a shower, got dressed, and went to his closet to check his arsenal. The back of his closet had a secret panel that unlocked with a magnet. Inside was a sawed-off, chrome-plated Remington 12-gauge pump shotgun, an AK-47, and various pistols. He grabbed his Glock 17 and the SIG Sauer P290 Two-Tone Sub-Compact 9 millimeter with integral laser sight, checking both pistols to make sure they were fully loaded. He glanced down to the street below to see if the detective's car was there, but it was all clear. Champa was on time for once, so Casey went out to meet him.

Champa's silver Aston Martin looked like a sleek beast on the wet streets, and he made it roar when they took off. It was still dark outside, with a light rain coming down and minimal traffic. For most of the ride, they both listened to the radio without speaking. Crush had received a text from Sean E Sean that he and the other guys had the fake cop cars and were in motion. Shin also confirmed that Al P. would be there, as well as the other cats. Casey hadn't heard from Petrosian the day before, which struck him as odd, but he knew where the meet-up was, so he wasn't gonna trip 'bout it.

A couple blocks from the warehouse, Champa hit a nasty pot-hole that had been hidden by water. They checked the damage after they pulled in; the rim was bent a little, but it didn't look like the tire was leaking. Still, it was enough to put Champa in a sour mood. He loved that car and always kept it in pristine condition.

Casey saw Petrosian's S600 Mercedes-Benz and a gunmetal gray Hummer H2 behind him and waved them into the ware-house. The rest of the guys were already there, and Sean and the others would be arriving momentarily. Casey took Mick aside for a private conversation before Petrosian stepped out of his ride.

"Your guys in place?"

"Yeah, four on the roof here, two on the roof across the street, and the other two are in the alley."

"Those guys know who our people are?"

"Yeah, it's my regular crew, they ain't gonna mistake any iden-tities."

Petrosian got out of his ride along with his two guys, and Casey made the introductions. All of Casey's guys were cool. They didn't put on attitude or a hard face; instead they all stayed mellow. The plan was to make Petrosian believe everything was good before they rocked him to sleep. Sean pulled up in the stolen Altimas with the other guys and then there was another round of introduc-tions. Casey checked the time—it was 5:45 A.M., they would need to move out in five minutes.

The plan was for Shin, Al, and Champa to be in one car, and ghost the two trucks as soon as they left the port, while Petrosian and Casey followed them, updating the rest of the guys on their ETA. The meeting place was thirty miles down the freeway, just before the Pennsylvania Avenue exit. There they'd make the trucks pull over, gaffle up the guys and take the transports to the ware-house, then unload them. The Pennsylvania Avenue exit was just two miles from the warehouse, meaning they wouldn't be out in the open with the cars for more than ten minutes max. Casey ran over the plan again to make sure everyone was clear on what was about to go down. No one had any questions.

They got to Port Authority just before 7 A.M., pulled into a dusty lot where Port Street met Corbin Road, and waited. Based on Champa's intel, they knew there'd be two six-car enclosed trailers pulled by semis. Now it was a waiting game.

Casey sat in silence, his strong fingers tapping the steering wheel. He felt the weight of his P290 in his jacket pocket as he looked for cops or anything suspicious.

"What time you think these transports will pull out?" Petrosian asked as he looked out his window.

"If the intel is right, thirty minutes or so. It takes 'em that long to load the cars into the transports."

"So, you think we'll be at the warehouse and unloaded by when?"

Casey was immediately suspicious of these types of questions, even though Petrosian had the right to ask. "With traffic and everything else, it will take about forty-five minutes to get to the warehouse; once there, we should have everything safely unloaded and the trucks ditched by eleven thirty or noon at the latest. Why, you got an appointment somewhere?" Casey fired back, trying to gauge the man behind his Armani sunglasses.

"Yeah, actually, my son's got a game at two P.M. today, and I never miss seeing him play. Growing up in Armenia, we never played basketball, or even knew it existed." He chuckled, then turned to look at Casey. "My kid can't get enough of it. He doesn't know it yet, but I got two floor seats to the Knicks game on Saturday."

Eyes narrowed, Casey looked at Petrosian, wishing he would shut the fuck up about his kid. Was this a plan to get into his head and put him off balance so he might hesitate in taking him out? Was this muthafucka for real?

"Matter of fact, this will be his first professional game he's ever seen. It's going to blow his mind—"

"You know what, I'm glad you got the rest of your day and week planned out, but right now, I wanna focus on this job, so let's cut the small talk, 'kay?" Casey said.

Petrosian shot him an expressionless look before bending his head down and remaining quiet. Taking his own boy to basketball games and attending events at school were things Casey had never gotten the chance to do. He was always too busy making scratch and keeping one step ahead of the law, and by the time it would have really mattered, he was behind bars. If Petrosian really valued his relationship with his boy, he should have thought twice about his line of work. Casey hadn't, and had paid the price. Back in the day, he was too damn cocksure and thought he could balance it all, but that had proved to be a disastrously wrong course of action.

The transports finally appeared, like two huge dinosaurs lumbering out of the port gates. They reached the corner, took a wide turn, and started their trip to the freeway. In the front seat of each cab were two men. Casey had expected only one driver per truck. *Okay, not good, but that can be handled.* The one bit of good news was there didn't look to be a security escort at all, but as he watched the trucks, something else hit him like a ton of bricks and made him start to sweat. *Shit!* His mind went into overdrive, and he started working the problem. He could feel Petrosian looking at him, but if the Armenian suspected anything, he didn't say it. After ten minutes of dissecting the problem, he pulled out his phone and dialed Champa.

"Champa."

"Yeah, Case?"

"Are all the phones handled?"

"All except one, and Shin and Al are seconds from gettin' it."

"Okay, tell me when it's good."

Casey waited, hearing Shin and Al talking back and forth to see if either one had a lock. In the background, he heard Al say,

"Got it, we good, yo." He then heard Shin call Jacob for confirmation.

"Crush, they're all locked in. We won't shut 'em down until we hear from you."

"Okay. Look, we got an issue."

"We do?"

"Those trucks don't have enough clearance to turn onto Alabama, they're too damn big."

"Shit . . . you're right. Fuck!"

"This is what we gonna do. Matter of fact, put me on speaker so Shin and Al can hear this, too."

"Okay, you're on."

"So, those trucks are way too big to be able to make the turn onto Alabama—that street's only two lanes. Here's the new plan: We're gonna flash the badges as planned and pull 'em both over. Champa, Shin, Alek, and me'll approach the trucks and do our thing. Champa and Shin will stay in the cab with the drivers and we'll move the other passengers into our cars and lay 'em down in the backseat foot wells. We'll all exit at Pennsylvania Avenue, then take the first left on Seaview and park in the middle of the block. Then we will have to unload the cars and drive them to the warehouse."

"Uhhhhh, okay, what about the transports and the truck drivers?" Champa asked.

"We're gonna leave them and these cars there. We got twelve guys total, so we got enough drivers for the cars, but we're not gonna be able to dump the transports."

"Okay, that'll work. Hell, I actually like it better than the other plan," Champa said.

"I'll call Sean and the Garcias. Champa, you call Mick and Big Rich and let 'em know what's up."

Casey hung up the phone and took a deep breath. He knew Petrosian would have something to say about this last-minute shit.

"So much for careful planning, eh?" Petrosian said smugly.

"Shit happens, dude—it's how you handle it that matters."

"Aren't you concerned about unloading the cars in the open? That's a lot of potential witnesses, Casey."

"Maybe, the south side of that street is a grass field, the other side is a five-story apartment building with views obstructed by the trees along that street. If you have a better idea, you best speak on it right now, Alek."

Petrosian said nothing and looked out his window. Casey picked up his phone and told Sean and the Garcias what was up while Petrosian called his men and clued them in. Petrosian spoke in Armenian, but Casey could tell by his tone he was talking shit. The change in plan put a big wrinkle into taking out the Armenians outside the warehouse. Casey wasn't at liberty to talk to his men and regroup, but he knew they'd realize this. Whatever happened at the warehouse would have to be on the fly.

Fifteen minutes later, they were at the checkpoint. Shin and Al P. disabled the drivers' phones, then pulled up next to the semis, where Shin flashed his fake detective's badge and had the trucks pull over. The drivers seemed unconcerned, until they saw the 9-millimeter pistols inches from their faces and realized they were getting jacked. Traffic whizzed by the whole scene, clueless that a hijacking was going down. All the guys wore sunglasses and baseball caps, not the best disguise, but sufficient. The two passengers were put in the backseats of the Altimas and told to lie down or get shot. Shin and Champa jumped in next to the drivers and immediately plugged the GPS Tracker Defense units into the cigarette lighters. The whole thing took less than five minutes. So far, so good.

The trucks followed Casey as he drove another mile to the Pennsylvania exit; from there it was only a block to Seaview Avenue, where they made a left. Toward the middle of the block, they spotted the rest of the crew waiting. Now it was just a race against the clock.

As soon as the trucks were parked, their hydraulic lift gate system started to open. Sean, Mick, and Rich ran into the back of the first transport, opened the doors of the individual cars, and turned them over, and plugged in the GPS blockers. The enclosed trailers echoed and rumbled from the engines of the high-performance vehicles. As the cars eased out, Casey couldn't help but be mesmerized; this was car porn at its best.

The same thing was happening in the second transport. A few cars slowed as they passed because it wasn't every day that you saw whips like these in the wild. Every time Casey flashed his fake badge, and the cars would reluctantly move on. Shin made sure everyone had popped in their GPS Tracker Defense units, and then the first six cars were off. That left Petrosian, Champa, Shin, Al P., and the Garcia brothers to handle the rest.

The trucks had three upper hydraulic racks that held the cars. Those were operated using a key at the mouth of the back of the transports. After they unloaded the first three cars from transport one, they drove two of the fake cop cars inside the transport with the truck drivers in the back while transport two was being unloaded. The Garcia brothers duct-taped the drivers' mouths and put black bags over their heads. They also took all of their licenses and let them know that they would pay them all a visit if any shit went down. The drivers got the message loud and clear. Big E and Hen gave them all a hard sock in the head to bring home their point. Nothing like a little physical violence to make sure niggas is paying attention! The Garcias and Shin closed the back of the first transport while the last of the other three cars were being unloaded, then bailed out.

Casey let it be known during all this that he was driving the Bugatti back. He got a text from Mick that they'd made it back with no sweat. That just left Champa, Petrosian, and Casey to wrap things up. Casey was tempted to handle Petrosian right then and there, but he needed the third car driven back. He didn't know how or when shit was gonna go down, but he knew it was imminent.

They loaded Sean's other two cars in the back and closed up the transport. Petrosian and Champa jumped in their cars and sped off while Casey jumped into the black and orange Bugatti super car. He inserted the key by the side of his door and felt the diffuser flap close, the rear spoiler retract, and the car sink closer to the road like a crouching tiger. The Bugatti had that new car smell and reeked of power and performance. He put it into gear and hit the gas. The 16-cylinder, 1,001 horsepowered vehicle rocketed down the street, sounding more like a jet than a car. Eight seconds and a quarter of a mile later, he was doing 140 miles per hour, but had to immediately slow it down to make a right. From there, Louisiana Avenue was a straight mile, which he ripped down in seconds. *This shit is fucking addicting!* Even on the wet streets, the car handled perfectly. Casey figured it took him about three minutes to get to the warehouse. When he arrived, all the guys were waiting, staring at the cars. After he pulled in, the doors quickly closed behind him. *Back to business.*

Casey checked his phone; it was ten after eleven. "When I drove down this street and I didn't see anyone, was that the same for everyone?"

All the guys nodded. Casey wouldn't really know if there was gonna be drama for a minute. Anything was possible; as soon as Petrosian bounced to his kid's "basketball game," the place could be crawling with cops. He wasn't gonna relax till he handed the cars over to the Chinaman's contact and had the loot.

Casey walked over to Al and told him to activate the drivers' phones and have Jacob monitor them. He wanted to know when they got picked up and what they'd be saying to the cops. Next on his agenda would be to take out Petrosian. As he walked to the Armenian, all Casey's guys had that knowing look that shit was about to go down.

Petrosian came over to him with a smile and a satisfied look on his face, his cell phone out. The man was completely clueless that he was about to eat lead. "Nice work, Casey, you handled this very

well. By the way, a friend of mine would like to congratulate you."
Petrosian handed the phone to Casey.

What the fuck? Casey's face screwed up as he took the cell. The
voice on the other end was unmistakable and totally unexpected.

"Hello, fuck face, thanks for doing my dirty work!"

Casey clenched his teeth as he heard Fordham's arrogant voice
on the other end. He yanked his piece and told Petrosian and his
boys to get on their knees. Which the Armenian did with a smile.

"I got my 9 pointed at your partner's face, muthafucka. Any last
words you want me to relay, pig?"

"Well, now, isn't that a coincidence—'cause I got my .357 pointed
at a pretty little nigger bitch. Can you guess who I'm talking about,
Crush?"

20

The moment Casey drew down on Petrosian, his whole crew pulled their gats as well. Casey's worst nightmare was coming true. The detectives must have told Fordham about meeting Carla at the diner and got the rundown on her. When he couldn't arrest Casey, this must have been his Plan B. In the background, he could hear Carla crying and screaming his name.

Fuck! Casey couldn't let his cool crack under this pressure or he'd be that bastard's puppet—he had to play hard all the way to the end. They both had something the other wanted, and Casey knew it was gonna be a winner-take-all day.

"Ain't you got enough trouble to be adding to it by pissin' me off, Fordham?"

"Wow, that's pretty tough talk, Casey! Are you saying you don't want to play ball? Maybe I should have a little fun with your lady, then call you back later, see if you changed your mind."

"Fuck you! Let's get to negotiatin'—that's what this really is all about."

"That's what I like to hear! Now, this is the only deal on the table, there ain't no other, so listen up: Alek and his two guys are gonna unload the cargo from those cars. Once they're done, you can keep the fuckin' cars. When he and the dope are safely back to me, I'll let your bitch go."

"Now, you listen carefully, muthafucka, you're dead and you don't even know it! You'll get your dope when my girl is safe. Just tell me where we're doing the exchange or go fuck yourself!"

Fordham laughed manically. "Okay, gangsta, you wanna play it like that, I'm game. Give the phone back to Alek."

Casey tossed the phone to Petrosian, who got up, confirmed everything, and hung up. Casey looked at his guys—all had their pistols drawn and had overheard enough of the conversation to know what was going down.

Petrosian smiled at Casey as he started walking to the cars. "The dope's under the floorboards, in the trunks, and in front of the passenger seats."

Casey looked at his guys and told them to start unloading the cars. The H was hidden under the carpet; whoever did the packing had done a excellent job of regluing the carpet so it wouldn't be detected. The heroin was in plastic bags about two inches thick. After thirty minutes of going through all the cars, a three-foot-by-three-foot pile of heroin stood in the middle of the floor.

"Da-yamn, that's worth twenty mil easy," Mick said as he stood next to Casey. "If it's cut correctly, maybe twice that."

Casey nodded, his mind working overtime to get them all out of this alive. Fordham's ass in the hot seat meant this haul was his last. If he had an ounce of brains, he was gonna cash out, get lost, and never be seen or heard from again.

Casey instructed the guys to load it all into Champa's car. Once the drugs were secure, Casey told his crew to hold down the spot.

Then he turned to Champa. "Look, brotha, this ain't your fight, so I can roll solo—"

"You carryin' twenty mil wortha China White in *my* muthafuckin' whip, and you even think I'm lettin' you go alone—nigga, please, nobody drives my shit but me!" With that, Champa walked to his car. "You comin'?"

Petrosian's S600 creeped out of the warehouse, with Casey and Champa following it. The Armenian had both of his guys hang back to make sure that they weren't followed. Champa's Aston Martin ran a little low to the ground 'cause of the weight they were carrying. When his muffler scraped the ground, Casey saw Champa grit his teeth at the sound. The Armenian was a slick muthafucka; he definitely had the upper hand.

They got on the freeway and drove for twenty minutes. Casey talked through all the potential scenarios, but none of them were foolproof or sounded great to him. Casey doubted that Fordham would allow him to walk, but Petrosian, on the other hand, knew that Casey had a lot of firepower that would come for retribution if shit went wrong. Being hunted by a crew as notorious as Casey's would only end one way. And cop or no cop, Fordham would be on the top of their list. His mind went to Carla and what she must be goin' through. If she was being beaten or, worse, raped, Casey knew he would lose his shit. If they were both lucky enough to survive this, she would most certainly never speak to him again. Champa and Casey agreed on a plan that seemed the least insane and left it at that.

Petrosian's car pulled off the freeway and drove a few blocks past several single-level warehouses and then down a dead-end street for about three miles into the entrance of a junkyard.

"Turn around so you can make a fast exit. I gotta feeling this ain't gonna go smooth."

Champa whipped the car around and kept the engine running as Casey got out. With every step inside, he was flying by the seat of his pants. These sonsofbitches had already laid out a careful plan and lured his ass right into it.

He walked up to Petrosian and gave him a "what now, muthafucka?" look. Out of the shack of an office sitting behind him, Casey heard Carla's voice call his name. He turned to see Carla traumatized and shaking. Her usually perfect makeup had run down her face, and her cream-colored pantsuit was torn and dirty.

She was relieved to see him only because she was scared for her life. He didn't say anything; he just walked up to her and held her tightly, then walked her to Champa's car and put her in the front passenger seat.

He turned around to see Petrosian and Fordham standing next to each other, staring at him. All the men approached each other simultaneously.

Casey was the first to speak. "You know where it's at—speak that gibberish to your guys to unload it."

Petrosian put two fingers in his mouth and whistled for his three men to come over. He snapped something in Armenian, and as they went to the car, Champa hit the gas and sped off. Both Fordham and Petrosian freaked out and along with three goons started firing at the car as it snaked up the road, but it was no use. After emptying their guns, they turned to find Casey holding his P290 in one hand, aimed at them. And a live grenade in the other.

"You know, I didn't think that shit was gonna work. I felt fucked up taking the risk, but Champa swore you guys couldn't be trusted and called it exactly."

Both Petrosian and Fordham fumed as they looked at Casey.

"Now, I know you recognize a 9 millimeter, but do you know a genuine U.S. Army timed-fuse hand grenade when you see it? Drop your shit on the ground and kick it all towards me."

"You're fucking with the wrong guys, Casey," Petrosian said calmly.

"I agree one hundred percent, you're bad news, but I'm no picnic, either. Now, Fordham, get in the trunk of the Benz."

"Not on your fucking life. You'll have to put a bullet in me if you want me in that fucking trunk!"

"Okay," said Casey as he leveled his gun at Fordham's foot and squeezed off a round.

Fordham's foot exploded in a bright red mass of blood. He fell to the ground and howled in pain and then started cursing at Casey as he clutched what was left of his foot.

"Now, I know that has to hurt! I can shoot the other foot and work all the way up to your balls—I got plenty of ammo, so it's your choice. Get in the trunk or get ready to feel some more heat."

Fordham's face twisted in pain as he hobbled to the trunk, leaving a bloody trail and running his mouth the whole time. For once, the muthafucka was feeling the other end of the punishment that he so often delivered. This was a small payback for his career of bullshit, intimidation, and torture that he'd laid out for years. The former chief detective finally got his ass in the trunk and stared defiantly up at Casey, *still* talking shit. Casey picked up one of the empty guns and checked it out to make sure it had no more rounds. He told the guys to toss their cell phones on the ground and stomp 'em. Then he shot out the tires on Fordham's car and the other one.

"Alek, come here, I need you to do something for me."

The Armenian looked at Casey with disdain and slowly walked over. "You're making this real bad for yourself, Crush. You could have walked away with your lady and the cars, but now—"

"Save that shit, take this piece, and knock your buddy out," Casey said as he tossed the empty pistol to Petrosian.

Upon hearing that, Fordham went ape shit and started yelling and screaming at Petrosian all sorts of threats, and that he had "better not do shit!"

Petrosian's head sank and looked up at Casey and saw that there was no way of getting around it. He walked up to the trunk, and Fordham held his hands in the air and squirmed to get away from the beating that was coming.

"Put your hands down or get shot!" yelled Casey.

"You're fucking dead, Casey!" Fordham screamed, his face beet red and the veins in his neck popping out.

Casey pointed his gun at Fordham's balls.

"No, no, no, no, no! Okay, okay, okay, okay, okay," Fordham said as he bounced around the back of the trunk like a Mexican jump-

ing bean. Then he slowly lowered his hands and squeezed his eyes shut.

Lifting the piece high in the air, Petrosian quickly brought it down, giving Fordham a solid wallop. The other man let out a yelp as blood trickled from the crown of his head. The detective groaned in pain as he danced on the line of unconsciousness. Casey peered over while watching Petrosian's squad to make sure they didn't try shit.

He glanced at Alek and said, "Second time's a charm?" Without hesitation, Petrosian thumped the chief detective twice with all his might.

"Yep, that did it. You mighta even have killed 'im. NYPD *ain't* gonna appreciate that! Toss your gun in the trunk and close it."

Petrosian obliged. Casey walked up to the driver's door on the Benz and opened it. "Get in."

"You're really fucking this up, Casey. It's not too late—"

"Yeah, well, I appreciate your concern—now, buckle up, I'm on a schedule," Casey replied as he got in the backseat. After he shut the back door and put his gun up against Petrosian's head, he reached forward and ripped the rearview mirror off the windshield.

"Now, let's go back to the warehouse, and no peekin' back here unless you wanna lose an ear."

As the car pulled out, Casey settled in the backseat and placed his pistol on his lap. He carefully put the pin in the grenade, holding his breath until it was secure again. Then he pulled out his phone and dialed Champa. "Where are you?"

"Heading back your way."

"What—? Why?" Casey asked. "Where's Carla?"

"Shin met me. He's got her and is taking her back to her place. I told him to stay with her until he hears different."

"How'd he know where we were and how'd he get here so fast?"

"When all that shit was goin' down at the warehouse, Al P. hijacked Petrosian's phone, listened in, and knew exactly where we'd landed. After Petrosian's men bounced, Shin and the other guys started heading to us."

"Al fucking P. using his head, thinking on his feet. Goddamn, is the world coming to an end? How far away are you, and who's watching the cars?"

"About two blocks. Mick's boys are still in place, watching over everything."

"Okay, well, we in route to the— *Fuuuuck!*"

In the second before the crash, Casey recognized the Hummer approaching. He felt the S600 accelerate and swerve toward the large SUV, and knew the impact was imminent.

As the two cars collided, Casey's body hurled forward and hit the passenger backseat and he saw stars. He held on to his piece, even though it discharged, but the grenade fell out of his hand and bounced around the backseat.

When his vision returned, the Benz was up against the concrete divider, its rear end crushed and the driver's-side windows broken. Casey tried to get his bearings as he frantically looked for the grenade. He found it on the floor and stuffed it in his jacket pocket. Stumbling out of the car, he fell to the ground. His ears were ringing, and a sharp pain shot up his right leg that almost made him pass out. His forehead was wet, and he wiped away the blood coming from it so it wouldn't go in his eyes. He heard Petrosian yelling like a maniac in Armenian and his guys responding, but couldn't see any of them. When he stood up, he felt like someone was putting an ice pick in his head, and he fell back to the ground, screaming, *"Ah, shit!"*

In the distance, he heard a car horn blaring, then skidding tires, and a flurry of gunshots. Casey slowly got up, his leg and head throbbing. His leg was badly bruised, but it wasn't bleeding; he saw the Hummer had lost a chunk of its back end but other than that, it looked fine. The gunshots were from Champa, who was unloading at Petrosian and his men from behind the armored door of his ride. Behind him, Casey recognized the Garcia brothers' car, which whizzed by him and fishtailed to a stop a few yards away. Mick and Big Rich jumped out of the backseat as the two brothers came out of the front, guns drawn and blazing.

Seeing he was outnumbered, and with Champa to the north and the others to the south, Petrosian bailed into the building with his crew right behind him.

Champa was the first to reach Casey. "Crush, you a'ight, man?"

"Yeah—just a little dizzy, my leg's a bit fucked up, though."

"You gotta cut and a helluva bump on your head, but the cut don't look too bad," Champa said as he gave him the once-over.

Casey's other guys blew past him in hot pursuit of Petrosian and his crew. Casey's head started to clear as he stood up just in time to see a car with a doughnut for a front wheel skid to a stop a few yards away. Three of Petrosian's guys jumped out and started firing at them. Casey and Champa dived behind the Benz and returned fire. Casey's P290 went dry and he tossed it aside and started firing the Glock. He tagged one of the guys in the neck, and blood came gushing out like he was a fire hydrant. Petrosian's guys took cover after seeing that.

Champa crouch-walked to the front tire of the S600, looking for a shot before realizing he was empty. *"Crush, I'm out!"*

Casey popped his magazine out, freed nine shells from it, and gave them to Champa, who loaded his piece with military efficiency.

There was a loud *crack* behind them. Casey whirled to see one of Petrosian's crew trying to flank them and raining lead down. Casey and Champa fell to their backs and returned fire, catching the gunman twice in the chest. The slide on Casey's Glock locked back, and he cursed himself for not being more careful with his ammo. Checking on Champa, he saw his brotha sitting against the tire and grimacing as he clutched his shoulder while blood slowly oozed out. Casey tossed his empty piece aside and crawled next to him to inspect the damage.

"Jesus, you a'ight? Move your hand, lemme see."

"Feels like—it went through," Champa said, his face contorted in pain.

"Yeah, you right. How you feel?"

"It hurts like a muthafucka, but other'n that I'm good. How many are left?"

"Two more out there," Casey said as he peered over the hood of the car. He spotted the other two guys talking as they prepared to attack. Glancing back at Champa, Casey saw he was close to passing out. "Hey, man, try and hold on," Casey said as he grabbed Champa's piece.

Champa mumbled something Casey couldn't understand. He checked the piece for ammo: it had five rounds. *Fuck!* That was playing it too close. He still had the grenade, but hadn't wanted to use it yet, but necessity made it his only option.

"Hold on, buddy, once I get this sorted, I'ma get you some help." Casey pulled the pin on the grenade, let the spoon fly off, waited a second, and lobbed it World War II–style at the other guys and held his ears. Once it went off, he would charge the vehicle and cap any survivors. He could hear the other guys freak out when they saw it coming at them and waited for the blast.

But nothing happened. After five seconds passed, he knew it wasn't gonna go off. *A fuckin' dud! I don't believe this shit!*

Casey checked on Champa again and saw his eyes rolling back in his head as he slumped against the tire. He checked the man's jacket and pockets, hoping he might have an extra piece, but no dice. *Shit, we're both fucked—wait a minute—Champa's whip! The piece Hans had rigged in his ride!*

Casey glanced out quickly, locating Champa's Aston Martin about twenty feet away. He knew he couldn't think about what he was about to do; he just had to do it. He scrambled to the back of the Benz and sprinted for Champa's ride. With every step, pain shot up his leg like he was running on a knife point.

Both guys opened fire as soon as he came out, peppering the road and cars with bullets. Casey turned and squeezed off three rounds as he stumbled backwards. One of his rounds tagged a guy in the head, making him disappear behind the car. Casey lurched into the Aston Martin, falling across the driver's seat as multiple shots hit the bulletproof glass.

Casey reached over, turned the ignition key one click, and said "Düsseldorf," expecting Champa's gun to pop out of the dash. Nothing happened. He cleared his throat and very clearly and loudly said it three more times, but nothing happened. *What the fuck!* Casey hit the dash like a maniac and tried to pry it open, but it was impossible. *Champa must have changed the muthafuckin' password!*

"*Sonofabitch!*" he screamed. He dragged himself out of the car and looked over the hood. His leg hurt, but he was so amped up— his heart felt like it was beatin' a million times a minute—that it didn't matter; he was in survival mode. He could tell his opponent was behind the front passenger tire, about thirty-five feet away.

Casey slowly got up, feeling his best chance was to draw the man out and tag him, but the dude wasn't goin' for it. *Maybe he's low on shells, too?* Casey looked at Champa, whose eyes were closed, but he could see his chest move, so he knew he wasn't dead.

Petrosian's man wasn't gonna be drawn out, so Casey lay on the ground and watched under the car, waiting for an opportunity to wing him. It'd be a tough shot to make, and he'd only have one chance at it. He knew the tension would get to the dude, and it would only be a matter of time until he changed position. A few moments later, the guy shifted his stance, and a foot moved into view. Casey carefully aimed at his ankle and gently squeezed off a round. The man howled in pain, and Casey took off for Champa. At his side, he tried to bring him back around.

"*Champa, Champa, wake the fuck up! I need the password! 'Düsseldorf' ain't workin', man! Goddamnit, Champa, help me out!*"

Casey looked over the hood and saw the last dude was still sufferin', but was keepin' a keen eye on him, as evidenced by the three shots that buzzed by his head. Casey shook Champa, who was drifting in and out; his eyes were rolling back in his head as he moaned in pain.

"*Champa, come on, buddy!*" Casey shouted as he shook him.

Finally Champa mumbled something. "Rat . . . Ratti . . ."

"*Rat? Is that it? Come on, don't give up on me now, man! Is it rat? What the fuck is it!*"

Champa's eyes looked crazy, like he was stoned or something, and he was starting to drool. It didn't look like he was gonna last much longer. He needed a doctor pronto, but Casey needed that goddamn password. In the distance, he heard the pounding of gunfire in the building behind him between Petrosian and his guys.

". . . Rat . . . Ratouie . . . Ratatouille . . ."

"*Ratatouille! Is that it? Jesus muthafuckin' Christ, Champa?*" Casey screamed. He shoulda known it'd be some crazy shit like that.

Casey got up and did his suicide run one last time and heard more shots; he felt one of the shots close enough to tug his coat. He blindly shot his last round in the direction of the shooter, then tossed the gun aside. He slid next to the car like a baseball player, and searing pain went through his whole body. It was so bad, he wanted to puke and he felt light-headed, a hot flash flooding over his whole body as he started to shake. He pulled his head together and crawled into the car and uttered the password.

"Ratatouille."

And like magic, there was an electric hum and the black SIG Sauer 226 popped up. "*Thank fucking God!*" Casey snatched it, and his confidence surged; he popped the magazine out—it had a full fifteen rounds. *Yes!*

He took a deep breath and exhaled. He knew that the dude had to be in some serious pain, and that would make him pretty disoriented. Casey braced himself, then got up and started running and firing at the dude, who was taken completely off guard. Casey's first few shots missed, but the fourth and fifth ones hit him in the upper chest and put him down for good. Casey trudged over and saw that both men had checked out.

Casey ran back to Champa and checked for a pulse. It was weak, but it was there. He then followed the gunshots to his crew in the warehouse, who were still battling Petrosian and his thugs.

When he got there, he saw Mick had been shot in the leg and had his shirt tied around it as a tourniquet. The other guys looked fine. The warehouse was mostly empty except for a couple of forklifts, a large Dumpster, and a dozen or so rows of twelve-foot-high empty industrial metal shelves. A few dirty windows high on the walls provided the only light.

Hen came over and gave him the rundown. "We got Petrosian cornered, and I think his other dude is dead or wounded, but I can't confirm that." Hen pointed in the direction where he thought Petrosian was, and Casey stared hard into the gloom, but couldn't see shit.

"Okay, Champa's outside with a shoulder wound, and he's pretty fucked up; he needs a doc right now!" Casey turned to Big Rich. "Call up your guy, find out where he's at, and get him to look at Champa and Mick right away! I'll hold shit down here. I figure we only got a few minutes left till the cops come anyway."

All the guys agreed except Mick, who had scowl on his face. "All y'all niggas can bounce, but I ain't leavin' till I get that nigga that shot me!" he spat as he leaned against the wall.

"Goddamnit, Mick, I don't have time to argue with you—you need to get the fuck out of here. Hell, I don't even know if Champa's car's even drivable."

"Okay, well, I'ma roll that dice!" Mick looked defiantly at Casey, who knew it was pointless to argue with him.

"Christ, Mick—just once, I wish you wouldn't be the biggest pain in my ass! A'ight, the rest of you get the hell outta here, I'll meet you at the warehouse later."

Hen and the guys split. Now it was time to smoke Petrosian out. Casey looked at Mick again and exhaled deeeply. His boy's whole pants leg was soaked in blood; he knew that shit had to hurt.

"Petrosian, you're done, man! Give it up and come on out!" Casey shouted.

"If you want me so bad, Casey, come on in and get me! The way I see it, the cops'll be here any minute now, so every second you stay here, you get closer to going back in the joint! I'm just a citizen defending himself from a notorious criminal!"

Casey looked at Mick and said, "He's right, you know. Got any ideas?"

Mick grimaced. "Shit, not a one that don't involve both of us gettin' our asses shot off."

Casey surveyed the room and ran different scenarios; his biggest impediment was not being able to see because of the damn metal shelves. He turned to Mick, who, if he was suffering, was doing a good job of masking the pain. "Okay, I got an idea. We're gonna push this first metal shelf down, and hopefully it'll cause a domino effect and give us a better line of sight. When they start fallin', I'm gonna go after him and hope he's distracted enough for me to get a shot off. You cover me and focus on takin' down his man if he's still alive."

"That shit ain't gonna work, but fuck it, let's try it."

Casey ignored Mick's comment, and both men walked to the first metal shelf, which was about twenty feet long and four feet wide. Casey and Mick pushed on it as hard as they could. They budged it a little, but it was obvious after a minute that it wasn't gonna be as easy as he'd expected.

"Let's try rockin' it back and forth and tip it over."

"Dude, that shit'll fall back and fuckin' crush us!"

"What the fuck are you talkin' about? It's gonna work perfectly—now, come on!"

Both men started rocking the metal shelf back and forth. The metal squeaked loudly as the shelves moved slightly at first. In the back of his mind, Casey knew Mick had a point, but this was the only option he could think of. The shelves started teeter-tottering back and forth, at first just a little, but then more and more, like an unsteady giant. Each time an end would hit the cement, there was a deep *thud*. Timing it just right was key. Casey and Mick were working up a sweat, pushing the damn thing back and forth.

"This one's it, Mick, so put your back into it."

The guys pushed with all their might, but the shelf didn't tip over. Casey almost panicked, as he thought it was gonna fall on them, which it almost did. The next time around they pushed, the shelf teetered on the edge, then fell as if in slow motion, hitting the next shelf, which slowly fell, and so on. Casey started creeping toward where he thought Petrosian was as the shelves toppled over, making a thunderous racket.

As he got closer, Petrosian and his guy Vladik burst from their cover and started running at Casey and Mick, blasting away as they snaked back and forth. Casey and Mick hit the deck behind one of the fallen shelves as they fired back. Bullets ricocheted off the metal shelves as empty casings popped out of Casey's 9 millimeter like popcorn. He saw Vladik go down from a hit to the chest; he was still moving but didn't look like a threat, especially when Mick capped him with another shot.

Petrosian ducked behind the Dumpster, then popped out from behind it and ran for the door, firing at Casey and Mick the whole way. Neither man had a clear shot, so Casey started pursuing him. Petrosian hit the door and darted outside, with Casey following. As he left, he hollered at Mick to make sure Vladik was done.

After poking his head outside fast to make sure the Armenian wasn't lying in wait to cap him, Casey took off in a zigzagging run toward the battered Aston Martin. Just as he reached it, a shot burst the front headlight, and he quickly hit the ground.

Petrosian ducked into the Hummer and turned the engine over. Casey carefully aimed and shot out the front tire on the passenger side. He heard a loud *whoosh* as the tire deflated and did the same to the back tire. Petrosian spilled out of the car and crouched low as Casey approached the back of the car. From the warehouse, he heard two loud shots. Casey assumed it was Mick taking out Petrosian's partner.

"*Casey* . . . I'm all out of ammo! You got me, man!"

"So toss the piece and come out where I can see you."

"You not going to take me out, are you? I don't want my boy to end up an orphan."

"You should have thoughta that before you tried your bullshit. I gave you a chance at being down, and you fucked it up."

"Come on, man, I had Fordham putting me in the cross! What the fuck was I supposed to do? You know how cops are."

Casey carefully watched Petrosian as they both circled the Hummer, each one trying to get the upper hand. Casey didn't believe he was out of ammo for a second and stayed low as he circled around the car, looking for a shot.

"That's not my problem—you bet on the wrong man, that's why we're here. Now you need to stop bullshittin' and show yo'self."

"What, and get executed? I'm not going to make it that easy for you. I tell you what—" In midsentence, Petrosian jumped up and took his best shot at Casey. Casey heard the crack of the pistol and felt the bullet graze his left bicep. His return shot caught Petrosian in the shoulder and spun him to the ground. Casey ran around the car and found Petrosian balled up, holding his shoulder and wincing in pain.

He smiled up at Casey. "Looks like you won, Crush."

Casey kicked his gun away as Mick limped out of the building. A small pool of blood was starting to form around Petrosian's shoulder. The wound wasn't fatal—Petrosian could easily survive it. Casey looked at Mick and told him they needed to unload the dope from Champa's trunk and put it on the backseat of the Benz.

Petrosian sat on the ground and yelled at Casey as Mick and he started unloading everything. "*You're not going to kill me, right? Casey!* Come on, I got a kid! I know you know what that's like. Casey, come on, man. Answer me."

It took both of them five minutes to load the other car. Casey got in the driver's seat of the Aston Martin, looked at Mick in the passenger seat, and turned the key. The Aston growled to a start. Mick started laughing with relief. Casey told him to hang tight and got out of the car and started walking toward Petrosian. In the background, he could hear the faint wail of sirens.

The Armenian started backing up, scrabbling across the ground as he saw Casey approach and raise his pistol. *"Casey, you gonna kill me in cold blood! What about my boy?"*

In truth, Casey didn't know what he was gonna do or say and just looked at Petrosian. He thought about what it was like growing up without his parents and about his own son getting killed. He and Petrosian were so similar—the only difference was that Casey had already traveled the road he was on, and knew what the ultimate outcome was gonna be.

He pulled the trigger, shooting the man just under the heart. Petrosian's expression turned from anger and fear to shock.

Casey kneeled down close to Petrosian's face as the man gasped for his last breath. "I only did to you what someone shoulda done to me a long time ago. If they'd did that, my kid would still be alive today."

Casey was consumed by a deafening silence as Petrosian's life departed.

Casey limped back to the car. In the background, he heard the sirens grow louder as they drove off. After five miles with no pursuit, Mick and Casey knew they were in the clear. There was no conversation on the ride back. Like Mick, Casey felt he'd already sealed his fate to go to hell. He called Hen, who told him all the guys were already at the warehouse and they'd be there shortly.

Casey then called Shin to check in on Carla. "Hey, Shin, how's Carla doing?"

"Ya know, as you'd expect, but she's getting better," he said in a hushed tone.

"Yeah. I appreciate you handling that. Everything worked out here, it was a fucking shitstorm, but I'll tell you about that later. Tell me straight up—do you think she'll talk to me?"

"I don't think so, brotha."

"Okay, just leave it be, then, stay as long as she wants you to."

"Okay, peace."

Not in this muthafuckin' lifetime, Casey thought as he hung up.

At 11 P.M. that evening, the Chinaman's emissary arrived at the warehouse. He identified himself as Dr. Jonathan Chou, and was dressed in a black, pin-striped silk suit, and wore rimless glasses. He looked like an accountant, not a criminal.

Dr. Chou and his crew checked each car over and were satisfied. He dropped two Louis Vuitton duffel bags at Casey's feet. He looked at Casey and his crew, none of whom had cleaned up from the events of the day yet, and raised an eyebrow. "Looks like you've had a quite a day, Mr. Casey."

"Yeah, well, the day's almost over."

"Indeed. Inside, you will find five million dollars. My employer appreciates the efficient and honorable way you have handled things. We will look forward to future opportunities to do business with you again."

The well-dressed man had five small transports to take the cars, and in less than thirty minutes, he had them all loaded and was gone.

Casey gave the guys their scratch on the spot, plus an extra $250K from what had been earmarked to be Petrosian's share. He told them he would reach out in a day or so to check in. It was a nice payday for everyone, and it was well earned.

Casey and Champa would each walk away with a little over $2.1 mil. Even so, it didn't come close to taking away the sting from losing his relationship with Carla and putting her in harm's way. She could have been killed, and his selfishness would have been the reason. He knew she didn't know the extent of his life and the risks it held for her; otherwise, she would have bounced long ago. As James Brown said, "He paid the cost to be the boss," and once again, it was too high.

He thought of Petrosian's kid and flashed back to hearing the news of when his own father had died and when he had been made an orphan. He had no doubt that he'd done the right thing, but it still sucked knowing there was yet another innocent victim that would suffer as a result of his actions.

On the way home, Casey called Hans and told him everything was good and that he would get him his $500K tomorrow and that Champa was gonna need a little work done on his ride and to put it on his tab. He checked in with Jacob, who said it was all over the news how Fordham was found unconscious and badly beaten in the trunk surrounded by dead Armenian drug dealers and an estimated twenty million dollars of pure, uncut heroin.

Somehow the satisfaction wasn't as sweet as Casey had expected it to be. Like Rono's death, it was a victory that would not be celebrated.

He hung up the phone and called it a night.

21

A week later, when things had quieted down a bit, Casey summoned Alejandro to meet him at the diner next to his apartment one morning. The criminal defender was dressed to a T in a sharp Armani suit and a cocky-ass smile on his face.

"You're in a great mood, Counselor," Casey said as he cut into his French toast.

Alejandro settled in and accepted a cup of coffee. "That's because I just got a settlement of two-point-three million dollars for that client you turned me on to—you know, that kid that got beat by the cops. They couldn't settle fast enough—easiest money I ever made."

"Yeah, I remember."

"I'm gonna clear a million bucks on that. I owe you, Case, so name your cut."

"I was hoping you were gonna say that. I don't need money, but I do need a favor."

"Name it and it's done."

Casey's foot pushed a Louis Vuttion duffel bag under the table toward Alejandro. The lawyer looked down and raised his eyebrows.

"That's two million cash. I need you to make sure Alek Petrosian's kid, Ara, never wants for anything . . . *ever*. School, a decent place to live, medical, anything. Whatever he needs, he gets. Keep my name out of it and don't fuck this up. Whatever way you need to set it up or handle it, I leave that to you. Just make sure it gets done and done right. After today, we're not ever speaking 'bout this again."

Alejandro stayed silent and just looked at Casey, searching his face. He already knew Casey was dead serious. He finally nodded. "Okay, Case, I know what you want and I can take care of it. I'll keep this between us, and it will never come up again."

Alejandro got up, reached down for the bag, and left the diner without saying another word. Casey finished his coffee and saw that his taxi had arrived. His leg still bothered him, but his ego wouldn't allow him to walk with a limp. He got in the backseat, almost choking on the thick cloud of incense, and rolled his window down.

"Take me to the parole office, Webster."

Casey walked into the waiting room, where the desk officer said Lomax would see him immediately. He buzzed him in and escorted him to his office. Lomax looked up from his papers and motioned for him to close the door. He looked like he'd lost about thirty pounds, but he was still fat. On his desk was a salad and a plastic bottle of water. He held up the paper so he could see the headline: DISGRACED NYPD CHIEF OF DETECTIVES DIES AFTER 7 DAYS IN COMA.

"How do you feel about one of New York's Finest checkin' out?" Casey asked.

Lomax grunted. "It's about time there was a little justice."

"Well, we win justice quickest by rendering justice to the other party."

"Who said that, Tony Soprano?"

"Mahatma Gandhi."

Lomax cocked his head and gave Casey a strange look. He would never understand a man like Casey, and vice versa. After reaching into his desk drawer, Lomax pulled out the Saint Jude's medal and tossed it to him. "As promised, Mr. Casey."

Casey caught the medal and put it in his pocket and nodded. Lomax dispensed with the usual line of questioning and got to what was on his mind. "Mr. Casey, I have recommended to the Parole Board that they give you an early release from parole. They have denied my request, but have consented to having it terminate assuming there are no incidents on your record in a year from now."

Casey could tell from Lomax's demeanor that he was disappointed he couldn't repay the favor.

"Okay, so what's the schedule for me checking in?"

Lomax leaned back in his chair. "There is no schedule or spot checks anymore. I just need to see you a year from now to sign some paperwork to make it official."

"Cool. What about interstate travel?"

"I'm going to assume that you won't do that, and unless you are picked up out of state, I guess I would never know. Other than that, you're free to go. See you in a year, Mr. Casey."

Casey rose, pleased with the way things had gone down. He also thought of the similarities between Lomax and himself: Both of them had gotten screwed by their partners and sent to prison. For Lomax, it was a professional prison, one he had no hope of escaping. But it also seemed that he'd found a kind of peace as a result of being exonerated and his old partner being exposed. That was something that eluded Casey.

Casey looked out the window of the gypsy cab as it rolled down the street; it looked like the rain was finally drying up. He felt like he'd won the battle, but lost the war. Once again, his personal relationships had suffered as a result of his lifestyle. He'd called and texted Carla a few times over the past week, but had gotten no response. When he called her that afternoon, he got a disconnected number and got the hint. She was done.

Webster dropped him off outside his apartment. Casey got out of the cab, strolled into the diner next door, and ordered some coffee.

I wonder what Miami's like this time of year, he thought.

EPILOGUE

Casey opened the door of the restaurant and felt the cold, brisk air on his face. The streets were empty except for a well-dressed man down the block having his nicotine fix under a streetlamp.

It was ten blocks back to his place, and Casey looked forward to walking off his meal, even though it was a workout at his age. Thirty years later, his leg still bothered him a bit, but not enough to stop him from this journey. His two sons and wife had opted to drive home because of the chill. He loved his family, but he couldn't deny that he also enjoyed the solitude of being alone. The boys were off in college now, which meant that he and Carla had a lot more time on their hands.

As he walked down the street, he got a call from Shin. "Happy seventieth, Case!"

"Thanks, boss man," Casey said.

"I wanted to be there tonight, but Carla said she was keeping it to just you and the boys."

"Yeah, well, she thinks I've had enough excitement in my life. Who knows—maybe she's right."

"I respect that. Look, I was just thinking 'bout things, and I wanted to let you know that I appreciate everything that you and Champa—rest in peace—did for me."

"Absolutely, man. You deserved it. The two smartest things I did was putting you in the cut those many years ago, then steppin' away and lettin' you handle things. You've taken it to levels I couldn't even have imagined."

"Thanks, Crush—you know, you're the closest thing I ever had to a pop. You always gave me respect and I don't think there was a day that went by that you didn't drop a jewel on me that I took with me for the rest of my life. That all said, what do you want for your B-day gift, brotha? You name it, it's yours, and I mean *anything*!"

Casey chuckled at his protégé. In the ten years since he'd passed the mantle, Shinzo had increased income twentyfold, and showed no signs of stopping. The Consortium had its hands in everything, from white-collar crime to political maneuvering—everything but drugs. Shinzo had kept that as his first rule, and it was still enforced to this day.

"I'm past the point of wanting things, Shin. I already got everything I'd ever need. But thank you."

"Well . . . okay, triple OG, I'ma still think of sumthin', though."

"All right, Shin, you do that." Casey hung up the phone and smiled. He may have been seventy, but he didn't feel it in the least. What'd his wife say the other day, "Seventy is the new sixty"? He thought about Champa and how it had been six years since he died. Like so many, he'd died of cancer. His passing was quick, a blessing in a way.

As Casey drew closer to the smoking man, he smelled the faint odor of the tobacco and could tell the man was wearing a tailored suit. He had an air of success and sophistication about him. *His father would no doubt be proud—*

The impact and sensation was not foreign to Casey in the least. He'd felt it two times before: the first when he was seventeen and the second when he was twenty-four. But this time it was different, not because of his age, but because he instinctively knew it was fatal.

The force of it knocked him to the ground. The last time he'd lain on the ground and looked up at the trees was when he was a boy, at the park with his father more than sixty years ago. The pain crept in quickly, and his breathing became labored. He felt his shirt dampen as it absorbed the blood welling from his chest.

The man walked closer and stared down at Casey, smoke curling from the silenced pistol held in a gloved hand at his side. His face was handsome and unmistakable, framed by curly, jet-black hair. Casey dimly noticed he was losing the feeling in his feet and legs. He didn't have to think of what to say, because he'd always known what the words would be.

"You did . . . what you had to do . . . and should have done. Have no regrets . . . Ara."

The weight of his actions some thirty years earlier had always troubled Casey. He had created an orphan to save history repeating itself. And every day afterwards, he'd known that eventually that debt would need to be repaid.

Petrossian's son's expressionless face watched Casey for another moment. He said nothing, then walked away.

Casey saw the air crystallize his breath above him and felt his mind start to shut down, as if detaching from his dying body.

I'm sorry, Antonio. . . . The wind gently blew across his face as he exhaled his last breath.